# ROSE

## BOOK ONE OF THE HOMELAND SERIES

# CHRISTINA WHITE

# ROSE

BOOK ONE OF THE HOMELAND SERIES

# CHRISTINA WHITE

# Dedication

This book is for everyone who used to read all the time as a kid, then life hit them, and they lost their reading spark.

May this book bring at least a little of that spark back. I hope you fall into this world and find yourself in at least one of the characters. Learn from their strengths and weaknesses and strive to learn from their mistakes.

# Prolog

Lightning struck again. As it did, there was another figure on the dock. He yelled something they couldn't hear, but his voice was filled with rage.

"Take the baby!" she yelled, thrusting the bundle into her sister's arms. "Get on the ship, do not come back for me, whatever happens. No matter what you see, you keep my daughter safe!"

The woman didn't respond; her eyes were locked on the man coming closer. She shook her, "Sister!"

She pulled her gaze away from the man and back to her sister. She swallowed hard and took the squirming child, "I will take care of her, I promise." With tears in her eyes, she quickly climbed the ladder onto the ship and looked over the railing.

The man moved closer to the woman on the dock, and she heard their voices.

"What have you done with my daughter!" the man shouted.

"My love!" the woman cried. "You aren't yourself. Come back to me, please," she reached out as if to touch the man's face, but he slapped her hand away.

"You've taken my daughter. Where is she?"

"When you are better, she will come back." She held out her arms as if to embrace him, but he didn't respond. Her arms dropped back to her sides lifelessly, "Mikal, please." The woman said something else, but her voice was too faint to hear over the storm.

Mikal jerked away from her and reached into his jacket, pulling out a long, thin knife. "Give me my daughter!"

The woman shook her head, and the man lunged forward. The knife hit the woman in the chest, and she fell to her knees.

The moment the woman's knees hit the ground, something strange happened to the man. He stood completely still, then, above his head, there was a small, almost incomprehensible movement. In the dark, there was a slightly darker mist, floating just above the man's head. It rolled off him like steam from a pond. He exhaled, and more mist came from his mouth. His shoulders relaxed, his face relaxed, everything about him softened. Then the man looked down at the woman on her knees.

"NO!" he shouted. He dropped to his knees and cradled the woman in his arms, rocking back and forth.

The woman reached up and touched his face. She spoke softly, "You're back." She smiled and continued, "Our daughter is safe. I love you." Then her hand dropped from his face.

The man gave a throat-tearing cry and clung to the woman's lifeless body.

Her sister watched horrified from the deck. The boat slowly sailed away into the storm as Mikal knelt on the dock, racked with sobs. Tears fell freely from her own eyes as she looked at the bundle in her arms.

"You're our only hope, little one," she said.

The baby looked at the woman and started to cry.

The woman held the baby closer and walked through the cabin doors. Once inside, the woman found some dry, warm blankets and changed the baby out of the wet, cold ones. She picked up the baby again and held it close to her chest, still crying.

A man entered the cabin, "Where to my Lady?"

She didn't take her eyes off the child, "Home."

The baby slowly fell asleep, and the woman laid it in a small cradle. She looked at the sleeping baby and teared up again. She gently touched the baby's cheek and whispered, "We are all counting on you, my little Rose."

# Chapter 1

She really didn't want to go to riding lessons. Sure, she loved riding in the county with Trent, but riding lessons in the yard with the other ladies was not her idea of fun. For one thing, she had to wear her riding skirts, long heavy things that you could hardly move in, let alone ride. Secondly, she was always forced to ride side saddle when riding with the other ladies in the yard. She couldn't ride freely like a boy, with both legs around the horse, like she did while she was with Trent.

"Rose! Come inside this instant, young lady!" hollered a feeble yet surprisingly forceful voice from just inside the courtyard. Lady Ann, an elderly woman who had been head maid for as long as anyone at Zehrah could remember, was the nicest lady you could ever hope to meet, unless you were running late, then you had better pray to whatever god you believed in and hope she didn't have her switch with her.

"Coming, Lady Ann, sorry," Rose called back from the nook she had liked very much ever since she found it a few years ago. It was hidden unless you knew where to look, but you could see the entire courtyard and the main road to Castle Zehrah if you were clever enough to climb your way up to it. It used to be a lookout point for the guards in times of war, but the kingdom hadn't been at war for ages before Rose was even born.

So the spot was seldom used unless it was by Rose herself, who frequently went there to read or draw or simply get away from everyone when she didn't much feel like talking or using courtly manners.

She hadn't been trying to avoid riding lessons; she had become engrossed in a new book her tutor had given to her a few days ago. She was only now starting it because the whole last week had been nothing but rain and thunderstorms, and she simply hated reading by candlelight indoors. She much preferred to be outdoors, not only while reading but she preferred to be outdoors for every activity. She would even sleep outside most nights if she were allowed.

Presently, she was scrambling down the stone wall that led up to her nook, and just as she reached the bottom jump, she heard another familiar voice ask, "What exactly are you doing up there, Lady Rose?"

She smirked and answered, "You know very well I'm not a Lady, and you apparently are no gentleman either. Aren't you going to help me down?"

Trent laughed and retorted, "I've never known you to need anyone's help, let alone mine."

Rose made the last hop down to the dirt of the courtyard, which was more mud than dirt after all the rain they had had, and turned around, straightening her dress. "Well, that's good for me, I guess. You're never around when I actually need you. You always turn up to annoy me, though, right on cue."

Trent smiled, "Well, I can't have it said that the Prince of Zehrah was 'ungentlemanly'". He gave a mock bow that was low enough for a king and held out his arm. "Please, milady, take me arm so I's can escort ye safely across this here courtyard and into yander castle there."

Rose laughed and gently hit Trent on the arm before taking his offer. He might have been the crown prince, but he was so agreeable that anyone could like him. He was also a relentless flirt with a carefree smile who broke the heart of every maiden who set eyes on him.

They reached the castle gate, and he bowed her inside, "Here you are, milady. Safe travels to ye in the future." He gave a flourish of his arm and spun on his heel back the way they had come. Rose stood in the gateway for a moment, watching as he stopped by the milkman's cart, pulled a flower out of a hanging basket, and presented it to the milkman's daughter.

The young girl squealed with delight and offered Trent a small wedge of cheese from her father's cart. Trent popped it in his mouth and ruffled the girl's hair before walking off to the main road away from the castle.

"Rose! Where are you?" came Ann's irritated voice from inside. Rose, not wanting to make Ann truly angry and suffer her wrath, lifted her dress and sprinted up the stairs to her chambers to change into her riding skirts.

***

Every muscle in Rose's back and legs was on fire. She didn't know who came up with the ludicrous idea of riding with both your legs on the same side of a horse, but whoever it was, she was silently cursing them for about the tenth time that afternoon.

"Lovely, absolutely perfect, Princess," gushed their riding instructor from the ground as he watched Trish trot around the arena like she had been born to do it. Trish simply knew how to be a lady, granted that was partly her job, but she had a finesse that just couldn't be taught; it was born.

She finished the small circle they had been wearing into the arena dirt for the last hour and came to a stop next to Rose. Rose straightened up as best she could with her aching back, knowing if she didn't, she would receive yet another disapproving glance from the instructor.

"Well, I think that will be enough for today, ladies. Very well done," the instructor praised while retrieving the mounting block for Trish. She waited patiently for the block while Rose simply slid out of the saddle while he had his back turned. She didn't care at this point; she was very hungry and very ready to be out of her riding skirts that were now sweaty and felt like they weighed a million pounds.

She thought longingly of the breeches she often wore riding with Trent and gave a little sigh, knowing she wouldn't be allowed to wear them to dinner with the King. She would simply have to wait till tomorrow morning. Trent had promised to take her riding before the guests arrived. She would have to be on her best behavior for an entire two weeks while they were in the castle.

Trish dismounted her horse, gave it a pat on the nose, and turned to Rose, "That was lovely, wasn't it? I simply adore riding Been. She is the sweetest horse."

Sometimes Trish was a little over the top with her princessness. Rose used to get easily annoyed with her when they were children, but the longer Rose knew her, the more she came to know that Trish was simply that way. Everything was the best, the brightest, the most fun, or the prettiest. If Rose hadn't shared a room with Trish their entire childhood and most of their teen years, she would have probably thought it was all a show for the court. But it wasn't, Trish had a very kind heart and wanted to always think the best of everyone and everything.

"Oh yes," Rose replied as she stretched her back and rubbed her shoulders, "simply marvelous."

"Oh, I'm sorry, Ro," Trish said with a slight grimace. "I know you prefer a different style of riding, but we really must look our best and put our best foot forward tomorrow for the Duke."

"Ah, yes, the dear Duke. How well I remember him."

"I'm sure he's changed. You know, we were children when we last saw him. And you didn't do yourself any favors the last time he was here," Trish said reproachfully.

They handed their horses off to a groom inside the stable corridor and continued down the stables until they came to Rose's horse, Raul. Raul was a very large horse, almost sixteen hands, and pure black except for one small sock on his back left hoof. Rose patted his neck and fed him a carrot from a bucket hanging across the lane from Raul's stall. "It wasn't my fault he thought he could beat me in a wrestling match. Even Trent tried to talk him out of it, but he wouldn't back down. I warned him he would lose, didn't I?" Raul tossed his head and whinnied. Rose laughed and said, "See? Even the horse agrees with me."

Trish gave a smile. "Well, I guess you did warn him, but all the same, you really shouldn't have been wrestling in the first place. It wasn't very lady-like."

"How many times do I have to say it? I'm not a lady!" Rose protested half heartedly because she had said it so often in her life, it was coming close to being her catchphrase.

"Well, not technically, no," Trish admitted. "You aren't a lady by birth, but you *were* raised in the castle like one. You would think you would have picked up *some* manners in all that time."

"You would think so, wouldn't you, Princess? After all my hard work and lessons, you *would* think she picked up on some manners," Ann said as she strode up to the two girls. "Come along, you two, we need to get you ready for dinner with the King."

They followed Ann up to their adjoined rooms to get ready for dinner.

Rose kicked off her riding skirt and left it on the floor while Trish gently folded hers and put it in the bin to be sent out with the wash that night. She walked over to the basin of water sitting on her vanity and washed her face with the cold water. "That feels good," she sighed.

Rose followed suit and washed her face and arms to get rid of the riding dust from the long afternoon. She had Trish sit in the small chair at the vanity and began to take down her long, golden hair. Rose had always been jealous of Trish's thick, wavy hair. Rose's hair was very pretty as well, but it was always determinedly straight and was a reddish brown color as opposed to Trish's light gold.

After she got all the dust out of Trish's hair, she pinned it back up in a simple but elegant style that was suitable for dinner and went to the wardrobe to pick out a dress for Trish to wear. "What do you think? Blue tonight?" Rose asked as she held out the skirt of a light blue dress for Trish.

"I think so, that one looks nice. You always did have a way with clothes, Ro."

Rose pulled the dress out of the wardrobe and laid it on the bed. It was a simple dress, but it was cut very nicely. It was fitted at the waist and flared slightly at the hips with tiny gold beads on the bodice. It had long gossamer sleeves so it wouldn't be too hot in this summer heat.

Trish rose from the desk, walked to the bed, and slipped the dress on. She turned and let Rose lace up the back of the dress and asked, "What are you planning on wearing?"

"I wasn't planning on anything, just the usual." Rose's usual was a gently fitted plain dress of varying colors. She usually went for comfort over style, but when she helped others pick out outfits, she did have a knack for making others look their best.

"Oh, come on, we don't eat dinner with Father very often. You can dress up a bit. How about this one?" Trish held out a beautiful green dress with leaf patterns on the bodice and sleeves that flowed into a silk skirt.

"Really, Trish, I'm fine wearing what I have; it's not a big deal."

"Nonsense," Trish declared. "You're going to look wonderful. Here, let me do your hair."

Trish spent the next fifteen minutes brushing out Rose's hair till it shone and then pinning it up in a delicate fashion that shaped her face nicely. She even put a gold pin in her hair that brought out the gold in Rose's otherwise brown eyes.

"You look amazing," Trish gushed. "You really should let me dress you more often."

There was a knock at the door, and Trent walked in. "Are you ladies ready to go down to dinner?" he asked, then stopped when he saw what they were wearing. "Were we supposed to dress up?"

The girls laughed, and Trish said, "We felt like looking pretty tonight for Father. You clean up nice yourself, brother."

Trent did look nice. He was wearing his guard uniform, a deep blue number with gold piping along the collar and sleeves. It had little gold tassels on the shoulders and matching pins on the sleeve cuffs. He wiggled his eyebrows and pulled at his collar, "Some say I do look rather dashing."

"And humble as well," Rose retorted. "Although I do have to say I think Trish is the prettier twin. You really couldn't pull off her dress."

"I wouldn't even try," said Trent. He held out both his arms, and Rose and Trish took one each as they started down the hallway to the dining hall.

"I must say I don't know why you bothered getting all dressed up for Father. Shouldn't you be saving your finery for the Duke tomorrow?" Trent asked.

"Oh, I'm sure there is enough finery for tonight and tomorrow, dear brother," Trish chided.

They walked down a side stairwell and came to another hallway on the lower floor of the castle. It wasn't a well-used hall. It was more for servants running about than it was for show, but still, it was well-lit with candles. They were almost to the door that would lead them into the dining hall when Trent stopped as he saw Ann hurrying down the hall towards the three.

"Well, hello, Ann," Trent said with a nod of his head. Ann caught up to them, and Trent took her hand and kissed it, "You are looking quite lovely yourself this evening. Goodness, I really will have to step up my dressing game with all these beautiful women about the castle."

"Hush, you shameless flatterer!" Ann gasped and lightly slapped Trent's hand away. Ann might put up a front with Trent, but she was absolutely smitten with him. Like he was her grandchild, not a prince. She might be a fierce creature to cross with everyone else, but Trent always seemed to know how to get on her good side.

Trent opened the door for Ann. Rose and Trish followed her into the dining hall, where several other visiting nobles were already seated at the long table. The palace had been getting more and more crowded as they prepared to welcome the Western Duke. It felt like every nobleman in the Eastern Kingdom was now in the palace.

Trent took the chair to the immediate right of the slightly larger chair at the head of the table. Trish took the one to the left with Rose sitting in the one beside her. Normally, this would have caused problems. After all, Rose was not a noble, nor a lady, as she often liked to remind everyone. She really had no place at court except for the one allowed to her by the king and the friendship she shared with his children.

Rose didn't know where she came from. She, like everyone else, assumed she was some farmer's daughter, orphaned by raiders that sometimes came to the kingdom from the north or west. All she could gather was that the queen had found her on her way back to Zehrah from a diplomatic visit to Bawvel Hall. Some nastier rumors were that Rose was the queen's bastard child from a lover across the sea. She has always looked more like the queen than even her own children did. Both Trent and Trish were fair-haired and green-eyed like the king. Rose, however, had brown eyes, although light, and the same reddish brown hair as the queen.

Those rumors were easily discredited with the simple fact of timing. Not only had she just given birth to the twins a mere six months before leaving for Bawvel Hall, but she wasn't gone long enough to become pregnant, carry the child, and return with an almost four-month-old for the child to be hers.

Rose was grateful she wasn't the queen's child. She might not know where she came from or who her father and mother were, but that was still better than being the product of the queen's unfaithfulness to the king. Especially a king like Garin.

Garin was a good king as kings go. He was fair, just, brave, and a good fighter to be sure. He was good at ruling and doing what needed to be done, but Rose would never be able to call him warm or loving. He was slightly more open with his children and his commanding lords, but even then, he was more kingly than fatherly or friendly.

If you did what was expected, you got an appraising nod and, sparingly, a word of praise. Rose didn't need more than her fingers to count the times she had actually seen him smile. If you did wrong, you could count on a harsh glare and a firm rebuke and, depending on the wrong, a firm lashing or prison.

Rose didn't know what would have happened if she were the queen's child, and she was wholeheartedly glad that she never had cause to find out. As grim and stately as Garin was, Queen Millesant was quite the opposite. She always wore a smile on her lips and spread happiness like the sun on a summer's day. She was a friend to everyone, noble or lowborn; it did not matter to her. She was like Trish in her ability to think the best of everyone she met.

It was very much agreed upon that the king was a different man when the queen was alive. Rose only remembered that man faintly from her childhood. The queen died when Rose was seven. She was about to have another child, but the midwives were concerned for her. The birth of the twins had not been an easy one, and she had lost a few children before they could be born. Rose remembered the queen being ecstatic about having another child in the castle. She had Rose, Trent, and Trish help her make the cradle and the hanging mobile to go over the crib. She often asked Rose, "Are you ready to be a big sister?" To which Rose would reply, "Yes! I'm tired of being the littlest one." This retort always made the queen laugh, and she would pat Rose on the head and tell her to run along.

Those were happy days for Rose. Probably the happiest of her life. Her life had not been bad, not by any means, but as a replacement to the queen, who was as good as any mother Rose could have asked for, she got Ann. Ann was kind, but she wasn't the queen.

Trish, Trent, and Rose all became much closer after the queen died. As the king fought his grief and pulled away from people, the three children pulled together and consoled one another. They had always been playmates, but after the death of the Queen, they became true brother and sisters.

A light chatter had broken out in the hall as they all waited for the king. Rose watched as Lady Alice blushed while her doting husband bragged about her to Sir Dane. Lady Alice's husband bred the finest horses in the kingdom, and they were often invited to stay at court. Lady Alice was just starting to show with their first child, and her husband, Sir Evenon, was already the proudest father in the castle. Rose smiled at the young couple. She had always liked Lady Alice and was happy for her. She had always wanted to be a mother.

A moment later, the King entered the hall. Everyone fell silent, and with a scraping of chairs, everyone stood to bow or curtsey to the King. King Garin nodded and waved for everyone to be seated. He sat down himself, and with another wave of his hand, the food began to be served.

Tonight wasn't a full feast, such as they would have tomorrow to greet their guests from the Western Kingdom, but still, the food was splendid. The main dish of venison was lightly seasoned with salt and butter, and an orange glaze on the skin. There were large buttery potatoes and carrots along with fresh brown bread and crackers.

King Garin was not often a man of excess, but he did enjoy good food. Zehrah had the finest cook in the kingdom and was often asked to join the nobles in the dining hall. He always declined, however, saying, "A cook's place is in the kitchen, not at the table."

The talking started up again as people began eating. They got louder and louder as dinner went on. Even with everyone talking and laughing around him, King Garin didn't look any happier than satisfied. Rose watched him for a few moments and stared slightly as he caught her eye. She nodded politely and turned away, only for her to see everyone else fall silent.

King Garin had stood up. His food was not yet half finished, so Rose assumed he wasn't leaving but intended to make a speech. This was odd.

The King was a man of action and few words; however, the King did speak.

"My Lords and Ladies, thank you for joining us for supper this evening. As you all know, tomorrow we will be having guests from Bawvel Hall joining us for the next fortnight." He paused and looked at Trish, who smiled at her father. "However, this is not merely a social call. The Duke comes upon my invitation with the intent of marriage to my daughter."

Rose couldn't help but look at Trish, who didn't look entirely surprised, which made Rose think she knew something about this announcement. Trent, on the other hand, looked like he had lockjaw and was about to break his dinner plate. Rose tried to get Trish's attention, but she was determinedly looking at her father.

"We will unite our countries as they once were before the great war. When the westerners arrive, plans will be set for the wedding and what is to come afterwards." The King sat down without even glancing at Trish again. Trish had a smile on her face, but it was not her usual happy smile, more like she had forced the expression on her face, and it would stay there forever, whether she was happy or not.

Not long after the end of his speech, the King stood to leave. Once he was gone, the noise in the hall swelled at once. A few were congratulating Trish, a few more were talking about what this would mean for the kingdom, and most were talking about where the wedding would take place.

Rose leaned over and whispered to Trish, "Did you know?"

"Not for certain, but I had an idea. Father has been talking about a princess's duties for a few weeks now. I knew it would be something like this," Trish said. "I always knew I would be married, and most likely it would be arranged. Does it matter who it's to?"

Rose gaped at her, "Well of course it does! Trish, how can you say that?"

"I'm sure father wouldn't match me with someone unkind," said Trish with a glimmer of her real smile coming back. "You'll be my attendant, won't you?"

Rose looked at her for a moment, "I will be honored to be your attendant when you are wed. Whether that be to the Duke or not, we have yet to see. I have to approve first, you know."

Trish laughed, a real laugh, "Yes, of course, it doesn't matter if a King and a Duke have already made an arrangement, if Rose doesn't approve, then it won't happen."

"Watch me," Rose said under her breath. She turned to look at Trent, who had finally unclenched his teeth. He looked at her and shook his head, exasperated. They were all used to his father declaring what would or would not be done, but it usually involved matters other than his sister. They would all talk later, she knew, in their chambers away from the Lord's and Ladies who all thought the idea of a royal wedding was nothing but exciting.

Lady Alice had walked over from her seat and put her hands on Trish's shoulders, "I'm so happy for you, Princess. Marriage is wonderful." She looked at Rose and saw the skepticism in her eyes. "Really, Rose," she said. "Look at Evenon and me. Our marriage was arranged, and I could not be happier." Her hand fluttered to her slightly swollen belly.

"Evenon is a dear, the Duke is not," Rose retorted flatly.

"Honestly, Rose, you're so prejudiced," said Trish with a hint of annoyance. "You have no idea of the Duke's character other than the one time we met as children. Please, you must get to know him before you pass judgment."

Rose looked into the Princess's eyes and saw angst and begging there. She knew she was making this harder on Trish than she needed to. If Rose didn't like the Duke, then she had only two choices: make life very difficult for Trish, or hold her tongue and let Trish be happy while she was not.

She made her choice right then that she would be nothing but grace to the Duke until he proved to be anything other than a gentleman. "You're right, Trish, I'm sorry. I should give the Duke a second chance."

Trish looked slightly taken aback by Rose backing down so easily, but she smiled and said, "Thank you, sister."

Rose, not in the mood for dinner anymore, made her excuses and left the hall for her chambers. She did not want to be around all the happy people who only saw this marriage as an exciting affair. She had a bad feeling about the next two weeks that she couldn't shake, but she couldn't explain it to herself either.

The only time she had met the Duke, he was an arrogant, spoiled child. But that was just it, wasn't it? They had been children. She supposed that any child of a noble family was bound to be at least a little spoiled. She had grown so used to Trent and Trish that she rarely ever saw them as royals; they were just her friends. Did that make her naive and spoiled?

Once she made it to her chamber, she decided there were too many thoughts in her head and she needed to be outside to let them all go, not sitting in her room mulling them over. She put on a simple dress and a shawl and went out to the grounds.

She first stopped by the stables to see Raul. He always comforted her and always let her rant without judgment. Raul, however, was sound asleep when she got to his stall, and she decided not to wake him with her troubles. He was a horse after all, and didn't need to be weighed down with human problems.

She left the stables, took a few turns around the yard, and decided there was nothing for it but to take an actual walk. She knew if she went out the main gates, which had already been closed for the night, she would be reprimanded by a guard, and most likely she would be turned away. It was almost dark, the sun had set, but there was still light on the horizon. There was a small side gate that was used by servants she would use instead. She walked around the side of the courtyard into the shadow of the castle and down a slender lane that ran along the castle wall.

Once she reached the gate, she realized she wasn't alone. Trent was standing by the side gate, either waiting for her or about to go for a walk himself. He looked up and saw her with a tired smile on his lips, "I take it, I'm not the only one in need of a walk?"

Rose nodded, and they walked out the gate together onto the rapidly darkening lawn of the outer castle. They would have to walk through the city streets a ways to get to the more secluded woods just beyond town. Some city people were fearful of the woods because they had wolves and other wild animals. Rose loved the woods. The smell of the damp earth and the sound of birds calling to one another made her relax instantly. The crickets were starting their nightly chorus, fireflies were blinking in and out of existence, and somewhere in the distance, a nightingale was singing her chicks to sleep.

The moon was only half full, so the path was slightly dark, but Trent and Rose had been in these woods so many times they could have found their way in complete darkness. They walked along in silence for about ten minutes when they came upon the clearing where they often took picnic lunches in the summer.

"I don't understand why Father would force Trish into a marriage without even meeting the man first," Trent burst out without warning.

"Trish said she had a suspicion this was coming. She said the King had been talking to her about duty for a few weeks now." Rose leaned against the lonely tree in the middle of the clearing.

Trent paced back and forth in front of Rose agitatedly. "The thing is, I didn't think Father wanted to make a deal with the Western King. I thought he was going to refuse,"

"You knew about this?" Rose accused before Trent could even finish his statement. She knew Trent sat on his father's council, and there were things he was not allowed to tell her, but this? Trish? How could he have kept that from her?

"No, I didn't know it was this," Trent said calmly. "I knew the Westerners were growing ever more bold in their attempt to expand their borders, but I didn't know any arrangements had been made. The king has no male heir, but he has always treated the Duke like a son. Either the king is trying to gain a foothold in Zehrah, or the Duke simply got tired of waiting to become royalty."

"If this is a scheme of the Dukes', surely it won't last," Rose said, growing hopeful even though she had promised to give the Duke a chance.

"I doubt it is just the Duke," Trent said. "Nothing has been said for certain, but I suspect the Western King has fallen ill."

"What makes you think that?"

"Father has invited him three times to discuss trade routes and the like, but he's refused them all. He keeps giving excuses about projects in his kingdom that need to be seen to, that are too important for him to leave."

"He doesn't even send diplomats?" Rose asked.

"None. The other problem is that there is talk of bandits in the north, so even if he sent a diplomatic party, they might not make it here." Trent rubbed his face with his hands, put his back against the tree, and slid down the trunk to sit on the ground.

"Why would the Northern Kingdom send raiding parties this far south? They have the desert to cross, and they hardly ever come this far south unless they sail down the coast."

"Bandits 'in the north' doesn't necessarily mean from the Northern Kingdom," Trent said. "It just means they are north of us."

That made sense, but Rose also thought it silly to name the kingdoms by their location if you weren't going to use direction to talk about them. The raiders mattered very little to her right now anyway. She was much more concerned with Trish's engagement.

"Are they already engaged, or has the idea just been talked about?" She asked. If nothing official has been signed, then there might be a chance the Duke wouldn't even like Trish, and the whole thing wouldn't even be an issue.

Trent shook his head, "Nothing is official or in writing, but that doesn't really matter. Even if the Duke hated Trish, he would probably still agree to marry her. He wants to be in charge."

"Well, he wouldn't be in charge here," Rose laughed. "Surely he knows that. The people love you, and there is no way your father would give him any power in his kingdom."

Trent gave a rueful smile and agreed, "No, he wouldn't have any power here, but he would be wed and next in line to rule the Western Kingdom. I think that's his main goal, and," he raised his eyebrows, "Everyone loves me? That's very forward of you, Rose."

Rose rolled her eyes, refusing to be distracted. She said, "I'm serious. He was awful as a child, and in my experience, people who are awful children usually grow into awful adults." She looked Trent in the eyes. "We can't let her marry him."

Trent took Rose's hand and said, "If he hasn't changed and Trish does not want to marry him, I promise you I will not let it happen."

Rose looked at Trent for a moment longer and realized she was being paranoid. She knew Trent loved his sister just as much, if not more, than she did. She knew he wasn't the king yet, but his opinions definitely had sway with the king. Everyone on the council respected him, and they were all glad to know he would be a great king one day.

"You're right," she relented. "I know you would never let anything happen to Trish." Rose leaned her head on Trent's shoulder and sighed. "Sometimes I'm so glad I'm not a royal."

Trent laughed, "My dear, you would be the worst royal to ever have lived." He put his arm around her shoulders and gave her a small hug. "Come on, we'd better get to bed if you still want to go riding in the morning."

Rose agreed, and they both got up and walked the path back to the castle. She knew as long as she and Trent were around, the King wouldn't be able to force Trish into anything she didn't want to happen. Sometimes Trish was too accommodating, especially when it came to her father.

Ever since their mother died, Trish seemed to think it was her job to make sure her father was happy. She would do anything to put a smile on his face, or to at least make his frown less pronounced.

Rose worried that Trish would be willing to agree to any number of things as long as she thought it was what her father wanted.

Trent walked Rose to her room, said goodnight, then headed down the corridor.

Rose went to the door that joined her and Trish's room and pressed her ear to it. She didn't hear anything, so she gently pushed it open.

Trish was on her bed, the blankets slowly rising and falling with her deep, sleeping breaths. Rose closed the door silently, changed into her nightgown, and went to her own bed.

She lay her head on the pillow and said a soft prayer. She didn't really know who she was praying to, but she said the prayer all the same.

"Please don't take Trish away. I don't know what I would do without her. She is so gentle and kind, and she doesn't know how to stand up for herself. She deserves the kindest, most gentle man to be her husband. Please help."

She whispered the last words of her prayer, then rolled over and drifted off to sleep.

# Chapter 2

Rose woke in a slightly better mood than when she went to sleep. At least she had her ride to look forward to; the rest of the day, she wasn't so optimistic about.

She got out of bed and dressed in her soft but sturdy riding pants, a loose-fitting shirt, and, to not draw attention to herself, she shoved all her hair into a cap. To any of the townspeople, she would look like a young man going on a pleasure ride.

She walked down to the stables, her heart lifting with every step. She was glad she talked to Trent last night. His assurance that nothing bad would happen to his sister was the only thing keeping her from panicking.

Raul was standing in his stall, waiting for her, and gave a gentle nicker as she approached.

"Ready for a nice trot?" she asked as she rubbed his soft nose.

She got a brush, unlatched Raul's stall, and began giving him a good rub down. Raul loved this, and when she got to his belly, he lifted his head in the air and stuck out his upper lip, tilting his head.

Rose laughed and put the brush away, then got her saddle off the pegs directly in front of Raul's stall. She saddled him, and when she started guiding him out of the stall, she saw Trent walk into the stables.

"Perfect timing," he said and walked to his horse's stall. Trent's horse was a beautiful creamy gold with a large white patch on her rump, with speckles of white running down her back legs to the knee. She had a dark mane and tail with high black socks and a gentle yet confident personality.

Trent quickly brushed and saddled Star, and they were off. They walked the horses until they got to the main road, then they trotted through the town. Once they got to a nice flat grassy meadow just outside the town gates, they broke into a gallop.

They kept a good pace until they crested the top of the first low hills that surrounded the town to the northeast. It was a bright, clear morning. When they reached the top of the hill, they could see a considerable distance.

The rolling hills were all covered with waving grass and wildflowers. Dotted with only a few trees here and there, it felt like you were in a sea of green waves. The wind blew from the west, and they could smell a hint of bacon on the breeze.

"Smells like the Cod farm is about to enjoy a nice breakfast, shall we visit them? I haven't seen Collin in almost a month." Trent turned to look at Rose, raising a hopeful eyebrow in question.

Rose shrugged, unsure, "Should we bother them? Didn't Anne just have her baby?"

"We won't be a bother," Trent said. "I'll see if they need any help with the morning chores, and we can ask if they need anything from town."

Rose suspected Trent's main objective was the bacon they could smell. The Cods had eight, now nine, children, so she doubted there would be many chores left to do, and the family came to town every week with their produce to sell.

Nevertheless, Rose agreed, and they turned their horses towards the farm. The closer they got, the better the breakfast smelled, and the hungrier Rose became. They made it to the little lane leading to the house, then stopped to tie the horses to the hitching post and walked to the front door.

"Hello the farm!" Trent called when they didn't see anyone.

"That's odd," Rose commented. "You can usually at least hear the children by now. They're always running around."

Trent nodded in agreement. He knocked at the door, and after a few minutes, the second youngest boy, Benjamin, opened the door. "Hello," he mumbled, his eyes downcast.

"Hello, Benjamin," Trent said. "Are your parents home?"

The boy nodded

"Are they alright?" Trent asked with concern rising in his voice. It wasn't unusual for a child to answer the door in this home, but why did he look so sad?

The boy shook his head and ran back into the house, leaving the door open.

Trent looked at Rose, and they both went inside.

The house didn't look out of order. At first glance, everything looked perfectly normal, but as they scanned the small living room and kitchen, they noticed things that were out of place.

There was only a single log in the rack next to the hearth, and the fire was down to embers. The curtains were all pulled shut, and there was only one other child in the house, Baily, the oldest girl, who was twelve.

She was standing at the sink and didn't seem to have noticed that anyone had walked into the house.

"Bailey," Rose called softly. "Bailey, is everything alright?" She walked over to the girl and looked in the sink. She was rinsing out a rag that was covered in blood, turning the water in the basin a dark red.

Rose tried to remain calm. The mother had just had a child after all, it wasn't uncommon for there to be bleeding after birth. However, the amount of blood did give her cause for concern.

Rose touched the girl's shoulder, and she started. The girl looked up at Rose's face and gave her a weak smile.

"Hello," she mumbled.

"Bailey, is everything alright? Is your mother fine?"

Bailey looked slightly confused, then looked at the rag she was cleaning, "Oh yes, Ma's fine." She paused, then said, "Pa's hurt."

Trent looked alarmed at this news, "What happened to him? Where is he?"

"They're in their bedroom, majesty."

Trent looked up the staircase, then at Rose. They didn't want to trespass in their home, but something was definitely wrong, and they needed to make sure Collin was alright.

Rose turned to Baily and squeezed her shoulder, "Is it all right if we go up and check on your Ma and Pa?"

Bailey gave a small nod and turned back to the sink.

Rose and Trent went up the staircase and looked down the hall. They could hear a deep, rough male voice talking slowly.

"You must bring in as much hay as you can manage, son. You'll need to have Thomas and Arthur help you. Then have Ava, Emma, and Benjamin bring in as much firewood as they can carry. Bailey will need to milk the cows and collect the eggs. Molly can help your Ma with the baby and cook meals for everyone." The voice stopped and gave a small, ragged cough.

Trent and Rose came to the open doorway and looked inside. The scene was not a pleasant one. Collin lay on the bed with his shirt off and a tight bandage wrapped around his ribs and another bandage on his right thigh. This bandage had a fist-sized blot of bright red blood.

Collin looked to the door. Upon seeing Trent and Rose, he started as if to rise, then gave a hiss of pain and lowered himself back to the bed. "My apologies, Majesty," he stammered, looking around helplessly.

"Don't be ridiculous, Collin. Stay where you are. What happened to you?" Trent walked over to the bedside to look closer at Collin's wounds.

Collin, still trying to sit as tall as he could, explained, "I was taking a wagon of fruit to market over in Penshaw, on my way back, I was attacked." Collin gave a wry chuckle and continued, "Lucky for me, I wasn't carrying any of the gold I made on the trip. I'd bought a new pair of plow horses that'll be comin' along next month."

Collin winced and put his hand to the bandages on his ribs, "They didn't much like not finding anything of value on me, so they decided to get their fun by beating me near to death. Then just outta spite, they sliced my leg as they were leavin'. I crawled back and got into the wagon, and Nelly's a good enough horse; she knew her way home. I got here bout two hours ago."

"The bandits didn't want your horse and wagon," Trent asked, looking furious. Rose knew how it must ride on him that the bandits had made it so close to home and were now attacking his subjects.

"They didn't seem interested," Collin shrugged, then winced. "Truth told, I don't think they even cared I didn't have any gold on me. They didn't try very hard to find any, even though it was obvious I had just been to market and sold all my goods. They seemed to enjoy the violence more than the thevin'."

Trent put his hand on Collin's shoulder. "I promise you we will find the men who did this. In the meantime, I'll send the doctor to see to your wounds. Are Anne and the baby doing well?"

Even through the pain, Collin's smile couldn't be dampened. "Anne's doing fine. A boy. That makes five boys and four girls." Collin gave a small laugh, "Anne's already talking about having another just to keep things even around here."

Rose smiled at the thought. Trent, on the other hand, was still grim-faced, thinking about the robbers. She knew he would not be happy until the men were found and brought to justice.

"I'll go check on Anne," Rose said, looking at the Cob's eldest boy, Bailey's twin, John. "John, we'll send help for the hay harvest and the wood, as well as the doctor."

Trent nodded, "We will send anything you need, Collin."

Rose left the men talking and walked to the room next door, the nursery. She lightly knocked on the door and heard a soft "Come in".

She pushed the door open and saw Anne propped up in a small cot bed, holding her newest child. She looked up and smiled, "Rose, it's so good to see you. Sorry I didn't answer the door, we've had a bit of a morin'."

"Don't be silly, Anne," Rose crossed over to the rocking chair and sat next to Anne. She peeked into the blankets to see a healthy baby, contentedly sleeping. His mouth was slightly open, gently breathing. "He has your nose."

Anne smiled, "And Collins' hair." The baby had a generous amount of black curly hair.

Rose chuckled, "All the boys look exactly like Collin, and all the girls are little miniatures of you."

"That's what everyone says," Anne smiled down at the baby again. "I think they all have a bit of both of us, though."

"Does he have a name yet?"

"Not officially, but I think we are going to name him Oliver, after Collins' father."

"That's a lovely name," Rose turned her eyes from the baby to look closer at the mother. "How are you doing?"

Anne looked good, granted a little tired, but that was to be expected. "I feel fine. I'm more worried about Collin than myself. I've done this a few times, you know."

"Collin will be just fine. Trent is going to send the doctor over and a few men to help with the farm work." Rose could see the relief in Anne's face. She was a strong woman, but she also knew all the hard work it took to keep a farm running, and Collin was one of the hardest-working men Rose knew.

"We greatly appreciate it," Anne took Rose's hand and gave it a firm squeeze. "I was concerned about getting all the hay in for the animals before it got too cold."

Rose patted her hand, "Don't worry about a thing. Just keep that baby fed and happy, and soon you can work on the next one." Rose winked, and Anne blushed slightly.

Rose stood to leave, but Anne didn't release her hand. "They will catch the men who did this, won't they?"

Anne's eyes were mostly concerned, but there was a spark of anger there as well.

"Trent won't rest until they are found. I wouldn't be surprised if he goes out looking for them himself."

Anne let go of Rose's hand and gave a nod. Very little upset Anne, but her and Collins' love was fierce, and someone threatening that love was cause for being upset.

Rose left Anne's room at the same time Trent was leaving Collins. They walked down the stairs together and filled the wood rack with dry wood. Rose also cleaned out the bloody sink and made lunch for the family.

They returned to their horses and started towards the castle. On their way back home, they stayed closer to the main road, wanting to return as quickly as possible to send help to the Cob farm.

They turned a corner and saw a large party of mounted men and a carriage being pulled by four horses on the king's road. Behind that were at least half a dozen more carriages and wagons, all headed towards the castle.

"The Duke?" Rose's question was more of a statement, but still, Trent nodded.

"We'd better get to the castle before they do, otherwise father will be furious." Trent turned Star's head towards a shortcut through the trees that would get them back to the castle well ahead of the large party on the road.

They got to the castle, dropped their horses off at the stable, and went straight inside to find the doctor. Normally, they both would have taken care of their own horses, but they simply didn't have enough time if they wanted to have people sent to the Cob farm today and be ready to receive the Duke.

"I'll go round up a few men to help with their farm," Trent said. "Can you get the Doctor and tell him what happened?"

Rose nodded and headed up the main stairs to the doctor's chambers. When she got there, the door was open and the doctor was seeing another patient on his way.

"Three drops of this every morning and night on the affected area.

If you run out and still have the rash, come back and see me next week."

A young man, whom Rose didn't recognise, nodded fervently to the doctor and then turned to exit the room. Upon seeing Rose, he blushed so deeply that he looked like a mummer with red face paint.

He gave the slightest of bows and practically sprinted from the room.

"Ahh, poor boy," the doctor sighed. "Well, it's his own fault for not knowing the difference between poison oak and a live oak." He shook his head. "My dear, if you ever find yourself in need of a privy in the woods, be sure you are knowledgeable of the forest around you!"

Rose laughed, "I'll be sure to remember that, Doctor."

"How can I help you, my dear?" The Doctor waved her into his sitting room and bid her sit down. "What ails you?"

"Nothing," Rose entered the room, but declined to sit; she had to be quick. "Doctor, do you know where the Cob family's farm is? About three miles north east of here?"

The Doctor nodded his head, "Yes, yes, I know it well. I delivered Collin there many years ago and helped with their twins. She just had another child, am I right?"

Rose nodded, "Yes, her ninth."

"Ninth! Good gracious, they will hardly need me. I could probably take birthing lessons from Anne," the Doctor chuckled and sat down at his desk.

"It's not Anne, she's just fine, it's her husband, Collin. He took some produce to Penshaw, and on his way back, he was attacked. He was cut on the thigh and said they kicked him around pretty badly. I'm afraid he has a few broken ribs."

The doctor stood up at once. He was an older man, but he was spry. "I'll go right away." He went into his store room that was just off the sitting room, and Rose could hear glass bottles clanking around.

The doctor came out of the room with his bag stuffed full of medicine, clean wrappings, and all sorts of other items. Rose didn't know what they were.

"Do you need a carriage?" Rose asked

The doctor thought for a moment, "I'd better take a cart. If Collin is too bad, I will need to bring him back here, and he won't be able to ride."

Rose shifted nervously. Normally, she would have liked to walk the doctor down to the livery herself and explain the situation, but she simply didn't have time. The doctor was an important enough man that he shouldn't have any trouble getting a cart.

"Doctor, I'm sorry I can't go with you, but on our way back to the castle, we saw the Duke's party on the main road." The Doctor cut her off before she could continue.

"Not to worry, my dear, not to worry. I know the way to the farm and have a friend in the livery who won't ask too many questions about me borrowing a royal cart."

Rose was relieved to hear it. Although the doctor worked and lived in the castle, he didn't have access to everything the royal family did, and that included free usage of the stables and livery.

"Thank you, Doctor," she touched the shorter man's hand that was holding his bag. "I'm sure Trent will be in later to see how they are doing."

"Not a problem, no problem at all," he motioned to the door and let Rose through first. "I'll see what damage has been done, then, if he's well enough, I will give him what he needs for the night and go back tomorrow morning to check on everyone."

Rose walked him down the hall and left him on the staircase. She headed to her rooms to get ready to receive the Duke.

Almost as soon as she entered her room, the door to Trish's room burst open, and Trish came in. She was in such a state of panic and nervousness that she could hardly get any words out.

"Where have you been!! I need my hair, my dress isn't, my shoes are..." She looked around frantically, then locked eyes with Rose and sank onto Rose's bed.

Rose went to her and hugged her, "Honestly, Trish, calm down. You're going to give yourself apoplexy."

Trish took a few deep breaths, then rubbed her eyes with her fist, still clutching a light green shawl, "I'm just so nervous. It's not every day you meet the person you're supposed to marry."

Rose decided it wasn't the time to argue about whether or not Trish and the Duke would be getting married. Instead, she said, "Well, technically, you've already met, and right now he's not here to marry you. He's here to see your father to *talk* about marrying you."

Trish looked at Rose blankly and then burst out laughing, "I suppose you're right. We met as children, even though that's not the same; we have met before."

"Also, you could walk down those stairs in a potato sack and you would still be the most beautiful thing in the whole castle." Rose smiled at Trish and continued, "But I do agree that your dress and your shoes do not match."

Trish was wearing a red dress, pink shoes, and still had the green shawl in her hand.

Trish looked down and gave another laugh, "You're right. This outfit is horrible."

Rose led Trish back into her room and sat her down at the mirror on her desk. She got a brush and started detangling Trish's hair and sweeping it up into a sleek hairstyle that would be able to hold her tiara.

"There," Rose said, "Now, which dress do you want to wear? Once we pick a dress, we can put the rest of the pieces together."

Trish walked to her wardrobe and looked over her options. There were several dresses that would all be appropriate, but seeing how nervous Trish was, Rose was preparing to give gentle hints in the right direction if Trish picked out something that wasn't.

Trish held out a long, soft yellow dress that had sleeves that came down to her elbows. "What about this one?"

Rose gave an internal sigh of relief and smiled, "Very pretty." She stood and went to the wardrobe as well. She picked out a small sapphire necklace that was set in a silver chain, along with silver shoes to complete the ensemble.

Once Trish was dressed, Rose went back to her room and picked out a simple green dress and tied her hair back with a leather cord. She knew no one would be looking at her today. She wouldn't even go if it wasn't expected of her and if Trish didn't need her so badly for moral support.

She went back into Trish's room and found Trish holding a portrait of her mother. Rose's heart went out to Trish, and she didn't know if she should go comfort her or if she should let her have her moment.

Trish looked up and brushed away a single tear on her cheek, "I'm fine, really. I just miss her. I never imagined being married and having children without her there to help."

Rose went to her and wrapped her in a hug, "She would be so proud of you, Trish. You're kind, smart, funny, and beyond beautiful." She pushed back slightly from the hug so she could look at Trish. "And even if you don't marry the Duke, I know you will find someone who is just as kind, smart, and funny as you. And if you're lucky, someone just as beautiful." She gently pinched Trish's chin, which drew a smile from her.

"Are you ready?" Rose asked.

Trish nodded and stood. She straightened her dress and took a deep breath. "Ok, I'm ready."

They left the room arm in arm and went to Trent's room to see if he was ready to go down to the grounds and receive their guests.

Trent opened the door. He had his dress uniform pants on, but not the shirt. Rose raised her eyebrows, "Do you normally answer your door half-dressed?"

Trent half smiled, "Only when I know it's you two."

Trish walked into the room. "How did you know it was us?"

"I could hear your clacking shoes halfway down the hall, and besides," Trent shrugged, "Who else would come to see me right now?"

Trish rolled her eyes, "A great number of people could be coming to see you right now, and my shoes aren't that loud."

"You sound like a graceful elephant on stilts."

Trish swatted at him, but he nimbly skirted away. He gave an agast look, "Well, that's not very mannerly of you, Princess. What would Ann say?"

Trent looked at Rose, who had come into the room, "I'd better put a shirt on, though, otherwise Rose might fall in love with me." He gave her a wink and went to his dressing room to finish getting ready.

Trish raised her eyebrow questionably, but Rose just rolled her eyes, "Last night I told him everyone in the kingdom loved him and he would be a good king, and somehow that has translated to *me* being in love with him."

Trish giggled, "You haven't a chance, dear brother." She called loud enough for Trent to hear. "Our Rose 'isn't a lady' and would make a rather controversial queen."

Rose snorted at the mere thought of her being a queen. She certainly would be controversial, to say the least. She was controversial, *now* let alone being the queen.

Trent walked out of his dressing room fully dressed this time and ready to go downstairs with the girls.

"Maybe this kingdom needs some controversy," Trent said, low enough that Rose wasn't entirely sure if he meant for her to hear. Before she could comment, he said, "Read,y everyone? Let's go meet our guest."

# Chapter 3

The trio walked onto the lawn to see a large crowd gathered. Along with a spattering of nobility, there was a mob of servants waiting to take care of the luggage and the horses.

"He's only staying for two weeks," Rose grumbled to Trent. "Does he really need all this?"

Trent rolled his eyes, "Try and be civilized, Rose. Even if he was only here for afternoon tea, he would have gotten the same greeting."

Rose knew very well that this was true, but she was not in a friendly mood. She took a deep breath, reminding herself of her promise to Trish. She would be nothing but friendliness, genteel, and gracious until the Duke proved he didn't deserve it.

The king came striding out of the castle to stand on the lawn with his son. Rose took a few steps back. She might be on equal ground with Trish and Trent, but she was not equal to the Prince and Princess.

Trish looked back at her and squeezed Rose's hand. As much as she didn't like it, she knew Rose wouldn't be presented to the Duke like her and her brother.

"I see Alice and Evenon," Rose said. "I'll go stand with them."

Rose turned and walked to the young couple standing a little to the left of the royal party.

"Do you need a seat, dear?" Evenon fussed. "Shade? It's mighty hot out this morning. Would you like a fan?"

Alice gave a gentle smile and shook her head, "I'm fine, dear, don't worry yourself. All women have babies; if they can do it, so can I."

Seeing Rose, Alice put out her hands and hugged Rose. "Not part of the royal greeting party then?" She asked.

Rose shook her head, "Not when other royals are about."

"That's alright," Alice turned to Rose, so they were side by side. "It's more fun to watch anyway."

While Rose agreed with Alice that watching would be more fun, she didn't want to leave Trish alone to meet the Duke. She knew she was being overprotective, but it was in her nature. She had always stood up for Trish when they were children, and the other girls tried to take advantage of her sweetness. Rose felt obligated to continue that role in such a trying time as meeting one's intended.

A crisp fanfare sounded, and the crowd hushed.

A squat man walked a little way down the lane that had been made by the welcoming party. "Presenting!" he bellowed. "The great and honorable Duke of Bawvel Hall and Heir to the Western throne!"

Rose raised her eyebrows in shock. Either the King hadn't known or he hadn't told Trent the Duke had been officially named heir. Or perhaps the Duke was being presumptuous and wanted to make a grand entrance, but he wasn't officially named heir yet.

Rose seemed to be the only one who questioned this title. Either no one else cared much, or they were too distracted by the enormous horse that had just trotted into view.

The horse was almost two whole hands taller than her already large Raul. It had feathered hooves that were as large as feast plates. He was a deep rust color with a black mane and tail. Although it was hidden with an ornamental bridle, you could see he also had a wide blaze running the length of his face.

The Duke himself was splendidly dressed, as much as Rose hated to admit it. He was wearing a cream colored loose shirt with black riding pants. He also had a long crimson riding cloak that was embroidered with gold thread and green beading.

When they came to the path leading to the king, the Duke slowed the horse to a walk. The Duke took his time walking down the path, his chin held high. He never took his eyes off the king, or maybe Trish?

If Rose had hackles, they would have instantly been raised. She felt this introduction screamed arrogance and pride. Surely he wasn't going to stay mounted to greet the king. It would have been an insult to a normal person, let alone to the King.

When the Duke got about halfway to the King, he halted his horse and swept his long riding cloak to the side, and dismounted.

The Duke was about the same height as Trent, maybe a few inches taller, but he was much more sturdily built. Rose was used to seeing royals either in good fighting shape or fat, but the Duke looked like any farmer who put in a long day at the plow or chopping wood. *Why would a noble need that many muscles?* Rose thought to herself.

The Duke walked the rest of the way to the king with a long, purposeful stride. Rose wasn't very well versed in fighting, but she thought she could see a grace in the Duke's walk that meant he would be a formidable fighter as well as being very strong.

He must have given his horse a signal, or it was incredibly well trained, because it did not move an inch from where the Duke left him in the middle of the isle.

Growing up with nobility, Rose had to learn all the formalities of court. There were many ways to show respect and many more ways to give offense. The first thing noble children learned was how to greet those of their better, equal, and lower ranks.

Everyone bowed to the king, but they were all in varying depths. A commoner would completely prostrate themselves on the ground when talking to the king. A shopkeeper or landowner would go down on one or both knees, depending on their previous relationship with the royal family or the prosperity of their business. A visiting noble would bend at the waist completely. A local noble, in good standing with the king, would bend slightly less. Higher-ranking nobility, such as a viscount or count, would give a nod of the head as well as a half-bend at the waist. The higher nobility would usually receive a nod back from the king, but never a bow. And lastly, although it rarely ever happens, two kings would simply nod to each other.

The normal greeting from a Duke to a king would be for the Duke to give a half-bow and a nod, to be returned with a nod. The Duke gave a deeper bow than exactly necessary, especially if he was claiming to be the heir, as well as a nod, and he stayed bowed. Either he was trying to show humility, or he simply wasn't used to his higher rank. Or, as Rose was willing to believe, his higher rank was a farce, and he didn't want to push his luck too far all at once.

The Duke spoke in soft but deep, carrying baritone, "Your grace," he straightened. "Thank you for this warm welcome. I look forward to getting to know you and your family over the time of my visit. It has been many years since my childhood visit, and I am glad to be in these beautiful lands again."

The King nodded and assessed the Duke. He seemed to like what he saw. "It is an honor to have you in our house again, Sir Edmund." The king gestured to Trent. "My son and heir, Trenton."

Trent and the Duke nodded to each other.

"And my daughter, Patrishia."

Trish gave a gentle curtsey as the Duke nodded. When he looked up, he gazed at Trish slightly longer than propriety would normally allow, and a light blush crept across Trish's cheeks. She held the Duke's gaze, which Rose was proud of, and the Duke gave a small crooked smile.

"It is an honor to see you again, Parishia," The Duke said. "You have grown only in beauty and grace since we met as children."

"Please," Trish said, "If we are going to be friends, you must call me Trish. Everyone does, except father when he is being formal." She turned to her father and smiled. "Shall we go inside? The sun is rather hot today, and you must be tired from your journey."

"I would greatly appreciate it," the Duke hesitated, "Trish. I'm sure the rest of my party would also appreciate being able to settle into their rooms and freshen up before dinner as well."

"Of course," Trish gestured for the servants to start unloading the luggage from the caravan. "We will show you to your rooms and take care of your horses. We have a wonderful feast being prepared for supper tonight as well."

"A feast sounds lovely," the Duke whistled, and his horse trotted to him. "If it's not too much trouble, might I walk this one to the stables myself? He's a bit strong-headed, and I don't want to overload a stable hand with his temper."

Trent spoke for the first time, "The stables are just over here. I can take you, and we can see if there is a stall big enough for him."

The Duke chuckled, "He is rather a beast, isn't he?" The Duke patted the horse on the neck. "Our stable master has been working with a few farmers to breed more sturdy battle horses. He's the firstborn of my own line, along with some very sturdy northern plough horses."

Trent and the Duke started in the direction of the stables. Trish turned to her father, gave him a quick kiss on the cheek, then walked over to Rose and Alice.

"What did you think of him?" Trish burst.

"Trish, I didn't even talk to him," Rose said.

Trish just stared at her.

Rose sighed, "He seemed friendly enough." Trying to be diplomatic, she added, "His horse was magnificent."

"Really, Rose? His horse." Trish said in the most sarcastic voice she could muster. "Were your eyes completely closed? He is gorgeous!"

"That he is," Alice chimed in. "Some people have all the luck, being a princess, being betrothed to a hunk." She giggled and gently squeezed Trish's shoulder.

"I think I'll go see if they need help with that horse," Evenon said, sounding slightly hurt.

Alice caught his hand, "Darling, there is no need to run off. He might be a hunk, but you are *my* husband." She stood on tiptoe to kiss him on the cheek, and his feelings seemed greatly mitigated.

"All the same, dear, I think I will go. It never hurts to meet new people. Especially if they have breeders who can make a beast like that one." Evenon kissed his wife and headed off in the direction of the stables.

Trish turned on Rose with a ferocity that she rarely had, "Tell me truly, Ro, what did you think?"

"I'm trying to reserve such opinions until they can be fully formed. You can hardly get to know someone during a formal greeting where everyone has scripted lines that they have practiced since birth." Rose was trying to live up to her promise and thought she was doing reasonably well.

Thankfully, Alice was paying attention enough to be able to raise Rose's concerns, "Did I hear his titles correctly? Did they call him the Heir to the Western Kingdom? I didn't know anything had been made official."

"Yes, that is what they said," Trish confirmed. "To be completely honest, I don't know myself if it's completely true or not. However, if it isn't written down officially, it's true enough in understanding. The western king has no heirs, brothers, or even cousins to take the throne. I think the closest relative he has is an uncle who is about to turn seventy or something."

Alice nodded and started to fan herself. "Do you ladies want to go inside? As much as I try to tell Evenon I'm perfectly fine, I am starting to feel the heat."

Rose and Trish agreed, and they all turned to walk back into the castle. They dropped Alice off at her rooms with her ladies' maid, who made a fuss about her being flushed and quickly got her a cold cloth.

"See you at dinner, Alice," Rose called through the door just before the maid shut it.

Trish took Rose's arm and they headed up the stairs to their bedrooms. "You know, if you are going to insist on talking to Edmund before giving me your opinion, then I'm going to have to insist that you talk to him as soon as possible. He's only going to be here for a fortnight."

"Yes, I know," Rose turned them down the hall. "I will talk to him as soon as I can, but I highly doubt I will be high on his social calendar while he's here." Rose partly didn't want to talk to the Duke and partly was dying to talk to him in an informal setting to get a better feel for his character.

He had seemed perfectly friendly in the courtyard, but like she said, all of that was scripted. Everyone knew what was expected of them and exactly what they were supposed to say. What would he say when he didn't have a script to follow?

***

Both girls had picked out their outfits last night. They knew there wasn't going to be a whole lot of time between meeting the Duke and the feast, so they had laid everything out before they went down.

Rose was wearing another green gown, but this one was much more ornate than the one she had worn that afternoon. This one had a hoop underneath to lift the skirts into a larger, but not unmanageable, circle around her legs. The beading and needlework were tiny, intricate pink and white roses all along the hem of the skirts, as well as the sleeves and bodice.

Rose didn't mind this dress as much as she thought she would the first time she saw it. For one thing, the wooden hoops holding the skirts away from her legs made the dress significantly cooler than a dress that touched her legs. Another reason she liked this style was that she could stand and sit with her legs any way she liked, and no one would notice. She was also grateful that she didn't have to wear Trish's dress.

If Rose's dress could be called ornate, then Trish's dress was opulent. It was the lightest blue the dressmakers could find, and it didn't have beads like Rose's dress; it had pearls and diamonds.

The hoop was so large that when she walked, you couldn't see the faintest hint of movement from her legs; it looked like she was floating.

The bodice was lace and pearl with sheer sleeves that went to her wrists. The sleeve ended in a small triangular swatch of fabric that went over her hand, like a small glove, only it was connected to a ring on her middle finger.

Her golden hair had taken three maids almost an hour to curl and pile onto her head in a fashion that would be able to hold up the crown that topped off the outfit.

The dreadfully heavy thing was almost six inches tall at its highest peak. The diamond in the center was about the size of a large walnut. The peak and diamond pattern went all the way around Trish's head, tapering down to about one-inch peaks in the back and only grape-sized diamonds.

Rose didn't know how Trish walked around with so many breakable things. If she had to wear that much finery all in one dress, she would be afraid to move an inch.

"Ro," Trish asked, looking at Rose in the mirror. "Does everything look alright?"

"You look amazing," Rose said honestly. Even though the dress would have been far too much for her, it looked lovely on Trish. "It's a good thing we aren't having lunch, you would blind everyone with all your diamonds."

Trish smiled and gave her dress a few more adjustments, "I hope the Duke doesn't like dancing too much. I won't be able to do more than three or four dances with this dress, it's just so heavy."

"Well, if you need to, just pretend to be faint," Rose suggested. "Then we can both leave."

Trish rolled her eyes at Rose, "As much as you protest, you always have fun at these parties."

"Only because it's so entertaining to watch some of the nobles try to dance." Rose stood and walked to the desk, "Remember last year's harvest feast when Lord Alen tried to dance after having half a dozen mugs of brown mead? I felt so sorry for that poor girl he was with."

Trish tried to hide a giggle behind her hand, "Don't feel too sorry for her, they are engaged to be married in a few months."

"Really?" Rose asked, astonished. Lord Alen had done one too many turns on the dance floor and, when it came time for the dip, he fell on top of the young lady. When helping her to her feet, he had vomited all over her hem.

"Oh yes," Trish continued. "Apparently, he went to the family's land after he sobered up and offered to work in the fields for a whole summer as an apology."

"Offered? He didn't actually do it then?" Rose asked.

"No, he did. That's how they got to know each other. I think it's rather romantic, if you can overlook the vomit." Trish gave a small sigh. "I don't think my story will be that lovely, being arranged and all."

"I volunteer to get the Duke drunk as a skunk if you are feeling a lack of romance." Rose offered, half joking, half serious. She wouldn't mind watching him make a fool of himself on the dance floor.

Just then, there was a knock on the door, and Rose went to answer it. Ann was there in her usual clothing, looking a bit hackled.

"Are you girls ready to go down?" she asked.

Trish stood, gave her dress one last pat, and said, "I think so, Ann, lead the way."

As she stood, you could see the dress in all its glory. Ann's mouth opened slightly, and her eyes went a little misty. She cleared her throat, gave a curt nod, then turned on her heel and led them down the hall to a large landing.

The grand staircase was rarely used, but whenever an important noble or visiting royalty was being feasted, it was customary to introduce everyone and have them make a grand entrance on the long sweeping staircase.

Rose thought it tantamount to torture to make the women walk down the stairs in their most decorative dresses with everyone staring at them, but tradition was tradition, she supposed.

Thankfully, she wouldn't have many people looking at her. She was always announced far before the king and his children, if she walked down the staircase at all. Today, Trish had asked her to join them on the staircase for moral support.

A small crowd of nobles had already gathered behind the double doors that led to the staircase, and everyone was lining up by rank. A herald was standing at attention by the doors, waiting for everyone to settle down. The herald had been at the castle as long as Rose could remember, and he knew absolutely everyone. He knew if people were out of rank and would gently guide them where they were supposed to be.

Rose said goodbye to Trish and went to take her usual place in line, third from the door, behind a few noble widows who had enough money to warrant an introduction but not so important to be with the current land owning nobles farther back.

Rose hardly ever talked to the first lady in line, but the second was Lady Esther. Lady Esther was the most interesting older lady you could ever hope to meet. She had been something of a confidant to the queen when she was alive, and after she passed away, Lady Esther was a grandmother of sorts to her children and Rose.

Through a course of sad and unlucky circumstances, Esther had been married three times but never had any children. Her first husband died three weeks after their wedding from an allergic reaction to a bee sting.

Her second husband was called to war after only being married for two weeks. He was at war for two years and was killed. Her third husband she was married to for thirty years, but they never had any children. Either because they didn't want any or couldn't have any, Rose didn't know.

When Rose took her place behind Esther, she gave her shoulders a gentle squeeze, "Hello, Lady Esther."

Esther turned slowly and smiled at Rose, "Oh, hello, dear! My, don't you look fetching."

"Wait till you see Trish," Rose said as she bent to receive Esther's kiss on her cheek.

"You'd better look out, my dear, looking like that, you'll soon have more suitors than you can manage!" Esther tweaked Rose's nose and patted her cheek.

Esther was somewhere in her seventies. She walked with a cane and, at first glance, you would think she was a feeble old woman, but when you got to know her, you soon found out her mind was as sharp as a blade and she had more spunk than many twenty-year-olds.

Rose laughed, "Not with you in front of me, Esther dear, you look ready to leave all the young lads heartbroken."

Esther laughed and patted Rose's hands, "You're shameless, you are." She said, but also gave Rose a roguish wink, then turned back into line as the doors opened for the first time that night.

The herald announced the first lady, then closed the doors again. A minute later, the doors were opened again, and the herald bellowed, "Lady Esther of Dufshire!"

Esther took her cane and walked slowly to the top of the stairs. She walked down the stairs like she had done it a million times, which she probably had, and even though her descent was slow, somehow that added to her grace.

Rose's name was called, and she went down the stairs as quickly as she could without being considered rude. She almost tripped on her hoop when she reached the last step and had to steady herself with the railing.

She looked up, and no one seemed to notice. Most of them were already looking back at the top of the stairs to see who was coming next, but out of the corner of her eye, she could see someone looking at her. It was the Duke. He had the smallest of grins on his face as their eyes met and he gave a very slight nod, letting Rose know he had seen her stumble.

Rose gritted her teeth and walked towards her seat. Unfortunately, it was at the same table as the Duke, and Trish had arranged for Rose to sit with them for the feast. Rose didn't know how she had managed it, but she must have begged her father and somehow impressed upon him how much she wanted and valued Rose's opinion when it came to the Duke.

Instead of walking directly to their table, Rose walked around the perimeter of the dining hall, taking her time to make sure her temper was in check before she had to sit alone with the Duke until everyone else was seated. She even stopped to say hello to a few people along her way.

She could feel the Duke's eyes on her as she took much longer than necessary to get to her seat. When it got to the point that the important nobles were being announced and Rose was running out of ways to delay being seated, she walked quickly up the few steps to the raised platform where the royal family would be eating, and sat down quickly.

She and the Duke were only separated by the space that was left between chairs to accommodate the ladies' large dresses. The king was to sit at the head of the table with Trent and Trish to his right, and the Duke and Rose were to his left.

She knew it would be considered rude, but she tried not to look at the

Duke and pretended to be extremely interested in everyone else walking down the stairs. Out of the corner of her eye, she could see the Duke's smirk slightly, and he also turned his attention to the stairs.

The herald announced a noble lady whom Rose had only met once. She was wearing a ridiculously large, bright orange, feathered dress. Her dress was so large that the man escorting her had to walk behind her because they wouldn't both fit on the staircase at the same time.

"Your country has strange fashion. Do you agree?" the Duke turned to look at Rose with a raised eyebrow.

In this particular case, Rose did have to agree that this was indeed a strange fashion. However, her mood was still contrary, so she retorted, "Do not blame the entire country for Lady Anita; she's always been a bit... ostentatious."

"She looks like a large fruit we have in my country that we call the sun fruit." The Duke sipped his wine.

Rose gave a grudging smile and also took a drink of her wine, "Last year was worse."

"Worse?" the Duke questioned, "I don't see how."

"Last year she wore an entire rainbow complete with little cloud shoes that you could see under her dress," Rose explained.

The Duke snorted, actually snorted, and then covered his mouth to try and cover his laughter. "Does her personality match her clothing, or is she trying to compensate for a boring demeanor?"

"If anything, her personality is almost worse than her clothes." Rose rolled her eyes. "Her clothes could be considered a work of art, if a little grandiose. However, Lady Anita lacks intelligence and tries to make up for it in theatrics."

"Ahh," said the Duke, nodding his head. "We are all trying to make up for something, are we not?"

Rose looked him in the eye for the first time. She supposed he was right, in a way. Everyone had insecurities they tried to hide with their strengths, but in Lady Anita's case, she was pretty sure it was just stupidity.

"What about you?" She asked before she fully thought about the question. "What are you trying to make up for?"

The Duke looked at her for another silent moment, then looked away. "I am trying to build something." He took another sip of his wine, and before Rose could process his answer, a trumpet blared at the top of the staircase.

"Announcing! His royal highness Prince Trenton and her royal highness Princess Patricia!"

Trent and Trish stood at the top of the stairs, smiling at the crowd below as everyone stood. They slowly and gracefully descended the steps together. Once they got to the bottom, they walked down the aisle leading to the high table. They nodded at the nobles closest to them as everyone bowed and curtsied.

When they reached the table with Rose and the Duke, Trent pulled out Trish's chair so she could maneuver her dress into position to sit. No one sat down yet because they had to remain standing for the King.

The herald announced the king, and he walked quickly and purposefully to the table. Once he sat, everyone else in the room sat as well, and servants began to serve the food.

The first course was rich, creamy tomato soup with toasted brown bread. Each table also had large bowls of garlic butter placed in the middle for people to share as they pleased.

Everyone started with their soup, except Rose, who liked to put the garlic butter on her bread while it was still warm so the butter would melt.

No one at the high table seemed particularly chatty that evening, so they sat in what would have been an awkward silence if it hadn't been for the food.

By the time the second course had come out, roasted chicken with pepper, salt, and lime, Rose thought somebody should take a stab at starting a conversation.

Thankfully, Trent rose to the occasion, "So, Edmond, how does our fair compare to your own?"

"It's very good," said the Duke. "We don't have a lot of chicken; we have more cattle and pork, but I must say it is quite delightful."

"I do love pork," said Trish. "We eat quite a lot of it during the spring, but in the fall we try to salt as much as we can for the winter."

"Do you raise many animals here at the castle? Or are they brought in from the fiefs?" inquired the Duke.

"We raise a fair few on the surrounding grounds," said the king, joining the conversation. "But the majority of the livestock and crops are brought in from the surrounding fiefs. Our kingdom, as you know, does not have very many precious metals, so many of our Lords pay their taxes in either grain or livestock."

"What a wonderful notion," said the Duke. "Our King demands all of his taxes in coin, preferably gold, although he doesn't raise his nose at silver either. I will have to give him the suggestion of this tax collecting. It seems reasonable if the people don't have coin."

"The people have coin," said the king. "I would prefer them to keep their coin and use it for what they wish. People are much happier to part with a pig or a cow because they know they can raise more. You cannot breed coin."

The Duke raised his wine glass in acknowledgement, "True, I suppose;

however, I didn't think the point of taxes was to keep people happy."

"The point of taxes," Trent said in an annoyed tone. "Is to support the kingdom and to be able to provide the people with what they cannot provide for themselves. Good roads, a strong military, and law. What good is a rich kingdom if your people die from ruffians on the road?"

Trent and Edmund stared at each other for a moment before Edmond nodded his head in agreement, "Wise words, my prince. You will be a great ruler someday."

The words were polite enough, but something behind them suggested that the Duke was calling Trent a child. Thankfully, Trish brought up another subject before anyone else could notice the possible rudeness.

"We have a lovely day planned for you tomorrow, Edmund. Do you like hunting?"

The Duke turned his eyes to Trish, "I do indeed. What game will we be hunting?"

"Stag, if we can find any," said Trish. "They are rather elusive animals, I'm told."

Rose wanted to roll her eyes, but she refrained.

Although she and Trish only went on official hunts once or twice a year, they had both gone hunting with Trent and a few of the nobles who frequented the castle more times than she could count. In fact, Trish was probably better with a bow than most of the noblemen in the kingdom; she just had a tender heart and never wanted to kill anything. Her shots always went wide or short when they were hunting, but if you gave her a target, she would hit it nine times out of ten right in the bullseye.

"Will you ladies be accompanying us then? I'm not sure if women frequently go hunting here. They often do in Westland," said the Duke.

"They don't often go," said Rose. "But yes, we were planning on going.

We have to make sure the men's tales are kept humble when they return. It never fails, they always see 'the largest stag you've ever seen' when we don't go with them."

Trish giggled, "They always seem to have better luck without us, don't they. Maybe that's why most men think women shouldn't go hunting."

Rose tried to cover her laugh with her glass but ended up choking on the wine. Thankfully, the main course was arriving, smoked beef with scalloped potatoes and sauteed green beans, so no one noticed.

The rest of the meal went about in much the same way, eating and talking about trivial things just to keep the conversation going. Rose got the since everyone was feeling each other out. They were perfect strangers after all, and they all wanted to get to know one another before they talked about anything too serious.

Eventually, everyone had finished eating, and the servants started to clear the tables. The evening was supposed to end with a ball, but first they were to go out onto the grounds to light goodwill candles and set them afloat on little wooden boats on the lake.

This was an ancient tradition that no one seemed to know where it started. Some say it started when the first kings separated the kingdoms to show they were still united, even though they were going their separate ways. Others said it was to honor their ancestors who traveled across the sea to settle the kingdoms.

Either way, Rose loved the tradition. Not for any particular reason other than the water looked so pretty with all the candles reflecting on its surface. Tonight was going to be the perfect night for it, too. There was no wind, and the moon was almost completely gone, meaning the sky would be very dark except for the stars.

Everyone followed the high table out onto the lawns down towards the lake. When they got to the lake's edge, Trish and the Duke exchanged boats and lit each other's candles, then pushed them gently onto the water. Everyone else lit their candles and soon, hundreds of pinpricks of light went gliding out over the black water.

The moment was so peaceful that Rose was almost hopeful for what was to come. The Duke hadn't given her any reason to mistrust him so far. She was almost enjoying his quick wit and eagerness to learn about the eastern kingdom. The entire dinner had either been jokes or him inquiring about Zehrah's traditions and customs.

A small sigh interrupted her thoughts, "What?" she asked Trent, who was standing next to her.

"Nothing," he said. "I was just remembering how much mother loved setting off the boats."

Rose gave a small smile, then reached out and squeezed Trent's hand. "Do you remember when we put a sparkling candle on Trish's boat on her birthday? She was furious."

She felt Trent's shoulders shake in a silent laugh, "I do believe that was your idea, not mine."

"Oh, really?" Rose asked. "And who was the one who talked the chemist into giving him the sparkler?"

Trent thought for a second, "Oh, that was me, wasn't it? I didn't put it on the boat, though. You slipped the sparkler into Trish's pocket that evening before we even went down to the lake."

"You were still an accomplice," Rose said, enjoying the memory. When Trish lit the sparkler, it looked like a normal candle at first because they had coated the top inch or so in wax. However, when it got a few feet offshore, it started sparking and popping like mad and eventually flipped the little boat over.

Trish had tried her best to keep up the act of a lady, but when the boat had flipped over, she chased Trent all the way back into the castle until he was able to lock himself in his room. The queen had given Trent and Rose a terrible scolding and made them apologize to Trish, as well as giving them chores every day that week.

Many of the candles were starting to burn out, and the grounds were getting darker and darker. Soon they all turned back to the castle. There was an excited buzz in the crowd as everyone was anxious to start the ball and the dancing.

As they turned to go, Trent leaned down and asked, "Save a dance for me?"

"I always do, don't I?" Rose said, then they walked back into the castle.

# Chapter 4

The ball did not get over until close to two in the morning. Rose woke groggily and wiped the sleep out of her eyes. She had never been one to sleep in much past sunrise, but on mornings like this, she wished she were.

She tried for a few minutes to go back to sleep, wanting to be well rested for the hunt that afternoon, but she soon gave up. The sun was shining through her curtains directly into her eyes, and she simply couldn't fall back asleep.

She quietly got dressed, knowing Trish would be asleep for at least a few more hours, and went down to the kitchens in search of breakfast.

Many nobles waited for breakfast in their rooms, but Rose liked to talk with some of the ladies in the kitchen. She may have been raised with the prince and princess, but she was never able to forget that she was more than likely a commoner who was in the right place at the right time.

"Good morning, Eva," she said when she saw a round-faced maid she had known for years.

"My, you're up early," Eva commented. "I thought everyone would be sleeping until at least noon. What time did you finally get to bed, Miss Rose?"

Rose wiped some remaining sleep out of her eyes, "I gave up at about midnight, but I didn't hear Trish come in till at least two." Rose liked how Eva always called her miss instead of lady. Of course, she would have preferred to just be called Rose, but a lifetime of training was not easily unlearned, no matter how friendly you are with one another.

"You'll be looking for breakfast, I'm assuming?" Eva said as she shifted the linens in her arms so she could pick up an empty bucket.

"I was just going to see what was left over from the feast. I don't need anything fancy. Here, let me take some of that," Rose said. She had learned many years ago that if she asked if a staff member *needed* help, they would always decline, but if you simply helped them, they usually didn't refuse. She supposed that needing help and wanting help were two different things.

They walked along the hallway to the kitchens in comfortable silence. Eva wasn't one for many words, although you could often find her humming or singing softly to herself, and Rose wasn't awake enough to start a rousing conversation.

They got to the kitchen, and Rose opened the door for Eva and let her through first. As much as Rose didn't think of herself as a royal, she knew it made some of the kitchen staff nervous to have her around. The ones she knew didn't mind her at all, but if there was a new cook or scullery maid, they might consider her presence an invasion of privacy.

"Come on in, Miss, it's just me and Jasper in here this early," Eva said, knowing why Rose paused at the door.

Jasper, a friendly, talkative youth, smiled at her and nodded, "Good morning, Lady Rose, how are you today?"

"Fine, just tired," Rose managed to get out despite the large yawn she was trying to cover. "How did you two get so unlucky to manage the morning shift after a ball?"

"Unlucky?" Jasper asked, pushing up his sleeve a little as he grabbed another dish to be washed. "Them's who worked last night are the unlucky ones. Having to keep track of all those drunk folk," he shook his head in amazement. "I don't know how they do it! Give me the livery any day over that ruckus, m'lady."

Rose had to agree with Jasper on that point. She liked watching the people dance and say things they normally wouldn't without the help of a few too many glasses of wine, but she preferred small groups of close friends.

Jasper finished his dish and took a towel off the table in the middle of the room to dry it and his hands. "You'll be wantin' breakfast? What'll it be? Bacon? Toast? Tomatoes and cheese?"

Rose shook her head, "Just anything that doesn't take effort to make. I wouldn't mind some cold chicken from last night if you have any?"

Jasper looked a little insulted, "I ain't going to serve a lady a cold breakfast. If it's something simple you want, I can fry you up some eggs."

"I'm not a lady, Jasper," Rose sighed. "Some cold chicken and bread will do just fine. Don't trouble yourself for me. Everyone will be waking up in a few hours, and you will be very busy with lunch as it is."

"Eggs it is then," Jasper said, completely ignoring Rose. She rolled her eyes as she watched him walk to the egg shelves that had no fewer than four dozen eggs on them.

"Just let him do it, Miss," Eva said as she folded the towels she had brought down. "He thinks he's going to be the next cook in this castle, and he definitely needs the practice."

Jasper looked like he wanted to stick his tongue out at Eva, but he simply squared his shoulders and started on the eggs. "You didn't seem to have a problem with your dinner last night, or your lunch and breakfast. Cook only has time for the fancy folk upstairs, so it's me that fixes most of the staff meals, and I ain't heard a complaint yet."

"Just because people are hungry doesn't mean you're a good cook," Eva said under her breath, so Jasper didn't hear.

Stifling a smile, Rose thought it was time to change the subject. "Any good gossip lately?" It didn't matter where you went in the castle or how private you thought your conversations were; the staff always knew everything.

"Not too much," Eva said. "Mostly everyone's been talking about the Princess's engagement."

Rose should have guessed that not everyone had her same reservations about the Duke. She didn't feel up to talking about him this early in the morning, no matter how well last night had gone.

"Did Benny ever ask Jasmine to go walking with him?" She asked to change the subject.

"He surely did," Jasper said as he threw some seasoning onto the eggs. "They did more than walking too. He managed to borrow a carriage from his friend in the livery, but the friend failed to tell ol' Benny the horse he let him borrow was still greener than spring grass. Jas musta thought the ride was a little too lively cuz she hasn't gone out with him since."

"Poor Benny," commented Eva. "He's a nice lad, but he isn't the sharpest one you'll ever meet."

Rose silently agreed. Benny worked in the stables, and he usually tried to do jobs that were too big for him. Many times, he had offered to rub Raul down for Rose, and she always declined, wanting to make sure it was done correctly. He was a nice enough lad, but nice just doesn't cut it sometimes.

Jasper got a plate out and slid what was supposed to be simple eggs, but had somehow turned into an omelet, onto it, then handed it to Rose.

She shook her head slightly, then took a bite. It was delicious. It had just the right amount of seasoning and was filled with onion, peppers, and fresh spinach. It also had small chunks of leftover chicken in it.

"Jasper," Rose said after swallowing her bite, "This is phenomenal! What were you talking about, Eva? This is delicious!"

Eva didn't say anything, but Jasper was glowing with pride. "Twasn't anything m'lady. It's just eggs with some extra stuff thrown in there."

"You can say whatever you like, this is the best omelet I've ever had." Rose looked at the sun starting to slant in the windows. "Jasper, if it's not too much trouble, could you make another one for Trish?"

Jasper looked surprised but eager, "Sure thing, no problem at all, everything's already out, it'll take me two minutes."

"Making the princess breakfast, now he'll never shut up," Eva grumbled into her towels.

By the time Rose was done with her omelet, the second one was ready to go. Jasper had put it in between two clay plates to keep it warm on her way back up to Trish's room.

Rose thanked Jasper and Eva and left the kitchen. She didn't see anyone on her way back to Trish's room. Everyone was still asleep.

Rose went into her room, then went through the joining door between her and Trish's rooms. Rose was a little surprised to see that Trish was already awake and dressed.

"Oh," she said and stopped. "Good morning, I thought you would still be in bed."

"I only woke up a few minutes ago," Trish said with a yawn and a stretch.

"I brought you some breakfast. Jasper made it, and it's wonderful." Rose handed Trish the plate.

Trish smiled in thanks but put the plate on the dresser. She went back to slowly brushing her hair.

Rose furrowed her brows, "Is something the matter?"

Trish put the brush down, "No, nothing's the matter."

Rose could tell she had more to say and knew the best thing to do was to be quiet and let her say what needed to be said in her own time.

Trish looked at Rose for the first time, "I'm not sure if I'm ready to leave."

"Leave where? For the hunt? That's not for a few hours, you still have time."

"No, not the hunt," Trish said, looking away. "I'm not sure I'm ready to leave here. The castle. You. Trent. Father. Last night was wonderful, and Edmund was amazing, but I think it's hitting me that once I am married, I won't see you every day. I don't think I'm ready."

Rose's heart went out to Trish. Whenever a young lady was engaged, everyone was always so happy for her, but many times they forgot what she was giving up and leaving behind. Especially if she was a royal. She was leaving her family, her friends, and her childhood all at the same time. She often went someplace she had never been before, to live with people she had never met, all while being expected to do a job she had never done and had little idea of how to do it, being a wife.

Rose went to Trish and hugged her around the shoulders. "I know it's scary, but remember that nothing has been set in stone yet and Westland isn't too horribly far away."

Trish made a doubtful noise in the back of her throat, "Rose, you know as well as I do that father liked Edmund last night. The match has been official for weeks now, even if no one has said as much, and Westland is a full two weeks' ride from here. You don't consider that to be 'horribly far'?"

"It's only two weeks when you are traveling in a full caravan. A rider could make it in eight days or so, probably less if she was in a hurry." Rose had never made the journey, but she had seen maps that didn't show any major ranges that would make the journey difficult. It was mostly grassy plains and a few forests once you got closer to Westland.

"'She'? Are you planning on visiting me then?" Trish asked.

"Of course," Rose said hotly. "At least you aren't going to the northern kingdom. That would take at least a month, and it's across the desert and mountains." Rose looked at Trish's still skeptical face, "What? You thought after you got married, I would never see you again?"

"Well, it's a long journey, and I know you don't like Edmund, and" Trish peeked under her lashes at Rose and stopped abruptly.

Rose was glaring at her, "Really, Trish, you think so little of me? For almost our entire lives, we have lived like sisters. Any ill feelings, no matter how strong I have for the Duke, could never surpass my love for you."

Trish's eyes brimmed with tears, "I know, I know," she almost whispered. "I'm just overwhelmed and tired, forgive me."

Rose squeezed Trish's shoulders, "Of course I do."

Rose pulled Trish into a hug, "Besides, I'm sure I'm going to need a reason to get out of this castle once you're gone. Now eat your breakfast before it gets cold. I'm going to get dressed for the hunt."

***

Rose was in the stables brushing down Raul before the hunt. Most of the nobles waited for grooms to catch, brush, and saddle their mounts, but Rose liked to do it herself. She had seen what not having a strong bond with your animal did, and she wanted to be able to trust the animal who could be the difference between her life and death.

She finished rubbing Raul down and was on her way to get his tack when she saw the Duke. He was unlatching the stall door to one of the biggest stalls they had in the stables, which was usually used for foaling, but that had been where they put the Duke's mount.

He grabbed a brush and started briskly rubbing down the beast. He even murmured to him softly and scratched under his chin, which the animal enjoyed greatly. It stretched its neck out as far as it could and raised its upper lip.

Rose smiled. Raul would do the same thing if you scratched him just under his left front leg. The more she saw of the Duke, the more she liked him. Any noble who looked after his horse couldn't be completely evil, could they? It showed that they didn't mind doing a hard task and that they didn't rely on their servants to do everything for them. It also showed that they valued the time spent with their animal aside from just riding. Furthermore, this wasn't just the necessary brushing you needed to do before putting a saddle on a horse. The horse seemed to like the Duke very much, and they were comfortable with each other.

Rose, not wanting to interrupt, quietly got Raul's tack and turned to head back to his stall. On her way out of the tack room, one of the stirrups slid out from her grip, and it banged on the doorframe. The Duke stopped brushing his horse and looked over at her.

"Good morning," he smiled. "Do you need help with that?"

"Oh, no, thank you. Sorry, I didn't mean to interrupt." Rose quickly gathered up her stirrup and started back towards Raul's stall.

Despite her refusal, the Duke had come over to her and held out his arms for the saddle. Rose looked at him and decided, since he was already there, to hand him the saddle, and she carried the bridal.

"Thank you, I really would have been fine though."

"I have no doubt," said the Duke, "but what kind of gentleman would I be if I didn't help a lady?"

"I'm not a lady," Rose whispered under her breath.

"Pardon?" inquired the Duke, looking at her.

"Nothing, just talking to myself," Rose said, blushing slightly. "I guess I've gotten used to people knowing I like to do things on my own. People rarely even offer help anymore."

They had arrived back at Raul's stall. "Well," the Duke put Raul's saddle over the stall door. "I would not like to intrude on your self-sufficiency. I assume you would like to saddle him yourself?"

Rose hung the bridle on the horn of the saddle and turned to the Duke, "I would. Thank you for carrying it for me." She smiled at him, "I will see you at the line-up, your grace."

She curtsied slightly, then opened the stall door and shut it between them. The Duke gave a small bow, "Are we to stand on such formalities? You may call me Edmund, as long as you do not mind me calling you Rose."

Rose considered for a moment, "Thank you for your help then, Edmund."

He nodded his head and went back to his horse's stall. She couldn't put her finger on it, but she was still uneasy about him. She didn't dislike him as much as she had a few days ago, but something in her gut was telling her that he wasn't who he was pretending to be.

She shook her head. She was being ridiculous. Was she going to hold a childhood grudge forever? People change, especially going from childhood to adulthood. They couldn't have been more than five and nine when they had met as children. Was she the same person she was back then? Of course not, so why was she expecting him to be?

She grabbed the saddle and slung it over Raul's back a little roughly. He grunted. "I'm sorry," she said, rubbing his nose. "I'm sorry, boy. It's not your fault. I wish you could give me your opinion of him. Animals are much better judges of personality than humans are."

He nickered as if he was chuckling.

"You're right," she gave Raul one last scratch on the forehead, then went to saddle him. "If we don't get a move on, everyone will have already left and been back again before we even leave the stables."

***

Once Raul was all ready to go, Rose led him out into the courtyard where everyone was gathering for the hunt.

She saw Trish with Been and went to her. "Hello, it looks like it's going to be a lovely day. Not too hot, I hope." Trish said as she shielded her eyes from the afternoon sun.

"It doesn't feel too bad right now, and it'll be the hottest here in the yard. Once we get into the forest, there will be a breeze, hopefully." Rose patted Been's nose.

"If not a breeze, I hope there is at least shade. I didn't bring a bonnet. I didn't want it to get snagged on any branches." Trish patted her hair.

Rose raised her eyebrows at her, "Planning on doing some cross-country riding, are you?"

Trish blushed, "Well, I-I thought we should stay with Edmund. I didn't know if he would prefer to stick to the trails or not."

"Just make sure he's in front of you. He should knock down any branches you might hit; he and his horse are so tall." Rose said. "I saw him in the stables this morning when I was saddling Raul."

"Oh," Trish raised her eyebrow questionably. "Did he say anything about last night?"

"No, he just offered to carry the saddle from the tack room to the stall." Rose paused before tacking on, "He also said we should call each other by our first names."

"Well, of course, you should," Trish said fervently. "You really should be friends with him, Ro. You'll be family once we get married."

"Dum, dum, dum dum," Rose hummed the wedding song under her breath, and Tirsh giggled.

"Good day, ladies," Trent said from his saddle as he rode over to them. "Did you get enough sleep after last night?"

"I did," Trish assured him. "But you know Rose, always up at the crack of day, no matter how late she stayed up the night before."

"Just because I got up early doesn't mean I didn't get enough sleep," Rose contradicted.

"Well, you both look lovely and ready to go either way," Trent said, dismounting. "Do you need a hand up?"

He bent to help Trish onto Been, and when she got settled, he turned to Rose. He quirked up an eyebrow in question.

"Rose?"

He knew she hated being thrown onto her horse like a child, but it really couldn't be helped when they had the side saddles. On her regular saddle, she could simply put her left foot in the stirrup and fling her right foot over the horse's rump. However, with the side saddles, you had to put your left leg in the stirrup, then get your right leg over the fixed and leaping head, then arrange your skirts over the saddle to make sure nothing was showing that shouldn't be.

It was easiest to have someone grab your right foot and lift you onto the seat, then hook your right leg over the fixed head and have the helper put your foot in the stirrup.

"Fine then," she murmured. "Be quick about it."

Trent chuckled as she lifted her foot. He grasped her foot firmly as Rose bounced on her other leg.

"One, two, three!" Trent lifted as Rose jumped off her left leg. Once she was in the saddle, she arranged her skirts, and Trent took her left foot and put it in the stirrup.

"Thank you," she said, looking down at Trent.

"It could be worse, you know, it could have been Lord Redmond again," Trent said laughingly.

Rose looked to her left and saw Lord Redmond getting ready to mount his horse. It looked like he would either need a leg up himself or a mounting block. The one time he had offered to help Rose mount was an absolute disaster. Rose had tried to politely decline his offer, but everyone else had been busy, and he had insisted.

Lord Redmond was not the youngest of lords, and he was rather fat. When he counted to three and tried to hoist Rose onto the saddle, his strength failed him, and he dropped Rose on the dirt.

After Lord Redmond's profuse apologies and offering to help again, Trent had come and helped Rose into the saddle. She had to endure months of Trent teasing her about not eating dessert at dinner for the sake of the poor lords of the kingdom.

"Very true, and others have been known to throw women *over* their horse instead of on it, so, again, thank you."

Trent smiled and patted Rose's knee, and then remounted his horse. He then turned to everyone else in the yard.

"Attention, everyone!" he called so they could all hear him. "We are about to set off on our hunt. Please remember to ride in groups of at least two. We will be in the southern part of the woods today. If you do get lost or injured, blow your horn, and help will come. Everyone ready?"

A cheer went up from the crowd, and everyone started for the gates. As the courtyard emptied, Trent came back to Rose and Trish.

"Father is not coming?" Trish asked. "I didn't see him in the yard."

"No, he told me I would be in charge and to get to know the Duke," Trent said as they started riding for the gates.

The Duke and a man servant were standing at the gate, either waiting for them or not knowing which group to join.

"Edmund," Trish called. "Come with us. We know the forest better than anyone, and we'll show you the way to the stag."

"Of course, Trish," Edmund said amiably. "But if you know where the stag is, doesn't that ruin the hunt?"

"Not at all," said Trish quickly. "He ranges the whole of the woods and is rarely sighted. But we have seen him a few times on other hunts that this group of nobles wasn't on, so we should have a head start."

Rose rode next to Trish and whispered, "You're rambling."

"Shall we be off then?" Trish squeaked and blushed.

"I think we had better," Trent said, trying not to laugh.

The five of them rode out the gates and into the woods a little behind the larger party of nobles. Trish, Edmund, and his servant rode in front, and Trent rode with Rose far enough back that their conversation could not be heard.

"I'm quite surprised at you, you know," Trent said as soon as they were out of earshot.

Rose furrowed her eyebrows, "Whatever do you mean?"

"You have yet to uncover a diabolical plot involving the Duke, therefore making it wholly unsuitable for him and Trish to be wed." Trent nodded towards the Duke.

Rose rolled her eyes, "Well, I've only known him for a day. Truth be told, I actually enjoyed his company at the dinner last night."

"Shocking! Rose actually likes someone."

If they had been riding closer together, she would have punched him, "I've put up with you my whole life. My being able to like someone shouldn't come as a shock. I didn't say I liked him, I said his company was enjoyable; there is a difference."

"I must admit I didn't mind his company either. Even when you and Trish took to the dance floor, he remained amiable and interested in our governing style." Trent continued to look at the Duke.

"But?" Rose asked.

Trent returned his gaze to her, "Like you said, we've only known him for one day. I'm," he paused.

"Reserving judgment." They said together.

They looked at each other and gave brief smiles.

"Well, we should go and take the lead. Trish is an excellent shot, but she can't track to save her life. We don't want to get too off track or else we won't have anything to show for this hunt." Rose said and gave Raul a tap with her riding crop to move him into a trot.

"Ah, there you are, Rose," Trish said. "I was just asking Edmund if he had time for much hunting while he is at home."

"I do," Edmund said. "However, I must admit I'm not much of a tracker. We are accustomed to hawking smaller game."

"Well then, how about you go with Rose, and I will go with Trent," Trish suggested. "That way, we can cover more ground, and we will both have an accomplished tracker with us."

"Excellent idea, sister," Trent said, smiling at Rose.

As much as she wanted to, Rose did not protest. It made the most sense. To keep things proper, she really shouldn't be riding out into the woods unaccompanied with a man. Trish and Trent together would not need to be accompanied, and with Edmund's servant with him and Rose, everyone was properly accompanied.

"Fine by me," said Rose. "Edmund, we can go south along this trail. Trent, you and Trish can go northeast on the main road."

Then all turned to the trails Rose had indicated and set on their way. After a few minutes of silent riding, Rose decided to try her hand at conversation.

"I never asked," she said. "What is your beast's name?"

"Dante," he said, patting the horse on the neck. "It means steadfast or enduring. I think he grew into the name quite well. How about yours?"

"Raul, I was told it means wise counselor," She laughed. "I didn't name him, but he certainly gives good advice."

Edmund laughed loudly, then must have thought it rude, "Forgive me, I really shouldn't laugh. As you saw this morning, I also tend to talk to my horse. They truly are the best listeners."

"I think it has something to do with them not being able to talk," Rose turned to look at Edmund and remembered they were not alone in their party. "I'm so sorry, I'm being terribly rude. What is your name, sir?"

"Grady isn't a sir," Edmund said before the servant had a chance. "He's been with my family as long as I can remember, and he is quite shy."

Rose looked at the older man. He might be shy, but Rose wasn't accustomed to ignoring the help like many royals were inclined to do. "It's nice to meet you, Grady."

The man gave the smallest of nods, then looked down at his horse and dropped a little further back from them.

"Sorry, I didn't mean to offend," she started to say to Edmund, but he cut her off.

"No offense, he really is just that shy. He prefers taking care of things quickly and quietly around the house. He also prefers taking care of books and ledgers as opposed to hunting. I wouldn't have brought him, but like I said, he's worked for my family forever, and I trust him implicitly."

"Well," Rose said, trying to save the conversation. "Let's be on our way then. The sooner we find something to shoot, the sooner we can get Grady back to his books."

They rode in silence for another fifteen minutes before Rose finally saw some markings on the ground. There were hoof prints in the dirt just a few paces off the trail.

She pulled back on her reins to stop Raul and dismounted.

"Did you find something?" Edmund asked, dismounting as well.

"Yes, come look," Rose invited. "See the hoof prints on the ground?"

Edmund stooped to get a closer look at the prints. "Are those stag prints? They seem awfully large."

"It's either the stag we seek or a boar, which we certainly do not seek. The tracks look very similar, to begin with, and these aren't very clear. Either way, these are at least a few days old. See how deep the tracks are? They were made when the ground was wet, at least two days ago."

"The animal could still be in the area, though, right?" Edmund inquired.

"It could," Rose said, standing up. "We can walk along this little trail and see if there are any other signs. If it is a boar, there will most likely be some rooting."

"Grady, stay with the horses," Edmund turned and got a nod from Grady.

Edmund gestured for Rose to lead the way, so she went ahead of him, and they walked single file down the skinny game trail.

"Where did you learn to track and hunt?" Edmund asked.

"I learned a great deal from Trent and books. Most of the noble ladies do not enjoy the activities and never join in the hunts, but one day, when I was about thirteen, I followed the men into the woods. I would have gotten into a great deal of trouble if someone other than Trent had found me." She smiled at the memory. "He told his father that he had invited me. I've been going with them almost every hunt since."

Rose held her hand up for Edmund to stop. He did. She was honestly a little surprised at how willing he was to let her take the lead. Most of the men she knew would have tried to stay in charge even if they knew nothing about hunting or tracking. Edmund, however, seemed to take her at her word that she knew a good deal about the sport and was happy to follow her lead. Yet another reason for her to like him.

"Blast!" she said. "It is a boar, look, see how the undergrowth is all plowed up?"

Edmund nodded.

"That's what happens when a large group of wild boar goes looking for grubs and roots. We might as well go back to the horses. We don't have dogs or spears, and I have yet to see the arrow that will bring down a boar." She turned to go, but Edmund was directly behind her. She almost bumped into him.

"Sorry," she took a step back. *Why was he standing so close?* "Did you want me to lead the way back to the horses? It's just down the trail, back the way we came in."

Edmund gazed at her for a moment, then nodded, "I shall follow you then."

Rose gave an awkward smile, then, seeing as he still hadn't moved, walked around him and back to the horses.

When they got back to the main trail, Rose took Raul's reins from Grady.

"Do you need a leg up?" Edmond asked.

Rose looked around, finding a good stump. She said, "Not to worry, this will serve as a mounting block."

Edmund took Dante's reins but waited for Rose to mount before he did.

"If we keep going along this trail, we might have better luck," Rose said. "There is a stream about a quarter mile from here where we might find more tracks."

"We follow your lead, Lady Rose," Edmund put out his hand again, gesturing for her to lead the way.

Rose nodded and tapped Raul with her crop. They walked the horses in silence. Rose was enjoying the sounds of the forest and didn't feel inclined to start up another conversation. She had done most of the talking so far and decided that if Edmund wanted conversation, he would have to think of something to talk about.

They had almost reached the stream when they saw a large tree blocking the road. Rose looked to either side of the road, but they were both surrounded by brush and sticker bushes.

"Well," Rose shrugged. "We can either go back or go over. What do you say, gentlemen?"

Edmund looked like he had no problems with going over, but Grady looked like he was going to be sick.

Edmund looked at Grady and said, "Perhaps Grady can stay here while we have a look around at the stream?"

"Yes, that will be fine," Rose said. "The stream is only a little further. It shouldn't take more than ten minutes to look around. If you don't mind waiting here alone, Grady?"

"I don't mind, ma'am," Grady said in a much quieter, almost whiny, voice than his announcing yesterday.

"Well then," Edmund said. "After you, Rose."

Rose loved jumping almost as much as Raul did; however, she would have preferred to do it astride. When she was side saddle, she couldn't grip Raul with her legs to hold on. She was entirely dependent on her balance and the one stirrup she had.

Nevertheless, she trusted Raul and knew he was an excellent jumper, no matter what saddle she was in. They turned to face the tree and started to lope towards it. Raul did a slight check of his stride, then went over the tree gracefully and landed gently, hardly jolting Rose at all. She was always surprised, as large as Raul was, how exceedingly graceful he was.

Edmund followed shortly after, not as graceful as Raul and Rose but skillful all the same. They only had to go about two hundred more yards before they came to the stream.

It wasn't large or deep, but it was swift and cool. It had a rocky bottom and was spring-fed, so the water was crystal clear.

Rose dismounted and let Raul get a drink from the stream. She walked along the banks going upstream, looking for tracks. The ground was very rocky right next to the stream, but became soft and grassy a little further up the bank.

Edmund had stayed with the horses, and Rose was glad. She preferred to track alone or with Trent simply because they had been tracking together so long that they hardly needed to speak to communicate their findings. She didn't like it when people hovered like he had done at the boar rooting.

She had gone a good way upstream without finding anything and decided to turn back to see if downstream would fare better. When she passed by Edmund, she took Raul's halter, and they walked the horses downstream in search of tracks or any other signs of the stag.

They walked downstream for five minutes when Edmund said, "Is there much chance of us finding any tracks on these rocks?"

"Not much, no." Rose conceded. "Should we turn back? Poor Grady might be tired of waiting for us."

"He probably is," Edmund said with a smile. "I told him he didn't have to come today, but he insisted. Something about needing to watch out for me around so many foreigners."

Rose laughed, "Well, you look like you can take care of yourself."

Edmund gave a crooked smile and shrugged, "All the men in my family are large. From my experience, it's not always the largest man who wins the fight but the most skilled. Although a man who is large and skilled is a formidable foe."

Rose nodded in agreement. She didn't know much about fighting, but she supposed he was right. She looked around for a place to mount, but there wasn't anything close by, just a rocky bank.

Edmund noticed her predicament and said, "It's no trouble to give you a leg up. I assure you, I'm strong enough to lift you."

Rose studied Edmund for a moment and admitted her need for a leg up. He certainly looked strong enough, and he seemed to be an accomplished horseman. Rose silently prayed he wouldn't use too much of his strength and throw her over Raul into the stream.

"If you don't mind, I could use the help," She said.

"Not at all," Edmund said. He walked to her, and she lifted her foot. He grabbed it and counted to three. She pushed off with her left leg and sat in the saddle. As her weight went to the saddle, she felt Edmund's hand slip off her heel and slide up her calf to the crook of her knee.

She thought it a mere slip, but he kept his hand on her leg far longer than appropriate and looked up at her. She stared at him, not knowing what to say or do but desperately wanting him to take his hand away.

"Sir," She started to say, but there were three loud horn blasts that covered her words.

The Duke jerked his hand away from her leg and returned to his horse.

Rose cleared her throat, "The hunt is over. Three blasts mean someone got the stag."

"Let's find our way back to Grady then, and head back to the castle." He started without waiting for her.

Rose took a moment to compose herself. She could feel her face flushing and her heart pounding.

What on earth was that all about?

# Chapter 5

Trent and Trish had gotten the stag. Rose wished they had stayed together. She didn't know what to make of the Duke's slip. Was it a slip? Were the customs different in Westland? Maybe Westland was more relaxed on propriety than they were. Whatever it was, she knew she was going to have to watch him more closely.

She knew she couldn't avoid him completely, especially if she was overreacting, but she wanted to be able to watch him interact with other people without him knowing she was around. She might have to ask some of her maids to keep tabs on him as well. The gentry was often much less careful around the servants, and it was a good way to get to know their character.

"Congratulations," the Duke called to Trish. "We should not have separated, then Rose and I could have shared the glory of the kill."

Rose smiled, inwardly cringing at the casual use of her name, "Well done, you two."

"Oh, don't be jealous, Rose," Trent said teasingly. "You can't win them all."

When Rose didn't reply, Trent walked over to her, "Is everything alright?"

"Everything is fine," Rose said, trying to arrange her face to agree with her words.

"Well, you don't look fine," Trent said, studying her. "What happened?"

"Nothing," Rose said quickly. "I'm just still reserving judgment."

Trent searched her eyes for a moment, then nodded. He knew he wouldn't get much more out of her surrounded by excited people.

"Attention, everyone," Trent called loudly. "We will give the stag to the kitchens to be prepared for dinner tomorrow. Tonight we have arranged for dinner to be served picnic style around the lake."

The men all nodded and started talking again. They were handing their horses to the stable boys and heading back to the castle to change for dinner.

Rose was grateful they weren't having another formal dinner. It meant she had time to take care of Raul and talk to some of the staff to see what she could learn about the Duke.

She led Raul to his stall and took off the saddle. She rubbed him down and gave him some carrots. When she bent to pick out his hoofs, she heard footsteps behind her.

She jerked up, afraid it might be the Duke, but it wasn't. It was one of the newer stable boys with a bucket of water for Raul.

He put the bucket in the stall and said, "I can take care of him, m'lady, if you would like."

Rose smiled at him, "That's alright, I'm almost done anyway."

The boy shifted his weight from one foot to the other, unsure if he should help anyway.

Rose took pity on him, "He could use some fresh hay in his stall. Can you run and get a forkful?"

"Yes, m'lady!" he said and scampered down the aisle towards the hay loft.

By the time he got back, Rose had finished with Raul and was scratching his ears. The boy was carrying such a large fork of hay that she was surprised he could even lift it.

"My, I don't think he needed quite that much," Rose commented as the boy shook the hay off the fork, spreading it evenly on the stall floor. "I don't think we've met before. Are you new to the castle?"

"Yes, m'lady. I was brought in last week," he said, taking a few pieces of hay out of the water he had brought.

"Brought in? Who brought you?" Rose asked.

"The guards, m'lady. I'm up from near Penshaw. My parents were farmers, m'lady," the boy said, looking at his feet.

"They *were* farmers," Rose asked, noting the past tense.

The boy glanced up at her for only a second, "Yes, m'lady. Raiders came to our farm and burned our house. I would have been with them, but I was in the barn taking care of Reddy."

He was an orphan. It was not uncommon for orphans to be brought to the castle if they couldn't be provided for in their village. Rose's heart went out to the boy; she knew what that was like.

"Who's Reddy?" She asked, not wanting to force the boy to talk about his parents.

The boy looked up at her like he had been caught doing something he shouldn't have, "Reddy's my pet, m'lady."

"Did Reddy come with you to the castle?" Rose asked.

The boy ducked his head again, "Yes, m'lady."

"Might I meet him?" asked Rose, smiling gently.

The boy looked up at her wide-eyed, "I...I well. He's not here, m'lady."

Fearing the worst, Rose asked, "He didn't come with you to the castle?"

"No, he did. He's just not here in the stables," The boy explained.

"Oh," Rose said, taken aback. She had assumed that when the boy said he was in the barn taking care of a pet, it was a horse or some other sort of farm animal. "Where is he?"

"In my room," The boy murmured.

"I would dearly like to meet him," Rose pushed. "Are your rooms very far away?"

"No, m'lady," The boy said resignedly.

"We can go now if you like," Rose said.

The boy nodded and started towards the stable doors.

Rose latched Raul's stall door and followed, "Say, I didn't ask your name. Mine's Rose."

The boy looked up at her, a little taken aback at being asked his name. Rose suspected most people probably just called him 'boy.' "My name's Joshua."

"A fine name," Rose smiled at him. Apart from generally liking to know the people who helped take care of her and Raul, Rose was hoping the boy would be willing to help her watch the duke. If royalty ignored servants, they doubly ignored child servants.

Joshua led her around the stables to a long, low building that had many doors. It was a dormitory of sorts for the children who worked in the stables and yards. The children who worked in the castle slept outside the kitchens and scullery.

He led Rose to the last door, farthest from the stables, and opened it.

Normally, there were four boys in each of the rooms, but it looked like Joshua was currently this room's only occupant.

"Do you stay alone?" Rose asked.

"Just me and Reddy," he said.

At the sound of the boy's voice, there came a strange squawking, laughing, panting sound from under his bed. Rose had never heard an animal make that sound and had no idea what it could be. She thought maybe it was a cat or dog if it wasn't a barn animal, but now she had no clue what it was.

Joshua leaned down and looked under his bed. "Come here, Reddy, we have a guest."

A small wiggling black nose poked its way out from the blankets hanging over the side of the bed. Following the nose was a muzzle that was reddish orange on top and white on the bottom. The muzzle opened to make that same strange noise, showing a pink tongue and sharp white teeth.

"Oh come now," Joshua chided. "Come on out. Lady Rose wants to meet you."

Two black paws stuck out, and Rose could tell the animal was stretching. Then Reddy came out sliding on his side, pushed by his back paws, and wiggling all over. His extremely fluffy, white tipped tail thumped on the floor as he presented his white belly to be scratched by Joshua.

It was a fox. Rose had only seen a handful of foxes in the forests around the castle. They were mostly nocturnal and extremely shy, so they were very hard to catch. Rose marveled at the way the fox curled up next to Joshua, acting like a dog.

Reddy was the size of a small dog or a very large cat and had beautiful red fur along the top half of his body and on his sides. His front legs were black, and his back legs were the same reddish brown as his back. His tail was so fluffy that it was almost as big as his body and had a white tuft at the very end.

Joshua managed to contain Reddy's wiggles and pull him up into a hug. "This is Reddy," He said, looking at Rose.

"He's very handsome. How did you manage to catch him? I've seen a few foxes around here, but only glimpses of them." Rose joined the boy and his fox on the floor.

"I found him when he was just a baby. His mama was nowhere around, and he was starving. I took him into the barn and gave him some milk from our goat. He's been following me around ever since." Joshua said proudly. "I haven't shown him to no one here because a lot o' folks don't like em. They sometimes go after chickens. But not Reddy, he's a good fox. He's never bothered any of our chickens, and he's real good at catching moles and mice and things."

"Will he let me pet him?" Rose asked, scooting a little closer.

"Sure," Joshua said. "Just be gentle and slow. Maybe let him smell ya first."

Rose held out her hand and let Reddy smell it. He wiggled his nose all around her hand, and she giggled when his whiskers tickled her arm. She must have smelled alright to him because he squirmed out of Joshua's arms and slid over to her.

She gently patted his head and worked her way to his belly. The fur on his back was sleek and coarse, but his belly and undercoat were delightfully soft and warm.

"I think he likes you," Joshua said.

"I think so too," Rose laughed as the fox tried to crawl into her lap for more petting. "Thank you for showing him to me. I can talk to the stable master and see if it would be all right for you to let him out. If he doesn't bother the chickens, I don't see why he should need to be cooped up in your rooms all the time."

Joshua stared at her wide-eyed, "Th...thank you m'lady."

"No problem at all," Rose said, playing with Reddy's ears. "You know I came to the castle much the same way you did. Everyone should have a friend."

Rose handed Reddy back to Joshua and stood up, "I hate to cut our time short, but I really should be headed to dinner. I'll come by tomorrow and talk again."

Joshua didn't say anything, just nodded vigorously and hugged Reddy around the middle.

***

Rose entered the castle through the kitchen doors. She wanted to talk to some of the scullery maids before she went to dinner. The more she could find out about the Duke, the more prepared she would feel at dinner.

A handsome man like the Duke would definitely have the maids talking.

"Good evening, Eva," Rose said

"Hello," Eva said, looking hackled. "What can I do for you?"

"Nothing," Rose said, slightly concerned for the girl. "Are you alright?"

"Oh, I'm fine. Just breaking up squabbles with some of the other girls." Eva said and sat on a stool.

"What were they squabbling about?" Rose asked, intrigued.

Eva rolled her eyes, "Any time there's a new lad in this castle, all the lasses think he's going to sweep them off their feet and carry them off. Even when this lad is engaged to their princess. They all want to fancy he will see them and be so stricken with their beauty that he will forget all about his intended."

Rose was surprised. Eva wasn't one to make speeches, but she seemed to be particularly opinionated about this behavior of the maids.

"Which maids were arguing?" Rose wanted to know.

Eva looked Rose in the eye, then quickly looked down, "Oh, the whole lot of them." She looked quickly at Rose again.

"I'm not trying to get anyone in trouble," Rose said quickly. "I was just curious. Everyone has dreams of a better life." Rose said and sat as well.

"Well, these dreams aren't even worth dreaming," Eva said, standing again and grabbing a towel. "They are all deluded if they think a Duke would look at them with her highness in the same room, or even the same town, for that matter. I've warned them time and time again not to go chasing after men." Eve put her hands on her hips.

"Man chasing only ends up one a two ways, heartbroken or pregnant, and nine times outta ten you get both." Eva slapped the towel back onto the counter.

"Eva," Rose said, going to her. "Surely some giggling maids don't have you this upset. Did something else happen?"

Eva wrung her hands. What could have happened that made her this nervous? She was usually open with Rose.

"Please tell me," Rose said, taking Eva's wringing hands into hers.

Eva sat on the stool again and said, "Well, one of the quieter gals, Emma, said...well, she said the Duke followed her down the kitchen halls this afternoon after the hunt and tried talking with her."

Rose could tell there was more to the story. "Go on." She prodded.

"Well, I don't know. Emma is real quiet, shy, and sorta plain, so she might have overreacted. She doesn't get much attention from menfolk.

Anyway, she said the Duke followed her down the hall and was flirting with her. Telling her she was mighty pretty to be a maid and things like that. Then she told him she had to get back to work, and he kissed her hand and winked, then left."

"Did he now?" Rose said, growing more and more angry as the story continued.

"Now, Rose, there's no need to get upset. I don't think the Duke did anything wrong. Emma probably just read too much into the conversation. He was probably just being nice, and a gal like Emma just didn't know what to make of it." Eva said quickly. "Please just let it be Rose. I don't want to start no trouble."

Eva's eyes were imploring, and Rose didn't want her to be any more stressed than she already was. "Of course, Eva, no harm done."

Rose left the kitchens and headed upstairs to get ready for dinner.

She was going to be talking to Emma herself.

***

A long, wide table was set up next to the lake so everyone could grab a plate and choose what food they wanted, then find a seat at a picnic table or on one of the fifty or so large blankets that had been spread around the lawn.

Rose didn't know why the nobility insisted on eating like this. She knew most of the nobles preferred eating indoors, but for some reason, they all put on happy faces and tried to act like they were having fun outside.

She suspected they were all trying to prove to one another that they *could* eat outside if an occasion arose where it was necessary.

Rose loved eating in the fresh air and truly enjoyed watching some of the noble ladies try to keep everything clean to no avail.

She had picked up some bread and cheese along with some dried meat and wandered to a blanket on the outskirts of the yard so she could watch everyone. One of the tricks to eating outdoors was to eat food that was easy to eat with your hands. Anything sticky or wet was a bad option. Someone should have told Lady Tia that before she dished up her food. Rose had to contain a giggle as the poor woman tried to balance her skirts, a ridiculous hat, and a large bowl of stew, all while sitting on the ground and still looking lady-like.

Absorbed in watching the lady, Rose didn't notice that Trent had walked over to her blanket.

"Might I sit down?" He asked.

Rose looked up, "Of course." She swept her hand over the blanket in invitation, "Join the party."

"Who are we watching tonight?" Trent asked as he sat.

Rose nodded her head in the direction of Lady Tia, "I'm taking bets on which happens first. Her hat falling off, her dress getting stained, or her choosing wisdom and going to sit at a table."

"What are the odds?" Trent asked as if there was an actual bid going on the situation.

"The hat is favored to win." Just as she said it Lady Tia's hat toppled off the back of her head and rolled down the little hill to the lake.

Rose slapped her hand over her mouth to stop herself from laughing. After she suppressed her giggling and Trent wiped a tear from his eye, he asked, "So, what happened during the hunt?"

Rose took a bite of cheese to give her some thinking time. Before she talked to Eva, she might not have said anything, but now she was more certain that the Duke's behavior wasn't an accident. She still wasn't sure if he meant any harm, but it looked like it was becoming a trend. Trent deserved the truth.

Partly avoiding the question, slightly wanting to gather more information, Rose asked a question instead of answering.

"How many ladies have you helped onto their horses?"

Trent looked taken aback, "Sorry?"

"It doesn't have to be an exact number, just a guess."

"I don't know," He said, obviously confused. "Hundreds probably."

"Hmm," was all Rose said.

Trent looked at her incredulously.

"If a lady slips or isn't very good at mounting, what's the easiest way to help her?"

"Well, a lot of the Ladies' issues with mounting is more the gentleman's fault than theirs. Either they were lifted too far or not enough." Trent said, still confused.

"True, I suppose. Still, out of those hundreds of times you've helped a lady, how many times have you been in the wrong? Has your hand ever slipped off their foot?"

Trent thought for a moment, "I'm sure when I was younger, I messed up a few times. It's not all that difficult. As long as you are strong enough to lift the lady, there is only one movement you need to make. You just straighten up with her foot in your hand and then stand there while she gets situated on the saddle. Why do you ask?"

Rose sighed, "I just wanted to make sure I wasn't overreacting before I told you."

He looked at her quizzically, "Told me what?"

"When the Duke and I went looking for the stag alone, we went down to the creek. We dismounted and were looking for tracks when we heard the horns. There wasn't any place for me to use a stump or log to mount myself, so he offered to help. When I sat in the saddle, his hand came off my boot and slid up my leg to my knee. Then he sort of froze until I said "Sir," and he jerked his hand away. Then he acted like nothing had happened."

Trent sat stiffly, "Wasn't his groom with the two of you?"

"He was until we came to a downed tree. He wasn't a good enough horseman to jump it, so we went on to the creek alone. I didn't think anything of it at the time." Rose said.

Trent looked irritated, "He shouldn't have let you two go off alone. His being there was the only reason I felt comfortable splitting off from the group in the first place. I wouldn't have gone if I knew he wasn't going to take his duties seriously."

"His duties?" Rose asked.

"As a Chaperone."

Rose snorted, "A Chaperone? What am I, ten?"

Trent looked at her with steel in his eyes, "The Chaperone isn't for the lady."

His answer took her aback. "Do you know something about the Duke that you haven't told me?"

Trent looked a little guilty, "No, not really."

Rose cocked an eyebrow, "What does 'not really' mean?" She demanded.

"When he was younger, before he was considered the heir, it was said he was...a ladies' man. But nothing untoward was ever rumored." Trent said.

Rose thought about that for a moment. 'Ladies Man,' could mean a hundred different things, ranging from whore monger to the ladies simply liking him because he was handsome. Of course, the ladies would naturally flock to a strong, good-looking man, especially when he was more attainable at his lower rank. On the other hand, Rose knew there was no scandal too large that the status of a Duke wouldn't be able to hide.

"We need to find out more about him," Rose decided. "As it stands right now, I don't trust him. I don't know him well enough to be able to blow off what he did as something innocent. And you know, Trish, she always wants to think the best of people until they have outright done something wrong."

Trent nodded in agreement, "I'll have to talk to him."

"No," Rose said quickly. "If he doesn't think we suspect anything, then he won't be as cautious. If we accuse him, he will know he needs to put on a better face." Rose thought for a moment. "Do you have a man you can trust to be subtle? Perhaps someone who could take him drinking or play cards or something that will get him to talk freely?"

Trent nodded, "I know just the man for the job."

***

Trish was brushing Rose's hair when she said, "I can't take it any longer." She put down the brush and forced Rose to look at her. "You've been quiet ever since the hunt. What happened?"

Rose had been quiet. She had debated all evening on whether or not to tell Trish her suspicions about the Duke. She had even gone as far as loitering around in the kitchen much longer than she normally would in the hopes that Trish would be asleep before she got to her rooms.

Trish kept staring at Rose with her arms crossed over her chest. Rose sighed and said, "I'm not sure yet. I'm still trying to make out the Duke's character."

"Did he do something on the hunt to make you so quiet?" Trish asked.

"Not really," Rose said, having to drop Trish's gaze. "I'm probably just being overly cautious."

"About what?" Trish pressed.

"About you," Rose retorted. "You're far too trusting of people. He's a handsome man, and he's probably used to women giving him whatever he wants." Rose took Trish's hands. "Just be careful, please. Please guard yourself against falling for him before you get to know him."

There, Rose had warned her without being too obvious. That's all she was going to do until she had further evidence of foul play.

"Oh, Rose," Trish sighed. "I don't know what makes you so jaded against strangers. You've always been that way. On the other hand, you are usually right about people. I don't always judge things as harshly as you do, but you're still usually right. I promise I will be careful of the Duke."

"I'm serious, Trish," Rose implored. "Your kind heart is what makes you you, but sometimes it gets you hurt."

"I know," murmured Trish.

Rose leaned in and hugged Trish. Sometimes she wished she could be more like her and see the best in people all the time; other times, she was grateful that she was able to look past what people show you and see who they really are.

*There has to be a balance somewhere,* she thought. A *mix between Trish and me.*

Rose broke the hug and sat Trish on the chair she had just vacated and started brushing her golden hair.

Ever the diplomat, Trish was able to change the subject without making the conversation awkward, "I spoke with Alice today, she said she was getting sick in the mornings."

Rose had noticed Alice hadn't been coming to breakfast, "Has she gone to the midwives? I never asked her how far along she was."

Trish picked up a pillow and put it on her lap. "She's only three months along. She also said one of the ladies told her that as much sickness as she was having might mean she was going to have twins."

Rose laughed, "I can't imagine someone as tiny as Alice having two babies at the same time; she'll be huge."

Trish laughed as well and put the pillow to her stomach, "Like this?"

"Probably bigger," Rose commented.

Trish's laugh turned into a yawn. She stretched and said, "I'm going to turn in for the night. Hunting always wears me out."

Rose stopped brushing her hair and said good night. She went to the adjoining doors and into her rooms. She was going to start getting ready for bed, but she was very awake. She wasn't the least bit sleepy. Unlike Trish, being outside all day usually invigorated Rose.

She decided to go for a quick walk around the castle, maybe she would go to the library and find a boring book that would put her to sleep.

She was still fully dressed but decided to put on her slippers instead of her hard shoes that would clack in the halls. She lit the lamp at her bedside and went out her door.

She had almost made it to the library when she heard a faint noise. It sounded like someone was gasping for breath. She held up her lamp a little higher but didn't see anyone. She went a few more steps and heard the sound again. She still didn't see anyone, so she turned the corner and looked down the hall to the library.

On the ground, huddled in the corner, was a girl who was sobbing but trying not to make any noise.

"Oh dear," Rose breathed and rushed over to the girl. "Are you alright?"

The girl looked up at Rose and gasped.

"No, no, don't be afraid." Rose sometimes hated being associated with the upper class. "What happened?"

The girl wiped her tears and took a deep breath, trying to calm herself,

"Nothing' mi'lady, nothin'"

"Are you hurt?" Rose asked, trying to get a better look at the girl. She could hardly see anything because she was so tightly crouched into herself.

"No, mi'lady," The girl said.

If she wasn't hurt, then someone had terrified the girl. "What happened?" Rose asked again, a little more forcefully this time. She shifted from a crouch to sitting on the floor, making it clear she wasn't leaving until she knew what had happened to the girl.

The girl's eyes went wide at seeing what would have been royalty in her eyes, sitting on the ground next to her like an equal.

"I, I," The girl stammered. "I was going back to the servin' girls' rooms when some men cornered me."

The poor thing, she looked terrified. Rose looked at her again, a little more closely, but didn't see anything amiss with her clothes or her face. "What happened?" She asked again, wanting the full story.

"They, I think they had been drinkin' mi'lady. They were talkin' about how all the ladies here were prettier than back home, even the servin' girls." The girl looked Rose in the eye, then looked back at the floor.

"Did they hurt you?" Rose asked.

"No," The girl almost whispered. "They didn't touch me, but back in my village, when I was, I was." The girl looked like she was going to burst into tears again.

"Go on," Rose gently prodded again.

"In my village, before I came here, a man, he," The girl swallowed hard. "A man attacked me, and I thought they were going to do the same thing."

The girl started weeping again and hid her face. Rose put her arm around the girl and held her until her sobs quieted down enough for her to speak again.

Rose tilted the girl's face up with her chin, "Did you recognise the men? Do they work here?"

Whoever the men were, even if they hadn't touched the girl, would be thrown out of the castle the second Trent heard about this. Trent held the laws of being a knight sacred and would not tolerate any mistreatment of his staff, or anyone for that matter, by his men.

"I didn't know them, miss," The girl gasped at her slip. "MiLady! Sorry, I didn't mean to..."

Rose cut her apology off with a wave of her hand, "It's no matter. Can you tell me what they looked like?"

"There were two miLady. A short older man and a very tall younger man. He was, well, he," The girl looked slightly embarrassed. "He had more muscles than a bull and had tan skin with dark green eyes."

Rose felt her heart stop. The Duke.

It had to be. There was no other person in the castle that fit that description, especially when paired with a 'short older man' who had to have been Grady.

"What did they say to you, exactly? Please, everything you can remember." Rose said hurriedly.

"The tall man came to me and asked my name. He didn't wait for an answer, then turned to the shorter man and said, 'See what I mean? even this serving wench is prettier than half the ladies in our court.' The short man agreed with him, then the tall man turned back to me and came so close I backed up against the wall to get away." The girl wiped a tear from her cheek before continuing.

"With my back against the wall, he put his arm on the wall and asked me, 'What do you say, pretty? want to come back with me to my rooms?'

I shook my head no, but that seemed to make him angry. Angrier than it should have. He grabbed my arm and said. 'I could make you, what do you think about that?' Then the small man said, 'Remember yourself, sir, you are supposed to be getting married here.' The tall man let go of my arm and said, 'Right, of course. Some other time then, pretty,' he leaned in so the short man couldn't hear what he said. 'When we are both alone and there is no one around to ruin the fun.' Then he brushed my hair behind my ear, and they both left laughing."

Rose was sick, absolutely sick. How could he? Trent must know about this, and they had to put a stop to the wedding. Trish absolutely could not marry this monster of a man.

Rose stood and helped the girl up, "Here, you're alright now. I'll walk you back to your rooms."

The girl nodded and let Rose escort her to the girls' dormitory. When she stopped at the door, the girl surprised her by taking Rose's hand, "Will you be alright, mi'lady? Walking alone?"

Rose smiled and assured the girl she would be alright. The girl looked reluctant to let her go alone, but also clearly wanted to be safe in her bed.

"I'll be just fine," Rose said again. "You go to sleep. Maybe have some warm milk."

The girl nodded and went into the room.

Rose thought about going back to her rooms and telling Trent in the morning what the Duke had done. Then she thought about how many other girls he might have a chance to accost before she told Trent and decided she had to talk with him tonight.

She practically ran to Trent's room, thanking the stars she had chosen to wear her slippers. When she reached his door, she knocked quietly. It was rather late, and she hoped Trent wasn't asleep.

Just as she was about to knock a second time, louder than the first, the door swung open. Trent was there fully dressed, looking like he hadn't even thought about going to bed yet.

"Thank goodness you're awake," Rose said. "I have to talk to you right now."

Trent only looked taken aback for a second and then pulled the door open wide enough for her to enter, and she burst inside.

She strode into the room and began pacing in the sitting room of Trent's room.

"Come on in," He said wryly and shut the door.

"The Duke is evil," Rose accused. "He can't marry Trish."

Trent sat at his writing desk and watched her pace, "Mind catching me up? Last I heard, you only mistrusted him. How did he go from that to 'evil' in such a short amount of time?"

Rose explained everything the girl had told her in the hall. The more she said, the more furrowed Trent's eyebrows became.

"So," She demanded when she explained everything. "When are we throwing him out?"

She had stopped pacing to stare at Trent expectantly, and in her opinion, he didn't look nearly as mad as he should have.

"Well," She said waspishly.

"The girl said he never touched her?" Trent asked.

Rose's mouth fell open. "Well, that's what she said. Then she said he grabbed her arm, but what does it matter? He can't go around accosting women and then act like the dashing Duke in the light of day."

Rose was seething, and Trent knew he needed to go about calming her down delicately before she bit his head off.

"I know, Rose, I know, just hold on," He wasn't entirely sure how to phrase any statement that wouldn't infuriate her more. "Will you please stop pacing and sit down? You're making me dizzy."

Rose glared at him for a long moment but didn't sit down. She did, however, stop pacing, and that was probably as good as it was going to get.

"I agree something has to be done, but if I go to Father and say 'the duke harassed a maid,' that won't change anything in his plans to see the two wed. If our end goal is to protect Trish, then we need something that Father will see as a reason to stop the marriage."

Rose crossed her arms and huffed. She paced the room a few more times, then sat heavily on a settee. "You're probably right," she said, then looked at him. "Do you have any ideas?"

Before he could say anything, there was a knock at the door. Trent rose wearily to open the door.

"Yes?" He said, opening the door.

"Your highness," a footman said with a bow. "The King would like a word with you immediately."

"Did he say what for?" Trent asked, running a hand through his hair.

"No, your highness. I was just told to fetch you and the lady Rose and bring you to the King's study as quickly as possible. I was heading to her chambers next, your highness."

The footman gave a deep bow and started to go when Trent said, "No need, she's right here."

# Chapter 6

What could the king possibly want with her at nearly one o'clock in the morning?

She had asked Trent that exact question the second the footman was out of earshot, but he hadn't known the answer. She was sure he was used to being summoned at all hours of the day and night by his father, but she certainly wasn't.

The King hadn't ever shown outright dislike for Rose, but she never felt very accepted by him either. Every time he looked at her, she always felt like he had a pained or sad look on his face. The only thing she could think of was if she looked enough like Queen Millesant that it made him sad in remembrance of her.

Trent was walking quickly enough through the halls that Rose almost had to trot to keep up with him.

The King's chambers were on the same wing as his children, but the King's study was almost at the complete other end of the castle. When they reached the study door, Trent looked as if he was just going to walk right in without knocking, but with a glance at Rose, he must have thought better of that plan and gave a firm knock.

"Enter," came the King's voice from the other side of the door.

Trent pushed the door open and strode in with confidence, but Rose entered behind him, trying to stay out of the King's direct line of sight.

There were two other men in the room with the King, Lord Peter, and Commander Evans. Lord Peter was just a noble on the king's council. Rose didn't think he held any special or weighty title, but Commander Evans was a different story. Commander Evans was the King's chief war advisor and trained all the knights in the kingdom's army.

Rose had always liked the Commander. She didn't often see him because he was a very busy man, but she remembered the day they had met. She had just turned eleven and, in a fury from having to sit and do needlework on her birthday, she had run to the stables intending to take her pony Pepper out for a ride even if it meant a horrible scolding from Ann.

Not even bothering to change into britches, or put Pepper's saddle on for that matter, she had mounted astride and, breaking every barn rule that she had ever been taught, trotted Pepper down the aisle and out to the small yard in the back of the stables.

She had planned on taking a side gate out to the woods, but not ten feet from the stable doors, she almost flattened the Commander with her pony.

"Whoa there," he had said with a deep, carrying but also calming voice. "Where are you two off to in such a hurry?"

Rose had frantically wiped tears from her eyes and murmured, "Apologies, my lord. I was just going for a ride."

"I can see that," He had said, trying to keep a smile off his face. "But seeing as we are still inside the castle gates and on hard cobble, maybe we shouldn't be going quite so fast. You don't want him to throw a shoe, do you?"

Rose had been ashamed of herself. She loved Pepper and knew it wasn't good of her to ride the old pony on the cobbles. Forget throwing a shoe, he could twist his leg or get a stone bruise and be lame for months, or have to be put down.

She wiped another tear from her cheek and slid off Pepper, "No, my Lord."

The Commander put his hand on her shoulder and stooped to look her in the face. The Commander was a large man to most adults, but to an eleven-year-old girl, he was huge.

"What's the matter, lass?" He asked gently.

"I hate sewing!" She burst out. "I'm horrible at it, but they make me sit for hours and hours and tell me everything has to be pretty. But when I think something is pretty, they always tell me it's not. Nurse always thinks everything and anything pretty has to be pink or purple." Rose pulled a face that was not at all lady-like.

"I like green, and blue, and brown," She said quietly.

"Why do you like those colors?" The Commander had asked.

She had looked at him, surprised by the question, but answered, "They are the colors of outside."

He seemed to like her answer and nodded, "You know, I've seen purple and pink outside too."

She wrinkled her nose, "On flowers, they don't do anything but wilt."

He chuckled at that, "Oh, now I don't know about that. I use flowers almost every day."

"What for?" she asked, knowing he had to be joking. What would a warrior like this man need with flowers?

He could see the clear skepticism on her face and answered, "Well, let's see." He put his finger to his lips in thought, "Lotus is pink and it helps bring a man's fever down, Lavender is purple and it helps with swelling, Echinacea is pink and it helps men who have a cough, and roses come in all sorts of different colors and they make my wife smile when I bring them to her."

Rose's eyes were wide. She knew herbs helped sick people, but she didn't know flowers did anything useful. She was still miffed about the sewing and didn't want to give up so easily, so she said, "What about sewing then? When would a soldier need sewing? That's what the laundry maids do."

The commander nodded in agreement and said, "They sure do sew a prettier hem than I can, but I do a fair bit of sewing myself. For one thing, you don't see many maids on the battlefield, and if I need something fixed, then I have to do it myself. I've also had to sew bits of me that weren't cloth."

Rose blinked. She knew healers used stitches to fix large wounds, but she had never thought of it as sewing. She felt ashamed. If she were being honest with herself, she mostly didn't want to sew because she was being forced to.

Seeing her downcast face, the commander tried for a bit of humor, "You'd better learn how to cook while you're at it, or anyone you're out on a journey with will complain as much as they do when it's my turn to cook."

He reached down and pulled Rose's chin up so she had to look at him. "Come on, lass, let's put your pony away and give him a carrot for that hard ride. Then I'll come with you to check on your stitches to see if they are up to scratch for battle."

Since that day, the Commander had always asked after her sewing any time he saw her and often gave her a flower from whatever part of the kingdom he had just returned from.

Rose had often been envious of his seven children, wishing she could have had a father like him.

The commander looked around Trent to give Rose a small smile as they entered.

"Good," the King said, "You're here. Both of you sit down."

Trent and Rose took seats at the long table the others were already sitting, and looked at the King, waiting for him to tell them why they were there.

"There has been another raid," The King said, cutting straight to the point. He had never been one to waste time with pleasantries.

"Where?" Asked Trent.

"North of Bridgeten," Commander Evans answered. "Just south of the river. There's a fair bit of farm land over there. We're assuming they were after the harvest."

"Assuming?" Trent questioned.

"It seems they didn't get a chance to steal much of anything," The Commander said with a smile. "The local farmers proved to be a little too much for them."

"Whether or not they managed to steal our crops is of little consequence," The King said with no hint of a smile. "We must put a stop to these raids immediately. Trent, you will go with Commander Evans to Bridgeten and find out who is responsible for the raids and put an end to them."

Trent looked slightly taken aback, "You want me to go? Now? To settle a few farm raids that weren't even successful?"

The King cocked an eyebrow at his son, "That's what I said. You need to be present in the kingdom. The people need to know that their ruler takes all their concerns seriously."

"But Trish," Trent started to say, but the King cut him off.

"Your sister will be fine without you for a few days. I will not stand for these 'few raids,' as you put it. A few raids become a dozen, those become hundreds, and then before you know it, you no longer have a kingdom because you've allowed mice to eat away at it like a block of cheese." The King looked hard at Trent and asked, "Is that what you want?"

Rose was impressed at Trent's ability to hold the King's eye and respond with a simple, "No."

"Very well then." The king turned to Rose and said, "You'll be going with them."

The King must not have told this plan to anyone else because everyone responded at the same time.

Trent said, "Father?"

The Commander said, "What?"

Lord Peter said, "The girl?"

and Rose barely heard herself say, "Me?"

The King looked her in the eye and said, "Yes, you."

"But father, why?" Trent asked. "She doesn't need to go to what could be hostile territory. She should stay with Trish. They are best friends, and you know this marriage deal is going to be hard for her."

"It is precisely because of Trish that I am sending her." The king finally dropped Rose's gaze and looked at Trent. "The Duke mentioned over dinner tonight that he felt he would be able to get to know Trish better if he could have time alone with her. Apparently, Rose interfered during the hunt."

Rose felt her jaw drop. They had separated, yes, but it had been Trish's idea for crying out loud!

"I didn't," Rose started.

"I will hear no more of it. We all know how opposed you've been to this marriage," The king practically growled. "You are going with Trent and Commander Evans, and that's final."

The King stood from his chair and walked to the door. He opened it, took a step through, then turned and said, "You leave in the morning." He thought for a moment, then corrected, "In a few hours, I guess. I suggest packing and getting an hour or so of sleep." Then he shut the door with ringing finality.

"Evans," Trent snapped. "What is going on?"

"Pretty much what his majesty said," the Commander said. "There was a raid on the farming communities north of Bridgeten. Nothing was taken, but the raids seem to be increasing and spreading. He does want you to see more of the kingdom, and not just see it but be a commanding presence." He shot a glance at Rose, "I'm not entirely sure why he wants Lady Rose to go."

"It's like the king said," came Lord Peter's nasally voice from the end of the table. "He feels she is interfering with the Duke and Princess Trish's courtship. And I for one agree." He stacked the few papers he had in front of him and strode for the door.

Rose couldn't help but defend herself, "I did not! Trish was the one who suggested splitting up on the hunt, and the Duke agreed."

"Well, whatever happened, the King was mighty upset about it." Commander Evans said. "We shouldn't be gone more than a week, I wouldn't think. Like I said, nothing was raided. We are just supposed to get more information and report back."

Trent rubbed his eyes wearily, "What time are we set to leave, Evans?"

"'About an hour after sunrise,'" the older man said as he stretched and stood. "We'd better be off to bed. You two don't need to worry about packing up your horses. I will have that seen to. Just get your personal items together and meet us outside the stables in the morning. Goodnight, all."

As he walked out of the room, he squeezed Rose's shoulder, then left. Trent slumped in his chair and looked at Rose, "Well, I guess we'd better get to bed." He sounded like a scolded child who had been sent to his room. In actuality, that was exactly what had happened.

They both stood to go when Trent said, "Don't worry too much about Trish. They can't do anything too life-changing in a week. All sorts of papers and agreements have to be signed in a royal marriage, and those alone take weeks to go over. Everything will be fine."

He almost sounded like he was trying to convince himself instead of Rose.

They walked together until they reached Trent's rooms. They said goodnight, and Rose headed to her rooms alone. She almost knocked on Trish's door to tell her what had happened, but she knew Trish had to be asleep.

She went into her rooms to change for bed and put a few traveling clothes in a saddle bag. She ended up not being able to help herself and peeked through the door that joined the two rooms. Trish was sound asleep.

Rose paced the floor a few times, then decided to write Trish a letter. Hopefully, they would see each other in the morning, but Tirsh was not a historically early riser.

Rose sat at her writing desk, staring at a blank piece of paper, not knowing how to begin. How did you tell your best friend, almost sister, that her intended was a scoundrel?

Rose took a deep breath and put her quill to the paper,

*Trish,*

*I might be gone before I see you tomorrow, but I wanted to tell you myself why I had to leave.*

*There has been another raid. This time, north of Bridgeten. I just found out tonight when your father summoned Trent and me to his study. He said the reason I had to go with the party was because the Duke told him that I was interfering with him getting to know you better.*

*Trish, he outright lied to your father and said it was my fault that we separated during the hunt.*

*Seeing as I won't be there to investigate, I can't look into the lie further, but there have been other events that have led me to distrust the Duke completely, and I do not think you should marry him.*

*Your father is only right to say that I was never as eager as everyone else seemed to be about you marrying the Duke, but I was willing to give him a chance and get to know him. What I have come to know has made me more sure than ever that he cannot be trusted.*

*I do not know about his political opinions, but what I have seen of him as a man makes him completely worthless in my eyes.*

*Please, Trish, promise me you will watch him closely and do not agree to ANYTHING until Trent and I get back.*

*Commander Evans says we should be back within a week, so you shouldn't have to bear this alone for very long.*

*I love you, sister,*

*Rose*

She folded up the letter and wrote Trish's name on the outside. She slipped the letter under their door and went to lie on her bed. She knew she should get some sleep, but she also knew it would be impossible.

What had the Duke said to the king to make him so mad at her? It had to have been more than just the hunt. Nothing had happened at the hunt. At least *she* hadn't done anything at the hunt.

Maybe the duke thought she would tell the king about him grabbing her leg, and wanted to be the first one to say something to make her look bad. Of course, it was a simple lie to tell. The king was right, and Rose hadn't made her dislike of the duke any secret, but the king also should have known that was only because she was concerned about Trish. She wasn't trying to take down the kingdom.

Rose rolled her eyes and huffed in frustration. Obviously, she wasn't trying to thwart the kingdom. She loved Trent just as much as she loved Trish and knew he was going to be a wonderful king. Even if she did want to harm the kingdom, what could she possibly do? She was a farm orphan who just happened to be found by the queen. If she had been found by anyone else, she would be just as inconsequential as every other farm orphan at the castle. She would probably have rooms next to Eva and be good friends with Joshua.

At some point, her frustrated musings turned into dreams. She was playing with Joshua and Reddy. They were running through the forest, having a marvelous time, when there was a horrible squeak from Reddy. His leg was suddenly in a clawed trap, and he was squirming frantically trying to get out.

"Just stay calm, I'll get you out," Rose said, trying to help the fox.

Reddy looked at her with terror in his eyes and said, "Help my queen! my leg."

For some reason, in her dream, a fox talking to her did not faze her at all, but his calling her 'my queen' confused her. "Don't worry, little one, I will get you out," She said and looked for the release on the trap.

She had seen these kinds of traps before and knew there should be a pin on the side of it that would release Reddy's leg, but she couldn't find it.

She felt around the other side, but there was nothing. She looked helplessly at Reddy and saw that the trap was changing. It had been bright silver, but it was slowly turning black. Once it was completely black, it turned to smoke and rose just above Reddy's head. Instead of being set loose, Reddy seemed to struggle all the more and squeak more frantically.

The smoke began to lower over Reddy's head, and he squeaked, "My queen, my queen! Help!"

Rose tried to grab Reddy, but he had turned to smoke as well, and the black smoke overtook him.

Rose stood and took a few steps away from the smoke. She was crying when she heard a voice say,

*Hmm, another tasty innocent. How much longer till I have the flower I seek?*

That's when Rose turned and ran.

***

She jerked awake as a maid opened her window and said, "His Highness asked me to wake you for breakfast, my lady." She gave a small curtsy and exited the room.

Outside the window, the sun had barely begun to rise. The birds hadn't even started chirping yet, and Rose groaned. She sat up and rubbed her eyes. She usually didn't remember her dreams, but this one, this one had been different. She shuddered; what a horrible dream to have right before leaving on a week-long journey. At least her dream hadn't had anything to do with travel. If it had, she might have refused to go.

She had only remembered a few of her dreams in the past, and they had never been pleasant. The first one she remembered having was two nights before the queen died. She had dreamt she was wandering around the castle calling out for her, but there was never any reply. The second was during a particularly bad storm where lightning had struck the stables and caught them on fire. She had dreamt Raul was trying to trample her after a ride. There was another one she had as a child, but it was different. She had that dream many times, but it was always exactly the same. There was a storm, a boat, and a woman who screamed. She could feel the rocking of the boat and see the storm, and she had always been afraid of boats because of it as a child.

She wasn't particularly fond of them, even now, but she could tolerate the short trips they had taken to East Bay, and the river boats didn't bother her at all.

Groggy with sleep, she rolled out of bed and got dressed. She threw the saddle bag she had packed over her shoulder and peeked into Trish's room. She was still sound asleep. Rose couldn't blame her. If she had the choice, she would be asleep too. She thought about waking her to say goodbye, but then decided against it. The letter was still on the floor, and that would be enough. Rose hated goodbyes, even if they were for as short a time as a few days.

Rose made her way down to the kitchens for breakfast. Trent and Commander Evans were already at a table eating.

"Mornin'," she said, tossing her bag onto the bench.

The commander laughed and said, "Good morning, sunshine! Are you always this grumpy in the mornings?"

Rose glared at him but didn't answer. Eva had just brought her some bacon and a roll with a large glass of cold milk.

Trent studied her out of the corner of his eye, "She isn't usually this crabby. Especially knowing she is going to be outside riding all day.

What's wrong?"

Rose swallowed a bite of the roll and took a long drink of milk. "What's not wrong?" She didn't feel like telling anyone about her dream. They would just say 'don't worry, it was just a dream,' which is the least helpful thing to say to someone who has just had a nightmare.

"Don't worry, lass, it's only a three-day ride and there shouldn't be much trouble," The commander said, taking a bite of bacon. " We are going to have Trip and Bennett with us, and they are ugly enough to scare any raiders off."

"Where are they?" Rose asked.

"They're loading up the horses," said Commander Evans, taking another bite of his food.

"We should probably go help them finish up," Trent said as he finished his biscuit. "The sooner we leave, the sooner we will be back."

Heartily agreeing with that statement, Rose downed the rest of her milk and took a biscuit to go.

It was a brisk morning for fall, and the cold air invigorated Rose. The ride out west should be very pleasant, barring any hostile raiders. If they were going for any other reason, other than the one they were going for, Rose would have been ecstatic.

Raul was tied to a post with four other horses. He nickered when he saw her, his breath going up in two streams of smoke in the cold morning air.

Rose went to rub his nose, "Good morning, ready for a long ride?"

Raul just pushed his head into her hand, wanting another scratch. She assumed that meant he didn't care what they were doing as long as he was with her.

She went to check his saddle and put the bags over the horn. The men had put a man's saddle on Raul, Trent's doing, she suspected, and it was a good thing they had. Rose hadn't even thought to bring riding skirts. She had put a dress in her bags, but she only intended to put it on when they got to Bridgeton. She figured she didn't have to act like a lady if she was going to be riding with four men on a military mission. Besides, she didn't want to be a burden and have the men feel like they needed to do everything when they got to camp, just because she was a girl.

She finished checking Raul's tack when she heard a sniffing sound at her feet. She looked down and saw Reddy and smiled. She had talked to the stable master last night after dinner, and to her surprise, he agreed straight away that it would be fine for the fox to be out.

"Of course!" he had said. "There was a whole family of foxes around our stables growing up, and never did I see a cleaner barn. Cats are good for mice and the like, but foxes will get moles, voles, rats, and even squirrels if they're fast enough. I'll tell the boy at inspection it'll be alright if he lets the creature out."

"Reddy! Get back here! You're not supposed to be wanderin'," Joshua stopped short when he saw the four men and Rose, who was petting Reddy.

He looked at each of the men, then looked at Rose, "Sorry, milady, he got away from me. I think he's excited to be outside, is all, he normally listens."

Rose smiled at him, "It's no problem, I'm sure he is enjoying his freedom."

"That's a fine-looking fox, young man," the commander said, crouching to the ground and holding out his hand for Reddy to sniff.

Reddy went from Rose to the commander, sniffing cautiously. Deciding the Commander smelled alright, Reddy rolled over to have his belly scratched.

Joshua looked at the large man and whispered, "Thank you, sir."

"You said his name was Reddy? A fine name for a fox," The commander smiled and turned to Joshua. "What's your name, lad?"

"Joshua," He said, looking at his feet.

"Another fine name. My second boy's name is Joshua," the commander said, giving Reddy another pat, then standing up, "We'd better get a move on."

The men turned to their horses and mounted, but Rose went to Joshua and ruffled his hair.

"Thank you, milady. Thank you for talking to the stable master. Reddy would say thank you too if he could talk," he smiled and patted Reddy's head.

Rose smiled, then it dropped as she remembered her dream. "Joshua, can you do me a favor?" She asked. "While I'm gone, if you get a chance, can you introduce Reddy to Trish? I think she would love to meet him."

Joshua looked up at her, "The, the princess you mean?"

Rose chuckled at his wide-eyed admiration, "Yes, the Princess. She's very nice and she would love to meet you as well as Reddy. Her horse is the palomino, a few stalls down from Raul's. She usually goes riding in the afternoons. Just hang around her stall, and tell her I asked you to introduce her and Reddy."

"I don't think I'm allowed to talk to the princess m'lady," Joshua said, looking troubled.

"Sure you can," Rose contradicted. "You just met her brother," Rose gestured to Trent, and he gave the boy a smile and a wave.

Joshua's eyes looked like they were in danger of popping out of his head, "That's...he's the..." then he bowed so deeply that he might as well have sat on the ground.

"Get up, Joshua," Trent said gently. "Rose is right, my sister would love to meet the fox."

"Yes, your majesty, highness, sir," the words came tumbling out of Joshua's mouth so quickly that Rose couldn't help but laugh.

She patted his shoulder, then turned to Raul, "We'll be back soon," she said to the boy and waved as they headed out of the stable yard and to the main castle gate.

Trent rode next to her and asked in a lowered voice, "Why did you ask him to show Trish the fox?"

"You know Trish loves animals," Rose said off-handedly. "You can hardly keep her away from anything cute and fluffy. She will absolutely adore Reddy."

Trent didn't say anything, just stared at her.

"Ok fine," She said, looking at him as well. "I figure the more things she has to be distracted with, the less time she can spend with the Duke while we are away."

Trent chuckled, "You are a diabolical woman. No wonder Father wants you to leave."

Rose squared her shoulders and kicked Raul up so she was riding next to the Commander, "How long till we get to Bridgeten?"

"It's about a three-day ride," He said. "Hard riding, you can make it in two, then the next morning."

She looked at him, "Let's make it a hard ride then. Don't slow down on my account."

He smiled at her slyly, " I wouldn't dream of it, Lady Rose."

"You don't have to call me Lady," She said. "I prefer just Rose, Commander."

"I'll call you Rose if you call me Evans," The older man said good-naturedly. "Everyone does."

Rose took this as an invitation to not only be friends like they had been for so many years but also to be a comrade. She had a feeling he wouldn't treat her like a helpless lady on this trip.

"Alright then, Evans," She said, pulling her hair back into a knot. "Last one to Bridgeten has to cook the whole way back."

Evans roared with laughter as they rode through the gates and onto the king's road west to Bridgeten.

# Chapter 7

The Duke watched out his window as the party left the castle gates. He took a long drink of his brandy glass and set it on the windowsill. He hated her. How could a jumped-up farm wench cause him, the future king of Westland, so much trouble? He was furious with her for being so alluring. It had almost blown their whole purpose here.

He took a deep breath, closed his eyes, and straightened his spine. It was no matter. The problem would soon be taken care of, and he would be there to console poor Trish of her tragic loss. He smiled to himself. Weeping women were so easy to manipulate. He almost wished he could continue his dance of wits with Rose a little longer, but he had more important, long-term plans to see to.

A knock came at the door, "Enter, " he called lazily.

Grady entered with a stack of papers in his hands, "Your majesty, sorry to bother you, but I thought you would like to know, your letter was received, and they are asking for more money."

Edmund rolled his eyes and poured himself another glass. "How much more?”

“One hundred gold, your majesty,” Grady said, putting his papers on the desk.

Edmund snorted, “That is absurd. This is what I get for being generous with those lazy bastards.”

“They said this job would be more difficult, your majesty. They said you’d be paying for their silence this time, not just the job.”

“Well,” Edmund said darkly. “You can tell them the reward for their silence is their lives. As far as the job,” he turned and looked out the window again. He could just barely see the riders on the horizon. “How hard is it to kill one little flower?”

***

They had been riding for hours, and Rose’s legs were just starting to hurt. She didn’t know how far they planned to go on their first day, but she would not complain if they stopped and ate a bit of lunch.

“How bout some lunch? Eh Evans? Give the horses a rest,” Trip called from a little way ahead of their group. He had been scouting ahead all morning, making sure they didn’t come upon any surprises.

“There’s a creek up ahead; we can water the horses,” Bennett said in his soft voice.

Their companions came as a bit of a surprise to Rose. Trip, who was shorter and as skinny as a rail, was the life of the party. He had whistled most of the morning and sang the rest of the time in a bright, clear tenor. Bennett, who was almost as tall as Evans even though he was only fifteen, was well muscled and quieter than a mouse. Rose hadn’t heard him say more than five soft, spoken sentences the entire time they had been riding.

Trip was a skilled tracker and archer. Bennett was a lord’s third son who wanted to train as a knight. Commander Evans had told her he was

116

shaping up to be the best swordsman he had ever seen and had personally asked for him to come along as his page.

"Sounds good to me, lads," Evans winked at Rose. "Let's give it a rest and have something to eat."

They all dismounted and walked their horses the rest of the way to the creek to stretch their legs. Rose's legs gave a slight wobble when she hit the ground, but thankfully, no one noticed.

Seeing as this was just going to be a quick lunch and not a full meal, Trip distributed dried meat and cheese from his saddle bags while Trent pulled out a loaf of bread and started tearing off equal-sized chunks and handing them around. Rose gathered everyone's water skins and went to the creek to fill them. Evans and Bennett took out a map, and Evans was asking Bennett's opinion on their fastest route.

Stooping to fill the skins, Rose took some water and splashed it on her neck. Even though her legs were sore, and she knew the morning was not going to be pleasant, she couldn't help enjoying herself. She breathed in a lungful of the fall air and sighed. She loved travel and adventure, but she rarely had the chance to do either.

She wasn't important enough to be a diplomat, so the only real adventures she ever went on were ones where she accompanied Trish or Trent. She had traveled more when the Queen was alive, but when she died, the King was determined to keep his children close.

As much as she wanted to get back to Trish, Rose was having a wonderful time away from the castle.

She stoppered the last skin and walked back to the men who were now all around the map.

She handed each skin back to its owner and looked at the map herself.

"Which way are we going?" she asked.

"Down towards Midway," Evans said. "It's the only way we can go," he pointed to the map that showed a forest just ahead of them. "If it were high summer, I would say we could cut through The Red Forest, but with it being fall, the road will be all washed out from the rains we've been having."

"We don't have any carts or wagons," Rose pointed out. "We couldn't make it on horseback?"

"Even in high summer, the 'road' isn't much more than a few wagon ruts that the merchants use," Trip said. "We can spend the night in Midway instead of on the road," he gave Rose the quickest of glances.

"I don't mind sleeping on the road," Rose said, nettled. "I just want to get to Bridgeten and return home as quickly as possible."

"No offense meant, m'lad.."

"Rose," She said forcefully. She had told him to call her Rose at least five times since that morning, and it was wearing on her nerves that he kept reverting to calling her "M'lady".

"Rose," Trip continued as if she hadn't said anything. "To be completely honest, we've come along much faster than I thought we would. I wouldn't mind having a soft bed to sleep in," he said, rubbing his back.

Evans tried and failed to keep a straight face. Rose narrowed her eyes. She couldn't tell if she was being made fun of, if Trip was being diplomatic, or if he really was impressed with her and really did want to sleep in a bed tonight.

"It doesn't matter either way," Trent said, looking at the map. "We are ahead of schedule, and we don't know what awaits us in the forest, so to remain ahead of schedule, we should take the road and go to Midway."

"Alright then," Evans said, slapping the map. "To Midway we go."

Evans rolled up the map, and everyone repacked their saddlebags. When they were all mounted again, they headed off in a more southerly direction towards Midway.

As they rode, they came upon the forest they had been debating whether or not to take the shortcut through. Rose's eyes widened. Every single leaf on every tree was a brilliant, shining red.

Evans chuckled at her expression. "See why it's called the Red Forest?"

"It's beautiful," Rose almost whispered. "What makes the leaves red?"

"They are only red in the fall," Evans explained. "The trees near Zehrah are mostly all conifers, meaning they keep their leaves in the winter. These trees are deciduous, meaning they drop their leaves every year. Before all their leaves fall off, they change colors. Most of these are red, but they can also be yellow or orange. I've even seen purple ones before."

The more she saw, the more she resented being kept in Zehrah all these years. She was realizing she knew almost nothing about the outside world. It both scared and humbled her, becoming aware that she didn't know even the simplest of things, like the different types of trees in their world.

What good were all those classes she had taken from Trish's private tutor if she hadn't learned anything? Sure, she could read and write and sew and curtsey, but what did any of that matter?

"Evans," She asked. "Will you teach me? Teach me about all the things I've missed with my 'princess' education?"

Evans looked sideways at her, considering, "I can teach you what I know, which, mind you, isn't much in the way of nature. I would have thought one of those books you like to read so much would have taught you a few things."

"I've been reading the wrong books, apparently," Rose said sourly. Most of the books she had read had been given to her by her teachers, and they had been poems, histories, or love stories.

"Well, you can't blame your teachers for that," Evans laughed. "If you can read, you can learn anything, and you've only yourself to blame for not using the library."

She supposed he was right and felt slightly ashamed. She could have gone to the library and found books on trees, but she never knew trees could be interesting other than to climb.

"Are they all the same type of tree?" She asked, wanting to bring the subject back to trees.

"No," Evans said. "They are all deciduous, but there are different types. Let's see, there's oak, maple, sumac, persimmon, and sweetgum. That's just a few, though. Mind you, there are hundreds. Maples and Oaks are the ones that turn the brightest red. If you want to know more about the plants around here, talk to Bennett, he's from Midway."

"He is?" Rose asked, surprised. "He didn't say anything. He doesn't say much about anything."

Evans nodded his head, "He's a quiet lad, but I'm sure if you asked him, he would be happy to tell you all about the different types of plants from around here. I don't think he's used to people caring what he thinks, and that's why he's learned to be quiet."

They continued to ride in silence for a while, Rose still taking in the beauty of the trees, when she noticed something. She couldn't put her finger on it until she realized how quiet it was. Trip had stopped whistling.

She stopped Raul, and Bennett almost ran into the back of her. "Sorry," he started, but she held up her hand.

"What's wrong?" Trent asked in a hushed voice, "Why'd you stop?"

"Trip stopped whistling," Rose said, and they all listened for a moment. After a few seconds of silence, they heard hoof falls coming back to them.

Evans dropped his hand to his sword hilt but didn't draw. Over the ridge, they could see Trip coming back to them at a canter.

"What's wrong?" Evans demanded.

"Nothing," Trip said. "Ro, do you have any more of that cheese we had for lunch?"

"I," Rose started, utterly bewildered by this question. She had assumed Trip had seen bandits or something of the like. "Yes, I do." She started searching in her saddlebags for the cheesecloth.

"Take your time," Trip said very quietly when he was next to Rose. "Keep looking like you can't find the cheese."

Trip looked at Evans and gave the smallest jerk of his head to call him over.

"Rose," Trip said quietly. "Say you can't find the cheese in a normal voice."

"I'm sorry I can't find it," Rose said.

"Now, say Bennett must have it." Trip instructed.

"It might be in Bennett's bag," Rose said.

"Ah, Bennett," Trip said in a normal voice. "You're big enough, share the cheese!" He waved Bennett over so they were all in a group, seemingly looking for cheese, when they heard the jingle of carriage bells.

"Don't look up as they pass," Trip said, rummaging around in Bennett's saddlebags. "Just look for the cheese, and don't find it."

They all continued to look in their saddlebags as a cart passed with an older man and a girl in the front seat. They rolled by with nothing more than a nod of acknowledgement to Trip, who looked up and nodded as well.

As their cart rolled on down the road, Evans looked at Trip with his eyebrows raised in question.

"What was that all about?" Trent asked.

"Probably nothing," Trip said, still looking down the road after the cart.

"If it was nothing, then why are we all looking for cheese?" Rose asked.

Trip finally looked back at everyone in the group, "The old man. He had a green emblem around his neck."

Evans, Bennett, and Trent all whipped their heads back in the direction of the old man and looked angry, but Rose was still in the dark.

"What does that mean?" she asked.

Trip looked at Evans as if to ask permission to explain, and Evans nodded.

"The green emblem is the sign of the northern kingdom's new deity," Trip said. "Well, I guess it's not new anymore. When the old king died and his son died shortly after, the king's brother took the throne. Ever since then, he's been introducing many new ideas and religions to the northerners that they didn't have before. The old king wasn't necessarily a religious man, but he knew right from wrong and was just and fair."

"So the old man was from the northern kingdom," Rose asked.

"Not necessarily," Evans said. "Some merchants wear whatever they think will help them on the road. Either because they actually believe in the emblem or because they know there have been northern raids in the area, and they are hoping they won't be attacked if they are wearing the symbols of the attackers.

"What does the emblem mean?" Rose asked.

Trip snorted, "If it means anything real, then I'm a jackalope."

Rose smiled slightly, "Fine, what do they think it means then?"

Trent entered the conversation for the first time, "The symbol is an upside-down tree. One side of the tree has leaves, and the other side is dead.

It's supposed to represent life and death."

"Why is the tree upside down?" Rose asked, puzzled.

"It's only upside down for people who are looking at you. When you look down at it while it's on your neck, the tree appears right side up. It's supposed to represent you knowing what is right and wrong and looking inwards for the truth." Evans explained.

Rose was confused, "I thought you said it was a symbol of their deity? What does all that have to do with a god?"

"Well, that's where it gets interesting," Trip said. "Supposedly, the northern king saw a shining man named Shawv who told him all about right and wrong and how deep down everyone knows the difference. The King claims that there shouldn't be a set law. There its every man's own truth about what the law should be."

Rose just looked at him, "How can that be possible? You can't just say everyone gets to decide what is right and wrong, then anyone can do anything and claim it was 'right' because they wanted it to be."

"That," Trent said, "Is exactly the problem."

Evans cleared his throat, "Either way, we had better get going. If there are raiders around, we shouldn't be standing here like idiots, and we need to get to the inn before nightfall in any case."

They put Rose and Bennett's saddlebags back together and headed on their way. Rose wanted to know more about this 'gods' symbol, so she rode next to Trent and started asking him questions.

"I didn't think the northern kingdom was particularly religious," She said.

Trent looked at her, "None of the kingdoms are, to be honest. We all have our laws and customs, and they have been enough for most people. You will occasionally get a group of people who have 'seen the light' and claim to follow a higher being, but it always comes down to them following a man who just wanted power. Every time that man has always claimed to hear from a god or an angel or some other being, and in some cases that man claims to be a god himself, those never last very long."

"What about the ones who claim to have heard from a god?" Rose wanted to know.

"Those seem to last longer," Trent said. "It's much easier to convince people you know something you don't than convince them you are something you aren't. The closer to the current laws they are, the longer they last. They'll change one or two things but keep everything else in line. That way it's easier to accept the few changes."

They rode in silence for a little while. Rose thought what Trent was saying made sense. Accepting a small change was much easier than accepting a large change. Why do it at all, though, she wondered.

"Have any of them lasted? Why do they keep doing the same thing if they all fizzle out in the end?" Rose asked.

"Oh yes," Trent said, looking at her. "Some of them last. Three of them have lasted for a long time."

"Which ones?"

Trent raised an eyebrow at her, "Really?"

"What?"

Trent rolled his eyes, "Didn't you ever pay attention to your history teacher? Religion is how the three kingdoms were formed."

Rose looked down, embarrassed. She hated her history lessons, partly because the man who taught them was about a hundred years old and sounded like he would die any minute, but mostly because she didn't want to hear about things that had happened hundreds or thousands of years ago. She wanted to go on adventures and make her own history.

"I listened sometimes, but I must have missed that lesson," Rose said, trying to defend herself at least a little.

Trent chuckled, "Some call it the first age, we were all one people who lived in a land far away from here. The land we came from was a paradise. Everything was alive! You didn't have to plant crops. Anything you wanted or needed just grew on its own. The people there lived to be thousands of years old and some didn't die at all. But one day, one of the younger men grew jealous of his brother and killed him. The elders found out about the murder and asked the young man why he had done such a thing. The young man said, 'In a dream, an angel spoke to me and told me to kill my brother, so I took his life.' The elders banished him from the land. He and his wife made a small boat and sailed to this land near the western kingdom. They had many children together, but the eldest three all wanted to be the next leader of the family. The eldest took after his father. He was cruel and always wanted more than he had. The second and third boys were more like their mother, who followed the old ways of their homeland. The brothers decided to separate and each took separate lands, starting the second age. The second brother traveled north to a land separated from his brother by a large desert, and the third went east to his own island, separated from both of his brothers by water. The three kingdoms are still separate, as you know, but they work together as best three such different places can."

"Why didn't the second and third brothers just fight the eldest and take over?" Rose asked.

Trent shrugged his shoulders, "I'm not sure. I would assume it was because of their mother and her beliefs. Rose, it's just a story to explain why there are three different kingdoms. I'm not sure how much truth there is to it. Although it did come to war many years later, the Great

War, you know."

Yes, Rose knew about the Great War. The northern and eastern kingdoms joined forces against the western kingdom because it had started the practice of slavery. The western kingdom had sailed to the other kingdoms' ocean villages and took their people and brought them back, and forced them to work on their farms and in their mines.

The Great War had been the last in the history books. It was significant enough that the kingdoms had decided to call it the start of the third age. There had been many small border skirmishes between the east and west kingdoms, but nothing like the Great War. The northern kingdom kept to itself after the war. In the past, they had traded their precious stones and minerals with the other kingdoms, but they stopped after the war, isolating themselves in their frozen mountains.

"But the northern kingdom has kept to itself for hundreds of years," Rose countered. "Why are they attacking all of a sudden?"

"I don't know, that's what we are going to find out hopefully," Trent said with a sigh. "All I know is isolation is fertile ground for bad ideas."

They switched between riding and walking for a few hours until they finally got to Midway. It wasn't much of a town. There was an ale house, an inn, a livery, and only four small houses.

The look on Rose's face must have shown her less than approving thoughts about the place because Trip said, "This isn't the whole town. It's more of an outpost, really, for travelers on the road. The rest of the town is a few miles south of here."

"The Inn's nice enough, though," said Evans. "And ol' May makes a delightful roasted duck."

# Chapter 8

They hitched their horses to a post outside the inn and went inside.

It smelled wonderful. Rose took in a deep breath, and her stomach rumbled.

"Well, I'll be," came a drawling voice. A short, dark woman threw down a rag behind the counter. "If it ain't my favorite soldier walkin' through my doors."

Evans gave a huge smile, "Hello, May! It's been a long time."

"It's been too long, sugar, how's Eve?" The woman came out from behind the counter, wiped her hands on her apron, and hugged Evans.

"Oh, she's fine, doing fine. She's probably glad to have me out of the house," Evans smiled.

May waved her rag at him, "I wouldn't doubt it, you ol' rascal. And the children? They all fine?"

"Yes, ma'am, all fine. Abigail just got herself a husband, if you can believe it."

May put her hand to her heart and smiled, "Well, of course I can believe it, she was always a pretty thing, but my, children grown and getting married makes me feel like an old lady."

"You'll outlive us all, May," said Evans.

May smiled but waved away the comment, "What can I get y'all to eat? Looks like you've been riding all day."

"That we have," said Evans. "You don't have any duck cooking, do you?" He raised his nose to investigate.

"You know I do," May called from the kitchen. "Y'all sit down and make yourselves comfortable. Theo'll see to the horses and your bags."

They all sat at a table in the back of the large open room closest to the kitchens.

A young girl came and asked what they would like to drink. "We have lemon water, regular water, fresh cold milk, and ale."

Trent and Rose ordered water, Evans and Trip got ale, and Bennett got milk.

A few seconds later, May came back with an enormous loaf of bread and a large dish of yellow butter. "Here you are, the meal will be out in just a few minutes," she said and headed back to the kitchen.

They tore a few pieces off the bread and dipped them in the butter. It was wonderful. It was still warm from the oven and had raisins and nuts baked into it. The outside was firm, but the inside was soft and smelled so good. Rose's mouth started to water even before she took a bite.

They were only halfway through the bread when the rest of the food came out. There were three whole ducks, a large bowl of mashed potatoes, cooked greens, and another heaping bowl of black beans.

"May, have a heart," Evans said, looking at all the food. "My poor horse has to get me all the way to Bridgeton."

May laughed merrily, "Well, I intended you to share with your friends there. Go on, dig in, food's gettin' cold."

They all started dishing up their plates. Rose took a leg, a wing, and a spoonful of every side. She was starving. She wasn't used to riding all day, and she didn't realize just how hungry it would make her. Their lunch had been good, but a person can only go so far on bread and cheese.

"Have a plate yourself, May," Evans invited.

"Oh, I've already eaten," May said.

"Well, have a seat anyway, and we can catch up a bit. How have things been around here?"

May pulled a chair over from the table next to them and sat, "Oh, this summer was the busiest I've seen in a few years, but things are slowing down now with winter comin'"

"I can see that," said Evans, looking around. "I don't think I've ever seen this place this empty.

May nodded, "Well, you're a mite late for the usual town crowd, but all the same, we have been slow."

"Any trouble?" Evans asked.

"Not here, no, but you do hear things," May said darkly.

"What things?" Rose couldn't help asking.

"I'm sorry, May, I've forgotten all my manners," Evans said and wiped his mouth with his napkin. "This is Rose, Trent, Bennett, and Trip." Each nodding in turn.

May's eyes stopped on Trent. "This can't be little Trenton," She said, putting her hand on her heart. "I remember you when you was just a tiny thing toddling around after your mama."

Trent looked surprised, "I'm sorry, ma'am, I don't..."

May waved her hand in dismissal, "Of course you wouldn't remember. I left the castle when you were just a babe. I knew your mama, she loved my cookin'." May smiled at the memory. "But when my daughter got married and moved down here, I went with her. How's your sister doin'?"

"She's doing well," was all Trent said.

"And of course I know the Bennett family," May continued around the table.

Bennett smiled at her and nodded, but didn't say anything. He was rather preoccupied with eating his meal.

May looked at Trip and gave a questioning look, "And you, son?"

Trip smiled and gave as much of a bow as he could while seated at the table, "The name's Trip, ma'am, and might I say I haven't tasted such a fine duck in all my days."

May threw her head back and laughed, "Oh, this one's a troublemaker!" She said and wagged her finger at Trip.

Trip winked and went back to his food.

May turned to look at Rose and said, "And you, young lady?"

Rose swallowed a bite of potatoes, "Rose, ma'am. Thank you for dinner, everything is excellent."

May continued to stare at her, "Rose, hmm," She put her finger on her chin in thought, then looked at Evans, "Not the orphan girl?"

Evans nodded.

May locked eyes with Rose. Rose stared back, unable to look away. May gave her a small, sad smile and patted her hand, then said, "So, what brings y'all down this way so late at night?"

As soon as she spoke, it was like a spell had broken, and Rose was able to look away. Did she know this woman? She was sure they had never met before, but there was something so familiar about her.

"We're here to investigate the recent raids," said Evans.

"Ahh," said May knowingly. "That's nasty business that is. Raids this close to winter's going to mean some poor folks going hungry."

They all turned to look at her. They were under the impression that the raids had been unsuccessful.

"What do ya mean, May?" Evans asked. "We were told they didn't manage to take anything. We heard the farmers drove them off."

"Aye, they did," said May, getting angry now. "But ever since they left, the fields are dying. As far as the farmers know, raiders didn't have a chance to touch the fields, but those barbarians must have done something. I've heard of three wheat fields that rotted right on the stalk. At least two vineyards had their grapes perfectly fine one day, and the next morning, all the grapes had busted like they do sometimes on a hot summer's day."

Everyone stared at her in shock. "And that's not everything," May continued. "Every single person who ate the potatoes out of farmer Ed's fields got dreadful sick, two little ones died."

They were all quiet. "They must have salted the fields," Bennett said quietly. Rose looked at him and remembered he was from this area and felt for him. He probably knew these people personally.

"Salting a field wouldn't make the whole crop die so quickly," said Trip. "It takes at least ten days to even start seeing the effects of the salt, and to be that widespread, they would have needed a massive amount of salt."

Evans nodded in agreement, "Our reports said the raids happened only a week ago and the raiders weren't in town for more than three days before the farmers ran them off." he looked at May to confirm his information.

May nodded, "That sounds about right."

"Where were the other farms that went bad?" Bennett asked. "Ed's place is almost ten miles from Bridgeton."

"I'm not sure of their names," May said sadly. "I'm sure Ed's was the farthest away from Bridgeton, for now that is. The first field was closest to

Bridgeten, and they keep getting farther and farther away as time goes on."

Trent leaned forward, putting his elbows on the table, "What could be causing trouble with the fields so long after the raiders left? Bennett?"

Bennett shook his head, "I'm not sure. Grapes can burst in the heat, but it hasn't been that hot lately, and the farmers around here have been farming all their lives, and their fathers' lives before them. They know how to take care of their produce."

It was the longest speech Rose had heard him make. She was surprised at the intensity and emotion in his voice.

"What about the grain?" Trip asked.

Bennett shook his head, "Grain will go bad if it's been too wet, but again, we've had a good year for crops. Whatever happened to the fields, it wasn't the weather."

"I can tell you what happened," May said quietly.

They all looked at her, but when she didn't say anything else, Evans said, "Go on."

May looked up at him, "You won't believe me even if I told you."

Everyone kept looking at her, waiting for her to continue.

May looked each of them in the eye before saying, "They cursed the land."

It was silent for a moment. Everyone looked at May in disbelief.

"Cursed?" Trent asked.

May gave him a hard look, "I know y'all are going to think I'm the village crazy lady, everyone I've told does, but listen here," she leaned closer to the table. "I've been around longer than you, so I've seen more and know more than you. This lad here's lived around these parts most his life, and he can't explain what's happened. None of the farmers can. If no one can explain what's goin' on, then maybe it's time to consider things you've never seen."

Evans leaned towards the table, "Have you seen this before?"

May shook her head, "Not this exactly, but I've seen curses before."

"What kind of curses?" asked Trip.

"Sometimes it's the land, sometimes it's on a certain person, sometimes it's on a particular family," May said. "It's never the same, and most people just chalk it up to bad luck, but believe me, it's not."

It was clear no one knew what to say about this proclamation of May's. Everything she had said *did* sound like bad luck to Rose. Bad things happened. There wasn't any way around it.

Everyone went back to their food after an uncomfortable silence. May sat and watched them for a moment with a pitying look on her face, like she felt sorry for everyone because they didn't believe her.

"I'd best get back to the kitchen and clean up the supper," she said as she stood. "Y'all can have whichever rooms you like. Except the last room on the right, that one's occupied."

When she had gone, they started talking, "Why wouldn't reports of the crops have been sent to the castle?" Trip asked.

Evans shrugged, "They might have been. They might have come after we left, or the King might have just been focused on the raid and didn't think the crops were worth mentioning."

"I don't think my father would dismiss the crops this close to winter," Trent said. "Next month, the yearly taxes are due, and over half the kingdom pays at least part of their taxes with produce or livestock."

"But what about this curse nonsense?" Trip said with a laugh.

"May's always been a smart, practical woman," Evans said. "And like she says, she's been around a lot longer than any of us, but still," He looked back towards the kitchens. "I don't think I believe in curses."

"Didn't the king say the farmers ran off the raiders without them taking anything?" Rose asked. "Maybe the crops were already bad, and that's why the raiders didn't bother taking them. How long does it take for a crop to go sour?"

They all looked at Bennett. He had gone back to this meal with gusto after May left and had to swallow a rather large bite of duck before he could speak.

"Later in the year, they can go bad in as little as a day. Especially the grapes," he said.

"That's a possibility then," said Trip. "They might not have had time to report bad crops if it only takes a day or two for them to be ruined. Also, we have gotten more rain than usual these past couple of weeks, maybe that did it."

They looked at Bennett again, "It's possible," He said. "But, like I said, the farmers around here know what they're doing. I don't think a few extra days of rain would have destroyed even one crop, let alone the amount May was saying."

"So you think it's a curse then," Trent asked, half joking, half serious.

Bennett shook his head, "I'm not sure what happened. We need to see some of the fields."

Evans nodded in agreement, "That's right, we won't know what's going on till we get there. Farmers have always been known to be a little on the superstitious side." He shot an apologetic glance at Bennett, who didn't seem to notice.

"We'd better get on to bed in any case," Evans continued. "We need an early start in the morning."

Just then, the young girl came back out from the kitchens. Rose wondered if she had been listening for them to finish.

"Don't worry about your dishes," she said. "I'll clean the table."

They all stood and thanked the girl and headed for the stairs.

****

"Bennett and I can take this room," Trip said, going to the room farthest from the stairs.

"That sounds fine," Evans said. "Trent and I can room together in this room, and Rose can take that one."

"That sounds fine to me," said Trent.

The men went into their rooms and told Rose goodnight.

Rose said goodnight and opened her door. The room was small but clean and warm. There were two beds, a small chest at the foot of each, one chair, and a lamp on the little table next to the door. The lamp was already lit, giving the room a warm glow. There wasn't a fireplace in the room, but the stone chimney from the kitchens went along the outside wall, keeping the room plenty warm.

Rose set her bag on the bed closest to the door and went to the window. She couldn't see much because it was so dark, but she could see the dark outline of the stables connected to the inn, and a candle was lit in one of the ale houses across the street.

She pulled the window open to let in a breeze and looked up at the sky. It was cloudy. Every once in a while, a tiny sliver of the moon could be seen, but other than that, the sky was completely dark. She sighed. Her first day of real adventure was coming to a close. She was exhausted, not just from the riding but from everything she had learned and not learned.

She didn't believe the raiders had cursed the land. How could she? It was too far-fetched to even consider. The farmers had probably just had a bad year and found something convenient to blame it on.

That thought made her wonder if there had been any raid at all. Was the whole thing being made up?

There was a knock at her door. "Come in." She said.

Trent walked in, leaving the door open. "I just came to see if you have everything you need," He said.

She smiled, "I'm fine. All I want right now is a bed."

He laughed, "Riding around the castle is one thing, but riding long distances takes a different toll."

"It does indeed," Rose said, rubbing her neck.

Trent leaned against the wall. "What do you think about all this?"

She sighed and sat on the bed, "I'm not sure what to think. I don't think it's a curse like May says, but something weird is going on. I think Bennett's right, we are going to have to see the fields and the town with our own eyes before we can make heads or tails of it."

Trent nodded, "I agree." He pushed off the wall. "Well, if you don't need anything, I'm going to head for bed, Evans says we are leaving at first light."

"Alright," Rose said. "See you in the morning."

***

Rose was riding Raul down a wooded path. The sun through the trees was warm on her face. All the leaves were red and orange, making it feel like she was in a fire.

She looked to her left and saw Trish. They smiled at each other.

They stopped at a perfectly round pool. The water was deep blue and seemed to have no bottom.

A dark shape came out of the trees.

It was the duke. He came up to Trish and took her hand. Trish smiled at him, and he smiled back.

He looked at Rose and smirked. He twirled Trish around like they were dancing. He was behind her now, and he put his hand to her cheek. Quickly, he covered her mouth with his hand. Trish tried to scream, but no noise came out.

Rose jumped to her feet, but when she did, they vanished.

She looked all around for Trish but couldn't find her. She called her name, but there was no answer.

She came to a clearing. The grass was emerald green and gently waving in the breeze.

In the center of the clearing, a grape vine came out of the ground. Rose went to it, looking at its beautiful purple fruit. She plucked a grape and popped it in her mouth.

She coughed. The grape was sour, like vinegar. She spat it out and gasped. The vine had turned black, and the darkness was spreading in strange spirals throughout the clearing.

Rose ran back to the trees and started to climb, trying to get away from the darkness.

She looked back down at the grass and saw that the spirals were making a clear image.

The upside-down tree.

The branch she was on shuddered. Her whole tree was turning black and falling.

She jumped to the ground and ran. As she ran, the animals that had lived in the forest started running with her.

*Queen!* they cried. *Save us!*

A tear trickled down her face as she ran. She didn't know how to save them. How could she stop such a horrible darkness?

"Hmm," a horrible voice said in her head. "How indeed. You know you can't, my little flower. You can't stop me."

Rose jerked awake with a scream. She was sitting bolt upright in her bed. The room was completely black, and she frantically searched for the lamp.

A squeak came from the door. Rose finally found the lamp and a match to light it.

"I'm sorry," she said. "I had a bad dream. I'm alright. Go back to sleep."

Whoever was at the door didn't say anything.

She turned around and gasped.

The light fell on a bearded, scared face, a mean face. Then she really screamed.

The man lunged at her with a knife. She backpedaled and fell over the second bed.

She didn't have anything to defend herself with. All she had was the lamp. She stood up as the man came around the bed. She hit him across the face with the lamp. The glass broke and oil spilled onto the floor. A piece of glass cut her hand, but she held onto the handle of the lamp.

The door burst open, and Evans and Trent came hurtling into the room. The man swung at Trent, but he blocked the blow with his forearm and punched the man on the jaw. The man staggered but stayed on his feet. Evans grabbed the man's arms and pinned them to his side.

"Rose," Trent called. "Rose, are you alright?"

"I'm fine," she managed to say in a very small voice. Her hands were shaking. She couldn't steady them, and she dropped the lamp.

Trip and Bennett came into the room then.

Trip swore, "Put out the fire, Bennett, help me." The trail of oil on the floor was slowly burning to a larger puddle. Bennett and Trip took the blanket off the bed and stamped out the flame.

Rose was starting to hyperventilate. Bennett came over to her and looked at her hand. He couldn't bandage it yet because there was a large piece of glass stuck just above her thumb.

"You're alright, lady Rose, I'll get some water to clean your hand and some bandages," Bennett said.

Rose's breaths were coming faster.

Evans told Trip to get some rope, and Trip dashed out the door.

Bennett said something to Trent that she couldn't hear and left the room.

Trent came to her and forced her to look him in the eye, "Are you hurt?" He demanded.

She shook her head, "Just my hand."

Trent looked down at her hand, and his jaw tightened. He put his hand on her cheek and said, "Breath, Rose."

She tried. It took a few breaths, but she tried to match her breathing to his, and it worked. She blinked back tears, and she nodded.

He looked at her again and saw she was regaining control.

He turned to the man Trip and Evans had tied to the chair and, in a voice she had never heard him use before, asked, "What, exactly, are you doing in my sister's room?"

The man smirked, "Your sister? Shame, she's a pretty little thing." The man's eyes raked over Rose for a second before Evans backhanded him.

The man spat blood and chuckled, "I wasn't gonna do nothing to her, just kill her."

"Why?" Evans demanded.

The man looked at him, "Like killin' pretty girls, I do."

Trent punched him again, "Tell us what you were doing in her room!" he bellowed.

The man's eyes were slightly out of focus, but he said, "Was paid o' course."

"Who paid you?" Evans asked.

The man gave a dark chuckle, "Don't know a name. Just a piece of paper telling me who and when."

"You have to know something," Trent said, breathing heavily. "Tell us now."

"What's in it for me?" The man asked.

Trent leaned in close and almost whispered, "You'll get a quick death instead of a slow one. Either way, we will find out who paid you."

The man shrank a little, "Doesn't sound like much of a deal."

"It's the best you're going to get," Evans growled. "Now start talking."

"Fine," the man said, spitting out more blood. "I've already spent the money anyway. The only name I know's..." the man gagged.

"What's wrong with him?" Trent asked Evans.

"I don't know," Evans said. "What's the name?" He asked the man, but the man couldn't talk. He was choking. On what Rose didn't know, but the man was trying to retch like he had swallowed his own tongue.

He shook so violently that his chair toppled over. He struggled a few more moments and started to seize. His eyes rolled to the back of his head.

Trent shook the man, "No! You're not going to die until you give us the name!"

It did no good. The man twitched two more times, then went still.

# Chapter 9

"**I**s she going to be alright?" Trent asked May as he paced around the dining room.

"I'm fine, Trent," Rose said for what felt like the hundredth time. "It's just a cut."

"She'll be fine," May said as she gently took out the last shard of glass from Rose's hand. "Her hand will be sore for a while, but she will be fine, no permanent damage."

"Who was that man?" Evans asked, as he took a long pull of ale.

May shook her head, "I don't know. He came in two days ago, paid up front for a week. He kept to himself, never said much. I assumed he was in for harvest work. He would leave every morning and be back for dinner, then go back up to his room."

Trip came down the stairs, followed by Bennett.

"Did you find anything?" Trent asked.

Trip shook his head, "Nothing. A strange amount of nothing. The only thing in the room was an extra pair of clothes. Not much for a man who was planning on staying a week. And there wasn't anything that could be used by a farm hand."

"I don't understand," Evans said while taking another drink. "Why would anyone want to kill Rose? What good would that do for anyone?"

The only person Rose could think of was the Duke, but she didn't want to tell everyone her suspicions. She really wanted to talk to Trent alone.

"I don't know," Trent said, shaking his head. "And how did they know we would be staying at this inn? We only left yesterday, but that man's been here for two days? This was planned ahead of time. Someone knew we were coming before we did."

"A spy," Bennett asked quietly.

"It's possible," said Evans.

"Even if it was a spy, why Rose?" Trent demanded. "Why not me, or Evans. We would have been much more significant targets."

Rose winced as May wrapped her hand in clean cloth. She took another sip of her drink. May had made her a concoction of milk, cinnamon, and willow bark. The cinnamon made the drink sharp, and the willow bark made it bitter, but it helped numb the pain in her hand, so she drank all of it.

"We need to report this to the king," Evans said, looking at Trent.

"We can't go back," Rose protested, putting her glass down. "We have to get to Bridgeten, find out what's going on, and then go home. If we head back now, we will have wasted two whole days. It's more likely there will be answers in Bridgeten than there will be in Zehrah."

"We still need to tell the king," Evans said. "I don't want to waste any time either, but we can't trust this to a letter, and we have to tell him."

"I can go," Bennett said. "I can go back and tell the king while you four go on to Bridgeten."

Evans considered for a moment, then shook his head, "I don't want you going back alone. Especially now we know something is brewing."

"I'll be fine," Bennett said. "I can leave at first light and be back by supper."

"I can go with him," Trip offered.

"No," Trent said. "We need you for the road ahead."

Bennett looked only at Evans, "I can go alone. What have you been training me for?"

Evans looked at the boy and seemed to give in. "Fine," he said gruffly. "Let's all get a few more hours of sleep, if we can. We will leave at dawn."

Rose thanked May for bandaging her hand, and they all went back upstairs.

Rose turned to open her room door. "What are you doing?" Trent asked.

She looked at him, confused, "Going to bed?" The smell of smoke and oil drifted out of the room. They had opened the window, but the smell was lingering.

Trent reached over her and pulled the door closed, "Don't be ridiculous. I'm not letting you out of my sight."

He put his hands on her shoulders and steered her towards his and Evans' room. Evans was on the bed closest to the window. Trent gently pushed her down onto the bed closest to the door.

"Sleep," He ordered and took the chair, placing it directly in front of the door. He sat and crossed his arms, waiting for her to lie down.

"I highly doubt I will be doing much sleeping after what just happened," Rose protested. "You might as well take the bed, and I'll sit in the chair. Really, you need to get some rest."

She heard a small snort and turned to look at Evans. Evans put his hands up in defense, "You're never going to win that argument, my dear."

"He's right," Trent said. "You're not. Try to get some sleep." He said in a gentler tone.

Rose wanted to argue, but she didn't have it in her. The willow bark May had put in Rose's drink was making her sleepy. It also helped the pain, but her hand still burned and stung.

"Fine," she said. "At least take the pillow." She tossed Trent the pillow, and he caught it. He put the pillow behind his head and relaxed a little in the chair, but still waited for her to lie down.

"Do you want me to put the lamp out?" He asked.

She shook her head, "No." She didn't want to be in the dark, even with Trent and Evans in the room.

She lay on her back with her injured hand out of the blanket. It felt hot. She lay awake for a long time, listening to Evans' steady breathing. She turned to see if Trent was asleep. He was relaxed and slouching in the chair, but he was still wide awake.

He smiled at her, "How's your hand?" He asked softly.

"It stings."

Trent nodded, "That would be the alcohol. It'll stop infection, but it burns."

Rose nodded. "Thank you," she whispered.

"I will never let anything happen to you," he said fiercely but quietly. "When I heard you scream, I," he shook his head.

"You called me your sister," she said.

"You are," he said matter-of-factly. "Family is more than blood."

She gave him a small smile, "I know. Trish calls me sister all the time, but I don't think you ever have."

"You screamed twice," Trent remembered. "What was the first scream about?"

Rose shuddered, "I had a bad dream, that's what woke me up. If I hadn't, I wouldn't have known he was in my room." She knew if she hadn't woken up just as the man had opened the door, he would have killed her. He might have slipped out of the room with no one the wiser. Trent would have found her the next morning, cold and still. She blinked back tears. She didn't want to think about that.

"What was the dream?" Trent's quiet voice pulled her out of her disturbing thoughts.

Rose thought for a moment, debating whether or not to tell him the entire dream. She decided she might as well tell him, even if he thought it strange. She told him the whole dream.

He was quiet for a minute, then chuckled, "Queen Rose, now there's a scary thought."

She wanted to throw something at him, but he already had her pillow. "Don't make fun of me, it was terrifying."

"I'm sorry," He said, looking abashed. "You're right. But it was just a dream, nothing is going to happen to Trish. As for the rest of it, you were just dreaming about what we've been talking about all day. It wasn't real."

She knew he was probably right. Everything in her dream was information she had been thinking about all day. But what about the dream she had about Reddy before they left? The two felt connected. The only similarity between the two was the animals calling her Queen. No, that wasn't the only thing, that voice. The voice that spoke was the same in both dreams. Great, she thought, she was queen of the squirrels and hearing voices. Maybe she shouldn't be on this trip after all if she was losing her mind.

A ripping snore from Evans jerked her out of her thoughts. Trent suppressed a snicker with his hand and shook his head.

"Even without your scream, I was about ready to sneak into your room anyway to get away from that."

Despite her dark thoughts, Rose had to stifle a giggle as well.

"Do you want me to see if I can find some ice for your hand?" Trent asked.

"No, it'll be fine," she said.

Trent nodded, "Well, try and get some more sleep if you can."

Evans snored again. Rose smiled, "I'm not sure if that's going to happen."

It took a while, but Rose eventually did slip back into sleep.

***

*"That was very stupid"*, said a velvety voice.

"I'm sorry, so sorry," whimpered the duke.

*Did I tell you to kill the girl?* Said the voice.

"No, I'm sorry,"

*You are not in charge here,* said the voice. *You do what I tell you to do.*

"Yes, of course, I'm sorry," said the Duke. "I just thought."

*You? Thinking?* The voice was amused. *Dear Edmund, if I needed you for your brain, I would have already lost the war.*

The duke was silent.

*You had better pray she isn't dead. I have other plans for her. Do not disappoint me again,* the voice ordered.

"No, never, of course," stammered the duke.

The door opened, and Grady came in, "I'm sorry, your grace, but there's news." He stopped talking and looked around. "Are you alone? I thought, I thought I heard,"

"Of course I'm alone, Grady," the duke snapped. "I don't pay you for your brain. What news do you have?"

"The girl," Grady said. "She's alive."

The Duke straightened in his chair, "She's alive?"

"Yes," Grady said. "The prince and the commander managed to kill the cutthroat before he could finish the job."

The Duke barely contained his relief, "It's no matter. I guess that annoyance will be around for a little while longer. What about the other plans?"

"Those are still in effect, your grace," Grady said.

"Good," the duke said, turning away from Grady. He used his sleeve to whip the sweat off his forehead. "Is that all?" he asked.

"As far as I know, your grace."

"Then leave me," the duke waved Grady away. When the door shut, he sank onto his bed with his head in his hands and sobbed.

***

"Wake up, Rose," Trent gently shook her shoulder.

Rose slowly opened her eyes, "Huh?" The room was still dark, but the hazy glow of sunrise was shining in the open window.

Trent smirked, "Wake up, sleeping beauty, it's time to go. The horses are already ready, we're just waiting on you."

Rose sat up a little and wiped sleep from her eyes. It took a second for his words to sink in. Rose glared at him, "Why didn't someone wake me up? I should have helped with the horses."

Trent quirked an eyebrow at her part surprise, part amusement, "We tried, three times. You kept saying 'I'm up' but didn't ever move."

"I did?" Rose asked, embarrassed.

Evans laughed from the corner of the room, "You sure did, Trip thought you might be dead, but you were drooling so he figured you were fine."

Rose's hand jumped to her mouth. There wasn't any drool, so she glared at Evans, who laughed even harder.

"Ha, ha very funny. " Rose said and got out of bed.

Trent handed her her bags. "How's your hand?"

Rose lifted her hand. It felt much better than last night. "It's stiff, but the burning's gone."

"That's good," Trent said. "May said she wanted to look at it before we left. Go ahead and get dressed, and I'll send her up."

Trent and Evans left the room and shut the door. Rose took her clothes out of her bags one-handed and shook them out. She wasn't sure how she was going to get all her clothes on with one hand. Her boots were definitely going to be a problem.

She took her nightgown off with no trouble and put her riding pants on, but couldn't tie the strings in front. She gave up on those and put her undershirt on when there was a knock at the door.

"It's May," came a voice from the other side of the door. "Can I come in?"

"Yes," Rose called, still messing with her shirts.

"Oh, let me help you, darlin'." May came and helped Rose put on her tunic and tie her pants.

"Thank you," Rose said, embarrassed at her lack of independence.

"No trouble, darlin'," she said, picking up fresh linen to wrap Rose's hand. "We can't have your britches fallin' down now, can we?"

Rose smiled, "Thank you for last night too, my hand feels much better."

May nodded and held out her hand for Roses'. She gently unwrapped the bandage, loosening a few places where blood had dried with water before peeling it off. Once the bandage was completely removed and May whipped off the dried blood, Rose could see the wound wasn't as bad as she had thought it was.

May looked over the wound and nodded approvingly, "The glass didn't go in too deep, which is good. If it had gone much further, it would have severed the muscle to your thumb and would have needed stitches."

"That's lucky, I guess," Rose said. "How long do you think it will take to heal?"

"As long as you don't overdo it, you should be able to use it gently this evening," May said. "Here, take this ointment and put it on every morning and night. Don't take the bandage off till you get to camp tonight, and, if you need to, use water to loosen the bandage like I just did now."

May handed her a small glass bottle that had an off white lotion inside. When she applied it to her hand, it tingled slightly but then felt wonderful. It smelled faintly of lemon grass and lavender.

May patted her knee and stood up.

"Thank you again for everything, and sorry about the floor," Rose said.

"Oh, don't you worry," May said, shaking her head. "It's nothing a quick scrub can't fix. We've got to take care of each other, us-" May paused like she wanted to say more, but just smiled.

"Us?" Rose questioned.

"Us girls, that is," May smiled and opened the door.

Rose was sure that was not what she was about to say, but May was already headed down the stairs. She picked up her bag and headed down herself.

The men were in the dining room finishing up breakfast and getting their bags ready to go.

"Ah, she lives," Trip said with a joking smile. "Here, we saved you some bacon."

He handed her a plate with four pieces of thick bacon and two pancakes. Rose nodded her thanks and started eating the bacon. She hadn't realized how hungry she was until she smelled the food. Apparently, almost being killed in the middle of the night worked up an appetite.

"Everything's ready to go," Bennett said, walking into the room from outside.

Evans went and shook his hand and patted his back, "I still don't like letting you go alone, but I know you've proven you can take care of yourself."

Bennett nodded and shook Trent and Trips' hands. He paused, unsure what to do with Rose. She wasn't entirely sure what to do either, but she gave him an awkward one-armed side hug, still holding her bacon. How were you supposed to say goodbye to someone who had helped save your life?

When she let go, she was sure Bennett's cheeks were tinged pink in a blush. He waved and practically ran out the door.

Evans chuckled, "Poor kid."

Rose busied herself with eating her breakfast so she wouldn't have to answer.

Trent took her bag and went to put it on her saddle. When he came back inside, he was carrying a small box.

"Here," he said, handing her the box. "I don't have time to teach you to use it now, but at least you'll have it."

She put down her plate and opened the box. It was a small dagger. It was in a leather sheath that could be looped onto her belt. She pulled the dagger out of the sheath to look at it. It was an odd metal she had never seen before with an ivory handle. The blade was only six inches long, but it was sharp on both sides.

"Thank you," She said to Trent. "Where did you get this?"

Trent looked up at May, "It was just something I had lying around," She said. "Looks like you'll be needing it more than I will."

Rose was surprised. She and this woman were practically strangers, and she couldn't see why she was giving her such a nice weapon.

"You really didn't have to..." Rose started.

"I know I didn't," May said with a small smile. "I wanted to. Like I told you, us girls have to stick together."

Rose didn't think that was the only reason this woman had taken such an interest in her. There had to be something else, but she didn't know what it was, and apparently, she wasn't going to have time to find out.

Rose smiled her thanks and went to put the dagger on her belt. Her bandaged hand made her fumble the buckle. Trent took the blade from her and helped with her belt. He hooked the sheath onto it easily, then refastened it around Rose's waist.

Again, embarrassed at how incapacitated she felt with only one hand, she muttered her thanks. She hoped she was going to be self-sufficient by tonight. There was no way she was going to ask any of the men to help her get dressed.

Trip knocked his knuckles on the table and stood up, "Well, shall we be off then?"

They all stood and went outside to the small stable connected to the inn. Rose checked Raul's saddle out of habit. You should never take someone else's saddling skill for granted.

She walked around to give Raul's nose a scratch. He bent his head to her bandaged hand and sniffed. The ointment May had given her made him sneeze and shake his head.

"I know," She said softly, so only her horse could hear. "Listen, I'm going to need some help today. You're going to have to be gentle with me." Raul just looked at her as if to say, 'aren't I always?'

Trent helped her mount. She suppressed a moan as she landed in the saddle. With the injury to her hand, she had almost forgotten she had also fallen backwards over a bed. Along with the soreness from riding all day yesterday, her legs were also sore from hitting the bed frame. Today was going to be a very long day.

The men got on their horses and thanked May again for the food and the hospitality. She waved them off down the small town road.

She stood in the doorway for several minutes after they had disappeared down the road. "That poor girl," She said quietly to herself. "Please, Aahva, watch over her."

She took a necklace she had tucked under her shirt and kissed it. She stood for a moment longer in the doorway and then went inside.

# Chapter 10

Rose stifled a moan. She hurt everywhere. She could tell Evans had been keeping the pace slow for her, but it wasn't helping much.

She thought her hand would have been what hurt the most, but it wasn't. It wasn't even the bruises on the back of her legs from falling over the bed. No, Rose knew she would have been in just as much pain no matter what happened last night. She was sore from riding all day yesterday.

Every step Raul took was painful. But she knew she had to keep going. She had to finish this ridiculous mission the king had sent her on, so she could get back to Trish.

When they stopped for lunch, she could barely get off Raul. She managed to slide her leg over his rump and get her other leg out of the stirrup, but when she hit the ground, her knees buckled. Trent was there to steady her.

"Thanks," she murmured.

"No problem," Trent said. He had been in an annoyingly good mood all day, and she couldn't figure out why. Maybe it was just that she had never seen him away from the cares of the castle. He stretched and took in a deep breath.

"Here," he said. "Why don't I take the water skins and you just rest a bit. I would suggest stretching. I know they'll hurt, but do a few squats too. It'll help."

She glared at him as he took the waterskins and went to the small creek they had stopped at.

"He's right, you know," Trip said, rummaging in his saddlebags for their food. "I remember my first long-distance ride." He grimaced. "I couldn't walk for three days after I got back. Honestly, I'm very impressed you even got on your saddle this morning."

He handed her a chunk of cheese, "Here, let me show you some stretches."

"Stand in between the trees," He instructed. "Keep your feet pointing towards the creek and try to twist your torso to look at the road."

She tried, but she only got halfway around when her whole back cracked. She gasped and let go of the tree.

Trip laughed, "Well, there's your problem," He said, still laughing. "You've hidden some firecrackers in your spine. Do it the other way now."

She did, and her back cracked again, but not as much as the first time. She let go of the trees and took an assessment of her muscles. They felt better, much better.

"Thanks," she said to Trip. "Where did you learn all this?"

"I've picked up different things here and there, but I learned most of it from my mother. She was an acrobat for the circus."

"Really," Rose said in surprise. She had only seen the circus once when she was twelve. She had been fascinated by the tricks and the magic shows.

"Yep," Trip said, going back to the horses. "She was a great acrobat, but she was best at trick riding."

Rose vaguely remembered seeing people ride two horses at once. They had stood on the saddle, almost fallen off the saddle, then flipped back on, and even done handstands on the saddle.

"Why didn't you stay with the circus?" Rose asked.

Trip didn't answer right away. Rose was about to take back her question, wondering if it had been a rude thing to ask, when he said, "My mother died when I was seven, and the circus didn't want to take care of me anymore. The ringmaster told me the only reason they kept me at all was because my mother brought in so much money with her act."

Rose was quiet for a moment, "I'm sorry, Trip. That– that's horrible."

Trip shrugged, "S'alright. Two days after I left, I met an old tracker in the woods who needed a young man to help him with farm and house chores. He taught me everything he knew, and now even the king calls me when need arises." He gestured to the horses, proving his point.

Trip busied himself with his saddle bags, and Rose knew the conversation was over. Trip was always so happy, you never would have known he had such a tragic past. Rose thought about her past. She had no idea who her real parents were, and she had never tried to find out.

She had asked the queen about them once, and all she had said was, "They lived far, far away from here in a beautiful place." But that was all the information she ever got about them. She didn't even know their names.

"Rose," Trent called. "Come over here for a minute, please."

Rose left Trip with the horses and went over to Trent and Evans, who were still by the creek.

"How are you feeling?" He asked.

She rubbed her neck, "Just wonderful."

Trent smiled, "You'll feel better on the way back. You're a good rider, your body just needs to get used to the exertion." He clapped his hands together, "But for right now, Evans and I are going to teach you a few things with that dagger May gave you."

She almost wanted to cry with the thought of even more exercising, but she also never wanted to feel as defenseless as she had last night. She was a good shot with a bow, but that had been of no use last night.

"Right," Evans said, taking his knife out of his belt loop. "The first thing you need to know about weapons: If you don't know how to use it, it's an extra weapon for your attacker." He looked at Rose very intensely. "If you aren't going to learn how to use your weapon properly, I would rather you didn't have one at all. Nine times outta ten, the person attacking you will have some idea of how to use the weapon you have. If you don't know how to handle yours, the attacker is just going to take it from you and use it against you."

Rose nodded her understanding.

"Right then," Evans continued. "Take out your blade."

Rose slid her dagger from its sheath and held it loosely in her hand, palm up.

"Look at my blade, see how it's only sharp on one side and the point? That means I can use the back side as a shield. I can attack and defend with my knife. Your's is sharp on both sides, meaning it's only for stabbing or slashing," Evans looked at her as if this should be particularly significant.

Rose quickly glanced at Trent.

"It means you need to attack first," Trent said.

"Oh," Rose said, feeling stupid. "Got it."

"Attack first," Evans said. "Or don't let them know you have a knife until it's too late for them."

Rose nodded again. She didn't want to attack anyone. She just didn't want to die.

"This is one area where it's an advantage to be a woman," Trent said. "Most men won't be expecting you to have a knife, let alone know how to use it. If they get too close to you, and you don't want them there, you can stab or slash them and run away."

"Correct," said Evans, who was in full teacher mode now. "The first, and most important, part of learning about the blade is knowing how to hold it."

He showed her how to hold the blade loosely but firmly in her hand. He told her to always hold the knife with her thumb on top of the blade, unless you were defending, but she couldn't do that with her knife, so it didn't matter right now.

If she was going to stab, she needed to aim for a fleshy part of the body; stomach, arm, leg, something like that. It wasn't a good idea for her to stab at the chest. It was just as likely that she would hit a rib or the sternum as she would hit something vital. It wasn't worth the risk. A quick stab, then run, that's all she needed to know for now.

With every instruction, Rose nodded her head. She wasn't sure how much of this quick lesson she was going to retain in an actual fight for her life, but Evans said if she practiced, it would come back to her.

"What I want you to do for the rest of the day is to practice holding the blade," Evans continued. "Hold it and don't cut yourself, don't cut your horse. Practice drawing and sheathing it over and over."

Rose wrinkled her lip. She wasn't sure her body would be able to do much more than focus on not falling off Raul, let alone handle a sharp blade.

Evans gave her a sympathetic look, "It'll help take your mind off your sore muscles." He patted her shoulder and said, "We'd better get a move on."

Trent followed her to Raul and helped her up, and they were off.

They had been riding for about ten minutes, Rose pulling the dagger in and out of the sheath over and over, when Trip came up to her and said, "Practice with it on your other hip too. When your hand's better, you'll need to be able to draw with either hand on either side of your belt. Everything you learn with one hand, learn it with the other as well."

Rose twisted her belt so the knife was on the other side and started practicing. She was not nearly as good on this side. She almost dropped the knife a few times before taking a break.

"I'm not very good at this," She said to Trip, who was still riding next to her.

"Are you kidding?" Trip said with a faint smile on his face. "You just started ten minutes ago. Did you expect to be a master in a day?"

No, she hadn't expected that, but almost everything she had ever done she was good at from the start: riding, the bow, being sarcastic.

"You need to practice patience as well as the blade, apparently," Trip said with a chuckle, and he kicked his horse forward to ride with Evans.

Rose knew he was right, but she was still miffed. She hadn't asked to come on this quest. Sure, she wanted to go on adventures, but she did not sign up for being an assassin's target and having all her muscles feel like mush.

She rode at the back of their party for the rest of the day, practicing with her blade. She was still much better on her right side, but she was getting better on her left. Just to switch things up, she had also put the sheath in the middle of her back and practiced drawing from behind.

She had been a bit overconfident in her first behind-the-back draw and accidentally cut her jerkin in the process. Thankfully, no one was behind her, so no one saw her mistake.

Her muscles still ached, but Evans had been right about the dagger being a distraction while they rode.

When Evans called a halt for the night, she was able to dismount without falling and was grateful for it.

Trip led her in another round of stretching, and she felt better. Trent had gathered some wood for a fire and had water boiling for a stew.

"It's not going to be as good as May's food, but we won't go hungry," Evans said as he stirred the pot and gave it a whiff. He sprinkled in a few more pinches of seasoning, then started ladling the stew into bowls and passing them around.

Everyone was quite eating for a moment, glad to be off their horses.

"We should be able to make it to Bridgeton before noon tomorrow," Evans said.

"Good," Rose said.

Trent nudged her with his shoulder, "Oh come on, your whole life you've been talking about how you wanted to go on adventures and see the world, and now that you're finally on one, you want it to end?"

Rose ignored him, "What's our plan when we get to town?"

"We'll see what all there is to see on our way in," Evans said. "If the fields are as bad as May said, then we should be able to gather some information on the way in. Once we get there, we need to talk to the lord and see what he has to say."

"We know the bandits aren't there anymore," Trent said. "We just need to find out the extent of what they've done and report back."

"So we shouldn't be there more than a day or two?" Rose asked.

"Probably not," Evans said, considering. "It all depends on what we find."

Rose nodded and tried to stifle a yawn.

"We should get some sleep," Trent said, looking at Rose out of the corner of his eye.

"Quite right," Evans said. "I'll take first watch."

They cleaned up their dinner things and packed everything away so they could leave first thing in the morning.

They didn't bring any tents. The weather had still been mild enough when they left, Evans had said they wouldn't need them. They also didn't want to burden the horses with any more than they needed, and they had all agreed they didn't want to be slowed by a pack mule.

Rose went to Raul to get her sleeping roll and blanket. She struggled with the knot, but not wanting any help, before someone could notice, she stuck one end of the knot between her teeth and pulled.

The roll and blanket came loose, and she just managed to catch them as they fell off Raul's back.

She found a piece of dirt that looked relatively comfortable near the fire and rolled out her pad. She took off her belt and put it right next to her as she tried to unlace her shoes.

"Here," Trent said, coming to her aid.

'I've got it," Rose said, irritated.

Trent watched her struggle a few more times, then knelt and gently pushed her hand away and unlaced her boots.

"You don't always need to be so tough, you know," He said quietly so only she could hear.

Rose looked at him, "Apparently, I do. If people are going to start attacking me in my sleep."

The muscles in Trent's jaw jumped, "You'll be fine tonight. We are all going to take turns standing guard."

"When's my watch?" Rose asked as Trent pulled her second boot off.

Trent looked at her in surprise, like the thought hadn't even occurred to him that she should take a watch.

She tilted her head at him, waiting for an answer.

"Um," he said. "Well, you're still injured, so we didn't give you one. We'll be fine." He said, trying to discount not giving her a watch.

Rose rolled her eyes. Trent shrugged and chuckled as he rolled out his pad next to her.

"We can't help it," he said after he lay down. "I see you as a sister, and Evans sees you as something of a daughter, so we can't help but try and make it as easy for you as possible. It's not an insult, we just like you."

Rose humphed and rolled over. She hated being coddled.

"Don't be like that," Trent said. "Look, you would be doing the same thing for Trish if she were here, wouldn't you? You wouldn't let her take a watch because you would want her to get a good night's sleep. You probably wouldn't let her gather firewood or water either, would you?"

She didn't say anything. She knew he was right.

"Is that because you think less of her? Or because you think she can't do the task?"

"Of course not," Rose said sharply.

"Alright then," Trent said. Rose could hear a smile in his voice. "We are just doing the same thing for you as you would be doing to Trish. It feels nice to be able to take care of people."

Rose rolled back over to look at him, "Alright, alright. You win. Thank you for your help."

Trent didn't look at her. He just kept looking up at the stars with a smug smile on his face.

"Thank you, Evans, Trip," She called loud enough so they could both hear.

They didn't respond, but she could hear their quiet laughter.

She stared at the stars for a moment, listening to the wind in the trees. She was very comfortable, even if she was on the ground. It only took her seconds to fall asleep.

***

She was dressed in a cream dress that gently flared from her hips to her feet with a long train in the back. The sleeves were sheer gossamer and billowed around her arms.

She was sitting on a white blanket in a field dotted with red and yellow wild flowers.

To her left was a doe and her fawn. To the left of them was a raccoon. On her right was a large red squirrel. To his right was a badger. Directly across from her was a mouse, who was sitting on the blanket so as not to get lost in the grass.

She was smiling at them, and they at her.

There was a basket full of food in the middle of the blanket that had huge purple grapes, bread, cheese, apples, oranges, and nuts.

They were all eating and having a wonderful time when the mouse's ear twitched.

He scurried across the blanket, and Rose held out her hand so she could pick him up and bring him to her ear.

"You must wake my queen," the mouse said in a tiny voice.

She laughed, "Why, dear friend? Everything is well."

"No, my queen, you are in danger," the mouse protested, still in his tiny voice. "You must wake up."

Rose rolled over in her sleep. When she opened her eyes a fraction, she was looking at the last few embers of their fire. She closed her eyes again and half listened, half tried to fall back asleep.

Nothing seemed to be wrong. If someone had tried to come into their camp, one of the men would have raised the alarm.

She was very warm and almost asleep again when she realized she needed to relieve herself. She tried for a few more minutes to go back to sleep, but now that she was awake, the urge to use the privy was growing.

She opened her eyes fully and looked at the sky. It was still dark, but there weren't as many stars in the sky. It must be close to dawn.

With a sigh, she quietly pushed her blanket down and looked for her boots. She slipped them on, not bothering to tie them. She debated for a moment whether she should take her dagger. What was the point of having it if she left it lying around? She put her belt on and stood up. Trip looked at her from the tree he was sitting against and mouthed, "You alright?"

She nodded and pointed down off the trail and said as quietly as she could, "Privy."

Trip nodded and leaned back against his tree.

She walked a little way down the road, then found a concealing group of trees to relieve herself in.

She was tying her pants when she heard a shout.

"Stay where you are, guard," a rough male voice said.

"Easy there, old man," said a nasally voice.

"Now," said a calm, silky voice. "Do you want your friends to be killed, little prince?"

There was a thud and a grunt, "That's what I thought, now, where is the girl?"

It was silent for three heartbeats.

"Where is the girl?" the silky voice asked again, but was less calm.

There was another thud, "Where is the girl?"

Silence.

"Surely you saw where she went, guard," said the silky voice. "Where is the girl?"

"Sure, the prince is very nice looking, but to call him a girl is a bit of a stretch," Trip said. Then there was another thump.

"I can see her bedroll, you imbecile," The voice said, losing its silkiness. "Out in the woods are you then, little girl?" He called.

Rose was frozen.

"Why don't you come on over here so I don't have to hurt your friends?"

Rose started towards the group.

"No!" Trent called out, "Run, Rose, Run!"

Another thud.

Rose crept closer, staying out of sight in the trees.

"We don't need the girl," said the rough voice. "We was just told to get the prince and the old man."

"Silence," snapped the silky voice.

Rose could see the group now. They had kicked up the fire and added wood.

There were seven men. One held Trip from behind with a knife to his throat, one held Evans, who had a gag in his mouth, and one held Trent with his arms locked behind his back.

One stood close to the fire, twiddling with a long, thin knife. Two were going through their saddlebags. The last just stood watching. He had a hood that came so far over his head that Rose couldn't see his face.

"What do you want?" Trent demanded.

The man with the long knife smiled, "I want you to tell me where the girl is."

"That's not going to happen," Trent said angrily. "Is there anything else you want?"

The man moved closer, "You know, I like your style." He stepped even closer to Trent, making him pull his head back.

"Not very many nobles do their own dirty work, I respect that."

"You can't imagine how much your respect means to me," said Trent dryly.

The man stepped back and laughed, "And you have a sense of humor! How nice."

"What do you want?" Trent asked again through gritted teeth.

"Let's just take these three and head north," The man holding Evans said in his nasally voice. "We don't need the girl, and I don't want to be standing around here all night looking for her."

"Alright," said the man with the knife, clearly annoyed. "Fine. We can take these three and go, leave the girl to be eaten by wolves, I don't care."

The man turned on a dime and threw his knife at Trip.

Rose gasped. She couldn't help it. The knife thumped into the tree, not an inch from Trip's head.

The second she made a sound, she covered her mouth with her hand, but it was too late. The man's head had whipped around in her direction, and he yelled, "Go!"

The man in the hood took off in her direction. She stood still for two heartbeats, debating whether to run or fight.

"Run!" She heard Trent yell, panicked. She ran.

She didn't know if stealth or speed would be better. She didn't want to leave the men behind. Maybe if she could hide, she could follow them later.

"Take the horses," she heard someone bellow, and she could hear Raul screaming over all the noise.

Distracted, her foot hit a rock and she fell. Her boot fell off because it wasn't tied. She quickly slipped it back on and tried to watch her feet better, but it was so dark she could hardly see anything.

She made it to the creek and crossed to the other side. She found a small trail. It must have been used by deer or some other forest animal because it was far too small to be man-made. She followed it, hoping it would give her a better footing.

She had no idea which way she was going; she just ran as fast as she could.

She heard crashing in the woods behind her. Was it only the hooded man? Were they all after her?

Branches whipped at her face and hair. Her pants got snagged on a bramble, and she had to stop herself from crying out as the thorns dug into her leg. She managed to rip her pants free, and in the next few seconds of silence, she realized she couldn't hear anyone chasing her.

"Please don't scream," a chilling voice said right in front of her.

She looked up. The man with the hood stood an arm's distance away.

"What do you want with me?" she managed to ask with a surprisingly steady voice.

"I don't want anything with you," the man said with no expression. "But I work for them, and they want you." He tilted his head back towards the camp.

"Just let me go," She said.

The man's lip twitched, "I'm afraid I can't do that. We were only told to acquire the prince and the commander, but if I let you go, you might run off and tell someone what we did."

He took a step closer. Her mind was whirling. How was she going to get out of this? She couldn't outrun the man. She couldn't win a fight against him. So she did what Trent had told her to do: take him by surprise.

She fainted.

She had seen women swoon in the castle, but, never having done it herself, she felt she might have over-exaggerated slightly.

She let her eyes roll to the back of her head and fell forward into the man's arms.

Either because he meant to or because it was just a reaction men had to swooning women she didn't know, but he caught her and tried to keep her upright.

He grunted at her sudden weight, "I'm not getting paid enough for this." He shook her, "Wake up, lady, I'm not carrying you back to the fire."

She didn't move. She was completely limp in his arms.

He growled in frustration and stood for a moment in indecision. With another growl, he shifted her weight and drew her legs up so he was carrying her in both arms. Her injured hand was curled between her chest and his, and her other hand was left to swing.

She knew she would only have a second. She drew her dagger and swung her arm back down as hard as she could, stabbing the man in the thigh.

"Ahhh," he yelled and dropped to his knees, freeing Rose.

The man had fallen face down in the dirt, clutching his leg. While he was still in shock, Rose quickly went behind the man and, putting her foot on his spine to keep him on the ground, managed to tie his arms behind his back with her belt.

She took one of his boots off, took his sock, and shoved it in his mouth.

"Please don't scream," She said, looking down at him.

The man glared at her. He wasn't screaming anymore, but she was sure that if he didn't have a sock in his mouth, he would have a lot to say.

Rose turned and ran back down the trail. She had made it to a large stream with fast-flowing water. She hadn't seen any sign of a stream this large on their way towards Bridgeton. She had no idea how far or long she had been running, but she could just see a faint glow on the horizon. She didn't know if the men were still chasing her or if they would have given up, taking Trent and Evans like they said they were paid to do.

She stood at the edge of the wood for a long moment listening. She didn't hear any sound of pursuit, but the stream was loud enough that it could be covering the sound. She took a hesitant step out of the woods. Nothing. She looked up and down the rocks lining the stream. Nothing.

By the faint light of the rising sun, she could make out short cliffs on the other side of the stream and what looked like a shallow cave. She looked at the water. It was about fifty feet to the other side, but the stream looked shallow enough that she could walk across.

She took her boots off, not trusting them in the water while untied. She put one foot in, and the water was icy cold. She took a few more steps, and the water was only up to her shins. She kept going. The water only ever came up to her knees. She sighed in relief when she got to the other side.

On the other side, there were a few feet of dry rock before the cliff. She looked up at the cave. It was higher than she had expected, but she was able to throw her boots onto the ledge and started climbing.

She took a deep breath and tried to imagine this was just the short climb to her favorite reading spot on the castle wall. She would make it to the top, then find her way to Bridgeten and find Trent, Evans, and Trip.

Her arms were weary and shaking, but she made it a few more inches up the cliff. Her feet were numb with cold from the water, which was making it very difficult to climb. She thought about going back down and just staying on the stream bed, but she had to get her shoes. She cursed her panic that made her throw them up there in the first place. She took a breath.

"You're fine," She told herself. "It's not that far, just keep going."

She found another handhold. She took another step. She found a handhold, she took a step, she slipped. She scrambled, trying to regain her footing, but she fell. She fell flat on her back, her head whipping back onto the rocks, and her world went black.

# Chapter 11

She sat at her window and dabbed her eyes. Trish had tried so hard to keep her tears in when Bennett had given his report, but a few had leaked out in her father's office. She had managed to make it to her rooms before the true storm came.

She hated that when she cried, her nose got all puffy, her eyes swelled, and her lips turned very red. Everyone always went on and on about how beautiful she was, but they had never seen her cry. A small tear here and there, but never like this.

She had stayed in her rooms for almost a week when her mother died. At the burial, she had worn a thick black veil so no one could see her face. Only her family and her maids had seen her truly cry.

She turned to her desk and re-read the letter Rose had left for her. Was this why she had been attacked? Her eyes fell on one line in particular,

I do not think you should marry him.

Trish already knew of Rose's mistrust and dislike for the Duke, but she thought Rose had been doing a decent job of keeping that between themselves. Something bad, really bad, must have happened for Rose to so adamantly insist she not get married to the duke.

Trish wanted to talk to Rose. She wanted to talk to Trent. Why did everyone always insist on telling her half-truths? Like she couldn't handle knowing things. She knew she had been kept sheltered, but still, that wasn't her fault.

Anger replaced some of her fear, "Really, Rose," she murmured to herself. "It would have taken you two more seconds to tell me what these 'other events' were."

She folded the letter angrily and put it at the bottom of her desk drawer. She stewed for a few minutes, then came to a decision. If they weren't going to tell her anything, then she would have to find out what was going on all by herself.

She checked her reflection in her hand mirror and grimaced. She took a handkerchief, wiped her eyes, and put on some rouge. Once she deemed herself worthy of the public, she took a deep breath and headed toward the door.

She opened the door and almost ran into someone who had been just about to knock.

"I'm sorry, Princess," the man said and took a step back.

Trish looked at him and gave the smallest of head nods along with a smile that could almost have been a smirk.

"Not at all," She said, holding out her hand. "You're just the person I was looking for."

The man smiled and bowed. He took her hand, "Then I'm glad you found me."

"As am I," Trish said, and the man took her offered hand. "Edmund."

***

Rose could hear a voice. It was a man's voice, but it wasn't one she knew. "Trent," She asked groggily.

Opening her eyes slightly, she could tell something was wrong. It was too bright, even in the shade of a small tree she was under. What time was it?

She tried to sit up, but a terrible pain in her head stopped her.

"Easy there, lass," a man said. "You got quite a bump on your head there."

"Where am I?" Rose asked. The man had an accent she had never heard before.

"Just south o' the river," The man handed her a cup of something warm. "Here, drink this."

Rose shook her head, "No, I have to, I have to find my friends."

"You didn't have any friends when I found ya," the man said.

"They were taken," Rose said, remembering. "We were on the road, and bandits came and took them. I got away. I have to find them." The more she remembered, the higher her voice got. She tried to get up.

"Easy, lass, easy," the man said, gently pushing her back onto the bedroll she was on. She hadn't noticed till then that she was on the ground. "I don't know where your friends are, but you can't go after them on foot in any case. Now, how's about telling me your name?"

"Rose," She said softly.

"Well, nice to meet you, Rose," The man held out his hand. "I'm Garrett."

Rose just looked at him for a second. He had bright green eyes that seemed to be telling a joke. His hair was a light red, and he had a large, rather bushy, red-blond beard.

She slowly stuck her hand out and shook his hand. His hands were rough, full of calluses that a person only gets from years of hard work.

She studied his face for a second more. He wasn't one of the men from last night, she was sure.

"Where am I?" She asked again.

"Just a mile or so south o' the river," Garrett said again. "I was out hunting when I saw you fall. Brought you back to the camp with me to make sure you were alright."

"Thank you," Rose said. She put her hand to the back of her head. It felt like someone had put an egg directly on the back of her head. She winced at a particularly tender spot.

"Like I said," Garrett helped her sit up gently, letting her lean against the tree trunk. "You've got quite a bump. There wasn't any blood, though, so you should be alright. You might be dizzy for a few days."

What was she going to do? She could barely sit up, let alone walk or ride. How was she supposed to save Trent if she couldn't go after them? Sending a letter to Zehrah would take too long. There was no telling how far the bandits could get in the time it would take to get a reply.

Her heart froze.

"How long have I been out?" She asked, panic in her voice.

"'Bout an hour," Garrett said.

She breathed a small sigh of relief. At least it hadn't been days. She tried to remember how long she had run from the bandits, but it made her head hurt. Either way, it didn't matter; she had to find Trent.

"I have to go," She said again. She pushed the blanket off her lap and tried to stand. "Thank you for your help, but I have to find my friends."

She managed to get to her feet, but her head swam. She almost fell over again, but she grabbed the tree trunk in time.

She had only felt like this one other time in her life. The first time she had been on a boat in the open ocean. The pitching of the waves had made her dreadfully sick. She was glad her stomach was empty, or she probably would have vomited.

Garrett stood; he was huge. Rose had to tilt her head back to look up at him, which did not do anything nice for her head.

"Don't talk nonsense, lass," Garrett put a hand on her waist to steady her. "You can hardly stand. Here, come over and sit next to the fire and tell me what happened, and we can talk about finding your friends."

Keeping his hand on her waist, Garrett took her hand that was against the tree and led her to a small fire and sat her on a log.

There were two other men that she could see. One was cooking breakfast over the fire, and the other was tending to their horses. There were five horses, though, so Rose assumed there was another man she couldn't see.

Once she sat down and had a warm drink in her hand, Garrett asked her to tell them what happened.

It took her a moment to decide what to tell these men. You couldn't just go around telling random people that the crown prince of a kingdom had been kidnapped. She knew nothing about these men. Sure, they were being nice to her, but still.

She remembered how Trent had called her his sister and how Evans thought of her like a daughter. That could work.

"My father, brothers, and I were traveling to Bridgeton," she said slowly. She was hoping any gaps in her story could be attributed to her head. "Just before dawn, some men came into our camp and took them."

She paused. How was she going to explain the random kidnapping of three grown men? Real bandits wouldn't have bothered. If they had been carrying goods, they would have just killed the men and taken the loot.

"My father's a," she paused again, thinking. "Diplomat. We were going to the castle. They must be holding them for ransom."

Garrett ran his hand down his beard. "If you were going to the castle, why were you headed to Bridgeten?"

Rose's mind scrambled for a realistic reason they would be going in the opposite direction from Zehrah. "My horse came up lame, and we were close enough to head back for another one instead of going on to Midway." Her head hurt too much to worry if that made sense.

Garrett looked skeptical, but he either didn't care or assumed she was still confused, "Do you know where the men came from?"

She looked up at him, "The north, I think."

"You mean they came to the camp from the north?" He asked. "Or they are from the northern kingdom?"

"Both," she said lamely. "Look, if you could just take me the rest of the way into Bridgeton, you can leave me there and be on your way."

"We aren't going to Bridgeten," The man cooking breakfast said. He had dark hair and a beard that covered most of his face like Garrett's.

Rose stared at him, "Why not? It can't be too far away."

"Bridgeten's got the plague," The man said. "We're going back north where we belong."

Rose could feel the blood run from her face. These men were from the northern kingdom.

"Stop it, Steven," Garrett said. "You're scaring the girl."

"What?" Steven asked. "It's the truth."

"You're from the north?" Rose asked shakily.

"We travel," Garrett said soothingly but vaguely. "We are headed that way to do some trapping and trading."

Rose's eyes darted from Garrett to Steven and back. "So, so you won't take me to Bridgeten?"

"Sorry, lass," Garrett said. "We won't risk Bridgeten."

Rose took a deep breath. "Fine, I understand. I'll be on my way then, thank you again."

"Now hold up there, lass," Garrett said with a hint of a smile. "I said we wouldn't take you to Bridgeten, I didn't say we wouldn't help you."

"What do you mean?" Rose asked.

Garrett looked at Steven, who shrugged and rolled his eyes.

"You see, we are trappers by trade and are pretty good at finding things," Garrett said. "If your father was important enough to be kidnapped, then I assume someone would pay to see him returned?" Garrett raised one eyebrow at her.

"Yes," Rose said slowly.

"Well then," he said, grinning. "What better people to help you get him back from northern kidnappers than some upstanding northern trappers?"

Rose blinked, "You want to help me?"

Garrett shrugged, "We were headed north anyway. Money's money. Helping a nice young lass like yerself doesn't seem a bad way to make some."

He stuck his hand out for Rose to shake. She hesitated for a moment. She didn't know these men, but something about Garrett made her trust him. He had helped her; he didn't pry with questions. She needed to find Trent, Evans, and Trip. She could probably do worse with companions than this lot.

Rose shook his hand.

***

Trish had gone down to the stables, tired of everyone's company. She was especially tired of her father. He had given her so many lectures about family duty in the last few days, she was starting to feel like he couldn't wait to be rid of her.

She felt sorry for Trent. She knew he bore the brunt of most of their father's lectures. Maybe her father just missed giving lectures to Trent, and she was the only one around who could listen.

Shivering slightly at the coolness of the stables, she wrapped her shawl closer around her. Fall had truly started to set in.

"Hello Bean," She gave the horse a sugar cube and rubbed his nose. "Sorry I haven't been out to ride in a while."

Not having taken any offense to a few days of rest, Bean eagerly nudged at Trish's pocket, hoping for more sugar cubes.

Trish giggled, "Stop it now, if you stand in your stall forever eating sugar cubes, you will get dreadfully fat."

Bean nickered softly, not caring in the slightest if she got a little fat. She continued to nudge at Trish's hand until Trish gave in and fed her the other cube she had brought.

"I'll take you out tomorrow, I promise," Trish said, scratching under Bean's chin. "I have a luncheon with Edmund."

She sighed. She had talked to Edmund for almost an hour yesterday, and she couldn't find anything wrong with him.

He enjoyed riding and hunting. He collected sand from every shore he had been to, which was quite a few. He didn't have any siblings, but he had an elderly mother whom he took care of. He thought growing up alone was a poor experience, so he wanted at least two children. He liked putting fresh flowers outside his window in the spring.

She couldn't imagine what he had done to make Rose mistrust him.

Lost in her thoughts, she didn't notice the small animal sneak up behind her. All of a sudden, she felt a tugging at her skirts. She looked down.

"Oh," she said in surprise. "Well, hello there." A small but very fluffy fox was trying to play with her boot laces.

She bent down to pat the creature on the head, but he kept tugging at her lace.

"Come now, that won't do," She said, trying to nudge him away. "You're going to ruin my new boots."

"Reddy," came a boy's voice. "Reddy, where did ya go?"

The fox's ears perked up, and he dashed down the stall lane.

A young boy, no older than ten, came around the corner and called again, "Reddy!"

He froze when he saw her.

"Hello," Trish said, standing. "Is Reddy the fox?"

The boy nodded his head slowly.

"He ran that way," Trish pointed down the aisle.

The boy nodded again and went in search of his fox. Trish followed him.

They found Reddy scratching at a small hole in the stable wall near the grain room. He was making a strange noise, half squeak, half growl.

The boy went and scooped up the fox like a cat.

"I'm sorry, m'lady," The boy said, giving an awkward bow with the fox in his arms. "He likes to come in here to catch mice, but he's only supposed to come after dinner."

Trish smiled at the boy, "It's no problem at all. I'm sure the stable master appreciates his keeping mice out of the feed room. May I pet him?"

The boy nodded and brought Reddy to her. She gently scratched the fox's head, and he turned his nose up to sniff her hand. He started to lick her fingers that still had some sugar on them from the cubes.

Trish laughed, "Do my fingers taste good, little friend?"

The fox nudged her palm open with his nose to get every last crystal of sugar on her hand. When he was done, she gave him another pat on the head.

"Thank you for letting me pet him," Trish said to the boy. She whipped her hand on her skirts, then held it out to the boy, "My name's Trish, what's yours?"

The boy froze with his hand halfway to hers, "Trish? The Princess Trish?"

Trish smiled gently and nodded. To her surprise, the shy boy shook her hand and smiled.

"I've been waiting for you," he said. "I started to think I wouldn't have a chance to introduce Reddy to you before she got back."

Trish frowned in confusion, "Before who got back?"

"Lady Rose," The boy said eagerly. "She asked me to introduce you to Reddy. She said you would want to meet him."

Trish smiled sadly, "She was right. He's a very handsome fox." Rose hadn't told her about a fox, but Trish was touched that she had taken the time to ask this boy to introduce them. She must have known how alone Trish would feel with her and Trent gone.

The boy stood there for a moment, uncertain of what to do. He started fidgeting with the dirt on the stable floor.

"I'm sorry," Trish said. "You must have chores to do, don't let me keep you. Thank you for introducing me to Reddy."

The boy grinned sheepishly, "I'm supposed to be mucking out the stalls. I only stopped to find Reddy."

"Well," Trish stood. "I don't want you to get in trouble on my account."

The boy nodded and started off to the other side of the stables.

"Wait," Trish called.

The boy stopped to look at her.

"I didn't get your name."

The boy blushed fiercely, "Joshua."

"It was nice meeting you, Joshua," Trish waved.

The boy gave a very small wave, then darted off to clean the stalls. He started in such a hurry that he almost ran into someone who had just walked into the stables.

"Whoa there, boy," It was the Duke.

"Sorry, Sir," The boy said, keeping his head down. The fox sniffed at the Duke and started to growl. It wasn't the playful growl he had used with the mouse hole; it was an angry growl.

The Duke didn't even glance at the fox but turned to look at Trish.

"Ah, there you are," He said, coming towards her. "I was wondering if you wanted to take a ride and have a picnic instead of a formal luncheon? You've been cooped up in the castle for days."

Trish was still looking at the boy and the fox, who were still looking at the duke. The fox continued to growl, and all the hair on his back was standing on end.

"Trish?" The duke said, trying to draw her attention back to him.

"Sorry?"

"Would you like to go for a picnic?" The Duke asked again.

"That sounds lovely," she said. She looked for Joshua and Reddy again, but they had gone.

***

Garrett had questioned her for almost an hour. He wanted to know every last detail of what had happened at their camp.

Trying to make up careful half-truths and remember them all was excruciating on Rose's head.

She had nibbled on a few crackers Garrett had given her and kept them down, so he allowed her to eat a few pieces of bacon as well.

When they were finally done talking, Garrett stood and stretched. Rose stood slowly and was happy to find that the world stayed where it was supposed to.

"Well, we'd better get on our way," Garrett said. "We need to go back to your camp. Do you think you can find it?"

"Go back?" Rose asked. "Shouldn't we head north?" She wanted to go after Trent, not back to their camp.

Garrett shook his head, "We aren't sure they were going north. For all we know, they are headed to Zehrah to collect their ransom money. We need to retrace their steps."

Rose huffed impatiently. Even though she had no idea how to track, going back seemed like a waste of time. Then again, arguing about it was a waste as well. She decided if she was going to trust these men, she would have to trust them completely.

She nodded, "I think I can find it. We weren't far off the road."

"Good," Garrett said, nodding. He called to the man who was saddling the horses and said something in a language Rose had never heard.

"Rose, this is Malcolm, Malcolm Rose." The man nodded at Rose. "He doesn't speak much of the common tongue, but he understands it well enough. He takes care of our horses and is our best tracker."

"Nice to meet you," Rose said.

The man nodded, "Nice to meet you." The man's speech was slow and heavily accented. It was also surprisingly high-pitched for such a large man. He was just as tall as Garrett but had blond, almost white, hair and no beard.

"Do you think you're up for riding?" Garrett asked.

Rose nodded, uncertain, but she wanted to get going. She was thankful she was used to riding Raul because all five of Garrett's horses were just as big. Looking at the horses again, she realized one was a mule.

"We will go slow," Garrett promised. He handed her the reins of a dark brown gelding.

"This is Trodaiche," He said, patting the horse on the nose. "But don't let that bother you."

"What does Trodaiche mean?" Rose asked, not knowing why a name should bother her.

Garrett glanced at her, trying to hide a smile at her bad pronunciation, "It means fighter in our language, but don't worry, Trod's as gentle as a lamb."

"Why the name then?" Rose asked as she rubbed Trod's nose.

Garrett laughed, "He was so big as a foal the breeder had high hopes for him, but when he got older, it was clear he only wanted to eat and lounge in the sun. He's as sure-footed as you could ever hope for, though. Do you need a leg up?"

Rose nodded, as dizzy as she had been all morning. She didn't want to risk looking like an idiot in front of these men by falling again.

Garrett helped her into the saddle, then mounted his horse, "This here's Valdar."

"He's beautiful," she said. He was a deep gray with speckles of white on his nose. "Who was riding Trodaiche before?" Rose asked when they were all mounted.

"No one," Garrett said. "It's always good to have a spare or two. We traded a particularly nice bear hide for these two," he gestured to the mule and the horse Malcolm was on.

"The mule's Angus," Garrett said. "I've never met an angrier animal in all my days, but he can carry a mighty heavy load of furs when it comes down to it. He only likes Malcolm."

Malcolm chuckled and said something in their language. Garrett laughed as well. He saw Rose's questioning look and explained. "The last person who tried to pet Angus lost a finger to his teeth, but he was trying to rob us, so I didn't feel particularly bad about it."

"Oh," Rose said, giving the mule a weary look. "I'll mind my distance then."

"Smart Lass," Garrett said with a wink. "Let's get a move on, then, shall we?"

***

There was hardly anything left of their camp. The only thing that marked it as a camp at all was a few burnt logs.

Rose stayed on her horse. Garrett didn't want her footprints to get confused with the bandits.

He had looked around for what felt like a very long time.

"Someone was bleedin' pretty bad," Garrett murmured to himself. He followed the blood a little way out of the clearing, "Wandered in bleedin' though, he wasn't hurt here."

Rose couldn't help but smile. Garrett looked up at her. "What?"

"Nothing," Rose stopped smiling. "One of the men followed me, and I stabbed him. That's probably where the blood came from."

Garrett raised an approving eyebrow at her, "I'm impressed, lass, you must have stuck him good for there to be this much blood."

He continued to look around. Steven came out from where they had tied the horses, "Looks like they took all the horses and tack. One of the horses put up a mighty fuss from the looks of it."

Rose winced. She hoped Raul was alright. She liked Trod. She had started calling him Trod because his full name didn't seem to fit, but she wanted her horse back.

Malcolm went to Garrett and started speaking quietly. Garrett nodded, then looked surprised.

"What?" Rose asked. "What is he saying?"

"He followed the tracks, and they all led north," Garrett said. "He also found a man not far from here, unconscious. He's wondering if he was one of your brothers or one of the raiders." Garrett looked at her questioningly.

Rose's heart instantly froze. Surely the raiders wouldn't have left one of theirs behind? He would know too much. He could give away their plans.

"Was he hurt? What was he wearing? Are you sure he wasn't dead?" Rose asked.

Malcolm shook his head, pointed north, and said something else to Garrett.

Garrett nodded again and came back to Rose and the horses. She waited for them to mount, then asked, "Well? What did he say?" She hated having to use a translator.

"He said the man was alive, we need to go see who it is before we will have any other answers," Garrett turned his horse to follow Malcolm.

They only had to ride for five minutes before she saw him.

"Trip!" she flung herself from the saddle and went to him. He had a few bruises on his face and a knot that could rival hers, but other than that, he looked all right. "Give me a water skin."

Garrett handed her a skin. She opened it and splashed some water on Trip's face. He woke with a jolt and a few choice words before he looked at her. "Rose?"

She nodded and smiled, "Yes, it's me, I'm so glad I found you, brother."

She hugged him quickly and whispered in his ear, "Go along with it."

She pulled back from the hug and looked him in the eye long enough for him to give the smallest of nods, "As am I, sister. Do you mind telling me what happened?"

"We were hoping you could tell us," Garrett said, dismounting. "Here," He said, handing Trip another skin, "This'll help more than the water."

Trip took a swig from the skin and coughed, "Yeah," He said with a laugh. "That'll help more than water. Thank you, friend." He put the cork back in the skin and handed it to Garrett.

"Tell us what happened," Garrett said, squatting next to Trip and Rose.

Trip hesitated, not knowing what story he was supposed to be 'going along with'.

Rose spoke hastily, "All I know is those men took father, Trent, and you, and now we are probably going to miss the royal wedding." She tried to put some pouting in her voice. The more she sounded like a spoiled daughter of a noble, the better.

Trip nodded slowly, "After you got away, they gagged, bound, and blindfolded us. They put us on horses and then headed towards the road. They didn't get very far and decided they didn't need all three of us. They pulled me off my horse and told me to go tell everyone we had been taken. Then the bastard hit me over the head." Trip looked at her and Garrett, "That's all I remember until just now when you all showed up."

Garrett stood and held his hand out to Trip, "Well, we had better get going if we plan on catching up with them. Can you ride?"

Trip took Garrett's hand and stood. He checked his balance for a moment, then nodded. "Why are you helping us?"

Garrett looked at Rose, then back to Trip, "The young lady said there might be some gold at the end of this rainbow."

Trip looked at Rose, "I'm sure there will be." He looked back at Garrett, "Do you have another horse?"

Garrett shook his head, "We'll have to ride double. Steven and Malcolm can scout ahead and follow the trail, we can ride a little behind and switch Rose between the two horses so neither one gets too tired."

Trip did not look comfortable with this arrangement. Seeing his face, Garrett backtracked, "Unless she's uncomfortable." Rose was surprised to see both Garrett and Trip blushing slightly.

"She can just ride with you, of course. Trodaiche's a strong horse. He should be able to carry you both with no trouble." Garrett patted his leg awkwardly.

Rose could tell that Trip objected, but not for the reason Garrett thought. Trip objected to her riding double with Trip.

She spoke up quickly before the moment could get too awkward, "It's alright, brother," she emphasized the word 'brother' and put her hand on Trip's arm. "I don't mind. Besides, it won't be for long. The next town we come to, we can get another horse."

Trip nodded again and cleared his throat, "Well, I guess there is no way around it, but" he squinted his eyes at Garrett, "I'll be watching you."

It was all Rose could do not to roll her eyes. "Right then, shall we?" She turned quickly and headed for the horses.

# Chapter 12

"Please," Rose said for what felt like the hundredth time that morning. "Stop fidgeting." f

"I'm not," Trip protested under his breath. He was as rigid as a rod, and he kept trying to slide as far forward in the saddle as possible.

"You're being ridiculous," Rose's patience had finally worn through. "This is a life-or-death situation to find your sovereign leader, and you're squirming like an eel. Surely you've touched a woman before."

"Of course I have," Trip hissed, and Rose could see his cheeks grow even redder than they already were. "But never a lady."

This time, Rose did roll her eyes, "I'm not a lady!" She whispered fiercely back at him. "I'm a nobody who got picked up by the queen as a baby. If it had happened to you, you would be a lord."

"Still," Trip started to protest.

"Stop it," She demanded. "The only person who's going to defend my honor is Trent, and I promise you he wouldn't mind the situation. You're supposed to be my brother, now start acting like it."

Trip thought about it for a moment, then relaxed marginally. They rode in silence for a few moments before he said, "He isn't the only one who cares about you, ya know."

Rose let out a snort. Garrett, who was a few paces in front, looked over his shoulder at them, raising an eyebrow. She smiled at him but lowered her voice, "Of course, he's not, but he and Trish are the only family I have, so he would be the one to ask."

She thought for a moment, thinking of something she had never thought of before. If she were to get married, who would the man have to ask for her hand? She smiled to herself, he would have to ask her and only her.

"Not that I have to ask anyone," She finished.

The longer they rode, the more relaxed Trip became in the saddle. Rose didn't think it had as much to do with their conversion as it did with the simple fact that it was extremely uncomfortable to ride so rigidly for hours on end.

They came to a stop at around midday. Trip gave Rose his arm so she could slide off the back of their saddle before dismounting. He winced when his feet hit the ground.

Rose didn't even try to suppress her small smile. "I told you," was all she said.

He glared at her before turning to take care of Trod.

Rose went to Garrett and asked how much farther to the river.

"We're at the river, lass," He said. "Can't you hear it?"

She stood quietly, over the sounds of the men tending to the horses and rummaging in their bags for lunch, she could faintly hear running water.

"Shouldn't we be able to see the bridge then?"

"We're not goin' to the bridge lass," Garrett said.

Confusion was evident on Rose's face, so Garrett continued.

"There are watchmen on the bridge. Both sides. There's no way the bandits would have been able to cross with hostages." Garrett shook his head, "No, we're going to the ferry. It's bout five miles upstream from the bridge."

"Aren't there watchmen on the ferry?" Rose asked.

"There are," Garrett said. "But the ferry watchman is more persuadable to look the other way when you have, eh...questionable cargo."

"Like nobles?" Rose asked drily.

"Can't say for sure," Garrett said. "Never tried to carry that sort of cargo myself," he smiled at her. "Anyone doing anything untoward is going to be taking the ferry, don't worry."

Wanting to know at least a little more about her guide, Rose persisted, "And what type of 'untoward' cargo is your usual?"

"Oh, my cargo's always toward," he said with a smile. "I just don't like paying taxes."

"Ahh," Rose said. She knew there were taxes on the large sea boats carrying goods from one kingdom to another, so she supposed it made sense that the goods coming over land would be taxed as well. She noticed that Garrett still hadn't told her what goods he normally carried.

At that moment, Trip came over, handing both Garrett and Rose a hunk of bread and cheese. They both murmured their thanks and went to sit with the others under a tree.

They all sat quietly, eating their lunch and enjoying a break from the saddle. Rose finished her cheese and lay back on the grass. She closed her eyes for a moment and breathed deeply. Other than being knocked unconscious, Rose hadn't slept since the night Trent had been kidnapped. Rose counted back and realized that it had only been about ten hours ago.

It felt like a lifetime.

She wasn't intending on falling asleep, but she was so tired and the grass was so soft that she slowly drifted away.

***

She laughed at the joke the mouse had told.

Rose was back in the field with wildflowers, wearing the long white dress.

The only difference was that there were two other humans with her.

Trent and Garrett.

Trent looked like his normal princely self, but Garrett looked nothing like Rose had ever seen him look before.

He wore a light cream colored shirt and pants, with a sword at his belt. His hair was combed back out of his face, and his wild beard had been trimmed to nicely shape his face. He wore a simple silver crown that was almost identical to Trent's.

He was laughing merrily at the mouse's joke as well.

"Is something wrong, Rose?" Trent asked.

She dragged her eyes off Garrett to respond, "Not at all, dear cousin."

Garrett turned to Trent and said, "She's not used to seeing me all fancied up, is all." He and Trent laughed.

"Garrett," She said. "Are you a prince?"

Even in her dream, she was confused. Garrett was a simple fur trader.

"Not technically, lass," Garrett said and winked at her.

"I don't understand," Rose said vaguely.

"Rose," Trent said. She looked at him, waiting for an explanation, but he didn't give one.

"Lass," Garrett said, and gently put his hand on her shoulder. She looked at him, thinking he would explain, but he didn't. Instead, he shook her slightly and said, "Wake up, sleepy head."

She looked at the mouse in confusion, and he said, "You have to find Trent." The mouse stood on his hind legs and bowed. "I'll see you again, but right now you have to go."

Rose looked back at the men, but they were gone. She was all alone in the beautiful meadow, and she didn't want to leave.

***

Her eyes opened, and she stared at the face just inches away from hers. It was so different from the one in her dream, but it was Garrett.

He gave a small sigh of relief, "Don't scare me like that, Lass, you were sleeping like the dead."

"Sorry," she said. "I must have nodded off. Is it time to go?"

Garrett nodded, "For the next few days, let someone know if you're going to go to sleep. When a person hits their head as hard as you did, sometimes they don't wake up if they fall asleep again."

"I'm sorry," Rose said. "I didn't know."

"S'alright," Garrett said, helping her off the ground. "You're riding with me for the rest of the day."

Rose nodded and shook the sleep from her head. Her dreams were getting stranger. The disturbing thing was, a few of them had been actual warnings. Now she didn't know if they were just dreams or visions or premonitions or what they were.

Garrett helped her into the saddle behind him, and they all started on the trail again.

Malcolm had gone ahead of them to follow the trail. Steven was riding a little way in front of them, pulling the small strips of cloth from the tree branches Malcolm was leaving for them to follow. Trip was a few horse lengths behind them.

Garrett was much more relaxed with Rose in the saddle than Trip had been. The only problem was that Garrett was also a lot bigger than Trip, leaving Rose hardly any room to sit.

They rode for almost twenty minutes in silence. To Rose's surprise, it wasn't an awkward silence either. During their lunch break, the wind had picked up, and Rose found herself grateful to have Garrett's huge shoulders blocking most of it.

"You never told me what your cargo normally is," She finally said.

She could feel Garrett chuckle, "You still on about that? Why so interested?"

She shrugged, "Just making sure you're not a crazy person or something like that."

He laughed, "Not sure if you can tell a man's crazy by what cargo he carries."

Rose disagreed but kept quiet, hoping he would answer. After a long moment, he said, "It's mostly furs and small wooden figurines. Malcolm loves to whittle, and he's pretty good at it, too."

Rose knew he was still avoiding the question and pressed, "Mostly?"

Garrett sighed, "The intentions behind our cargo are good, but it's not exactly...legal. Are you familiar with the Great War?"

"Yes," Rose said.

"Do you know why it started?" Garrett asked.

"The northern kingdom and the eastern kingdom started taking slaves," Rose answered.

Garrett nodded, "That's right."

"You're a salver," Rose said, appalled.

Garrett turned to look over his shoulder at her, his eyebrows knit together in surprise at her quick assumption, "Course not."

"But," Rose started.

"I just wanted to make sure you understood why we do what we do," Garrett said. "After the Great War, the Northern and Western kingdoms stopped taking people, but the Northern kingdom didn't stop having slaves. They simply started using their people."

Rose was shocked. She was silent, so Garrett went on, "They don't call it slavery, o'course. They are 'servants', but they are slaves in everything but name. During King Douglas' reign, most of the slaves were let go or allowed to work for money, but when Graham came into power after King Douglas, that changed."

"So," Rose asked hesitantly. "What does that have to do with you and cargo?"

"For the last five years, Malcolm and I have been finding people who want to leave the northern kingdom and bringing them across the river to the Western and Eastern kingdoms," He said matter-of-factly. "Steven joined us a few months back. He and his mother were trying to leave the kingdom, but she died before they could make it. He decided to stay with us and help others."

"I'm sorry," Rose said softly. "That's horrible."

"It is," Garrett said gruffly. "If King Douglas' son hadn't died, he might have been able to stop it completely."

Rose remembered her dream, with Garrett looking every bit as royal as Trent. She shook her head slightly. The dream didn't mean anything. She was royalty in her dream, and she knew for a fact that wasn't true.

She decided it was time to change the subject, "After we cross the river, what's the plan?"

"I'm not sure," Garrett said. "It depends on why the bandits took your father in the first place. If they just wanted ransom money, they wouldn't have taken them very far across the border. If they were trying to start something between the kingdoms, then they would have taken them to the mountains."

Rose considered that maybe she should tell Garrett who was really taken. He was operating on a very loose version of the truth, and it might change his plans if he knew who they were looking for.

"We'll have to talk to ol' Kenneth before we can make any real plans," He continued.

"Kenneth?" Rose asked.

"He's the old man who runs the ferry," Garrett explained. "I've known him most my life, and he will usually give me information about others comin' and goin'."

"How much longer until we get there?" Rose wanted to know.

"We should be there by nightfall," Garrett estimated. "If we're real nice, Kenneth might even let us sleep in the stables." He chuckled wryly.

***

"What do you mean, my son has been taken?" Garin said in a dangerously low voice.

The Duke bowed his head and explained, "I had arranged for some larger presents for the princess to be brought by boat after my arrival. When they arrived at the ferry, the captain saw a large group of Northmen with two blindfolded and bound men."

"And how does that make you certain it was my son?" Garin demanded, losing patience.

The Duke nodded again and continued, "My men did not recognise him as your son, but when they described the two men to me, I knew it had to be your son and Commander Evans. They said one was young with blond hair, the other older, tall, and wearing the armor of a knight."

"What about the other two?" Garin asked. "The girl and the archer?"

"They didn't mention them, your majesty," the duke said. "Perhaps the northerners only wanted high-value hostages."

Garin considered, "That description could have been anyone. There are plenty of tall knights and plenty of young blond men."

The Duke nodded, "Of course, your majesty. I could very well be wrong, but I thought you should know all the same, considering young Bennett's report."

The king's office was quiet for a moment. No one had been told about the report Evans's squire had brought back.

"How did you know about that?" The king demanded.

The duke hesitated, "I didn't know it was a secret, Your Majesty. Patrisha was melancholy during our lunch, so I asked her what was bothering her. She told me."

The first time he had called the king's daughter "Trish" in front of the king, it was not received well, ever since the duke had been calling her Patrisha whenever he spoke with the king.

The king was silent for longer than the Duke was comfortable, and he decided he needed to take control of the conversation.

"I'm sorry, your majesty," He said with another bow. "I overreacted and am causing you undue stress. You've surely heard from the party and know exactly where they are." He gave another bow and turned to exit the office.

"Wait," The king called. The duke couldn't completely suppress his grin, but mastered his face before turning to face the king again.

"As a matter of fact, we haven't had any communication with the group, except for Bennett." The king ran a hand over his beard. "Peter?"

"No, your majesty," Lord Peter said from the corner of the office. "We haven't had any communication since Squire Bennett arrived."

The duke waited patiently for the king to make up his mind on his own. He didn't think he could push anymore without the king getting suspicious of his motives.

After a long, silent minute, the king finally spoke, "Alright. If you say they were seen at the ferry, that should be easy enough to check. Peter, arrange for two groups to leave immediately."

"Two, your majesty?" Peter asked.

"Send one to Bridgeten and the other to the ferry. Tell them both to ride without stopping and send a letter once the Commander and my son are found." The king said and stood.

"Yes, your majesty," Peter said, bowing.

"Your majesty," the Duke said and bowed as the king exited the room. Once he was gone, the duke turned to go himself and allowed himself a small but triumphant grin.

***

They got to the ferry just before sunset. The sun made the water of the river look like liquid gold that shimmered and danced in the current.

"Hello, the house!" Garrett called as they approached.

A moment later, an elderly man came hobbling out with a cane and a lamp, "Who goes there?" he demanded in a frail, crackly voice.

"You don't recognize my voice?" Garrett said. "I'm hurt, Kenneth."

The old man looked up at Garrett, "You never know what trouble may be about these days, my lad. Never hurts to check, plus my hearing isn't what it used to be, ya know."

"Nonsense, old man," Garrett said with a laugh and dismounted. "You could hear someone whisper on the other side of the river as long as there was a coin to be earned."

The old man gave a grin that was missing more than a few teeth and said, "Aye, you might be right there, s'good to see ya, Garrett."

The men clasped hands and patted each other's backs. They were obviously old friends.

Rose was coming around Garrett's horse when Kenneth said, "Ya can put the horses in the stable. Be careful, though, the last group that came through left a wild one they didn't want. I've never met a meaner horse in my life. I'll put the kettle on for ya and see what food I can scrounge up."

Kenneth toddled back into the house as the rest of them headed for the small stables just a little way upstream.

As they approached, Rose could hear an extremely unhappy horse cry and kick the walls.

"Kenneth wasn't kidding," Garrett said. "The poor beast sounds mad."

Rose listened to the cry again and ran for the barn. There was a chance, a small chance, but still a chance, and she was sure she recognized that cry.

She threw the stable door open. Garrett and the other man yelled at her to stop, but she didn't care.

It was Raul.

He looked up at her and whinnied again, tossing his head. She went to him immediately and stroked his soft velvet nose. She made small shushing sounds to him, and a few tears oozed from her eyes.

Garrett and Trip stood in the doorway. Garrett looked like he was about to give another warning, but upon seeing Rose and the horse, it died in his throat. Trip, of course, recognized Raul immediately.

"I'm so sorry I left you," Rose whispered to the horse over and over. "Are you alright? Did they hurt you?"

Raul gently butted his head to her chest and softly nickered. She scratched behind his ear as he started sniffing at her pockets.

Rose laughed gently, "I'm sorry, friend, I don't have any sugar cubes on me just now."

Raul snorted disappointedly.

"You can have all the sugar cubes just as soon as I find some," Rose promised.

"I take it this is your horse then," Garrett said from the stable door.

Rose nodded, wiping the tears from her cheeks.

"Well, that works out perfectly," Garrett said and brought the other horses into the stable. "I'm sure Kenneth won't mind getting him off his hands."

They bedded down the other horses, and Malcolm unloaded the mule. Once everything was settled in the barn, they went to the main house for some supper.

"I'll be back before I go to sleep," Rose promised Raul, who seemed perfectly content now that he was with his rider again.

Back in the house, Kenneth had set a kettle of tea to boil and had a large pot of stew cooking on the embers in the fireplace.

Kenneth himself was bustling around the small kitchen, opening cupboards, trying to get enough bowls for his guests. Every time he found one, he handed it to whoever was closest to him. Rose's was more of a plate with a small lip that would hopefully keep the stew in place.

There was no way they would all fit at the table, so they dished up the stew and went to the front lawn, where there were half a dozen chairs and a few benches that were normally used by people waiting for the ferry.

They used their laps as tables and dug into the hardy, if not a little plain, stew.

"So, Garrett," Kenneth said after they had some time to enjoy their dinner. "What brings ya back my way so soon? It's only been a couple o' weeks since you crossed."

"True," Garrett said, bobbing his head. "We didn't stay as long as planned, but something important came up."

"Does that important thing have somethin' to do with your pretty companion here?" Kenneth said, gesturing to Rose.

"O'course," Garrett said, putting his spoon in his empty bowl. "The lady here seems to have misplaced her father and brother. A group came to their camp just last night and carried them away."

"Why didn't they take her?" Kenneth asked. He asked Garrett, but then he looked at Rose.

"They tried," Garrett continued with a grin. "She was too much for em. She gave one of them a pretty good poke with a knife."

"Did she now?" Kenneth said approvingly to Rose. "Well, good for you, miss."

Rose grinned, embarrassed, "We know they came this way because they left my horse with you."

Kenneth's eyes went wide, "That terrible beast is yours? That's no fit horse for a lady. He nearly took my arm off when I tried to put him in the stable." Kenneth shook his head darkly. "Then all day he's been trying to knock down all the walls he can reach."

"I'm sorry about that," Rose said. "He was probably trying to get back to me. He's really very gentle."

Kenneth gave her a skeptical look, "I'll have to take your word for it then."

"I can pay you back anything you paid the other men for him," Rose said quickly.

Kenneth waved her offer off, "I didn't pay anything for him. He refused to get on the ferry, so the men just left him. Said he'd been fighting them the whole way here, and they didn't have time to deal with it."

"Did they say where they were going?" Trip asked.

Kenneth shook his head, "Naw, they didn't. After I took them across, they headed for the coast, but that's all I know."

Garrett was nodding in understanding. He saw Rose's look and explained, "They're headed for Seawalk. Either to stay or to get past the desert, then travel by boat the rest of the way to the western side of the northern kingdom. The desert's unpassable this time o' year, and the only other way up there is to take a ship down the river between the eastern and western kingdoms, then take another ship back up the coast."

"How long would it take them to get to Seawalk?" Rose asked.

Garrett considered, "It's about a four-day ride up the coast."

"Why wouldn't they take a ship?" Trip asked. "It would be faster than riding."

Garrett nodded, "It would, but ships are very expensive, and I doubt kidnappers would want to waste their ransom on a ship." Garrett chuckled, "Unless you've got the king himself, it wouldn't be worth it."

Trip's eyes shot to Rose. She clenched her jaw.

"Well," Rose said. "We can cross the river tomorrow, then see if we can follow their tracks to a boat or up the coast on land."

"There's no need," Garrett said. "We don't have to go all the way to the coast. I know a path that will get us to Seawalk faster than taking the rocky coastline. We might even beat them there if we're lucky." He sat back in his chair, impressed that he would be able to catch up with the kidnappers so quickly.

Rose glanced at Trip. Trent might not be the king, but he was the next best thing, and the bandits might very well have been willing to hire a ship to get them as far away from the western kingdom as quickly as possible.

The kidnappers wanted something from Trent. Otherwise, they would have just killed him. Rose also knew it had to be something other than just money. Even if they gave Trent back to the king in perfect condition, it would still be a death sentence for them. You don't just kidnap the crown prince on a whim. No, something major was going on, and Rose needed to find out what it was.

"Shouldn't we check the coast?" Rose said as nonchalantly as she could. "Just to make sure?"

Garrett tilted his head, "There's really no reason. For one thing, we don't have the money to hire a ship ourselves, so we would still have to travel on land to Seawalk."

Rose chewed her nails. He might be right, but still, she had to know where Trent went for certain. She didn't have time to go running around the whole continent looking for him.

"Is there no way we can catch up to them before they make it to the coast?" Trip asked.

Rose looked at Garrett hopefully, but he was already shaking his head, "It's only half a day's ride from here to the coast. If they left around midday, they would have already been there and gone."

Rose looked at Trip for a moment, then sighed. After a minute of silence, Garrett spoke.

"I think your best bet is to head to Seawalk by my route," Garrett looked her directly in the eye. "Unless I'm missing something."

Rose held his gaze. He knew. He might not know exactly what he knew, but he did know she wasn't telling him the truth.

Rose had to drop his knowing stare, "No," she said. "Let's go with your plan. After all, you do know the way better than we do."

She stood, she wanted to be alone, "I'm going to check on Raul before I go to bed. Goodnight, everyone."

They all murmured goodnight as she headed for the barn. She could hear Malcolm say something in his language, and Garrett responded, "Indeed! Kenneth, do you think we could have another bowl of that delightful stew?"

The sun had truly fallen, now making it dark in the barn. Rose had to feel for the lamp that was hanging by the stable door and light it.

Raul looked up at her expectantly. She went and fondled his soft nose, "I'm sorry, boy, I still don't have any sugar."

She took a brush off a hook on the wall and started currying her horse. He probably hadn't been brushed since he had been taken, meaning he was put in this barn, soaked in sweat.

"I'm sorry," she whispered again and started gently working over the horse's body with the brush. She enjoyed the simple rhythmic process almost as much as Raul did. After a while, she was surprised to feel her eyes prickle and a tear trail down her face. She whipped at it quickly.

"There's no reason to cry," She said firmly to Raul. "We'll find them, Trent and Evans. We have to." She ended in a whisper.

Raul's ears pricked at the barn door. Rose turned and saw Garrett standing in the doorway.

"Talkin' to horses is a sign you're goin' crazy," Garrett said.

"It is not," Rose said, turning back to brushing. "You're only crazy if the horse starts talking back."

Garrett chuckled, "I guess you're right about that." He walked to Raul's stall and picked up another brush, "May I?"

Rose nodded, and Garrett came over to Raul's other side. He let the horse smell his hand and gently rubbed his nose, "There now, you're not as wild as old Kenneth said."

They brushed in silence until Raul's coat shone. Rose hung her brush back on the peg and took a comb to start on Raul's tail. Garrett hung his brush as well and then leaned against the stable wall.

"Look, lass," He started. "I don't pretend to know exactly what's going on here, but I do need some information."

Rose glanced at him and went back to Raul's tail.

"I understand keeping your business to yourself," He said. "Believe me, I do, but if I'm going to be taking my men all the way to Seawalk, I feel like I ought to know the level of danger they might be gettin' into."

Rose stopped combing and looked at him, "You're right." She said, and he was. She couldn't just expect this man to do whatever she said without question. He had people of his own to look out for, and as a northerner, he had no obligation to help save the eastern prince.

"My father," she paused. When they found Trent, the ruse would be up anyway. If Garrett were going to harm her, he would have already done it. Furthermore, he had no reason to re-kidnap Trent. He would already have what he needed to collect a ransom when they found Evans and Trent.

She started again, "Well, my brother actually, He's worth a boat."

Garrett nodded slowly, "I see, and might Rose not be your real name?"

Rose was confused for a second, "What do you mean?"

"Might your real name be Trish?" Garrett asked quietly.

Rose's mouth hung open, and her eyebrows furrowed. How could this fur trader from the northern kingdom possibly know what only the castle staff and Trish's closest friends called her? In every official document, every diplomatic introduction, Trish was always called Patrishia. Even the king called her Patrishia.

"No," Rose finally managed to answer. "My name is Rose."

Garrett looked like he was going to protest, but she cut him off, "How do you know Trish?"

"We met when we were children," He said, smiling fondly at the memory. He studied Rose for a moment, "Come to think of it, she was a mite blonder than you are, and rather pale. Her eyes were blue as well."

"What do you mean you met as children?" Rose demanded. "The princess hardly goes around meeting commoner children in the northern kingdom."

Garrett's eyebrow raised, "Who said I was a commoner?"

Rose started to say something, then stopped, then started again, "But you're a fur trader."

Garrett laughed, "That I am, but that doesn't mean I started that way. How do you know the princess then? Are you a lady in waiting or something?"

"I'm not a lady," Rose blurted out before she could stop herself. Garrett looked at her questioningly, "I'm an orphan, I was raised in the castle."

"Well, there ya go," Garrett said. "People's fortunes can go down just as easily as they can go up."

They were quiet for a moment. Garrett pushed off the wall, coming around Raul so he could see all of her.

"Well, if you're not Trish, then I think you might be over-stating your brother's value a little." He said gently. "No one short of royalty would warrant a ship. We'll head north in the morning and find your brother. Kenneth fixed up the couch in the house for you, he said the barn wasn't suitable for a girl as pretty as you. "

"He is royalty," She whispered as Garrett shut the stable door.

Garrett looked at her with pity in his eyes.

She looked him in the eyes, "He's not really my brother, but we grew up together like family."

"Who?" Garrett asked.

"Trent," Rose said. "Trenton Zehrah, Crown Prince of the Eastern Kingdom."

# Chapter 13

She told him everything. There was no point in keeping it from him. He listened carefully, only asking a few questions. When she was done, he rubbed his chin thoughtfully.

"This is all very interesting," Garrett said.

"Which part?" Rose asked after he didn't elaborate.

"All of it. The entire situation." Garrett said. "We don't hear much official news in our line of business, but we do hear plenty of gossip. With this information, some of the gossip now makes sense."

"What gossip?"

"All last year, we have heard that several western kingdom caravans had been traveling up the coast to the northern kingdom," Garrett said deep in thought.

"What?" Rose hadn't heard anything about the western and northern kingdoms being any closer than they were to the eastern kingdom.

Garrett shrugged, "We thought it was just village talk. Any party with more than two wagons always generates a lot of gossip, especially in the smaller towns."

"Why did they think the parties were from the western kingdom?" Rose asked. "Did they fly a banner or have Western soldiers?"

Garrett shook his head, "No, they never said anything quite so obvious. They just said the people looked like they were westerners."

"What does that mean?" Rose asked, frustrated. "People from the eastern and western kingdoms look pretty much the same. They might be slightly darker, but that's quite an assumption to make from just seeing a group pass through your town."

Garrett shrugged again, "I assume it has more to do with large parties traveling through their town at all. It follows logically, seeing as the parties were on the western coast of the northern kingdom, that the parties were western."

Rose eyed him, skeptical.

"Anyway, it's not so much what the people are saying but what you've told me." Garrett continued. "You said the Princess was getting married. She wouldn't be getting married to anyone less than royalty, and the Western Kingdom is the only place that has any royals to wed. Secondly, the prince has been kidnapped by the north. It looks to me like we might have a second great war on our hands."

Again, Rose was baffled by this man's knowledge of politics and his intimate knowledge of the royal families.

"How do you know all this?" She asked.

Garrett looked at her and smiled, "Like I said, I wasn't always a fur trader. Anyway, you should probably get to bed. This information won't change our plans. We still need to go to Seawalk as quickly as possible."

Rose started to protest, but realized he was right. They had to get to Seawalk and get Trent. Garrett walked her to the house and said goodnight, then went back to the stables.

Trip was sitting on the front porch, "I didn't figure you would want to be left alone. I can sleep on the floor if you want." He phrased his statement like a question, but it was obvious he wasn't going to leave her.

She nodded, "Thank you, Trip."

She laughed quietly when she opened the door. Trip had already set up a place for him to sleep in the corner of the room, right next to the door.

"If I want?" she said jokingly to him.

He shrugged, embarrassed, "Like you said earlier, it's Trent I have to answer to if anything happens to you. I don't think he would take kindly to my letting you be alone all night in a stranger's house. With the stranger in it no less."

Rose smiled in agreement, "You're probably right. Anyway, I needed to talk to you alone. I told Garrett everything."

Trip didn't look surprised, "We were going to have to eventually. I don't know if I woulda trusted him if he blindly agreed to go so far as Seawalk without some information."

"Malcolm and Steven don't know, though, he thought it best," Rose said.

"Doesn't he trust them?' Trip asked.

"He does," she said. "He just said if anything were to happen, the less they knew, the safer they would be."

Trip nodded, "Smart." He went to the lamp Kenneth had left on the table for them, "If you don't mind, I'm beat."

She nodded, and he snuffed out the flame. Once her eyes adjusted to the dark, she watched the stars until she fell asleep.

***

Trish was in her room looking at the stars from her balcony. She sighed. She missed Rose. She couldn't count the number of times they had sat on the balcony dreaming of their futures, often falling asleep outside.

Trish would always talk about being a queen married to a handsome king and having five children in a castle. Rose changed her dream every other day. One day, she was going to be an adventurer who discovered a new land, the next, she was going to be a pirate ship captain. One time, she even said she was going to be a mighty dragon slayer, and they had gotten into a horrible fight about whether or not dragons were real.

Trish's maid came into her room and called her name.

"Yes," Trish said, moving from her couch on the balcony.

"His highness would like to see you," The maid said with a curtsey.

Trish frowned. It was very late, "Right now?"

The maid froze, "I think so, your grace. His accountant just told me to fetch you quickly."

Trish sighed and threw on her dressing gown and slippers. What could her father possibly want that was so urgent it couldn't wait till morning?

She knocked gently on her father's office door. "Come in," came his voice from the other side.

She pushed the door open and walked into the room. Her father was pacing behind his desk, his accountant was sitting in a chair in the corner, and, to her surprise, Edmund and Grady were both there as well.

"What's wrong?" She asked, glancing at each face in turn. Her father's accountant looked frazzled, but that was his normal expression. Edmund looked grave and pulled out a chair for her. Grady looked... almost smug. She couldn't quite tell.

Her father's face was blank. It was a mask he liked to don when he was angry and maybe even scared. It was his king face, and Trish hated it when he wore it around her.

"Your brother has been taken." He said, looking at her.

"What do you mean? By who? Where has he been taken?" Trish didn't mean to ask all her questions at once, but they just came out.

"We don't know," Edmund said.

She looked at him, then back at her father. Alliances or no, surely it wasn't a good idea to let another kingdom know the crown prince had been kidnapped.

"We don't know by whom or what for, but we suspect the Northern Kingdom is behind it," the king said. "They were seen being taken across the river."

"They?" She asked.

"Evans has been captured as well." Her father said, gripping the back of his chair.

Her mouth fell open, about to ask another question, but she paused. It was bad enough that Trent had been taken, but Evans as well. Someone was trying to start a war.

"Father," she said tentatively. "Father, might I speak with you alone for a moment?"

He just shook his head. He didn't even look at her. "There's no time. You're leaving with the Duke in one hour."

"What?"

"He's taking you to the western kingdom to hide you. No one outside this room will know you've left or where you're going." The king sat behind his desk. "Someone is trying to start a war, and I will not have my only other heir kidnapped as well."

"Surely I'm safer here than I am on the road," Trish protested. "Father, please, let's talk."

"No." He said forcefully but more gently than he had been a moment ago. "I know you're scared, dear, but no one will know where you've gone. They won't know where to look for you."

"Father, please," was all she could say.

To her utter surprise, her father smiled at her like nothing was amiss. "Besides," He said, reaching over the desk and patting her hand, "You would have been going to the western kingdom soon after the wedding anyway. Hurry and pack now, you need to leave well before sunrise."

***

Rose woke to a loud rooster crowing. She opened her eyes and jolted upright. The rooster was sitting on the window ledge right next to the couch she was sleeping on.

He stretched out his neck, puffed out his feathers, and let out another ear-splitting crow.

"Alright, Alright," Rose said to the rooster. "I'm awake!"

The rooster made to crow again, but she nudged him off the ledge and onto the lawn. He ran off towards the barn, flapping his wings in indignation.

"Sorry 'bout him," Kenneth said from the stove. "As soon as I can get another one, he's going to make a mighty fine supper."

Rose laughed. She stretched and sat up on the couch, looking out the window. The sun had just started to come over the hills to the east. She looked over at Trip, who was somehow still asleep, and quietly folded the blanket she had been using and put it over the back of the couch.

Kenneth brought her a large bucket full of water, "Here ya go." He put the bucket just inside his bedroom door. "I usually just wash in the river, but thought you'd like something a little more private and warm."

She thanked him as he handed her a clean towel as well. She went into the room and shut the door and window hangings.

She hadn't realized just how dirty a person got running through the woods and falling off cliffs. The water was tinged brown just from washing her hair.

She felt like a new person after she was done. She regretted not having clean clothes to put on when there was a soft knock at the door. She froze.

"I brought your saddle bag from the barn," came Garrett's voice from the other side.

She quickly wrapped the towel around herself and went to the door. She opened it, just enough to hold out her hand for the bag. He chuckled and handed it to her.

"Thank you," She said quickly, then shut the door again.

The only other clothing she had brought was the dress she planned on wearing in Bridgeton. She sighed, Oh well, at least it was clean.

She put on the dress. She debated whether or not to braid her hair back, but decided it would dry faster down. She ran her fingers through her hair, working out a few stubborn knots, then went out to the main room.

Immediately, she wished she could step back into the room and close the door again.

All the men were dishing up plates of eggs and sausage, and they all turned to stare at her.

She self-consciously tugged at her dress, then, red as a tomato, demanded, "What?"

Steven, Malcolm, and Trip quickly turned their attention back to the food, but Garrett continued to stare at her.

Old Kenneth chuckled then continued putting eggs on Trip's plate, "S'nothin' Miss, these lads just aren't used to seeing a falcon turn into a swan." He handed her a plate with some eggs on it, and she quickly went to the front porch to eat.

Garrett sat next to her and didn't say anything. He still had that smile on his face, and it was starting to annoy her.

"As soon as I wash my other clothes, we can use this dress for rags as far as I'm concerned," She stabbed her sausage with a fork.

Garrett shook his head and chuckled, "A falcon indeed. Both beautiful birds, you know, and there's nothing wrong with either of them."

Rose rolled her eyes, "Was there some sort of bird analogy meeting I missed this morning?"

Garrett looked at her out of the corner of his eye, "Kenneth might have gotten the swan part wrong, though, you're more like a hissing goose."

Rose swallowed her retort, knowing it would just lead to more teasing, but glared at him. She shoveled the rest of her breakfast into her mouth as quickly as she could, then went to wash her dirty clothes in the river.

***

She hung her wet clothes on the back of Raul's saddle and walked him out into the yard with the others. She grinned slightly as Kenneth's face turned doubtful.

"I promise," she told him, "he won't be any trouble while I'm here."

He mumbled something she couldn't quite hear, but it sounded like, "We'll see about that."

The ferry was too small for all six people and their horses, so Kenneth took Malcolm and Trip with their horses first. He then came back for Steven, his horse, and Angus. Then came back another time for Rose and Garrett.

On the first crossing, Rose had asked Garrett if they should help. After all, Kenneth was an old man.

Garrett smiled and shook his head, "No need, Kenneth doesn't do any work, he lets the river do it all, watch."

There was a large rope tied from one tree on their side of the river to another tree on the other side. Attached to the large rope were two wheels with smaller ropes coming down to the ferry, one tied to each end. Once Trip and Malcolm got on the ferry, Kenneth let the rope tied to the end closest to shore loose. The current of the river pushed that side of the ferry downstream, and Kenneth tied off the rope again. The water continued to push the ferry at an angle to the other side of the river without Kenneth having to do anything other than untie a knot.

"He's a genius," Rose said under her breath.

"That he is," said Garrett. "But he mostly just got tired of pulling that ferry across the river every day."

"I've never seen a ferry work like that," Rose said. "I've only seen ones pushed with a long pole."

Garrett nodded, "Most of the time that does work, but this river is too deep and swift for that. Kenneth used to have a rope tied at chest height, and he would pull it back and forth with a winch in the middle of the ferry, but as he got older, he tried to find easier ways to operate. This one works the best."

Kenneth came back for them a final time, and they loaded Raul onto the ferry without any problems.

Kenneth shook his head in disbelief and chuckled, "I'll never doubt you again, miss."

When everyone was across, they all said goodbye to Kenneth. The men all shook his hand, and Rose hugged him, "Thank you for keeping Raul."

"Of course, lass," he said, patting her cheek. "You be safe now, his majesty needs ya I think."

Rose gaped at him, but he turned back to the ferry and started off towards the other side of the river.

She was going to kill Garrett! Hadn't they decided they weren't going to tell anyone about Trent? Hadn't it been his idea in the first place? Why would he go and tell the man who saw countless people every day? Not to mention that Kenneth's clientele wasn't exactly made up of law-abiding citizens.

"You coming, lass?" Garrett hollered after her. The men were already on the top side of the bank, headed east.

She whipped Raul around and headed towards the sea.

# Chapter 14

They followed the river for almost two hours before Garrett took them on another path heading north, and "path" was a generous word. They had to go single file, and even that was almost too much for the trail they were following. There was a sheer rock cliff to their left and a drop-off on their right. They could see the top five feet or so of pine trees that were over one hundred feet tall.

Rose made the mistake of looking over the cliff down into the trees and experienced a horrible swooping sensation in the stomach she had never felt while climbing the walls at the castle.

"How long are we going to be on this cliff?" She called to the front, where Garrett was riding.

"Not too far," he said, not looking back. He kept his eyes on the trail.

"How far is 'not too far'?" She demanded.

She swore she could hear the grin in his answer, "About another half hour or so. And keep your voice down, there are lions in those trees."

She rolled her eyes. She had never seen a lion, but she had seen pictures of the great cats that prowled the edges of the red desert. She also knew there was no way an animal that large would make it to the tops of these trees.

If they made it off this death trap, she would add it to the list of things she was going to kill him for.

Slowly, very slowly, the cliff grew less and less steep. Eventually, they were riding on more of a hill, and they were able to spread out.

It was too soon to stop for lunch, but Malcolm told Garrett they needed to give the horses a rest from straining to keep on the narrow, rocky path for so long. They all dismounted and walked their horses for another hour.

Rose tried to talk to Garrett, but he was walking with Malcolm and Steven, and she didn't want to assume he had told them about Trent, even though he had told Kenneth.

Her chance arose when they stopped for lunch. Garrett had volunteered to fill their water skins, so she offered to help.

She handed him a second skin to fill and asked, "I thought we weren't planning on telling anyone about Trent?"

He looked up at her accusatory tone, raising an eyebrow, "We did."

"Then why did you tell Kenneth?"

"I didn't," he said, stopping the second skin and holding out his hand for the next. "What makes you think I told him?"

She couldn't believe he was denying it, "When I said goodbye to him, he said, 'You be safe now, his majesty needs ya I think.'"

Garrett didn't say anything, which infuriated her even more. They were the only two who knew about Trent, besides Trip, but she knew Trip would die before he told anyone what they were doing.

"You're going to deny telling him?" She asked heatedly.

He stoppered another skin and looked at her, "I didn't tell him anything about Trent."

"Oh, so he was calling you 'majesty,' I take it," she said sarcastically. She handed him the last skin, but he didn't say anything.

There was silence until Garrett stood from the creek with the last full skin, "My father died when I was young, and I never knew my mother. Kenneth is as close to family as I have; I would never put him in danger by giving him such a secret."

His look was so intense that Rose almost backed away from his glare, "On top of that, I would not put this mission in jeopardy. I only knew Trish briefly when we were young, but we were good friends, and I wouldn't hurt our chances of finding her brother even if he wasn't the crown prince of a kingdom."

"Then what did Kenneth mean?" Rose believed him, but she had to know what Kenneth was talking about.

Garrett shrugged, "Maybe you misheard him." He took the full skins from Rose and headed back to the others. "He does have a bit of a strong accent."

Rose watched him go in confusion. What on earth was his problem?

***

They broke from lunch and rode swiftly until dusk. They kept the same forced pace Evans had used on their way to Bridgeten.

When they got to camp, Rose was tired but not exhausted like she had been that first night at May's. They had started a small fire and cooked a couple of rabbits that Trip shot with his bow.

When she finished eating, she went to her saddle and retrieved the knife Evans had given her, "Trip," She asked, walking back to the fire. "I know we don't have much time, but is there anything else you can teach me that will help when we get to Seawald?"

Trip looked at her doubtfully, "I can teach you what I know, but I'm no great fighter. There's a reason I chose the bow."

"I can help," Garrett offered.

Rose was surprised at his offer. They hadn't spoken since lunch. She simply nodded her thanks.

"She's a woman," Steven said as he grabbed another piece of rabbit. "She shouldn't learn how to fight."

"No," Garrett said. "She shouldn't have to, but I would rather her learn skills she never has to use than to find herself needing skills she never learned."

Trip nodded his agreement and stood, "I've seen you practicing while you're riding, which is good. Knowing how the knife works is half the battle."

He took her a little way away from the fire and showed her how to jab and thrust with the knife. Garrett watched them but never interrupted. Soon it was too dark to continue, even with the low flame of the fire.

"It's time for bed," Garrett said, standing. "I'll show you a few things in the morning. Trip's good, but I can tell he's not been in too many fights, no offense." He glanced at Trip apologetically.

Trip shrugged, "None taken, you're right of course." He stretched and said goodnight to them and headed to his bedroll.

Garrett looked at her, "You'll need to know how to do more than just thrust that knife into someone. There is a technique, which is important, I know, but when you're fighting for your life, there are no rules. A knight might be able to fight every man in the room and win, but if he's stabbed in the back by a knife he doesn't see, then all his talent is useless."

Rose nodded, "Thank you for helping. I know I won't be much help in an actual fight, but," she sighed, "I hate feeling helpless."

Garrett smiled gently at her, "From the little I've seen, you're somewhat of a natural. You're athletic and have good balance; I doubt you'll be useless."

She gave a small, sheepish smile. He had every right to be mad at her from that afternoon, but he was offering to help her. She could tell he was still slightly irritated, but he seemed willing to forgive and forget.

They walked back to the fire and took out their bedrolls. Garrett said goodnight and went to lie next to Malcolm. She took her roll and laid it by Trip, who was close to the fire.

She knew she had heard correctly. Kenneth had said 'his majesty,' and he had to be referring to Trent. She supposed, for the sake of finding Trent, she would have to put it aside and trust that Garrett truly hadn't told Kenneth anything.

She pulled her bedroll closer to the dying embers of the fire and closed her eyes. When had life become so complicated? It had been less than a week ago she had stood with Alice in the castle yard waiting to meet the Duke. Before he came, everything had been fine, almost boring.

She knew she couldn't blame everything that had happened to her on the Duke, but it made her feel better to have someone to blame. She wondered what Trish was doing, if she had met Reddy yet. She wondered if Trent was alright. She wondered who had taken him and why. She wondered if Bennett had made it back to the castle all right.

Somewhere in her troubled thoughts, she fell asleep.

***

"Oh, Ro! I missed you!" Trish ran to Rose and hugged her tightly.

Rose rolled her young eyes. Trish had only been gone for three weeks; must she always be so exuberant?

"I have so much to tell you!" Trish gave a girlish giggle. "I met a boy," she squealed again and took Rose's hand, practically dragging her to their bedroom.

"Trish darling," her mother called after them. "Don't forget about your lunch with your father!"

Trish didn't look back but called down the stairs, "Yes, mother!"

Trish swung Rose into the room, shut the door, and locked it.

Rose raised an eyebrow. They weren't allowed to lock the door until nighttime, and Trish was a strict follower of the rules. Whatever she had to tell her must be important.

Trish, breathing heavily from their dash to the room, turned and looked at Rose but didn't say anything.

After a few seconds without any explanation, Rose said, "So, what about a bo.."

Trish rushed at her and clamped her hand over Rose's mouth.

"Shh," Trish glanced nervously at the door. "Come over here."

Trish unclamped Rose's mouth again, and Rose rolled her eyes as Trish dragged her out onto the balcony.

"I met a boy," Trish said, eyes sparkling with excitement.

"You've met hundreds of boys," Rose said, tired of the suspense. "What makes this one so special?"

Trish made them sit as close to the edge of the balcony as they could before she whispered, "I'm going to marry this one."

She sat back and expectantly looked at Rose.

Rose stared at her, "You're seven."

Trish deflated a little, "I know, but Rose, he was absolutely perfect." She sighed and looked dreamily into the sky.

She launched into a minute-by-minute explanation of their visit to the northern kingdom. How the boy had given her flowers when they arrived, how he played games with her. He had read her one of his favorite books, and he took her for a walk in the forest that had the biggest trees she had ever seen. He took her to look for a wisp, which she didn't think was real, but it was still fun. They had ridden their horses to a beautiful waterfall. He was a very good rider. He was very handsome, he had red hair and freckles, he was a prince, and she was going to marry him.

While Rose thought all of this sounded fine, she also thought marriage was a bit of a stretch for meeting someone only once, and for someone who was seven years old.

"Are you going to see him again?" Rose asked. "Or is the wedding tomorrow?"

Trish pursed her lips at Rose, "Obviously, we wouldn't be married until we're grown up, but yes, I am going to see him again. He's supposed to come down and visit during the winter. It's very cold up there, and he said he wouldn't mind being someplace warmer for a change."

"Don't your parents have to decide who you marry?" Rose asked. "You're a princess."

Trish grinned in a diabolical way Rose had rarely seen on her face, "I think that's why Mother took me to meet him."

Trish took Rose's hand, "Nothing was said, of course. I think they wanted to see how we got along before they made anything official."

"What's his name?" Rose asked, realizing Trish hadn't said it yet. She had only said a revenant 'he'.

Trish handed her a letter from the boy. Rose didn't bother to read it but skipped to the bottom, where he had signed his name.

I hope to see you again soon,

Gar

Rose wrinkled her nose, "Like the fish?"

"No," Trish said, giving her a stern look. "Gar! It's short for Garrett."

Rose's dream shifted.

Rose ran to their room. She opened the door and found Trish on her bed, crying.

"Trish, I'm so sorry." Rose went to her and lay on the bed next to her.

"He's gone," Trish sobbed.

Rose sat and rubbed her back. Eventually, Trish's tears ebbed enough for her to speak.

"They said he drowned," she shook her head in disbelief. "He told me he was a strong swimmer. He told me about swimming in the rivers and the lakes, and one time he even went in the ocean."

"Even the strongest swimmers can drown," Rose said, giving Trish another hug. "I'm so sorry."

Rose held Trish as she cried. They eventually fell asleep huddled together.

***

Rose woke gradually. The bird song was getting louder and louder as the sun came up over the hills. She sat up and stretched. She looked over to where Garrett's bedroll had been, but it wasn't there. She looked around the camp but didn't see him.

Her dreams were out of control. She knew this last one, at least, was a real memory. She had been mad at Trish for almost two weeks because all she could talk about was this boy whom she was supposedly in love with and going to marry.

Maybe this forgotten memory was why Garrett had been royalty in her other dreams. Surely it couldn't be real, though, for all she knew, Garrett was a very common name in the northern kingdom, and every other boy was called Garrett.

*Besides*, she thought to herself, *that Garrett is dead.* That was the whole reason the uncle had taken over the kingdom. He was the only heir left after the king died.

She gave her head a shake and pushed the thoughts from her mind. Maybe she was going crazy. She stood and walked over to Raul, who was hobbled with the other horses.

"Good morning," She said, rubbing his nose. "Did you sleep well?" She took out a sugar cube from her saddlebag and gave it to him.

As he munched happily on the sugar, Rose saw Garrett walking toward her.

"Good morning," He said quietly, not wanting to wake the others.

"Good morning," she replied, taking out two apples from her saddle bag and handing one to Garrett.

He shook his head in refusal and said, "I already ate. Are you ready to practice?"

"Practice?" Rose asked.

"Fighting," Garrett said.

"Right," Rose pulled her knife out of her pocket.

Garrett shook his head again, "You won't need that."

Rose looked at him in confusion, "I thought you were going to show me how to use the knife?"

"No," Garrett said as he started to stretch. "I told you I was going to teach you how to fight."

"I don't think I'm going to be much of a boxer," Rose said, putting her knife away.

Garrett chuckled, "I wasn't planning on teaching you boxing."

"Wrestling?" Rose asked.

"Not exactly," He said.

"Does it have a name?" Rose raised an eyebrow at him.

Garrett's lips twitched almost into a smile, "Not that I know of. Stand over here, please."

He took her by her shoulders and walked her a little way away from the horses. He stood her next to a tree, gestured for her to stay, then walked back down the hill.

"How am I supposed to practice fighting if you're way over there?" She asked, miffed.

She had never been given any training in fighting, the bow, yes, but fighting hand to hand was another matter entirely. She was hardly older than five before any nurse or maid would scold her for fighting with Trent or any of the other boys in the castle who had made her angry.

She started to turn around to see where he had gone, but he said, "Keep looking forward, this is part of the training."

She turned and folded her arms to her chest. She had no idea what was going on, and she didn't like it. He was supposed to be teaching her how to fight, not how to play hide and seek.

"Alright," Garrett's voice came from farther back than it had before. "When you hear anything, I want you to raise your hand on the side where the noise came from. When you think I'm close enough to touch you, hold up both hands."

"How is this teaching me how to fight?" There was no answer, "Garrett?" She almost turned around again, but she heard a twig snap, then silence. Taking a deep breath, she held up her right arm.

She held up her right and left arms a few more times. Each time she held up her arm, she hesitated a little longer. She was so focused it was hard to tell what was normal nature noises and what noises were Garrett's.

A few silent moments later, she heard a shoe scuffle to her left. She held up her left arm. A longer silence had her straining her ears. She was hardly breathing. She forced herself to take a deep but quiet breath.

She heard something to her left, but she couldn't tell if it was Garrett or just the wind in the trees. She hesitantly held up her left arm.

She waited for almost thirty seconds with no noise at all before she said, "Garrett, I really can't.."

"You won't hear anything if you keep talking."

She jumped and whirled around. He was directly behind her with a huge smile on his face.

"How long have you been standing there?" She demanded.

He shrugged, "Almost a minute. I was already behind you the last time you raised your arm. You started well, then you were trying too hard."

She held up her hands in defeat, "I couldn't tell if it was you or an animal or the wind. I didn't want to be too jumpy." Her face grew slightly red with embarrassment. She hated being bad at things, even things she had never done before.

Garrett nodded, "That's because you were listening for me."

Rose gaped at him, "That's what you told me to do!"

Garrett shook his head, "No, I said 'when you hear anything' to raise your arm. If you had raised your arm every time you heard a noise, you would never have been wrong."

She squinted her eyes, "So every little noise is an attack? A squirrel finding a nut, a bird calling, the wind blowing?"

She had said it sarcastically, but Garrett was nodding his head, "Exactly, you're a fast learner."

He turned to head back to the camp, leaving Rose completely confused by the horses.

"Wait," She called after him. "Not everything can be an attack. If I jump at every sound in the forest, I'll never get anywhere."

She caught up to him and tugged on his sleeve to make him stop.

"You have a bow, right?" he asked.

"Yes," Rose answered hesitantly.

"Are you any good at it?"

"I'm a fair shot," she said.

He nodded, "When you were learning how to shoot, did you only shoot at targets?"

"We did during lessons," she said, nodding her head.

"Is that the only time you ever shot your bow?" he asked, skeptical.

"No," she said, shaking her head. "Trish and I would go out into the woods and shoot anything we could see. We practiced all the time."

"Exactly," Garrett said and started walking away again.

"Hey!" she said, going after him. "Are you going to explain or just keep walking away from me?" She was mad now. He was being deliberately unhelpful.

He sighed, "When you were just learning, you practiced on everything you could see. You needed to test your aim, the draw weight, and what the wind did to an arrow. It's the same with listening. You have to listen to everything, all the time, and check what every little sound is until you can tell what things are without having to check," he paused. He looked at her and saw the stubborn set of her lips and continued.

"You have to hear and identify everything before you can afford to ignore anything," Garrett finished.

"What does listening to noises have to do with fighting?" she was close to shouting.

"You're used to castle fighting," He said. "In the real world, very rarely will you know you're about to be attacked unless you're paying attention. Especially because you're a woman."

"What does that have to do with anything?" She asked.

Garrett sighed, "A man will attack another man in the middle of a crowded tavern, but have you ever seen a man attack a woman outright?"

She thought for a moment, "No, I haven't," she had to admit. She remembered the girl she found in the hallway; her stomach gave a turn.

"Unfortunately, we live in a world that has a large population of people you have to listen for in the dark," He gave a small shake of his head. "There is evil in the hearts of men."

"Why couldn't you just tell me that?" She asked.

Garrett looked her in the eye, "I was hoping you would figure it out if you took a few seconds to think about it."

"Are you calling me stupid?" She was on the verge of hitting him.

"No," He said, infuriatingly calmly. "You let your anger take over, and you don't think straight when you're mad."

That made her swallow her next retort. She couldn't think of anything to say that would negate his statement, so she just stood there and ground her teeth.

Garrett put his hand on her shoulder and gave a gentle smile, "The real trick to fighting is to not start one in the first place." He squeezed her shoulder and went to the fire, where everyone else was getting breakfast ready.

# Chapter 15

"You're majesty, please. I will beg if I have to, but please stop." Evans said with his hand covering his eyes.

Trent banged his fist on the door again and yelled, "I demand to speak with your leader!"

Evans groaned, then went to the door, "If you want to bang on the door again, you will have to hit me."

Trent growled and started pacing, "How can you be so calm? We've been kidnapped."

"We have not," Evans said, sitting back on his cot. "We are men, we are being held for ransom."

"It's the same thing," Trent said, walking from the door to the small barred window. He could see the ocean, smell the salt and fish, but that did little to tell him where they were.

"It is not the same thing," Evans said, lying down. "Look at this room. It's not as grand as your castle chambers, but trust me, this is not a room you are put in if you are being held hostage or if you've been kidnapped."

Trent continued to look out the small window. Evans had a point. Their room, although not an honored guest room, was tidy and comfortable. There were two cot-like beds with blankets, a chair and desk, and candles that were pushed through a small slot in the door every morning and night. They even had a small privy.

They had been fed every morning and evening with the coming of the candles as well.

It was the lack of knowledge that bothered Trent so much. The servants never said anything when they brought the food, despite Trent's demands to be allowed to talk to someone in charge.

He got far more information from listening at the window than he did yelling at the door. They were clearly in a large city, and the cries of merchants selling their goods started early in the morning and didn't stop till sunset.

There was a particularly loud fish merchant directly below their window who liked to comment on the shoppers as they passed. Trent couldn't see the shop, but he gathered that people who bought his fish were praised vehemently, while those who didn't had every family member they knew cursed to the sea.

When he wasn't trying to pound down the door or listen at the window, Trent lay on his bed trying to remember their journey here, wherever here was.

He remembered the attack on their camp. He remembered yelling for Rose to run. He remembered trying to fight the men, but there had been too many, and one of them had hit him over the back of the head. After that, he remembered nothing until two mornings ago.

Neither he nor Evans knew how long they had been unconscious. Evans knew from years of being a knight that getting hit on the head would only render a man unconscious for a few hours at most, not nearly long enough to get to a large city from where they had been.

Evans' theory was that they had been given an herb to keep them unconscious until they had arrived in this place. Neither of them could remember anything about their journey at all.

That meant they could have been traveling for a day, a week, a month. Trent shuddered at the thought. Surely his father would have done something if they had been gone for any amount of time. Then again, maybe he had. Trent didn't know anything about the outside world except what the fishmonger shouted to his customers.

"Ah! Grady! My old friend! Back from the south so soon?" The monger chuckled, a deep rumbling sound. "All the better, those southerners smell worse than my fish! What can I get for you today?"

"Be quiet, you fool," a whiny voice said, almost too low for Trent to hear. "No one is supposed to know I'm here."

"Why not?" The fishmonger asked in a marginally softer voice.

"Because," The whiny voice said with an edge. "I'm supposed to be with the Duke and his bride on their way to the western kingdom."

Trent's head snapped up, and he made eye contact with Evans. They both jumped up and put their ears close to the window.

"I hadn't heard the happy news!" the monger said. "Congratulations to his highness!"

"Be quiet," Grady hissed. "Did the other carriage arrive yet?"

"Two days ago." There was a thud and a scrap. He must have gone back to chopping his fish. Trent strained his ears to hear every word that was said.

"Good," Grady said. There was a clicking sound. "Keep them for another five days, then have one of your boats take them back to

Bawvel Hall."

There was a groan from the fishmonger, "Now, my friend, this is hardly enough to feed them. Considering how precious the cargo is, I would think his majesty might be a little more appreciative of my services."

There were a few moments of silence, then a clicking sound, a groan from Grady, and then more clicking.

"That's more like it," The merchant said.

"Five days," Grady said. "Then cut them loose."

"As you say," The man said again. "Fresh fish! I have halibut, cod, and eel! Best in the city! Fresh fish!"

Trent jumped at the man's booming voice. He had been listening so intently to the conversation.

"Evans," he whispered.

"I know, lad," Evans said gruffly, patting Trent's shoulder. "I know."

"We have to get out of here."

***

The sun was setting, and Rose could see the small town blinking into existence. Every few minutes, another candle was placed in a window or a lantern was lit by a door.

"Is that Seawald?" She asked Trip.

"No," he said. "Seawald is much bigger. I'm not sure this village even has a name."

She turned to Garrett, assuming he would know, but Garrett turned to Malcolm. Malcolm shrugged his shoulders and said something in his language.

"It doesn't have a name for a map," Garrett said. "It's people just call it Hjem."

"What does that mean?" Trip asked.

"Home," Malcolm said quietly.

They rode down the hill towards the town. It was wedged into two cliffs looking out towards the sea. Many of the houses were built right into the rock, but they were all painted a vibrant color, none exactly the same.

Children were running and playing in the streets, and mothers were yelling out the windows for them to come in for dinner. The easy laughter of the children made Rose smile. It was good to remember not everyone's lives were as complicated as hers had become.

There was a long, low building in the middle of the town that had no walls, only a roof and pillars to hold it up.

Garrett saw her looking, "That's where the fishermen come and set up their stalls. They trade fish, and caravans come to trade goods from farther inland. Trading ships also like to dock here in hard weather and will often sell some of their goods."

A little further to the left was a two-story building that was clearly an inn. Every window had a candle, and Rose could hear music coming from the common room.

It looked like a very cozy, inviting place. Rose was surprised to see a frown on Garrett's face. "What's wrong?"

"It's very crowded," he said. "Maybe we should stay somewhere else." He turned to Malcolm and said something quietly in their language.

Malcolm shook his head and replied in the same language.

"Good point," Garrett said. "Let's head down to the inn. I'll see if they have any rooms; everyone else waits outside."

His tone was nervous, almost harsh. He turned and saw Rose's questioning face and amended, "It's so crowded it doesn't make sense to have everyone go in." He smiled at her, but it was forced.

Why was he so worried? Normally, he was the picture of joking ease.

He trotted over to the inn and hitched his horse to the post. There was only one other horse on the post. All the other guests' horses must be in the stables.

Rose shivered. It was still summer here, but the wind coming off the bay was strong. As she rubbed her arms, she looked around the town. There was a smithy and a carpenter directly across from the inn. A few houses dotted the lane going through the middle of the town. Other than that, there wasn't much. Rose guessed most of the trading was done down at the docks.

Garrett was inside for almost ten minutes before he came out again. He looked irritated and smug at the same time, "They're full up except for one room." He glanced at Rose, then continued, "There's room in the barn, though, apparently it has a rather nice loft."

"What about dinner?" Steven asked.

Garrett nodded, "It's fish stew and oysters with some bread if we like. There is a table in the far left corner of the room if you want to head in while we take care of the horses," he looked at Rose.

"I can help with the horses," she said. She partly didn't want to go into the crowded inn by herself and partly wanted to look after Raul herself.

"We won't be long," Garrett said. "If you don't go in, we might not have anywhere to sit. A trading ship is in port with a broken mast. They've been here for three weeks, according to the innkeeper. I told the man you would be coming to save us a table."

"Very well," Rose said. She took her rucksack off Raul and turned to go into the inn.

Garrett reached out and caught her hand. "You have your knife on you?"

"Yes," she said. "Why?"

Garrett shrugged, "Just in case. Sailors can get a little..." He cleared his throat, "rowdy."

He turned back to the horses and went to the stables to the side of the inn.

Rose squared her shoulders and went into the inn. The noise and smell hit her in the face like a wall. A short man was playing a lively jig on his fiddle, and all the men in the room were banging their mugs on the table in time.

The smell of the seafood was strange to her, but it smelled appetizing enough. There was a small desk just off the entrance with a tall, fat man standing behind it.

"You with the lad what just came in?" The man asked.

Rose nodded and started to speak, but the man spoke again, "Right this way."

He took off at a quick pace, and Rose almost had to jog to keep up with him. The man wove his way in between tables with ease, probably from years of practice, and led Rose to two tables in the very back of the room that had been pushed together.

"Sorry bout the present dining conditions, ma'am," he said as he laid out napkins around the table. "We've been full ever since that blasted boat came in, good for business, mind you, but still, I'll be happy when it's quiet again."

Without giving Rose time to respond, the man dashed off through a swinging door that must have led to the kitchens.

Rose sat with her back to the wall so she could see the whole dining room and the stage with the fiddler. He was still singing the pounding jig, and the men were now singing along. Rose winced as they started the chorus. She had heard the song before, but she shuddered to think what

Ann would have done if she had ever dared to sing it.

As the chorus ended and they started on another verse, a pretty young woman backed out of the kitchen with a pitcher in both hands. She turned to look at Rose and said, "I'll be right with ya, miss, just one moment."

She hurried away, filling mugs as she passed by the tables. She was very good at her job. It almost looked like she was dancing as she moved in between the tables, avoiding the swinging arms of the men who were singing along to the song.

A few of the men watched her as she poured the drinks, but none of them made any attempt to grab her like some men did to serving maids. As far as Rose could tell, none of the men even talked to her.

She eventually made her way back to Rose, "What can I get ya, miss?" She said breathlessly.

"I'm waiting for my friends to come in from the stables," Rose said.

The maid nodded, "Pops said there were more coming. Can I get ya anything to drink while ya wait? We've got ale, wine, cold milk, and water."

"I'll just have water, please," Rose said, smiling at the girl.

She smiled and nodded, then whisked back into the kitchen.

Rose turned her attention to the fiddler again. He had started a slower song, and the men were settling down. As she watched, she noticed that she also was being watched. Without the distraction of the raucous song, the men were now turning to see who the newcomer had been.

A few of the older men just glanced at her and turned back to the fiddler to enjoy the music. Some men looked curious, and some men looked interested, but there was one table of men that looked dangerous.

There were five men at the table, two who looked like they could be brothers with light colored hair. One had a tunic with no sleeves. His arms were covered in tattoos. One was noticeably smaller than the rest. He had reddish hair and looked into his mug instead of at Rose. The last one was tall, even sitting down, with black hair and dark eyes. He looked directly at Rose.

He gave a small half smile, then stood and walked over to Rose's table.

"Hello," he said. He didn't do anything but stand there and stare at Rose.

After an awkward moment, Rose felt she had to respond, "Hello."

The man's smile widened, "It looks rather lonely back here in the corner. Why don't you come join us over there?"

"No, thank you," Rose said, forcing herself to smile. "My brother and our friends will be here in just a moment."

The man clicked his tongue, "That's a shame, we're a fun bunch to be around."

Rose had to work hard to keep the grimace off her face. "I'm sure you are, but in any case, it doesn't look like there is any room at your table."

The man put a hand on the table and leaned closer to Rose, "We could share a seat." He winked and licked his lower lip, "I wouldn't mind having someone as pretty as you on my lap."

The man started to sit down, but there was suddenly a hand on his shoulder, dragging him back away from the table.

"What about someone as pretty as me?" Garrett asked. He had a smile on his face, but there was steel in his eyes.

"Get your hand off me," the man spat, his voice going from low and seductive to shrill and harsh in a second.

Garrett took his hand off the man's shoulder and held his arms out in a placating way, "I'm sorry, my good sir." He said, not bothering to keep his voice down. "I thought you wanted someone pretty to sit on your lap.

I'm far prettier than the lady here, so I didn't want you to feel slighted by having to settle for the second-best-looking person here."

Most of the men in the room whooped with laughter. Garrett smiled at the man, and he glared back.

"Sit down, Rasp, and shut up," a burly middle-aged man said from the front of the room. "You're ruining the music."

Several men coursed their agreement and told Rasp to sit down. Rasp took a good look at Garrett, Steven, Malcolm, and Trip and must have decided it wasn't worth a fight.

He smiled at Garrett and said, "My apologies." He gave a short mock bow and headed back to his table. Once he sat down, Garrett and the rest of the men sat down next to Rose.

Rasp looked back at Rose with that same half smile and winked again. His eyes were dark, but Rose could have sworn for a second they were completely black. She blinked and tried to look again, but Rasp had already turned to watch the fiddler.

Before she had time to question what she just saw, Garrett said, "Making friends, Rose?"

She instantly prickled, "I was just sitting here, and he came and talked to me. What took you so long?"

Garrett shrugged, "The barn is as full as the Inn."

Just then, the serving maid came back out of the kitchen. She turned to face the table and gave Rose her water when she saw Garrett. Her smile instantly brightened, "What can I get you gents to drink?"

Garrett turned to tell the maid he would take ale and smiled back just as brightly as she was smiling at him. Rose had to focus on not laughing or rolling her eyes. Obviously, there was at least one person here who thought Garrett was prettier than she was

***

They had finished their stew, which was good, but Rose preferred beef and venison to fish, and they were sitting, enjoying the music. Their table never wanted for anything, but the maid seemed to be spending a lot of unnecessary attention on their table.

After her fifth visit, Rose couldn't help herself. Once the kitchen door had swung shut, yet again, she whispered to Garrett, "Did you bribe the innkeeper for all this special attention?"

Unruffled, Garrett just smiled and said, "You know, if you worked on your manners, people might be nice to you, too."

Rose snorted into her water, "Besides," Garrett continued, "it's been established that I am, in fact, the prettiest person in the room." He batted his eyelashes at her. She had to slap her hand over her mouth to keep from laughing and ruining the fiddler's final ballad.

The man had an impressive number of songs in his repertoire for such a small town. He played all types of songs, love songs, ballads, jigs, drinking songs, and he never played a sour note as far as Rose could tell.

Rasp hadn't stayed long after he sat back at his table. The burly man who told him to shut up had stood and talked to him briefly, then the entire table left with sour looks on their faces.

Rose had all but written off the darkness in his eyes. She had imagined it, or it was a trick of the flickering lights. At the moment, she was too full and sleepy to give it much thought.

The fiddler played the last few notes of the ballad he was performing, and everyone clapped loudly and cheered. Garrett even stuck his fingers in his mouth and whistled shrilly. The fiddler bowed over and over and put his hat out to the end of the stage for tips.

Slowly, the tables turned back to talk amongst themselves, or they headed up to their rooms. Rose was just about to suggest doing the same when the burly man came over to their table.

Garrett looked up at the man and said, "Thank you for earlier. I think you stopped a fight in the making."

The man nodded and said, "I thought so." His voice was deep and loud. Rose was sure all the other people still in the dining room could hear him. "I'm the captain of these men. I figured it was time to step in."

Garrett nodded his thanks again and said, "Would you like to join us for one last drink before bed?"

The captain waved off the offer, "I'm headed back to the ship, but thank you. I just wanted to let you know I sent Rasp and his crew back to the ship as well. You shouldn't have any more trouble with them tonight."

He hesitated, then asked, "You're just staying the one night? I can only keep them on the ship for so long. I plan on heading out the day after next, as long as our mast is fixed, but it would be best if you didn't stick around." He looked at Rose, then quickly back to Garrett.

"Just the one night, Captain, we are leaving first thing in the morning," Garrett said.

The Captain nodded, obviously relieved, "Good, that's good." he sighed, "I only have a few of my normal crew with me and these new men, I just don't know."

"Trouble?" Garrett asked.

"Well, you saw what they were like." The captain said. "They like to drink and sing, and they don't like working. I had to pay this crew twice what I would pay my men."

"What happened to your men?" Trip asked.

"They've all taken up with the Royal fleet," said a tall, slender man who had been sitting at the Captain's table during dinner.

The captain nodded, "This here's McKinnen, my chief mate." McKinnen dipped his head to everyone in greeting.

"They've all been called to work for the Royal Fleet in AyZer. Only a few captains and their top officers were allowed to keep trading," McKinnen said. "Our trade is livestock, horses, mostly."

"That explains why the stables are so full," Trip said.

McKinnen nodded, "A country always needs good horses, so we were told to keep trading when most of the other ships were called to serve the fleet."

Garrett looked shocked, "I've never heard of the Northern kingdom having much of a fleet. When did they start drafting men?"

The Captain answered, "Early last year. After all the crews came back to the capital to trade their goods, the men were told they had to sign up for the fleet or they would be arrested."

Garrrett looked like he wanted to press the subject further, but Malcolm mumbled something in their language, and he bit back the question he had been about to ask.

"Times are tough all around," the captain said to Garrett, patting his shoulder. "Well, McKinnen, we'd better head back to the ship."

They said goodbye and left the inn.

Steven put his mug down and stood, "I'm off to the loft, first light?" he asked Garrett, who nodded distractedly. "Goodnight then."

The maid came back from the kitchen then. She had changed out of her apron and put her hair up in a top knot. She smiled at Garrett and said, "Your room's ready." She looked at Rose, "It's not the best of rooms, miss, but it's cozy and clean. Are the rest of you staying in the barn then?" She looked back at Garrett.

Malcolm nodded, but Trip and Garrett hesitated. There were still some men from the ship in the room.

"I'll be staying with my sister," Trip said, louder than needed for the maid to hear.

Rose looked around the room. No one was looking at them, but quite a few ears seemed to be listening.

Rose hid a smile by taking a drink. Was poor Trip going to sleep at all until they found Trent? She was grateful for his words. She was glad the captain had sent Rasp back to the ship, but she was sure some of these other men would be very interested to hear she was in a room alone.

The maid nodded, "Have a good night then." Very boldly, she looked at Garrett and said, "I stay in the rooms on the back of the inn, on the ground floor." She saw Rose's raised eyebrow and lost some of her nerve. "Pops serves breakfast, and it's easier to get up early if I'm already here. If ya need anything, just let me know." She blushed, said goodnight again, and then left.

"This Inn has excellent service," Garrett said, chuckling.

Rose stuck her fingers in her water and flicked it at him.

"You leave that girl alone," Rose scolded him. "Not a single man here touched her, and there is probably a good reason."

"No one touched her because she's the innkeeper's granddaughter and her father is the carpenter across the street who is fixing their mast," Garrett said, standing. "Besides, she's far too young for me. Still," he said with a laugh, "the inn still has excellent service."

Rose rolled her eyes and stood as well, "I'm off to bed then. Trip, you can have the bed this time, I have my bedroll."

Trip started to protest, but Rose held up her hand, "You can't protect me if you're half dead with exhaustion."

Trip looked like he was still going to protest, but Rose cut him off,

"Come up in ten minutes, and I will already be asleep." She stifled a yawn, proving her point nicely.

Trip sat back and agreed.

Rose went to the room. It was at the very end of the hall on the second floor. The maid had been right; it wasn't much of a room. There was a bed shoved into the corner of the room and a wash pail on the floor.

There was hardly enough room for Rose to lay her bedroll out next to the chimney and still give Trip room to walk to the bed.

She went to the pail and splashed some water on her face. It was cold, but it felt good. She washed her face and neck, then changed into nightclothes. She settled into the bedroll and, true to her word, was asleep before Trip came into the room.

***

Everything was black. Rose was wandering around blind.

*This is stupid,* she thought to herself. *I need a candle.*

Suddenly, there was a small pin of light close to her hand. It looked like a small flame sitting in her palm. It didn't burn her; there was no heat at all. It wasn't a candle, but it would work. She held her hand up to try and see what was around her. There wasn't anything.

She walked a little way, and slowly, grass formed under her feet. Soon there were bushes, then trees.

The more she looked around, the more things there were to see. The light from her hand was also getting brighter.

She sat on a fallen log and continued to look around. There was something on the edge of the light that was moving in the dark. It didn't have a shape. It was just darker black than the rest of the darkness.

"Who's there?" She called quietly. She wasn't sure she wanted the thing to answer.

"Come now, flower," said an inky velvety voice from the dark. "You know me."

"No, I don't," Rose protested louder now. "Who are you?"

"I'm not sure that's the right question, flower," The voice said. The shadow was starting to get more solid.

"What do you mean?" Rose asked.

"Well," the voice said. Rose could tell it was enjoying her confusion. "'who' implies I'm a person, I am not."

"What are you then?" Rose said.

There was a soft chuckle, "That's not exactly the right question either."

The dark shape drifted into the light. Its form was vague. It swirled and moved, not giving it a definite shape.

"What's the right question then?" Rose asked.

"Oh, now that, that is an excellent question," the shadow said, gliding closer.

Rose stood, "Are you going to answer me or just play with words?"

The shadow shook and the voice chuckled, "Ah, you humans, so impatient. It's one of your best qualities. It makes my job so much easier."

"What's your job?" Rose asked.

"Another excellent question," the voice said. "I suppose 'job' might not be the right way to describe it, no, my delight, my joy, my purpose would be better ways to phrase what I do."

"And that would be," Rose asked. She was equally frustrated and scared.

The shadow moved ever closer. The longer Rose looked at it, the more defined its shape became.

"I bring out the most human parts of people," The voice said. "I'm sure you've seen me before. I was there tonight in Rasp when he was speaking with you. I was there when that man followed you out of the camp and you stabbed him. I was there when your father killed your mother. Ah, that last one was particularly lovely."

Rose cringed back, "You're evil."

The shadow was now in the shape of a woman, completely black, but it was a woman's silhouette. It laughed.

"Yes, I suppose you could call me that, but I'm so much more. I'm many things that are perfectly fine. It's not my fault you humans take everything too far." The shadow reached out to touch Rose's face, but she jerked back.

"Don't touch me," She shrieked. "I don't want anything to do with you; leave me alone."

The shape chuckled and, starting from its feet, the black swirled into color. When it reached the shadow's face, Rose froze. She was looking at herself.

"I'm already with you, flower, I'm with everyone," it smiled.

"No," Rose yelled. She tried to run, but her feet were glued to the ground.

"Don't go," the shadow said in her voice. "Your mother thought she could save you from me by sending you away, but she was wrong. I'm in the heart of every human, and most don't even know I live there." The thing smiled with Rose's lips.

Rose screamed, or she tried to. The thing put its hand, Rose's hand, over her mouth and said, "Shh, really all this drama for something that has already happened, something that is inevitable. There's really no point."

Rose's eyes whirled around, trying to find a way to escape. On the log was the mouse. He was holding the flame that had been in Rose's hand;

she reached for it.

The thing's eyes followed her hand, "No!" it shrieked in its velvet voice.

It put its hand around Rose's throat and squeezed. Rose reached for the flame. She couldn't breathe. She was inches away. She looked at the mouse and, with her last breath, gasped out, "Help."

The mouse took one step, and Rose's fingertips touched the flame.

# Chapter 16

Rose woke up gasping, her fingers went to her throat. It took her a minute to remember where she was. She saw Trip in the bed and relaxed; she was awake.

The first light of dawn was coming in the small window above the bed. The red light made her think of the flame and the mouse, and she shuddered.

She wrapped her blanket around herself, but it didn't help. Shaking, she stood and threw her cloak over her nightdress. She had to leave the room. She knew it was a bad idea, but she didn't care. She had to get out of this small room and see the sky.

She snuck down the stairs towards the kitchen. She heard someone banging pots and pans, getting breakfast ready. She poked her head in and saw the maid from last night.

"Good morning," Rose said, and the maid jumped.

"Oh! Sorry, miss, I hope I didn't wake ya."

"No," Rose said. "Is there a place I can change? My brother is still asleep, and I don't want to wake him."

"You can use my room, miss," the maid said. "It's just over here." She led her to a side room just off the kitchen.

"Thank you," Rose said, "I'll just be a minute."

"Take your time," the maid said. "I can bring you some hot water if you'd like to wash."

"Don't go to any trouble," Rose said. She wanted to say thank you again and realized she didn't know the girl's name.

"It's Lilly, miss," The girl smiled and went back to making biscuits.

"Thank you, Lilly," Rose said and shut the door.

The room was small but tidy. There were little knick-knacks Lilly had collected over the years on the walls.

Rose quickly changed and went back to the kitchen.

"Has anyone from our party come out of the barn yet?" Rose asked.

The girl's cheeks blushed pink, "Not that I've seen, miss."

The blush made Rose think the girl had been specifically looking for at least one of her friends. Rose just smiled and nodded and headed out to the barn.

She went straight to Raul's stall. Garrett had been right, the stable was full. She guessed the trading had been good this year for there to be this many horses on one boat.

He knickered a greeting, and Rose threw him some hay for breakfast. The familiar task of taking care of her horse was calming her nerves.

Or at least it was until a large hand gently touched her shoulder and she almost jumped out of her skin.

She spun around with the pitchfork in her hand at hip height, ready to skewer whoever had touched her.

Garrett jumped back and held his arms up, "Whoa there. Sorry, I didn't mean to startle you. I called your name, but you didn't respond." Rose was still frozen in fright and kept the fork raised.

"I'm sorry, Rose, really," Garrett said. Taking in her white face and her shaking hands, he said, "Are you alright? What happened?"

He was serious now. Thinking Rose's reaction meant something more dire than a bad dream. Rose slowly shook her head and put the fork down.

"I'm fine," she tried to say, but it came out as a rasp.

Garrett cautiously walked towards her and put his hand on her shoulder again, "What happened?"

"I," Rose tried, but her voice broke. She hated crying, and above all else, she hated crying in front of people. "I," she tried again, but she couldn't get her words past the lump in her throat.

"It's alright," Garrett said. "You're safe with me."

For some reason, his words made her tears run over. She dropped her head, trying to hide her face. She gasped for breath, and the tears flowed.

It took her a second to realize he was holding her. His arms easily wrapped around her, making her feel like a child.

Slowly, her cries subsided, and he released her. He took her by the shoulders and held her at arm's length,

"Can you tell me what happened?"

"I, I had a bad dream," She stammered. Saying it out loud, it seemed like such an overreaction. She knew he was going to make fun of her or call her a girl.

"That must have been some dream," he said. "Do you want to tell me about it?"

She looked at him, surprised. That wasn't the reaction she had expected.

"I used to have horrible nightmares when I was a child," He said, leading her to his horse's stall. He got a brush and started currying his horse. He gestured for her to sit on a bale of hay in the corner of the stall.

"I would start screaming and my eyes would be open, but I was still asleep. My father called on every doctor he could find, but none of them could do anything." He looked at her and gave her a small smile. "I eventually grew out of it, but I remember how terrible they were."

She nodded and hugged her arms around her legs. She didn't think her dreams were just dreams, not anymore. The dream was telling her things she couldn't possibly know.

"Do you want to talk about it?" Garrett asked gently.

Rose looked at him. What on earth could she tell him? "I don't know,"

Suddenly, the barn door flew open with a bang, and there was Trip looking around wildly. When he saw Rose, he looked like he was going to kill her or cry in relief. Rose couldn't tell which.

"I woke up and you weren't there," Trip said, marching towards them. "Don't do that." He said, slumping next to Rose on the hay bale she was sitting on.

"I'm sorry, Trip," Rose said, feeling instantly guilty. "I woke up and didn't want to wake you." She put a hand on his shoulder.

"You could have left a note," he said. "I thought that bast," He looked at Rose and changed his words, "I thought that thug Rasp had come back and kidnapped you or something."

"I'm fine, really, I'm sorry," Rose said.

"If I lose you, it'll be my head," Trip said. "I'm quite fond of my head, so I would appreciate it if you would help me keep it attached to my shoulders."

Rose couldn't help but smile slightly, "I don't think he would actually kill you."

Trip snorted in disagreement, "If Trent didn't, Trish would."

Rose laughed at that, "You might be right about that."

"Well," Garrett said, "now that we're all accounted for, shall we go in for breakfast and be on our way?"

Trip nodded and headed out of the barn, mumbling to himself. Rose could have sworn she heard "Royals" at least once, but she couldn't be sure.

She turned to Garrett and said, "Sorry for the hysterics, I'm fine, really, just a bad dream."

He looked at her, not buying her cavalier words, "Anytime."

"Thank you, Gar," Rose said as they walked to the door.

Garrett missed a step, and she looked back to see if he had tripped on something, but he just looked at her and smiled, then held the door open for her.

***

"Almost there," Evans said. "I've almost got the handle."

"Good," Trent whispered back. "Hurry if you can."

Evans gave a quiet snort, "If you think you can do it better be my guest."

They had taken all the candles in the room and melted them next to the fire, so just the wick was left. They tied all the wicks together to make a rope of sorts. There were bars high on their door, and Evans was trying to lift the handle from the outside.

Trent had slid the tray that their food came on under the door so Evans could use it as a mirror and see the door handle.

"Almost," Evans said. "Damn!"

"What?" Trent asked breathlessly.

"I have the handle, but there's a lock on it," Evans said, stepping off the chair he was standing on.

He shook their makeshift rope loose and pulled it back up through the bars.

Trent slid the tray back into the room and put it on the desk. He went to his cot and slumped.

They had known there was a possibility that there was a lock on the outside handle, but there wasn't a handle at all on their side of the door, so Evans had thought there might be a chance the door wasn't locked.

"Now what?" He asked.

Evans shook his head, "I'm not sure. Even if we could get out the window, there's no way down."

"Well," Trent said, scrubbing his face with his hands. "At least we know we will be out of here in four days."

Evans nodded and took a drink of water from the jug given to them that afternoon. He grimaced. They had both agreed they did not want to be sedated again, so Evans had put charcoal from their fire into the water.

He assured Trent it would stop any poisons or herbs from being absorbed in their stomachs. It made the water gritty and taste foul, but it was worth the peace of mind knowing they couldn't be rendered unconscious again.

"Do you think they've sent someone to look for us yet?" Trent asked Evans.

"I'm sure they have, lad," He said comfortingly. "Even without us missing, remember we sent Bennett back to report about Bridgeton and the man who attacked Rose. They would have had to have sent another party to check on Bridgeton at least. They won't find us on the road or in the town, so they will have to send out more parties."

"What about Trish?" Trent said. "They had to have been talking about her. I don't believe my father would have sent her off to be wed without me being there."

He also didn't believe Trish would have gone without talking to him or Rose first. Trish was sweet and everything a princess should be, but she had a stubborn streak to rival a mule when she put her mind to it.

That meant if she was with the duke, headed west, that she had been kidnapped. And the man had said, 'his bride,' did that mean they were already married? No, it couldn't, he wouldn't allow it. He got up and started pacing again.

"There's no sense in worrying about things you can't fix, lad," Evans said. "When we get out of here, we can find out what's going on, and then we can figure out what to do. You're going to drive yourself mad if you keep pacing like a caged cat."

"I know," Trent said, stopping at the window. "You're right, I'm sorry. I just feel so helpless."

He wished he had done more. He wished he had talked to his father about Rose's suspicions about the Duke. He had spent his whole life doing whatever his father had told him to do, but he realized now that was a mistake.

If he was going to be a ruler after his father, he needed to start making his own decisions. He needed to trust his instincts. He needed to pay more attention in meetings and know what was going on in his land.

He thought back to the Cod farm, how could attacks like that be happening, and he knew nothing about it? He wondered if his father knew about it. He spent so much of his time away in his office, Trent was starting to wonder how much he knew about his kingdom.

He missed Rose. He smiled to himself. She would probably have already found a way out of this, or she would be pacing a hole in the floor right along with him.

Four days, he told himself. Four days, and he was going to be out of this room. He was going to go home and fix what needed fixing.

*** 

"Your majesty," Bennett said when he entered the King's office.

The king was sitting at his desk. His chin was resting on his steepled hands, and he looked deep in thought.

He didn't say anything, and Bennett had to stop himself from fidgeting nervously. He hadn't seen the King since he delivered the news about the man who had tried to kill Rose in the inn.

"Are you a King's man, Bennett?" The king asked, finally looking at him.

"Of course, your majesty," Bennett said. "I'm not a full knight yet, but I intend to serve the realm however I can."

"I fear the realm is in danger," The king said. He stood and went to the window.

Bennett didn't know how to respond to this. He thought that observation was rather obvious with the crown prince having been kidnapped, but he didn't think voicing that opinion would be wise.

"I'm not just talking about my son," The king said, coming back to his chair. "I do not like both my children being taken from me within a week's time. It feels," The king paused, "planned."

Bennett didn't know what to say, so he thought it best to keep quiet until the King came to the point.

"Evans speaks very highly of you," The King went on. "He seems to trust you implicitly. Is that trust well-founded?"

"Yes, your majesty," Bennett said. He was not bragging he was simply telling the truth. Bennett did not like playing with words like some of the other lords or knights. He was raised to say what he meant and to mean what he said.

The King studied him for a moment longer, then said, "Good. I have a job for you."

***

After a quick breakfast of biscuits, eggs, and gravy, they packed their saddlebags and headed north once again.

The land had gone from mountains and sheer cliffs to rolling hills and then to open prairie. Rose was glad not to be on the cliffs anymore, but the ocean breezes droned on relentlessly.

"How much further to Seawald?" She asked, having to raise her voice so Garrett could hear her.

"We'll camp tonight, then we should be there by tomorrow afternoon," he said.

"Do we have a plan when we get there?" She asked.

He smiled grimly, "I thought you could come up with one, seeing as I'm just a guide."

She refrained from rolling her eyes, "Well, I suppose the first thing to do will be to find where they are being held."

"If they're still there," Garrett added helpfully.

"Yes," she said with an edge to her voice, "if they are still there. The second thing to do is to find out who took them in the first place and why."

Garrett nodded but didn't say anything.

"Then I suppose we have to get away," Rose said.

She knew that wasn't an actual plan. It was just what needed to be done.

"So we're winging it," Garrett said and looked at her. "My favorite type of plan."

Rose sighed, "I don't know how to make a plan when I don't know any details."

"Well," Garrett said. "You do know some things. You know the commander of your army and the crown prince have been kidnapped."

Rose looked over her shoulder to make sure no one could hear them. Trip and Malcolm were riding not far behind them, but with the wind, she doubted they could hear. Steven had ridden off to scout ahead.

"Yes," Rose said, not knowing how that obvious information would help.

"You also know that the kidnappers knew this information, correct?" Garrett asked.

Rose nodded, "Well, they called Trent the prince, so they at least knew that. I'm not sure if they know who Evans is."

"So," Garrett continued. "From that information, we can assume this was not a random kidnapping or robbery. They have taken the prince for a reason. What reasons are there to take a prince?"

"There aren't any, really," Rose said. "Other than to start a war or hold him for ransom."

"Exactly," Garrett said.

Garrett had the very annoying habit of making her feel like a child when he did this. Even more annoying was that she didn't think he was doing it on purpose. He truly thought they were on the same page, and she understood what 'exactly' was supposed to mean.

"I don't quite see how that information is supposed to help me," Rose said. She was proud of herself for keeping a sarcastic tone out of her voice.

"We'll come back to that," Garrett said. "What else do you know?"

"We know they went north," Rose offered. She thought this was a blatantly obvious statement, but then she thought back to him teaching her to listen. If she said everything, then she wouldn't be wrong; maybe it would work here, too.

Garrett nodded, "Go on."

She racked her brain for more, less obvious information.

"I know they went north, but I can't help but think this has something to do with Trish's possible engagement to the duke. It feels like that was the first event here, not Trent being taken." She said. It felt good to voice this opinion. She had been so focused on finding Trent that she had put the Duke at the back of her thoughts.

"What makes you say that?" Garrett asked.

Rose shook her head, "Things were strange before Trent was taken. We were attacked the night before in an inn. A man came to my room and tried to kill me." She shuddered.

Garrett slowed his horse a little and looked at her, "You didn't tell me that."

"It didn't seem as important as finding Trent," She said. She scrunched her eyebrows in concentration, "But now that I think about it, the men who came to our campsite were also looking for me. They eventually decided they could just take the men, but they had specifically been looking for me as well."

She was quiet for a moment. Extremely few people even knew she had gone with the party to Bridgeton. She had been called to the king's offices in the middle of the night and left before sunrise that morning. Why would a group of people who were out to kidnap the prince and hold him for ransom have been looking for her? And how would they have known that she was even there?

"What if this isn't about Trent?" Rose almost whispered.

"Hmm," Garrett said. "An interesting thought. If it is a diversion, it's a rather big one."

Rose was thinking hard now. They had wanted her out of the way. The king had said so when he told her to go with Trent. But it hadn't been the

King's idea; it was the Dukes.

The duke had told the king he would be able to get to know Trish better if Rose weren't there. He had said Rose had interfered during the hunt.

"The Duke," She said it like a swear word.

"What?" Garrett asked.

"The Duke," Rose said again. "The man who's supposed to be marrying Trish. He wanted me out of the way. He's from the western kingdom. What if–" Rose started but stopped, not wanting to think of the possibility.

"Go on," Garrett nudged.

"What if the north isn't involved at all? What if the plan is to make it look like the north took Trent, then the united eastern and western kingdoms go to war with the north, and then the Duke could rule everything?" Rose hadn't realized she had stopped riding.

Garrett stopped with her, "That would be a rather bold plan." Rose could tell he was skeptical, but it looked like he was also thinking about the possibility.

"Everything alright?" Trip asked as he and Malcolm approached.

"Fine," Garrett said. "We were just trying to think of why your family would have been kidnapped and taken so far north."

Malcolm must have known more of the common language than he let on if Garrett was still going with their made-up noble kidnapping story.

They all started riding again. They rode in silence. Rose's brain was swirling with possibilities and connections she had missed before.

By the time they stopped for the night, she had come up with a hundred different diabolical plans the Duke could have been working on. She had to remind herself often not to let her imagination run away with her.

They had set camp and eaten dinner when Garrett came to talk to her.

"Are you doing alright?" He looked concerned. She had been almost silent since they had talked on the road.

Trip had already laid out his bedroll on the other side of the fire. Malcolm was checking one of the horse's hoofs, and Steven was taking the first watch.

She shook her head, "Just thinking. I'm missing something, probably more than one thing, and I don't know how vital that piece of information is. It's driving me mad."

Garrett was quiet for a moment, "I've been thinking too. I know you think this Duke is the cause of everything, but I wouldn't put it past the northern king to grab power." he reached down and started snapping a twig in half, then half again, throwing it onto the fire.

There was a bitterness in his voice that she didn't quite understand, "What makes you say that?"

"Because I know him," Garrett said, staring into the fire.

"How?" Rose asked. How could a fur trader, who lived hundreds of miles from the capital, know the king?

Garrett looked at her for a moment. He looked at her face so intently, it felt like he was trying to see what she was thinking.

He looked back at the fire and saw that Trip was listening to their conversation. Garrett threw a few more twigs into the fire, "I knew him when I was young. I wouldn't put anything past him. He is a cruel man."

"I always heard his brother was a great king," Trip said. "Can two brothers really be so different?"

Garrett looked up at him and gave a derisive snort, "They aren't true brothers. They were half, same father, different mothers. M," Garrett paused but quickly went on, "The old king had a mistress. They were raised in the castle side by side, but they were taught very differently. You would be amazed at how much influence a mother has over a son."

Rose was confused, "How did an illegitimate son become the king? I've never heard they weren't true brothers."

"It was all kept very quiet," Garrett said. "The staff were the only ones who knew, and they were told to keep quiet or face imprisonment. The queen eventually became ill and passed. After her passing, the king remarried the mistress."

They were quiet, listening to the sound of the fire crackling.

"If only the staff knew," Trip asked. "How do you know?"

Garrett hesitated before answering, "My father grew up in the castle, he told me."

Before the silence could get too awkward, Malcolm came over and told Garrett something in their language. Garrett nodded, got up, and said, "All that to say I wouldn't rule out the northern kingdom in being party to any skulduggery that is going on."

***

Trish had been riding in her carriage for three days. She wanted to get out and ride, but every time she asked, she was told it was too dangerous, someone would see her.

They only let her out at night, and that was only to walk from her carriage to a wagon that was only a few steps away, where she could lie down and sleep.

Edmund had visited her often, but that did not do much to raise her spirits. He seemed distracted when they talked. He didn't seem interested in what she had to say. It felt like the only reason he was coming to talk with her was because he had to.

She had worked the drapery over her window so she could see a sliver outside. The sky was bright blue with a few large puffy clouds. The air was brisk, and the leaves on the trees were starting to change from green to orange, gold, and red.

She slumped back in her seat, folding her arms across her chest. What did it matter if she didn't sit up straight? No one could see her. She resisted the urge to groan or bang on the door. She had even managed to refrain from asking 'how much further,' a fact that she was proud of.

Even though she didn't like the situation, she was still going to behave according to her rank.

There was a shout from the driver, and the carriage rolled to a stop. She pulled the curtains as far back as possible, but all she could see was sky and grass.

There was a knock at the carriage door. "Come in."

It was Edmund. She forced herself to smile, "Have we arrived?"

"Almost," Edmund said, patting her hand. "I know this must be dreadfully dull for you, my dear, but it's for your safety. You don't know how dangerous things can be."

She raised an eyebrow ever so slightly, "Maybe if someone told me where we were and what was happening, I would understand better." She did not like being talked to as if she were a child.

His charm dropped for just a second, but Trish saw something dark flash behind his eyes, "Of course, dear. We are just half a day away from my kingdom, and we've stopped because one of the wagons broke a spoke."

"Well," Trish said. "That will probably take a while to fix. Might I get out and stretch my legs in the meantime?"

"That's not a good idea," Edmund said and started to leave the carriage.

She quickly grabbed his hand on the handle, "Edmund." She smiled her most winning smile, "I *need* to get out of the carriage for a moment."

She stared at him, waiting for him to catch her meaning, "Oh, well, alright then, be as quick as you can."

"Thank you," She said and smiled again.

He helped her down the carriage steps and handed her a black cloak, "You can wear this, and Rob here will go with you."

He gestured to a guard she had seen briefly during her nightly walk from the carriage to the wagon.

"There's a wood just over there," Edmund said, pointing to the south.

*Obviously.* Trish thought, but just smiled. They had been traveling on a road that ran just along the forest for the last day. Everything else, as far as she could see, was prairie land. The long waving grass looked like a yellow ocean.

She turned to walk around the carriage without waiting for her guard to show the way. She went into the woods, breathing deeply. She could tell it was an old wood by the smell and the size of the trees.

She went in farther than necessary, and the guard kept following her. Days of irritation at being cooped up in that carriage and that wagon finally broke through, "Did you plan on helping me hold up my skirts as well?" She rounded on the guard.

He looked embarrassed, his cheeks turned slightly pink, "No, your highness, my apologies, I'll wait here then."

"Thank you," Trish said. "And I would appreciate it if you would turn around."

The man cleared his throat and nodded, then turned back to face the road.

Trish continued walking deeper into the woods. She finally stopped when she could barely see Rob standing guard.

There was a convenient stump that she sat on, draping the cloak around so it couldn't be seen from behind. If anyone did see her, it would look like she was squatting.

She sat and sighed. She didn't really have to relieve herself. She just wanted out of that carriage, and this was the only way they would ever let her out. She stifled a giggle. If she truly needed to relieve herself as often as these men were letting her, Ann would have sent her to the kitchens to eat a whole wheel of cheese.

Trish sat there for almost five minutes before Rob called, "Are you alright, your highness?"

Trish turned to see if he was still turned around. He was so she called back, "Fine, just looking for some moss."

She kept looking at him, and he didn't turn around. She chuckled to herself again. Really, men could be so funny sometimes. Just because she was a princess didn't mean she didn't use the privy like everyone else. Surely they must know that. Whatever the case, she was going to use it to her advantage as long as she could.

The wood was very quiet. She closed her eyes and breathed deeply. It smelled of pine and dirt, moss and rotting leaves. She had always loved the woods. It reminded her of her childhood running around with Trent and Rose before any of them had responsibilities.

She remembered her mother liking to take long walks in the woods, looking for berries and wild flowers.

She wiped a tear from her cheek. She missed her mother. She knew if her mother were still alive, she wouldn't be here. Her father had changed after her mother had died. He had turned cold, dark. Sometimes Trish could be speaking to him, and he wouldn't hear her at all. He could be looking right at her and not see her.

She had always tried her hardest to make him laugh, to bring him back to his old self. Sometimes it would seem to be working for a short time, but he would always slip back to being sullen and distant.

He was a good king; he ruled fairly and made sure his people were taken care of, but the man he had been had died with her mother.

She wiped another tear from her cheek and rose. She couldn't sit on this stump crying all day. She remembered the last letter from Rose. She was going to do everything in her power to find out everything she could. Anything that might help Trent or her father know what type of alliance they might be getting into with the Duke.

She turned to go back to the carriage when she heard a twig snap. It wasn't a loud noise, but she turned to see what had made it. She didn't see anything, but she got the sense that something was watching her.

There was a loud groan and a hearty round of congratulations from the road. They must have fixed the wheel.

She turned and started walking back to the road, but she still felt like something, or someone, was watching her as she went.

# Chapter 17

After their failed escape attempt, Trent and Evans tried to busy themselves with other things.

Evans had used the melted wax from the candles to make a chessboard on the floor. Trent had asked, through the door, for some paper that morning, and a few hours later, some was slid under the door.

They tore up the paper and, using a charred stick, wrote the different names of the chess pieces on it.

They were currently two to three. Evans had won the last match, putting him in the lead.

Trent thought the commander had a slight advantage when it came to chess. Most people just played it as a game, but it was remarkably close to what the generals used on the battlefield.

"Your move, lad," Evans said. His knowing smile told Trent he thought he had gained the upper hand.

The only reason Trent had won two games was that Evans was a terrible poker player. He might be good at chess, but he did not know how to keep a straight face.

Trent supposed he didn't have to hide his intentions when he was in a command tent, discussing his plans with other leaders.

Trent slid his rook three squares to the left. It was now directly in front of Evans' queen.

Evans looked at the board, "But I..." he started. He looked up at Trent, who was grinning wolfishly, and rolled his eyes. He looked at the board again and swished his hand over the pieces of paper so they scattered.

"Don't look too smug, lad," Evans said. "You'll kindly remember who taught you how to play this game."

"I owe all my victories to you," Trent said and gave a sweeping bow as he picked up the pieces. "Shall we play again?"

Evans grunted as he stood from the floor, "I don't think my back or my pride can take another game." He stretched and went to the window.

Nothing had changed outside their window, but Evans liked to listen every half hour or so to see if they could learn anything more about where they were.

The day before, they had heard someone speaking a different language. Trent didn't know it, but Evans said it sounded like some of the northern languages he had heard.

He said that because of the size of the northern kingdom and because of its weather, many small, isolated towns often developed their own dialect. Sometimes they got so strong it almost sounded like an entirely different language.

Trent went to his bed and lay down. He let one leg swing off the side and started tapping it on the floor. He did not like waiting. He thought he would prefer torture to this, but their captives didn't seem to want any information out of them at all.

They still had not been spoken to or been able to speak to anyone. Trent had wondered their first day why no one had come when he had been banging on the door so loudly. Surely someone in the street had heard. If they could hear the people on the street, the people on the street had to be able to hear them.

Evans had said there were many reasons. Someone could have heard and come to ask, but was told a lie or to mind their own business. People could know who was up here, but Evans didn't think that as likely. Or, the most likely case, people had heard, but they knew the owner of this building and were too scared to mention anything.

"Evans," Trent said, sitting up on his cot.

"Hmm," Evans grunted, not turning away from the window.

"In chess, you don't win until you checkmate the king," Trent said.

"Yes," Evans looked at Trent.

"But the most powerful player is the Queen," Trent looked at their makeshift board on the floor. "When I was little, you used to play handicapped, you would start without your queen."

"What's your point, boy?" Evans asked, coming over from the window.

Trent was on the floor putting the papers on their squares. "The man at the window said they were going to release us. Why? What was the point of taking us if they were just going to let us go?"

"To start a war," Evans said. "To get a ransom, there are many reasons."

Trent laid the last piece of paper on the floor. He took a knight, a bishop, and a pawn and held them in his hand.

He held up the pawn, "Rose."

He held up the knight, "You."

He held up the bishop, "Me."

He reached down and picked up the paper that said 'Queen', "Leaving the path clear for the queen, Trish."

***

Trish sighed. They had been sitting in the courtyard for almost half an hour, but she hadn't been allowed to get out of the carriage.

She didn't know if they had reached their destination or if they were just stopping for the night. She assumed they weren't in the western kingdom because they had only been traveling for three days, but they had also not stopped in any towns so far. They had camped on the road.

She heard footsteps clacking on the cobblestone, and the carriage door opened. "So sorry for the wait, Trish," Edmund said.

Trish put on a smile, "Not at all, what's going on?"

"We've stopped for the night, but the inn didn't have enough rooms. We had to uh," Edmund gave a slight smile. "We had to convince some of the other patrons to find other lodging."

"I don't mind sleeping in the wagon," Trish said, which was partly true. She didn't mind the accommodations. What she didn't like were the circumstances.

"Nonsense," Edmund said, waving off her words. He held his hand out to help her out of the carriage. "You deserve a real bed after such a long journey."

When she stepped down from the carriage, instead of letting her go as was proper, Edmund put his other hand on her lower back and started guiding her towards the inn.

She let go of his hand, thinking that would be enough to remind him she did not need his help, nor was it proper for him to guide her into the inn, but he kept his hand at the small of her back.

Her back stiffened. Maybe he was just being protective, after all, it was nighttime, and they were in a small town in the country.

The inn was small but well-kept. The owner came over to the door when he saw Trish and Edmund enter, "Your room's all ready for ya, ma'am." The man said. "You can head on up, and I'll bring supper along shortly."

Trish started to say she didn't mind eating in the dining room, but Edmund cut her off, "Thank you, good man. Right this way, darling."

Before she could protest, Edmund guided her up the stairs and went down a hallway. He opened the second door on the right and motioned for her to enter. She went into the room and looked around. There was a bed, a desk, and a changing screen in the corner. The bed had a flower-patterned blanket over it, and there were flowers on the bedside table in a vase.

She heard a click and looked back to see Edmund locking the door.

"What are you doing?" Trish said, all courtly manners gone from her voice. She backed up further into the room.

Edmund turned towards her, his arms outstretched placatingly, "I'm sorry, I know this is all very untoward, but it is necessary, I assure you."

"Why?" Trish asked. "What's going on? Where are we?" The days of being kept in that carriage with no one to talk to had worn on her.

Edmund motioned for her to sit on the bed, but she hesitated. She wanted answers, but she also figured being contrary was not the best way to get them. The more suspicious she acted, the less she would be told. Fine, she could be a dimwitted noble if she had to. From her experience, people tended to tell you more if they thought you were stupid.

She sat down and sighed, "I'm sorry." She put her head in her hands and shook her shoulders a little to make it look like she was crying. "So much has happened, and I'm just scared."

"It's going to be alright," Edmund said in a soothing voice. He came over and sat on the bed next to her.

"Can you tell me where we are?" Trish asked, sniffing her nose.

"We're in Lockinge, it's the first city you come to in the western kingdom after you cross the river," Edmund said. "I am sorry about your having to ride in the carriage this whole way, but I didn't feel it was safe for you to be seen until we were across the border."

Why would I be any safer in your country than my own, Trish thought.

"I've told the innkeeper we are married and you weren't feeling well and asked him to bring your dinner up to the room." Edmund stood and went to the window. "I feel better in my country, but I didn't want to take any risks this close to the border."

"Of me being seen?" Trish asked.

Edmund turned from the window and smiled at her, "Exactly."

Trish looked around. A thought came to her, "You told the innkeeper we were married?"

"Yes," Edmund said. "Only to avoid questions about you traveling with a group of men."

"We're not," Trish had trouble getting the words out. "We're not sharing this room, are we?"

"No, no, of course not," Edmund said with a chuckle. He went to a door in the wall that Trish had assumed led to a privy. He opened the door, and she saw another room. "I'll be staying here."

Trish tried to contain her relief. Thankfully, there was a knock at the door breaking the awkward silence, "Your dinner, sir and madam," came a voice from the other side.

Edmund went to the door and opened it. "Thank you." He took the tray from the maid and took it to the desk.

The maid was an older woman with a kind face. "Enjoy your meal, madam. I hope you are feeling better. If you need help undressing for bed, just let me know."

"Thank you," Trish said. "If you could come back in an hour, I would greatly appreciate it."

The older woman smiled and nodded as she shut the door.

"Well," Edmund said. "I'll leave you to it then. I'm going to go to the common room with the other men."

"Good night," Trish said, and she sat down at the desk.

As soon as the door closed, she stood back up. She listened for his footsteps to fade away, then quickly went to the door and locked it.

She went to the adjoining door and quickly stuck her head in to look around the room. It was almost the same as hers, but there were two beds and a large wardrobe.

There was no one in the room. She looked at the other side of the door to see if there was a keyhole to unlock it from their side. There wasn't; there was just a latch on both sides.

She would be able to lock the door, and none of the men would be able to get in unless they knocked the door down.

She shut the door and locked it. Then she went to the window. It was too dark to see much, but she could see they were in a small city. There were plenty of people still on the streets going to and from a pub next door to the inn.

Further into the city, there were houses with candles lit in the windows, but that was about all she could see.

Trish went to the dinner tray and took a roll. She then flopped on the bed and moaned. It had been four days since she slept in a real bed.

"I'm not made for cross-country travel," She muttered to herself. "This is what Rose likes to do, not me."

She stretched her neck and back, which ached from sitting in the carriage for days.

There was a soft knock at the door. Trish sat bolt upright.

It couldn't have been more than five minutes since Edmund left. It couldn't be the maid.

"Hello," She called tentatively.

"I have wood for the fire, madam," came a soft male voice.

Trish went to the door and unlocked it. There was a tall man with a bundle of wood under his arm and a hood over his head.

He didn't wait for Trish to let him in, but instead, he almost pushed past her and shut the door and locked it again.

"What are you?" Trish started to say, but the man turned back to her and put his finger over his lips.

"I'm sorry for the intrusion, your majesty, but I need to be quick," The man went to the fireplace and started stacking the logs he had brought.

"How do you," Trish started to ask, but she couldn't finish her sentence.

The man took off his hood and turned to face her. It was a surprisingly young face considering the size of the man.

"Bennett?" Trish whispered.

The young man nodded, "I wasn't sure if you would recognize me, it's very helpful that you do, we don't have much time."

They had only met one time in her father's office. Trish had seen the young man a few other times trailing Commander Evans around the castle grounds, but they had never been introduced.

"Your father sent me," Bennett said quickly.

"My father? Why?" Trish asked.

"He doesn't entirely trust the Duke," Bennett said. He put his last few logs into the fire. "I tried to talk to you in the woods, but you left before I had a chance."

"That was you?" Trish was in shock.

Bennett stood and nodded. He had stoked the fire to a merry glow.

"Listen," He said, taking her hand and leading her to the bed. "I don't know if you will be taken all the way to Bawvel Hall. I've heard some of the guards talking, and it sounds like you're being taken to a smaller outpost. They think it will be easier to hide you there."

"From who, from Trent? Or from my father?" Trish asked.

"I don't know," Bennett said, shaking his head in frustration. "I've been following close behind your caravan. Whenever you get where you're going, I'll stay close."

Trish was grateful. Not only knowing there was someone from home so close by, but the knowledge that her father hadn't completely abandoned her made her eyes well with tears.

"It'll be alright, your majesty," Bennett said, misinterpreting her tears. "When you get to the outpost or the castle, we will need a way to communicate."

Trish nodded.

"If you get there during the night, place a candle in the window and don't let it go out. Make sure it burns all night. If you get there during the day, hang a red cloth from the window so I will know which one is yours." Bennett said.

"Alright," Trish said.

"After the first day, make sure there are shutters or curtains on your window. If there aren't, ask for some; they should be accommodating." Bennett said. "If your window is completely shut or open, I will know you're alright. If you open just the right shudder, I will know you need me to come to you. If just the left is open, it will mean you are going out of the castle, and I can talk to you outside the grounds."

Trish nodded that she understood.

"Right then," Bennett said, standing. "I should go, I was able to sneak in through the kitchens, and I need to go before the common room clears and things aren't as busy."

"Thank you, Bennett," Trish said, grabbing his hand. She didn't know how to put into words how grateful she was that he was here. "If you need anything, let me know as well, food, shelter, clothing. I will make sure you have it."

Bennett nodded and went to the door. He cracked the door and looked out to make sure no one was in the hallway, then left silently.

Trish watched from her window until she saw a dark shape leaving the inn and heading back towards the woods.

***

"There it is," Garrett said. "Seawald."

Rose was surprised by the size of the city. There was a huge bay that had more ships than she had ever seen. Like the other smaller seaside villages they had seen on their way north, the docks were the busiest place. Houses and shops were going up the hills in a crescent shape, all facing towards the bay.

On the northernmost side of the bay, there were sheer cliffs that blocked the majority of the wind, leaving the bay almost pond smooth.

They were on the southern hills where they had a view of the whole city. She could smell the fish and seaweed and salt.

"How are we going to find him?" She asked. "I thought the eastern kingdom was big, but this place." She let her sentence hang.

"It's not as big as it looks," Garrett said.

She eyed him skeptically. She tugged at her dress. She had decided she should wear it while in the city, but it was very annoying and confining after days of wearing a loose shirt and pants. She had also taken the time to comb her hair. It had almost taken her half an hour to work out all the snags.

"Really," he said with a grin. "It's not that bad. Most of the city is the market. Remember, only a few families stay here year-round. Most of the lodging is for rent when ships come into harbor or trade."

"Still," Rose said. She didn't see how they were going to find two people in a city this size. Especially two people who were bound to be well hidden.

They continued down the hills towards the heart of the city. The closer they got, the louder it became. Rose could hear merchants yelling at people to buy their goods. There were so many smells of different spices and baked goods that she almost couldn't smell the fish anymore.

There were silk traders and jewelers who kept trying to catch Rose's eye, but she followed closely behind Garrett. He was so big that he parted the crowd easily. Trip followed behind her, and Malcolm and Steven took up the rear.

She didn't know what he was looking for, but he seemed to be completely ignoring most of the merchants.

The market was a mix between an open market and shops. You would walk past three or four tents or tables, then you would come to a shop door.

Garrett only seemed to be interested in the permanent shops. Finally, he said, "Ahh, here we are, follow me."

He turned to go into what looked like a mix between a smith and a jeweler's shop.

It took Rose's eyes a second to adjust to the darkness of the building. When they did, her eyes widened. There was every type of precious jewel you could think of in display cases lining the walls. Rubies, sapphires, emeralds, and diamonds. There were many stones Rose didn't even know the name of.

Trip gave a low whistle, "There's more finery in here than the entire royal vault."

She walked along the cases looking at the stones. Some were by themselves, some were set into necklaces or earrings. On the back wall, there were dozens of blades hung on pegs. They all had jeweled hilts and scabbards.

Garrett walked to the counter and rang the small silver bell sitting there. Nothing happened.

"They can't just leave all this untended," Rose said.

"They don't," Garrett said. He walked around to the back side of the desk to a door that led out of the shop.

"What are you doing?" Rose hissed. "You can't just go back there."

He ignored her and went to open the door. "Malcolm, Steven, stay here."

They both nodded. Garrett opened the door and went to the back of the shop. Rose stood there and blinked at the door as it swung closed.

She went for the door. "What are you doing?" Trip asked.

"He didn't tell me to stay here," She said and followed after Garrett.

The back of the shop was dark and smelled of smoke. The only light came from an opening where large bellows let out their smoke in the middle of the room. The fire had gone out in the bellows. There was a long workbench along the left wall covered in more jewels and silver or gold fastenings that hadn't been set yet.

"Carlos," Garrett called.

"You know the owner," Rose asked.

Garrett jumped slightly. "What are you doing in here?"

Rose shrugged, "You didn't tell me to wait."

Garrett rolled his eyes and sighed, "Yes, I know the owner. We often trade. Jewels sell for a good bit of money, but they don't keep you warm during northern winters."

"He buys your furs," Rose said.

Garrett nodded. He walked to another door that was at the very back of the workroom. The room was even darker than the workroom. Rose couldn't see anything in the room, but there was a low growling.

Garrett said something in the language he spoke to Malcolm, and the growling stopped. A large dog came slinking out of the shadows with its tail tucked between its legs and its ears flattened back.

"Come here, boy, what's wrong?" Garrett asked.

The dog's ears perked up as it came and smelled Garrett's hand. He had a black muzzle and black around the eyes, the rest of his head was light brown that went over his shoulders and down his front legs. There was a large black patch on his back, making him look like he was wearing a saddle. His heavy tail wagged a little as Garrett patted his head, but it quickly went back between his legs.

"Where's Carlos, boy?" Garrett asked.

The dog gave a small whine and went back into the room.

Garrett stepped back into the shop and found a candle on the workbench. He lit it and went into the room.

He looked at Rose, "You might want to stay out here."

She ignored him and followed into the room. With the light of the candle, she could see that there was blood smeared on the wall. They turned a corner and saw the dog lying on the floor next to a man. The man was curled up facing the wall.

"Get out of here," the man croaked, then coughed. "He'll bite your leg off, he will."

Garrett went to the man and set the candle on the ground. "He won't be biting anyone. He only looks scary. Carlos, it's me, Garrett."

The man turned his face to look, "Garrett?"

"What happened to you?" Garrett asked, helping the man sit up.

He only got a few inches off the floor when the man groaned and clutched his stomach. Rose looked down. The man was drenched in blood.

"Rose," Garrett said urgently. "Get Malcolm, tell him to bring his bag."

Rose ran from the room back to the main shop.

"Malcolm," Rose said as she ran through the door. She stopped. There were two guards in the shop now, and they looked like they had been in the middle of questioning the men.

"What's going on?" Rose asked.

One of the guards, the younger of the two, looked at her. He looked a little surprised.

The other one kept his eye on Trip but said, "These men say they're with a young lady who came to pick up a brooch she bought." He turned to look at her, "Is that true?"

She glanced at Trip, who nodded his head ever so slightly, "Yes." She said simply. She didn't want to say too much in case it contradicted anything Trip had already told them.

The young guard looked like he was satisfied with that answer and ready to leave, but the bearded one who had spoken to her looked suspicious. "And what would a southern lady want with this scum shop?"

"Scum?" Rose asked, raising an eyebrow. "This shop has the finest jewels I've ever seen, north or south."

The man scoffed, "Not talking about the jewels, talking about the owner."

"What's wrong with the owner?" Rose asked.

"Nothing, my lady," the other guard said with a slight bow. "We'll just be on our way. We only came in because this shop hasn't been open today, and we wanted to make sure these men weren't thinking of stealing anything."

The other guard spat on the floor, "Let um take what they want. The owner's not coming back, that's for sure." The man gave a dark chuckle.

"That's enough, Marik," the younger guard snapped. He seemed to be in charge despite his youth.

"What happened to the owner?" Rose said in a more forceful voice.

"He's gone, my lady," The young guard said.

The bearded guard chuckled again, "Oh, he's gone alright, gone to the crows."

"He's dead?" Rose asked, raising an eyebrow.

"We believe so, my lady. I'm afraid you'll have to buy your brooch elsewhere," he bowed to her again. "Have a nice day."

He went to the door, and the bearded guard looked back at Rose, "The man ran afoul of the good graces of Mevusha." He looked Rose up and down, "I suggest you don't do the same."

The younger guard rolled his eyes and held the door open for the bearded man. He swaggered out the door, and the young man looked back, almost apologetic, but shut the door without saying anything.

Trip looked at Rose, "They must not care if we take anything if they are just going to leave," he went to the window.

Steven went to the back side of the counter and started picking up jewels, "The man is dead, why not?"

"He's not dead, put that back," Rose said. She went to Malcolm, "Garrett needs you, bring your bag."

He nodded and followed her to the door, "You two stay up here in case those guards come back." She looked at Steven, who was still looking greedily at the jewels, "The man isn't dead, don't steal anything."

She went through the door and showed Malcolm where Garrett and Carlos were.

"What took so long?" Garrett demanded. He had managed to move the man from the floor to the low bed that was against the other wall of the small room.

"There were guards," Rose said.

Garrett's head snapped up, "What?"

"They thought we were robbing the store," She said. "They think he's dead." She gestured to the man Malcolm was now working on.

They had cut away the shirt to show a stab wound that was clearly infected. The smell when they pulled off the shirt almost made Rose vomit.

"Rose," Garrett said without looking up at her. "Send Steven to find the strongest liquor he can and some clean cloth. You and Trip can bring the horses around the back; there's a stable."

She nodded, grateful for a reason to leave the room. She told Steven to get the liquor and cloth, then helped Trip move all their horses around the back of the shop.

Trip didn't ask any questions, but he seemed upset about something.

"What's the matter?" Rose asked when they were bringing the last horse and the donkey around.

"Steven," he said. "When you left, he said something in their language, then shoved a handful of jewels in his pocket. He doesn't say much, but the more I see of him, the less I trust him."

Rose nodded. She had never felt as comfortable with Steven as she did with Garrett or Malcolm, but there was nothing they could do about it. He was Garrett's friend, and she trusted Garrett, so she had to trust Steven.

When all the horses were settled, they went back to the shop. Steven had returned, and Malcolm was still working over Carlos.

He looked much better. They had cleaned off most of the blood, and the wound was now covered in clean white cloth. He was drinking some of the liquor Steven had brought.

"Can you tell us what happened, Carlos?" Garrett asked gently. He was sitting on the floor at the head of the bed.

The man took another drink and said, "Those damn guards are what happened." His voice was raspy and low. It looked like every word hurt him.

"Why would a guard stab you?" Garrett asked.

"Cuz they's mean that's why," The man said.

"Carlos," Garrett said in an exasperated voice. "Guards don't just go around stabbing respected shop owners. What happened?"

The man looked around like a kid who had been caught doing something naughty. He sighed and said, "I was trying to get into the brothel down the way. They said they were full up, so I tried to get in through the back way, and the guards came and ruffed me up."

Garrett eyed Carlos skeptically, "A brothel was full? Couldn't you just have waited ten minutes?"

"That's what I was thinkin'. I said I didn't mind waiting, but the madam said they were full all night. I thought the madam was just being difficult. I was ahh," He stopped, looked at Garrett, cleared his throat, and said, "I was well watered, but I was fine."

Garrett snorted, "You were drunk, figures. Why did you want in so badly? There are at least three other establishments you could have gone to."

Carlos gave the smallest of smiles, "There's a new girl there I saw the other day, I took a liking to her and wanted to talk with her."

"Talk," Steven scoffed. "Because that's what men do in brothels."

"How could an entire brothel be full all night?" Trip asked. He was rubbing his chin like he was thinking hard.

"I asked that very question, sir," Carlos said, looking at Trip. "I said, 'I've not seen anyone come or go from here for four days, how's it that you're full?' That's when they kicked me out."

Four days. Rose looked at Garrett and knew he was thinking the same thing. If they had taken Trent and Evans by boat, they would have been here for about four days.

"Thank you, friend," Garrett said. "Rest now, Malcolm will stay with you if you need anything."

Carlos nodded, "Feed the dog, will you? Poor thing hasn't left since I came back."

The dog, who had been lying quietly on the floor, looked up. Garrett patted his leg as he stood and said, "Come on, Jack, let's get you something to eat."

# Chapter 18

They went back to the shop. Steven went to look after the horses.

"Four days, Garret," Rose said as they went through the door. "A brothel hasn't had anyone come or go for four days?"

"You think that's where they're keeping them," Garrett said. It wasn't a question.

Rose nodded. She looked at him, trying to will him into agreement with her eyes.

"It's a good place to start at least," Trip said. "Aside from the four days, guards don't usually knife people for trying to get into a brothel's back door."

Garrett nodded but didn't say anything.

"How do we get in?" Rose asked. She didn't direct her question at either of them in particular.

Trip shrugged, "It doesn't look like being a normal patron will get us in. Unless they were only opposed to Carlos being drunk."

Garrett shook his head, "A large portion of their business is because men are drunk. They wouldn't have cared if he fell into the building as long as he had gold to pay."

"Can we sneak in?" Rose asked. "Go in a window or something?"

Garrett shook his head again but didn't suggest another plan.

"Then what do we do?" Rose asked, frustrated.

"I have an idea," Garrett said quietly.

"What is it?" Rose asked, willing to hear anything at this point. They were so close to finding Trent.

Garrett looked at her. Was he blushing? It was hard to tell under his beard. He cleared his throat, "You're not going to like it."

"Does it matter?" Rose asked. "We have to find them. I'll do whatever it takes."

"We won't be able to get in from what Carlos said," Garrett said, pointing between himself and Trip. "But you might be able to."

"How?" Rose asked.

Garrett looked at her like the answer should have been obvious.

"Wait a moment," Trip said, suddenly pushing off the wall he had been leaning against and strode towards Garrett. "No, absolutely not."

The men stood facing each other. Trip only came up to Garrett's shoulders, but he looked like he was about to hit him.

"Trip," Rose said reproachfully. "What are you doing?" She tugged at his elbow, trying to pull him away from Garrett.

Garrett held his arms out, "It was just an idea, she said whatever it takes."

"Not that," Trip growled, still standing toe to toe with Garrett.

"Will you please tell me what this plan is?" Rose said, exasperated.

Garrett looked at her over the top of Trip's head, "I was wondering if the brothel might be hiring any new girls."

Rose's mouth fell open, "You want me to pose as a–a prostitute?"

Garrett nodded, "It's most likely the only way we will get in. If Trent and the Commander are the only two men in the building, you'll be perfectly safe."

"We don't know if they are the only men in there," Trip snapped. "Just because this Carlos person hasn't seen anyone coming or going doesn't mean no one is there."

Rose dropped Trips' elbow and turned away from the men. They continued to argue, but she didn't listen to anything they were saying.

Was she willing to do anything to get Trent back? She shook her head. Of course she was. That was a stupid question. He was like a brother to her. She would die for him. Besides, she wouldn't actually be doing anything salacious. She would just be dressed differently.

She and Trish used to play dress up all the time when they were kids. Rose rolled her eyes at herself. Of course, this would be nothing like that.

She was going to at least hear the rest of Garrett's plan before she said yes or no. "What's the rest of the plan?" She asked quietly.

She was surprised they had heard her question over their arguing.

"It might not even work," Garrett started.

"What's the plan, Garrett?" Rose asked, looking at him.

"Well," he said. "First, we need to go shopping."

***

"I look ridiculous," Rose moaned.

She had stayed at the shop to try and do something with her hair while Garrett went to the modiste to find a dress.

He had come back with an extravagant ruby red dress that was trimmed with black lace on the hem and sleeve cuffs. The corset had black opals sewn into the fabric. They were heavily beaded at her waist and got sparser, but bigger, as they moved up to her chest. There was a ruby the size of a chicken's egg sewn directly over her heart.

"Come out so I can see," Garrett called through the door.

"I can't," Rose called back. "I can't get the lacing on this damn corset to tie right."

There was a pause. "Do you need help?"

"You are not helping me put my clothes on," Rose spat at him through the door. She tugged on the laces again, but it was no use. She couldn't tell if they were tangled or hooked on one of the stones.

She stomped her foot then sighed, "Fine."

The door opened slowly, and Garrett poked his head in. If Ann could see her now, she would have heart failure. "Just hurry up, is it snagged or twisted?"

Garrett took the laces from her hands and adjusted them. He had to loosen them a little, then re-tie them. He tied the extra lace into a bow, "There," He said, and stood back.

"I don't even want to know where you learned how to tie a lady's corset," Rose said and turned to face him. In all honesty, the dress wasn't all that revealing. True, it was a lower cut than she was used to, but it was more the shape and color than anything that made it stand out.

"I tie my boot laces every morning," Garrett retorted. "It's not that different."

He looked at her, studying the dress.

"Well?" She asked briskly.

"It looks good," Garrett said. "Can you pull it down a little?"

Rose tugged at the skirt, but she didn't see why. The hem was already touching the ground.

She looked back up at Garrett, who was staring at her.

"What?" she asked, her eyebrows furrowed in confusion.

"I didn't mean that part of the dress, Rose," Garrett said. She could tell he was holding in a chuckle.

Rose could feel herself blushing. She gritted her teeth, "That part of the dress doesn't go down. That's the whole point of a corset, to keep things up."

"Fine," Garrett said, his smile breaking through. "I guess you will just be a modest prostitute."

"This is hard enough as it is," Rose lectured. "Do you have to make fun of me on top of everything else?" She put her hands on her waist.

Garrett's joking smile turned to a soft one, "The reason I can so easily make fun of you is the very reason you have nothing to worry about. You're so innocent; your honor is so impeccable that this will do nothing to it."

Rose wasn't sure if that was logical, but she appreciated him trying to make her feel better.

He had a change of clothes too. He was wearing a beautiful dark blue jacket and a fresh white shirt. He was supposed to be posing as a nobleman who had a mistress he needed to get rid of.

He fit the part well. Rose had grown used to him in his simple traveling clothes, but he seemed to fit in the finery as well.

"Ready," He asked, holding out his elbow for her.

"No," She grumbled.

He laughed, and she took his arm.

It was late afternoon and there weren't many people on the streets. The market had closed half an hour ago, and the nightlife of the city hadn't started yet. Most people were home eating supper.

They walked quickly down the street towards the brothel. Rose was surprised at how large it was. Carlos had said it was the nicest place in town, well, the cleanest place at least, but she didn't expect it to be a two-story building.

Garrett opened the door and let Rose enter first. There was a girl, close to Rose's age, sitting behind a desk, reading a small book. She was wearing a very frilly, very pink dress. She looked up when the door opened and had to lean back to look at Garrett.

She gave him a flirtatious smile, "I'm sorry, sir, but we're full up till tomorrow night."

Garrett smiled back just as flirtatiously and said, "That's alright, miss, I'm here for a different matter. Is the owner about?"

The girl hesitated, "I can look, may I tell her who's calling?"

"Just let her know a gentleman has a business proposition for her," Garrett said with a wink. "We'll wait right here."

The girl looked like she wanted to say something else, but thought better of it and went quickly up the stairs.

"Why tomorrow?" Rose asked quietly. "Are they being moved?"

Garrett nodded with a frown, "Probably, it's a good thing we got here when we did."

They waited in the lobby for almost ten minutes when the girl came back down the stairs, "Madam is in her office, if you'll just follow me."

Rose expected the girl to go back up the stairs, but instead she led them outside around the building to a small lean-to. The room was so small that Rose didn't think Garrett would be able to stand all the way up.

The girl opened the door and waved them inside.

"Thank you, Lilly, you may go," said a woman's voice from inside the room.

The girl almost ran back to the brothel. Rose raised her eyebrow at Garrett, but he just shook his head and went into the room.

There were two chairs and a desk in the room, but nothing else. The woman behind the desk was dressed in black from head to toe like she had just come from a funeral. She was working on a ledger book and didn't look up at them. She gestured for them to sit with her pencil.

Garrett took it in stride and sat down, waiting patiently for her to acknowledge them. Rose was starting to get irritated.

The woman wrote a few more numbers in her ledger, then folded her hands under her chin and looked at Garrett, completely ignoring Rose. "What can I do for you, sir?" She sounded bored.

"I have a girl for you," Garrett said, holding his hand towards Rose.

The woman finally looked at Rose. She looked her up and down. It was like she was looking at a horse she might buy, trying to judge if it would be a good investment. Rose wanted to squirm in her seat to get away from that stare, but she forced herself to sit still and look at the woman.

"How old?" The woman asked, turning her attention back to Garrett.

"Twenty," Garrett said.

"And why are you trying to get rid of her?" the woman asked.

"I've been traveling, but I have to return to my home," Garrett said.

The woman smirked, "The wife doesn't approve of your traveling companion?"

Garrett smiled back, "The wife doesn't know, which is why I need to get rid of her before I see anyone I know."

"I see," the woman said. "How long has she been with you?"

"Two months," Garrett said. "That's another thing, I plan on coming back for her. And I want her back the same way I sold her to you."

The woman raised her eyebrows, "And how is that?"

"Mine," Garrett said. His voice had become ominous. This was more of a threat than a condition.

"You don't want her to work?" The woman asked, sounding bored again. "If she doesn't work, I'm afraid I can't afford to keep her."

Garrett put two stones on the table, a ruby and a diamond, "I do not share with other men." He leaned back in his chair, "This should more than cover any boarding expenses you will endure because of her. Keep her as a kitchen maid for two weeks; if I haven't come back for her by then, you can do whatever you like with her."

"Why not just put her up at an inn?" The woman asked.

Garrett was quiet for a moment, "If it's too much of a burden for you to keep her, then I can." He reached for the stones on the table and started to stand.

The woman's hand shot out so quickly it made Rose jump. She swiped the stones off the table and smiled at Garrett, "Not at all. It's no trouble."

Garrett nodded slightly, "Good. Two weeks then." He stood and turned towards Rose.

She looked up at him, trying to keep her eyes from pleading. He put his hand on her shoulder and squeezed it, "Until next time, dear."

He opened the door and walked through. Before shutting it, he turned back and said, "Oh, one more thing. If she is mistreated in any way before I come back," His eyes darkened, and his voice dropped to a low growl. "You will not live to see the next day."

The woman gave a slight nod to show she understood. She didn't look scared, though. She looked like she was used to being threatened.

The door closed with a snap, and the woman returned to her ledger book like nothing had happened. She worked in the book for a few more minutes, then shut it and looked up at Rose, "You must have done quite a number on that one." She grinned and stood. "Men think they are kings of the world even when they have to pay their subjects to say so.

Come along."

She walked around the desk and opened the door. Rose stood and followed. She looked for Garrett on the street, but of course, he wasn't there. He was probably already back at the jewelry shop.

"Did he give you a name?" The woman asked.

"My name's Rose," Rose said.

The woman looked at her out of the corner of her eye, "Rose, that's your real name?"

"Yes," Rose said, confused.

"Hmm, it'll work, I suppose. I usually have to change my girls' names," The woman opened the door to the brothel. "No one wants to sleep with a woman who has the same name as their daughter, sister, or mother."

The girl in the pink dress stood to attention, but the woman didn't come in any further than the door frame.

"Lilly, I still have work to do in my office. Take Rose here to the kitchen and find her some supper. She'll be working in the kitchen with Jade for now."

Lilly gave a quick bobbing curtsey, "Yes, madam."

The women left without another word. Rose stood in the lobby awkwardly. The girl Lilly didn't seem to be in any hurry to take her to the kitchens. She looked Rose over just like the woman had.

Finally, she said, "Alright then, follow me." She led Rose through a door to their right that led to a large open room. There were tables and chairs set up all facing a small stage at the end of the room.

"We usually have shows every night. Singing, dancing, and the like," The girl said, not looking at Rose. "Do you have any talent?"

"Not really," Rose said. She had been taught all the court dances, of course, but she had a feeling that wasn't the type of dancing performed on this stage. "Why isn't there a show tonight?"

"Oh, we've been closed all week," Lilly said nonchalantly. She kept going across the room towards a swinging door.

"Why?" Rose asked.

Lilly waved her hand dismissively in the air, "I'm sure Jade or Trixie will tell you, the girl never shuts up." She pushed open the swinging door with her back and let Rose in front of her.

"Jade," She called to the empty kitchen.

A second door at the far end of the kitchen opened. A blond woman came in carrying an apron full of eggs. "Yes."

"This here's Rose, Madam told me to bring her to you," Lilly left Rose just inside the doorway and went back across the stage room without another word.

Once again, Rose felt herself being evaluated, looked up and down by Jade.

She set her eggs into a basket on the large center table. "How long have you been working?"

Rose didn't know how to answer this question. "Sorry?"

Jade raised an eyebrow at her, "Not long then. Well, it's a good thing we're closed right now. Here," She held a spoon out to Rose. "Stir the stew for me while I candle these eggs."

Rose took the long wooden spoon and went to the large pot in the fireplace, and started stirring. The stew smelled delicious. It was potato and ham with all sorts of spices that Rose didn't recognize.

"Oh, hello," said a small voice from behind her. She looked up and saw a girl who couldn't have been older than thirteen.

"Trixie, Rose, Rose, Trixie," Jade said by way of introduction.

Trixie went to the table and put two large onions down. She got a knife and started peeling and chopping the onions.

"Angel's complaining that she's tired of feeding the guests," Trixie said.

Jade rolled her eyes, "That girl will complain about anything. She hasn't had to do anything all week except walk up a flight of stairs, and she still manages."

"I think she's mad because she hasn't gotten any tips all week," Trixie said.

Jade snorted, "Probably, every other girl here is having the best week of their lives, but she's mad."

Trixie looked nervously over at Rose but still said in a normal voice, "She's been sneaking out at night. Peach and Cinnamon told me yesterday at breakfast that she snuck back in just before sunup."

Jade started stacking the eggs on a table that ran along the inner wall of the kitchen, "She's going to get kicked out, or beaten, if she doesn't stop. Madam does not take kindly to being stolen from."

Trixie nodded vigorously and rubbed her shoulder like she knew what happened to people who stole from the madam. She gathered up her chopped onions and brought them to the fire. Rose moved aside so she could dump them in the stew.

She got a poker and dragged a cast-iron pot out of the coals on the side of the fireplace. She gathered her apron and grabbed the handles, then took it to the large table. She flipped it over, and a beautiful round loaf of bread came out, perfectly browned.

Jade watched her with approving eyes, "Good job, it's better than last time." She took the bread and flipped it right side up. "See how it keeps its shape?"

Trixie nodded and grinned, "The last one fell in on itself." She blushed a light pink.

Jade laughed and mussed the girl's hair, "Go call everyone to supper."

Trixie nodded and left the kitchen.

Jade sat down with a sigh, "You can pull it off the fire and let it rest a minute."

Rose pulled the pot on its swinging arm away from the fire and went to sit by Jade, "She seems awfully young to be in a place like this."

Jade blew a quick breath out of her nose, "I've seen them as young as six or seven." Her face turned sad, "I try my best to keep them in the kitchen as long as I can, but eventually they are all sent to a room. Trixie was supposed to go last week, but then we closed. She'll be going to a room after they leave."

Rose didn't want to ask anything that would make the other girls suspicious, but she had to find Trent and Evans. "You and Trixie both said this place was closed, but the Madam said it was full."

Jade nodded, "Of course she did. You can't go around telling people a brothel is closed, they'll all think there is a disease and men won't come back for months."

"Is there a disease?" Rose asked, slightly alarmed.

"No," Jade said. "Two rich men paid Madam to let them use the place for a week. We were told to tell anyone who asked that we were full."

"Two men," Rose said. "Why? What are they doing if no one's worked in a week?"

Jade put her hands up, "I don't know, and I don't care. I stopped asking questions a long time ago."

Rose didn't have a chance to ask any more questions. Girls of varying ages were filing into the kitchen for supper.

Everyone dished up their stew and then went back out to the stage room. After everyone was finished, Trixie gave Rose a bowl and told her to help herself.

Rose followed Trixie out to the stage room and sat next to her to eat. Most of the girls were chatting and eating quietly, but there was one who kept looking over at Rose.

Rose leaned over to ask Trixie quietly who it was. Trixie looked up, then looked back down at her bowl quickly, "That's Angel, just ignore her, she's always in a bad mood."

Rose tried to ignore the stare coming from Angel's table, but she couldn't help but look up every once in a while to see if she was still being looked at.

The third time she looked up, Angel had a wicked grin on her face. She called out, "So, where's the new girl from?"

Rose looked at Trixie, who kept her head down, then glanced at Jade, who looked bored, "South of here."

Angel laughed, "Everything's south of here." She studied Rose for a moment, "I saw the man who brought you in." She gave a low whistle. "That was a fine lookin' man, rich too, it looked like. Why'd he dump you here? What'd you do? Get pregnant?" She snorted.

"No," was all Rose said.

"Did the wife find ya then?" Angel said, laughing with the others at her table.

"No," Rose said again. "He's coming back."

A few of the girls laughed, but most looked at her with pity in their eyes.

"If you think that man's coming back for you, you're stupider than you look," Angel leaned back in her chair. "Which would be quite an accomplishment."

Rose grit her teeth but didn't say anything. She forced herself to remember what Garrett had said: the best way to win a fight is to not get into one in the first place.

Rose tried to go back to eating her stew, but the Angel girl didn't seem to be done with her yet, "You think you're better than us? With your pretty dress and your rich patron?" Angel stood and walked to where Rose was sitting. She laid her hands on the table and leaned towards Rose, "It doesn't matter how rich they are, darlin', you're still a whore."

"If you're done with your supper, go put your bowl in the sink," Jade said lazily. Angel turned to look at her. "And if you're not, go back to your table. Your perfume's clogging my nose."

Angel tried to stare Jade down, but Jade had a look of absolute indifference on her face. Angel gave the table a slight shove, then went back to her table.

Soon, everyone went back to eating. They started leaving in groups of two or three, most thanking Jade for the food, then heading down the hall to their rooms.

Angel sat at her table even though she was finished with her food, looking at Rose now and again.

"Come on," Trixie whispered to Rose. "You can help me with the dishes." Rose followed her to the kitchen and sighed.

They washed dishes in silence for a while when Jade came in. Angel came in the door after her, "I don't see why I have to take them food every night." She sneered at Rose, "Make the new girl do it, she's not going to be here for very long, right?" She tossed her bowl into the sink, making water splash all over Rose's dress.

Rose took a deep breath and clenched her jaw.

"I've had about enough of your attitude," Jade said angrily. "You'll take the food because that's what I told you to do. If you have a problem with it, you can talk to Madam. I'm sure she'd love to hear about your nightly routine that's interfering with your work here."

"It's alright," Rose said quietly. Everything in her was screaming to not let this girl have her way, but she needed to find Trent and Evans. "I can take the food."

"See," Angel said smugly. "She wants to." She turned on her heel and swept out of the room before Jade could say anything to the contrary.

Jade shook her head as the door swung closed, "You know you're never going to get on her good side, right? There's no point in trying." She said to Rose.

"I won't be here for very long anyway," Rose said. "I mostly just wanted her to leave."

"Suit yourself," Jade said, some of the pity the other girls had shown leaked through her aloof demeanor.

"What's her problem anyway?" Rose said, washing the bowl in her hands. "She seems quite satisfied with the life she chose."

Jade raised an eyebrow at her, "And what life might that be?"

"Being a–" Rose started, but she wilted under the glare Jade was now giving her.

"A prostitute?" Jade asked.

Rose gave a small nod.

Jade shook her head in disbelief and pointed the spoon she held at Rose like a sword, "Let me tell you something. I don't know where you came from or how you got here, but none of these women chose to come here. No one chooses to be a prostitute."

"But you said she," Rose started.

"She what?" Jade asked hotly. "She's going out doing her own work?

Yes, she is, do you know why?"

Rose shook her head.

"She has a seven-year-old daughter. She managed to find a local family who would keep the child, but she has to pay them monthly so they don't kick her out. If she misses even one payment, her daughter will most likely be brought here." Jade's eyes flashed with anger. "You're awfully judgmental for someone who has almost the same story as Angel. She had a rich young man once. He told her he loved her, told her he would marry her, and told her he would bring her to his castle. She believed him. She loved him. She got pregnant and he kicked her out. Her family wouldn't take her back. She came here so she wouldn't starve."

There was a brief pause, but Jade wasn't done. "Lilly out front was the last of seven children. Her father married her off to a man who was twice her age and never talked to her again. Her new husband liked to gamble, and he lost all their money in one night. He sold her to Madam so he wouldn't be put on a rowing ship to pay back his debts. She hasn't seen any of her family since."

Jade put her spoon down, and her voice lowered, "And Trixie here, do you think she chose this? She's twelve years old. She showed up four years ago in the dead of winter. Frozen almost to death, skin and bones. She smelled the stew and came begging for a mouthful of bread. Half of these girls were sold, and the other half had to choose between this place and death."

Jade took a deep breath to calm herself, "Now, I hope your young man comes back for you, I truly do. I will not judge any of your choices you've made in life so far because I don't know what drove you to make those choices. You should do the other women here the same courtesy."

Rose was silent.

"Here," she held out a tray with two bowls of stew and a loaf of bread.

"Take this upstairs and don't come back to my kitchen until you've changed your attitude."

Rose took the tray and nodded. She hadn't ever felt so small. "Which room are they in?" She almost whispered.

"Up the stairs, third door on the right," Jade said.

Rose went out of the room without another word. She had to steady her hands. The tray was shaking.

She took the food to the room Jade had told her and slid it through a hatch. There wasn't any noise coming from the room. She wanted to knock and let them know she was there, but she held back.

They had decided to make their rescue in the early hours of the morning. Everyone would be asleep, and it would make for an easier getaway if they could run during the day instead of the night.

She studied the door. It wasn't barred, which Rose found strange. She looked at the handle and saw it had a keyhole.

Rose grimaced. Now she had to find a key. It was most likely kept by Madam.

She gently touched the door, inwardly promising Trent and Evans she would be back, then went back downstairs.

# Chapter 19

She went into the kitchen, but Jade was gone. Trixie was laying out a bedroll next to the dying embers in the fireplace.

She turned and smiled when Rose opened the door, "Jade asked me to show you to your room." She started towards the door

Rose stopped her, "Is it all right if I stay here with you?"

Trixie stopped, "Umm, I guess so." She looked confused. "You want to stay in the kitchen?"

Rose shrugged, "I just don't want to be alone."

Trixie gave a small smile and nodded, "Sure, here, I'll get you a blanket."

She came back with a thick brown blanket, "It's kind of scratchy, but it's thick and warm." She handed it to Rose.

"Thank you," Rose said. "Is there a privy?"

Trixie shook her head, "There's an outhouse in the back. The key's hanging on the wall in the lobby."

Rose chuckled, "You have a key for the out house?"

Trixie nodded seriously, "It's only for the girls; none of the men are allowed to use it. They used to have trouble with that rule, so Madam put a lock on the door."

"Alright," Rose said. "I'll be right back then."

She went to the lobby and found the key easily enough. It was hanging on a peg behind Lilly's desk.

She went outside and around the building to the back. It was cold. She shivered, and her fingers had trouble with the key in the lock.

Instead of going all the way around to the front of the building again, she went into the kitchen through the back door. She went towards the swinging door to put the key back in the lobby, but Trixie said softly, "You can just leave it on the table. Most of the girls don't leave at night. They won't need it."

Rose laid the key on the table and went to the fireplace next to Trixie. She laid the blanket over her legs, but she didn't lie down.

It was quiet for a long time, and she thought Trixie had fallen asleep when she asked, "Does it hurt?"

"Does what hurt?" Rose asked.

"You know," Trixie asked, propping herself up on an elbow. "Working."

"I," Rose started, now knowing what to say. "I don't..."

"The others all say the first time hurts, but after that you get used to it," Trixie said in a small voice.

Rose's heart broke that a girl so young could have this conversation with nothing more than passing curiosity.

"Jade said you came here four years ago," Rose changed the subject. "What happened?"

Trixie lay back down and looked at the ceiling, "I grew up on a farm.

We never had much money, but we had a little house and a barn. Papa used to take our apples to the market and sell them." She smiled fondly at the memory.

"One year, it rained and rained for weeks. When harvest came, there weren't very many apples on the trees." Her smile faded. "Papa tried to sell anything he could find in the house, but it wasn't enough to pay the taxes. Mama went to town to see if she could find any work washing or sewing, but there wasn't any."

She paused and took a deep breath, "I don't know exactly what happened, but one night Papa woke me up in the middle of the night and told me to hide in the barn. I heard men shouting, and then there was a loud crash. They set the house on fire. I could see the flames from the hay loft."

Trixie was quiet for a long moment. "The men came into the barn and took all the animals, but they didn't find me. The next morning, I went looking for Mama and Papa, but I," Her voice broke. "I couldn't find them."

Rose quickly swiped at a tear. Jade had said her story was close to Angel's, but her real story was closer to Trixie's. She was an orphan. She didn't know what had happened to her parents, but without the queen taking her back to the eastern kingdom, she very well could have ended up exactly like Trixie.

"I'm so sorry that happened to you," Rose whispered.

"Thank you," Trixie said in an equally quiet voice. She rolled over to look at Rose, "It'll be alright. I like most of the girls here, and we all help each other." She gave a small smile, then turned back towards the fire.

Something in Rose snapped. How could this girl, this child, talk about the rest of her life in this place so calmly? She had only been here a few hours, and already she was dying to get out.

"Trixie," Rose said, her voice hard.

"Hmm,"

"What's your real name?" Rose asked.

Trixie turned back to Rose and propped herself up on an elbow. She looked Rose in the eye for a moment as if no one had asked her that question before. Finally, she said, "Adelaide."

"That's a beautiful name," Rose said, smiling at the girl.

"Papa used to call me Ade for short," she smiled.

Rose looked at her for only a second before she knew what she had to do, "Do you want to leave here, Ade?"

***

"So," Trent grunted as he did another pushup. "Do we have a plan?"

"Yes," Evans said, sitting on his cot.

Trent stopped his workout and sat back on his heels. "Are you going to tell me the plan?"

They hadn't gotten any candles with their meal that evening. They didn't know what to make of that. Evans supposed it was because they were going to be moved tomorrow, and they didn't feel like wasting any.

They were both still awake in their room, not able to go to sleep. Evans seemed relaxed, but Trent had to keep moving to distract himself from the uncertainty of tomorrow.

"The plan," Evans sighed, "is to come up with a plan after we see where we are taken."

"I don't like that plan," Trent said.

"Then come up with your own plan," Evans retorted.

Trent rolled his eyes and went back to doing pushups.

He had gotten to twenty when Evans suddenly said, "Stop."

"What?" Trent asked.

"Just stop," Evans said again, getting off his cot. "Listen."

Trent listened. There was a small squeaking sound coming from the door. It sounded like metal scraping on metal.

"What are they?" Trent started to whisper, but Evans held a finger to his lips. They both moved closer to the door. Evans put his ear to the door where a knob would be if there was one on their side of the door.

"I think someone's trying to unlock the door," He breathed.

He motioned for Trent to stand to the side of the door, and he did the same. Both men had their backs pressed against the wall when it opened very slowly.

A woman poked her head inside. She looked towards the cots in the corner of the room and opened the door more.

She slid into the room, leaving the door open.

She took a few steps into the room. Trent looked at Evans and nodded. Trent stepped out from the side of the door and grabbed the woman. He put his hand over her mouth and grabbed her around the waist.

Evans shut the door. The woman had given an initial grunt of surprise, but she didn't struggle. She breathed deeply, or sighed, Trent wasn't sure.

Trent looked to Evans, "What do we do with her?"

The woman mumbled something under Trent's hand. He grabbed her more tightly and hissed, "Be quiet."

The woman sighed this time. Trent felt her shoulders try to shrug, but he was holding her tight enough that it was an awkward movement.

He felt something wet and squishy slide between his ring and middle finger, "Eck." He gasped and dropped the hand he had on the woman's mouth. She had licked him.

"Really," The woman said, straightening her skirts. "I snuck into your room, dummy." The woman turned to face Trent and Evans.

He couldn't see her face in the darkness, but Trent knew from years of hearing that tone of voice whenever she had outsmarted him or beaten him at a game, "Rose?"

"What was your plan exactly?" Rose said with her hands on her hips.

"I," Trent started. "I didn't have one. What are you doing here?"

"Rescuing you, of course," Rose scoffed.

The door came open again. "Is it all right to come in now?"

"Come in, Ade," Rose said quietly.

Ade came in holding a candle. "Who's this?" Evans asked.

"This is Ade," Rose said. "She's helping me. What?"

Trent had been staring at her since the candle gave light to the room, with his jaw almost hanging. "What are you wearing?" He asked.

Rose's eyes narrowed, "A dress."

"I recall most dresses having a little more fabric," Trent said.

"I didn't have a choice," Rose said, her voice rising and her cheeks reddening. "Do you know what this building is?"

"Easy, Rose," Evans said. "You'll wake someone."

"You two have been in a brothel for the last four days," Rose hissed. "They are saying two rich gentlemen bought the place out for a week and wanted privacy. This was the only way I could get in." She gestured to her dress.

Trent opened his mouth to respond, but Evans cut him off with a wave of his hand, "We can talk later. Do you have a plan to get out of here?"

Rose nodded, then held her hand towards Ade, "Ade's lived here for four years. There's a back stairwell we can take to get out. Trip and a few friends who helped us get here are in a shop down the road waiting for us."

"Trip's alright?" Trent said, with obvious relief in his voice.

Rose nodded, "He's fine. We found him the day after you were taken. We need to get going."

She looked at Ade, "Follow me," the girl said, and turned to open the door.

*****

They went down the stairs as quickly and quietly as possible,

"When we get to the bottom," Ade whispered, "we just need to follow the shadows of the other buildings until we get to the jewel shop."

"Sounds like you've done this before," Evans whispered back, mussing her hair.

Ade smiled widely. She had taken to Evans immediately. Most children did. Rose marveled at how most men, hardened soldiers even, would cower under Evans' gaze, but children just laughed and ran to hug him.

They came to a door at the bottom of the stairwell. "Let me go first," Ade said.

"No," all three of them whispered back in unison.

Ade put a hand on Rose's elbow, "If anyone sees me, they'll just think I'm sleepwalking. They say I do it all the time." Ade's mouth twitched up at the corner. She slowly pushed the door open and stepped out. It was silent for a few seconds, then the door opened, "Come on." Ade said.

They cautiously went through the door one by one. They followed Ade to the next building, staying in the shadows. The moon was only a sliver, but it was enough to see where they were going. The town was quiet, but the never-ending beating of the waves on the shore made it seem loud to Rose.

They had two buildings to go, and Rose was starting to relax. This had been far easier than she thought it was going to be.

Ade, still in the lead, passed the edge of another shop and gave a quiet yelp. Her head jerked to the side. She was pulled around the corner of the building out of sight, "Aren't you supposed to be in the kitchen?" a low female voice asked.

"Let her go," Rose hissed. She turned the corner quickly to see Angel with a fist full of Ade's hair, pulling the girl's neck back so she could see her face.

"Ahh, two chicks out of the roost," Angel said smugly. "Madam will love to know about this." She made to grab Rose as well, but Trent and Evans came around the corner.

Angel froze for a moment but quickly regained her smug manner, "If it isn't our reclusive guests." She smiled, but it wasn't the least bit friendly.

"Let the girl go," Evans said in a low, threatening voice.

"Hmm," Angel said, pretending to think. "You know, I don't think I will. I've heard some very interesting things about you two, and I'm sure Madam will reward me very nicely for giving you back."

"Let the girl go, or," Trent started, but Angel laughed.

"Or what?" She looked Trent up and down. "All I have to do is raise my voice, and ten guards will be here in a matter of seconds."

She sauntered closer to Trent, still holding Ade's hair. She put her hand on Trent's chest and looked up at him through her lashes, "So what exactly is your plan? Your majesty."

Trent's eyes widened in shock. Angel chuckled, "You know, men always complain that women like to chatter, but I've never met a more talkative person than a boastful man who thinks he rules the world." She rolled her eyes, "You were only in town one day before I knew who you were. That idiot Grady would not shut up."

Rose's heart sank, "Grady? The duke's man?"

"A duke, eh?" Angel said with a shrug. "That explains how he could tip so well. But it doesn't matter, back to business." She took in a deep breath of air.

"Wait!" Rose said, moving towards her, but Trent had already clamped his hand over her mouth.

Angel didn't seem to mind at all. It almost looked like she had planned for this to happen. She droped Ade's hair and staired at Trent.

"Now what?" Trent asked, looking to Evans.

Evans shrugged his shoulders, "Whatever you do, do it quickly." He was scanning the surrounding darkness wearily.

Trent looked at Rose. Rose clenched her jaw, "The only reason we're still here is because she thinks we can offer her something better than Madam."

Angel quirked her eyebrow at Rose and mumbled something into Trent's hand.

"Let her talk," Rose said. Trent lowered his hand slowly, ready to clamp it back over her mouth if she made a false move.

"You're smarter than I took you for, new girl," Angel said.

"What do you want?" Rose asked.

Angel huffed angrily, "I take it back, you are just as dumb as I thought you were. You're a naive little girl, no wonder you found yourself in a whore house."

"I'm not a whore," Rose said.

"Of course you're not," Angel said sardonically. "Of course you're not. If you were, you would know there is only one thing a woman like me wants."

"Which is," Rose asked, trying to control her voice.

Angel snorted, "Why don't you have the child tell you? She knows more about this world already than you ever will."

Rose looked at Ade.

Ade's eyes swam with tears, but she smiled weakly at Rose, "Freedom."

Rose met Angel's eyes. They were hard and determined, but underneath, they were also terrified. They were the eyes of an animal in a trap. She needed this standoff to work just as much as Rose did.

"You can come with us," Rose said.

Angel shook her head, "I can't leave until." She snapped her mouth shut and shook her head. "I can't leave."

"Your daughter," Rose said very quietly.

Angel's eyes flashed, but she didn't say anything.

Rose looked down at her hands. She didn't have anything she could give this woman. She... wait a moment. She turned so her dress caught the small amount of light the moon shone down on them.

She quickly reached under her skirts and pulled out her knife. She cut the threads that held the ruby in place, and a few opals came off as well. She held the stones in her hand out to Angel, "Will these be enough to get you out of here?"

Angel's eyes widened, and she nodded. She held her hand out for the stones.

Rose pulled her hand back, "If you come with us, I can get you more. We need to know everything you learned from Grady."

Angel shook her head and clenched her jaw, "I can't leave."

"Just down the road to the shop," Rose said.

Angel looked Rose in the eye. Rose didn't know what she was looking for, but after a moment, Angel nodded, "Deal."

# Chapter 20

"Garrett," Rose said when they went in the back door of the shop. There wasn't an answer. "Garrett," Rose called again, slightly apprehensive. No answer. There was a soft clicking, and the dog came trotting around the corner.

It came up to Rose and licked her hand, "Where are they, Jack?" Rose asked, patting the dog's head. He gave a small whimper and went back into Carlos's room.

Rose followed the dog into the room. It was not a pretty sight. There were bloody clothes strewn all over the floor and a large pile in the corner.

Carlos was lying on the bed with his head hanging over the side, throwing up into a bucket. The vomit looked to be mostly blood.

"What happened?" Rose asked. Carlos had looked better when they left.

Trip sprang up and looked like he might hug Rose, but he stopped when he saw Trent and Evans. "Thank goodness you're back." He shook both men's hands and patted Rose on the shoulder awkwardly.

Garrett looked up at her and shook his head, "I don't know. He seemed to be getting better. He slept for a little while, but he woke up and started this." He gestured towards the bucket.

Garrett stood, and Malcom took over taking care of Carlos. "Where's Steven?" Rose asked.

"He went to get water," Garrett said. He rested his hands on Rose's shoulder and looked her over, "I'm glad you're alright." He squeezed her shoulders, then looked up at Trent.

"Let's go into the workshop to talk," Garrett said.

Rose looked down at Ade, who was petting Jack in the doorway, "Ade, stay right here, alright? Don't go into the room just yet." Rose didn't want the girl to have to see all that blood.

Rose looked at Angel. She didn't know what to do with her. She was planning on giving her some of Carlos's jewels in payment, but with him in this state, she wasn't going to be able to ask him or work out a way for her to pay him.

"I'll stay with the girl," Angel said.

Rose nodded and followed the men into the workshop.

The workshop was pitch black. The only light came from the vent in the roof above the bellows.

Trent, Evans, and Trip were standing in the small, dull circle of light. Garrett was standing just outside the light, waiting for Rose.

Evans and Trent were having an intense whispered conversation. "It's not possible, Evans, drop it," Trent said as Rose and Garrett came into the light.

"What's wrong?" Rose asked.

Neither said anything, but Evans was studying Garrett intensely.

Rose looked between Evans and Trent. Trent just shrugged his shoulders, and Evans continued to stare at Garrett.

"Alright then," Rose said slowly. "We need to come up with a plan to get out of here. The sooner the better, I think. Once we pay Angel, I don't think I would trust her to..."

"What's your name, sir?" Evans burst out, cutting Rose off.

"Evans," Rose said reproachfully, but Evans took a step closer to Garrett.

"What's your name, lad?" Evans insisted. Trent looked embarrassed and a little angry.

"My name is Garrett, Commander Evans," Garrett said quietly.

Evans raised his eyebrows, "You know who I am?"

"I had to tell him," Rose answered before Garrett had a chance. "The others don't, though, so keep your voice down, please, Evans."

"What's your father's name?" Evans continued his questioning, completely ignoring Rose.

Garrett took a deep breath, "My father's name was Hamish of Clan Righ. I am who you think I am, Commander."

"But that,that's impossible." Trent stuttered, "You're dead."

"He's the spitting image of his father," Evans said. "I knew him well; he was a great man."

Rose held up her hands to stop the conversation, "What are you talking about?" She turned to Garrett and looked him in the eye, "Who's your father?"

Garrett looked at her, his eyebrows scrunched together in confusion, "You don't know?"

"How exactly would I know a fur trader's father?" Rose asked, annoyed.

"But in the barn," Garrett said gently. "You called me Gar, I thought you figured out who I was."

"What," said Rose, completely flummoxed. "Your name's Garrett. I didn't think it was too far of a stretch for a nickname."

"I thought Trish must have told you about me," Garrett said. "I signed all my notes and letters to her with Gar."

"But," Rose started. She felt so stupid. Her dreams had been trying to tell her, but she had refused to listen. He knew Trish, he had intimate knowledge of the northern royal family, he was well spoken, and he knew about politics.

"How are you alive?" She finally asked.

"My sword master saved me," Garrett said. "He had discovered a plot by my uncle to kill me, so he took me into the woods one day and told me everything he had heard. He told me to run away and get out of the northern kingdom, or I would be killed. He told everyone in the castle that I had fallen off my horse into the river and drowned."

Garrett gave a dark chuckle, "They didn't look for me very hard. I stayed close to the castle for almost a week in the woods. When no one came for me, I knew the master had been right. I left and never went back. I met Kenneth a few weeks later, and he took care of me."

"Why didn't you go back?" Trent asked, speaking for the first time.

"I thought about it," Garrett said with a shrug. "I'm afraid it comes down to being young and hurt. I was angry that no one came to look for me, not even the staff that had taken care of me. I was only eleven at the time. By the time I had grown up enough to regret leaving, it was too late." He shook his head.

"What do you mean?" Rose asked.

"My uncle had changed so much in the kingdom. Hardly any of my father's old court had any power. Even if I did go back, no one would believe my story," Garrett said. Rose could hear the frustration in his voice.

"But why not," Evans said briskly. "I recognized you easily enough. Why shouldn't they?"

Garrett gave a small, sad smile, "My father was a good king, but he didn't spend much time out of the castle with the people. He preferred to delegate his kingdom to the lords, letting them rule their land as they saw fit, trusting they knew their different territories better than he did. But like I said, all the lords that would have recognized my father no longer have any power. It would only take my uncle saying I was a liar, and I would be killed."

"Kenneth knows," Rose said softly after a few moments of silence. "Who else knows?"

"Just Malcolm," Garrett said. "Steven tends to talk a lot when he drinks, so I thought it best he didn't know."

"Hey, hey, I think he needs help," Angel called from the room.

Garrett didn't hesitate; he went straight into the room to help Carlos. The others stood looking at each other a little while longer. Evans finally spoke, "We need to get out of this town and back south as soon a possible. Once this fellow is taken care of, we need to go. I think we might be in greater danger than I first suspected."

Rose started to ask a question, but Evans held up his hand, "I don't have time to explain now, let's see if we can help in here."

***

Trish looked out her window at the ocean. She breathed in the salt air and sighed. Bennett had been right, they weren't at the main castle, but they were a few miles north in a seaside castle that used to be used as a military outpost.

She had done as Bennett instructed with the shudders and hoped he could see her window. Her room faced the ocean, and there wasn't much land between the castle and the small rocky beach.

Edmund had told her to make the castle her home, but he wanted her to stay on the grounds. There was a small private walk that led to the beach that she was permitted to walk down, but he had asked her not to stroll the beach without an escort.

They had traveled much faster once they were in the western kingdom. True to his word, Edmund had abandoned the carriage, and Trish had ridden a horse for the rest of their journey. She had tried very hard not to look for Bennett, but every once in a while, she couldn't help looking towards the woods and thinking she saw movement far in the branches.

Bennett hadn't talked to her since the inn. She didn't expect him to, but it was hard knowing there was at least one friendly face so close but so unreachable.

She had been in her rooms much of the morning, and she had finally worked up the nerve to go down for lunch in the dining hall. She was supposed to be gathering information after all, and she couldn't do that hiding away in her rooms.

She went to her door, took a deep breath, and opened it.

The castle was small as far as castles go, but it would have been quite large as a military outpost. Trish tried to remember everything Commander Evans had ever said about military encampments to her father while she had been in a few meetings. She wasn't technically allowed to be at the meetings, but Trent would often let her in through a back door, and as long as she was silent, no one ever kicked her out.

She guessed this castle would have held at least fifty men. There were two long barracks down in the yard, as well as about twenty rooms in the actual castle itself.

There were a large number of towers compared to the size of the place.

Trish supposed that was on purpose, so there could be lookouts over the sea.

She made her way to the kitchens and found some bread and cheese for lunch. There wasn't supposed to be a cook coming until this evening. Trish looked around the silent room and decided to take her lunch with her on a walk around the grounds.

She went out into the yard, and there again it was silent, so she went out the open gate and went down the path that led to the beach. She had only gone a little way down the path when it split. One path went to the beach, and the other led to a lighthouse she could see up on a little hill.

She debated for a moment. Edmund hadn't mentioned anything about a lighthouse. Maybe he didn't think it would hold any interest for her. He couldn't have been more wrong.

She turned towards the lighthouse. After all, Edmund hadn't said anything about it, so if he didn't want her to go there, she could always claim ignorance about it being off limits.

The tower was in bad shape. The door was hanging on one hinge, and most of the paint had been stripped off by sand and salt.

Trish ducked under the door and went into a small living space. Charts and maps were hanging on every inch of wall space. There was a desk with an old compass and a telescope, and some more maps.

A protractor and a charcoal stick were sitting on the desk like whoever used to use this light house had just finished making a map, got up, and walked out.

Trish turned to her right and looked up the stairs. She could only see a short distance up the spiral staircase, so she took a few steps. They groaned under her weight but seemed to hold. She took a few more cautious steps. The steps protested but held firm.

Ten steps up there was a small landing with a window. The landing didn't have anything interesting on it, so Trish continued up the stairs.

There was a small hatch door that opened after a few good pushes. It led into a circular room. There were no walls but glass windows that let her see in every direction. In the middle of the room, there was a small fire grate that had a rounded metal backing that could roll around the fire on a track.

Trish tried to move the reflector, but it was rusted. She was looking out towards the ocean when she heard the stairs groan. She whipped around and soon saw Bennett's head coming out of the hatch.

"Well," he said, putting down three squirrels he had shot. "You found me faster than I expected."

"Bennett," Trish gasped. "Isn't this a little too close to the castle? They are sure to come out here."

"They already did," Bennett said. "Two of them came here this morning and looked it over. They won't be coming back. They just checked to see if everything was still sound."

"But what if," Trish started.

"If anyone does come back here, I will be able to see them before they get here," Bennett said reassuringly. "I won't be spending much time here anyway. I just need a dry place to sleep."

"Alright," Trish conceded. "Is there anything you need?"

"No," Bennett said. "I can get food well enough, I'll be fine. You probably shouldn't come up here very much, though. It might make them suspicious."

Trish nodded in agreement, "I won't."

She looked out the windows again, "This is a beautiful view, though."

"I would think your seaside window was just as good," Bennett said.

"It is," Trish sighed. "But this feels like a hideout, not like a prison."

She looked back at Bennett. "Have you found anything out?"

Bennett shook his head, "They keep talking about a plan and that it's going well, but they don't ever say what the plan is. I don't know if they are talking about you or something else."

They talked for a few more minutes, then Trish got up, "I should probably go, I don't want them to come looking for me."

Bennett agreed and told her not to worry about him. Trish went back down the stairs and headed towards the castle.

She was just entering the gates when she ran into Edmund. "Oh, hello." He said.

"Hello," Trish said. She had already thought up what to say if anyone asked where she had been. "I went up the path and picked some of these flowers for my room. This place could use a woman's touch."

Edmund looked at the small bouquet she had picked on her way back and smiled, "It could indeed. The cook just arrived and said supper would be ready in an hour."

"Wonderful," Trish said. "I'll go up to my room and change then."

She walked past Edmund and couldn't help but smile to herself. There was something satisfying about keeping a secret, especially when it was right under someone's nose.

***

Rose stepped into the room and almost gagged. The smell was horrible.

Carlos was curled up on the bed, vomiting blood into a bucket, and Malcolm was speaking rapidly to Garrett in their language.

"What can we do to help?" Rose asked Angel.

She shrugged, "I don't know. He was bad when we got here, but it looks worse now." Her eyes were locked on Carlos. "If he's sick, we all need to get out of here before we get whatever he has."

Rose's eyebrows scrunched together in confusion. Carlos was looking better when she had left. Were his injuries causing this, or was it something else?

Evans stepped into the room and looked at Carlos, "How long has he been like this?" He looked at Garrett.

Garrett turned from Malcolm, "He started vomiting about an hour before you got here."

"And he was fine before that?" Evans asked.

"Not fine exactly," Garrett said. He explained about Carlos's injuries.

Evans nodded, then knelt by Carlos. He looked into the man's eyes and felt his forehead, "Has he had anything to eat or drink since you arrived?"

Garrett nodded, "We gave him some soup and water."

Evans stood, "You trust this man?" He asked Garrett, gesturing to Malcolm.

"With my life," Garrett said with an edge to his voice. "Why do you ask?"

"I think this man has been poisoned," Evans said. "If he started vomiting over an hour ago, then he doesn't have long."

"What?" Garrett said. "That's impossible."

"You said there was another man?" Trent asked.

"Yes, Steven, but I trust him as well," Garrett said.

"When did he leave?" Evans asked.

"A few minutes before you got here," Garrett said. "He went to get water."

Evans nodded, "We need to leave, now."

"We can't just leave him like this," Garrett protested angrily.

"Did the other man know who we are?" Evans asked.

"No," Rose said, cutting off Garrett, who looked like he wanted to yell at Evans. "He thinks you're my father."

"Hmm," Evans said. "Still, he might have overheard something. We need to go." He reached out for Rose's wrist, but she pulled it back.

"Garrett's right, we can't just leave him like this," She looked at Trent and Evans. "If it weren't for him, we wouldn't have known where to find you two."

Evans gritted his teeth. She knew two sides of him were at war, the side that wanted to help and the other that wanted to get Trent and her to safety.

There was a tense silence in the room. It was broken by a small voice from the door, "Mr Carlos?"

Everyone looked at the door and saw Ade, white faced with her hand on Jack's head.

"Hello, dear," Carlos choked from his bed. Rose looked from the girl to the man on the bed and was filled with rage.

"This is the girl you were trying to see at the brothel?" Her eyes sparked with fury. She spun towards the bed. She wanted to hit him, but Garrett gently caught her hand in his.

"What's wrong, Mr. Carlos? Are you sick?" Ade asked. She moved closer to the bed with Jack.

"I don't think I'll be able to bring you sweets for a while, dear," Carlos said, coughing into his sleeve. It came away red.

He looked at Rose, "I know what you're thinking, but you're wrong. Yes, this is the girl I was going to see, but it wasn't what you think."

"Then what was it?" Rose asked through her teeth.

"I told you I just wanted to talk to her, she." He winced and grabbed at his stomach. Rose thought he was going to use the bucket again, but after a moment, he lay back. "Before I moved here, I had a wife and daughter. They both died of consumption."

He coughed again, and some blood bubbled on the corner of his mouth, "I saw Trixie outside the building a few weeks ago, and she looked, she looked." His eyes filled with tears, and his voice cut off. "She looked just like my Dianna looked, my little girl," He couldn't continue.

Ade slowly walked to the bed and knelt. She pulled a small handkerchief out of her pocket and handed it to Carlos. He looked up at her and smiled, "I wanted to take you from that woman. I wanted you to live with me here in my shop, if you would want to."

Ade smiled, "That would have been wonderful, Mr. Carlos, but I think now we all need to leave Seawald."

Carlos nodded and smiled, "Yes, my dear, I think you do." He patted her hand and dropped it. He looked around at the others in the room, "You all need to leave."

He patted the dog on the head, then reached into his pocket. He pulled out a silver key and handed it to Garrett, "You know where the safe is, here, take what's in it and give it to the girl."

Garrett took the key and nodded. He gripped Carlos' hand in his, "We will take care of her."

Carlos nodded and coughed again.

Angel looked at Carlos, "What's the point of having a safe? All your jewels are out on shelves for anyone to take."

Carlos waved a feeble hand, "Those are all fake, glass mostly. They are good enough for this town, but any real jeweler would be able to tell what they are."

Angel snorted a laugh and walked out of the room.

"What are we going to do about him?" Trip asked.

Carlos lay his head back on his pillow, "Just leave me, it won't be long now."

Rose believed him. His voice was so soft she could barely hear him, and his breathing was growing more ragged.

"Look," She said, turning to Evans. "Even if we leave right now, where are we going to go?"

"Back home, of course," Trip said.

Evans shook his head, "They'll be expecting us to go south once they find we're gone. Into the country is our best bet, then we can work our way back down."

Garrett nodded, "We could go north to the river. It can take us far enough west to get away, then we can head south again."

"You can all go wherever you want. I'm leaving." Angel had walked back into the room. Her pockets were bulging, and she had a bag slung over her shoulder that was clinking.

"What are you doing?" Rose asked. "You heard Carlos, those are all fake."

"Well," She smirked. "I don't plan on selling them to reputable jewelers, so it doesn't really matter, does it? I hope to never see any of you again. Goodbye." She bobbed her head, turned on her heel, and walked out of the room.

Evans stared at the empty door frame with his eyebrow cocked, "Do we need to worry about her?"

"I don't think so," Rose said. "She's going to get her daughter, then she's going to get as far away from this place as she can. Still, if someone offered her money for information, I'm sure she wouldn't hold back."

There was a small murmuring from the bed. They turned and saw Carlos mumbling unintelligibly. It didn't sound like he was speaking the common tongue.

"What's he saying?" Rose whispered to Garrett.

Garrett knelt by the bed, "It's a prayer, he's saying 'Aahva save me.'"

"What's Aahva?" Rose started to ask, but Carlos started shaking. He seized for only a few seconds, then went still. Rose saw his lungs exhale for the last time. On his last breath, there seemed to be a faint light that went up from his mouth.

Rose turned to Trent, "Did you see?"

Bang! There was the sound of smashing glass and loud voices all around.

"Are you still alive, old man?" Came a voice from the shop. It was one of the guards from the other day.

"Go," Evans whispered urgently. "To the horses, now!"

# Chapter 21

Evans swooped up Ade and carried her to the horses tied up outside the shop.

Garrett untied the mule and smacked it hard on the rear. The angry creature took off running down the back alley on his own. Rose hoped he would be safe.

They were going to be one horse short. They had only brought five, but there were six adults and Ade.

Someone could double up with Ade without a problem, but if they were going to be running, having two people on a horse would seriously slow them down.

"Did Carlos have a horse?" Rose asked Garrett as she hurriedly saddled Raul.

"No," Garrett said.

Trip and Malcolm had already saddled and mounted their horses. Raul and Stevens' horses were saddled, but no one had gotten on.

If they were going to have to fight their way out of town, they needed their best fighters free to do so.

"Trip," Rose said. "Take Ade. Evans, take that horse, Trent, you go on Raul. I'll ride double with Garrett."

Rose knew Garrett could fight, but she didn't know what he could do while on horseback. Evans and Trent had been trained to fight on war horses.

No one argued. The clatter of hooves on stone filled the alley as they ran full speed through the streets.

An angry shout came after them from the shop. Rose looked back as she held tight to Garrett and saw at least ten men holding torches in the alley.

"We need to split up," Rose shouted in Garrett's ear.

She could feel him shake his head in protest.

"There are seven of us," Rose shouted over the clamor they were making. "We're going to be extremely easy to find once they rally and get a party looking for us. Once we get to the high road, we need to split up."

They continued down the alley as far as it went. They would have to go on the main road to get out of town.

They slowed down as they approached the road. Thankfully, almost all the houses on this end of town were empty. They were empty, or their inhabitants weren't going to stick their heads out in the middle of the night to see why six horses were running at breakneck speeds down their street.

"I don't hear anyone pursuing," Trip said.

"They will be," Evans said darkly. He turned towards Garrett, "The river you mentioned, how do we get there?"

"The main road leads right to it," Garrett said. "The river starts where the road ends."

"We need to split up," Rose said. "We're too easy to find all together."

"If it comes to that, we will," Evans said. "For right now, we need to stick together. If they do send a force after us, we stand a better chance together."

"I don't think they know we are gone yet," Trent said. "When they came to the shop, they only called out for the owner. If they knew Evans and I were missing, they would have sent out everyone by now."

"They saw us running away," Rose protested.

"It was dark," Trip said. "They wouldn't know who they were chasing."

"And you don't think they are going to check on the two most valuable prisoners they've ever had," Rose spat back.

"We need leave," Malcolm said with a very strong accent.

Garrett nodded, "He's right. We'll make for the river. If we get separated, so be it, but everyone needs to head to the river, it's straight north of here."

A bell rang in the middle of the town. It was a deep resonating note that could be heard all the way on the outskirts of the town. It was struck over and over. No one would miss hearing it for miles.

"I think they know we're gone," Evans said. He looked at Garrett, "We'll follow you."

Garrett turned his horse towards the main road and took off at a gallop. Rose had to clutch at his waist to stay on.

She peeked back under her arm to see if the others were following; they were. Malcolm was directly behind them, Trip and Ade followed, while Trent and Evans took up the rear.

They rode this way for several minutes, only slowing to take corners on the road, and Rose was just starting to hope they could make it to the river, when she felt something fly past her ear.

"They have archers," Evans yelled from the back. "Into the trees!"

Garrett pulled his horse to the left side of the road and went into the trees. It wasn't a thick forest, but it was better than the open road.

They continued mostly north, but they had to go much more slowly, trusting the horse to pick the best path through the trees.

"Are you alright?" Garrett asked. "Not hit?"

"I'm fine," Rose gasped. "Is everyone still behind us?"

"I don't know," Garrett said. "But we have to continue towards the river, it's our only hope."

It was quiet for a moment, except for the pounding of the horses' hoofs, when Rose heard another horse coming up behind them. She turned to see who it was and screamed.

A man with a club was right behind them and gaining quickly. He raised his club to strike, she ducked and shoved Garrett down the best she could. The man flew past them as Garrett pulled them to a stop.

Garrett pulled out a long sword from his saddlebags and faced the attacker who had wheeled back around to come at them again.

"Get off," he said frantically to Rose. She didn't hesitate. She knew she would just be a liability on the saddle. She slid off and went behind a tree to stay out of the way.

The man with the club charged Garrett. Garrett let go of the reins and moved his horse with only his legs. He ducked the club again and slashed at the man with a vicious back swing of his sword.

The man howled in agony and slumped onto his horse's neck. Garrett swung his horse around and pressed his advantage. The man barely got his club up in time to take Garrett's next blow.

Garrett gave a series of hammering blows that nearly unseated the man. The man kicked out, trying to make Valdar bolt, but he was too well-trained.

The horse side-stepped, pressing into the man at Garrett's nudging. Garrett gave one last slash of his sword, and the man went limp.

Garrett quickly grabbed the reins of the horse and pushed the man out of the saddle.

"Rose," he called, but she was already running towards him. "Here, get on." He handed her the reins, and she swung up into the saddle.

"Are you alright?" Rose asked breathlessly.

"Of course I am," he said, and to her surprise, he smiled slightly. "He only had a stick."

They took off riding north again. The forest was eerily quiet after all the commotion. Rose couldn't help but look over her shoulder every few seconds for another attack. None came, which, if anything, made her feel more anxious.

If no one was following them, then they would be after the others.

"How much further to the river?" She asked when Garrett stopped suddenly.

"It shouldn't be far," Garrett said, looking around as well. Rose could tell he was straining to hear anything else in the woods, any sign of the others.

Garrett half rose in his saddle and turned to look behind them.

"Do you see anything?" Rose whispered, her eyes searching the woods.

"Something's wrong," Garrett said slowly. She was about to ask what, but he held up his hand to silence her.

There was a twang and a thud. Garrett grunted in pain.

"Garrett," Rose gasped. She nudged her horse towards him.

"I'm fine," He said through gritted teeth. "Ride!"

He kicked Valdar forward, and she followed. They were galloping through the trees, branches wiping past dangerously.

One smacked Rose on the face, and she felt a trickle of blood run down her cheek. Garrett seemed to be leaning close to his horse's neck. She wasn't sure if that was because he was hurt or if he was just trying to dodge branches.

She wanted to check on him, but there was no way to do that without stopping. She was sure he had been hit with an arrow.

They came upon a small clearing, and Garrett stopped. Rose almost ran into them, but she pulled her horse to a stop as well.

They could hear people coming through the trees behind them.

"You have to run," Garrett said, panting.

The glare she gave him was lost in the darkness, "If you think for one second that I'm leaving you here."

"You have to," Garrett said fiercely. "You don't have a weapon. You'll be no good when they catch up to us."

"I have my knife," Rose protested.

"Knives are no good on horseback," Garrett said. He tore the hem off his shirt and wrapped it around his shoulder tightly.

"You're hurt," Rose said. "Let me help."

He shook his head, "The arrow just grazed me, I'm fine. Go now."

"I'm not leaving," Rose said, tears welling up in her eyes.

"I'll be better off if you go," He said, smiling at her again like this was just a game they were all playing.

"And you're going to send me off into the woods, unarmed and alone?" she asked, trying to turn the argument around on him.

"You'll be fine, the river's about three hundred yards that way," he pointed to the far end of the clearing. "Can't you hear it?"

She couldn't hear anything over the roar of blood in her ears.

"Look, do you want me to die tryin' to defend ya?" He said roughly, his northern accent coming out in his distress.

"I'm not," Rose started to say, but that was all she managed to get out. Garrett leaned over and slapped Rose's horse on the rump hard.

The beast shot off towards the north, almost unseating Rose. She tried to rein him in, but there was no stopping him. She could only hold on for dear life and try to dodge branches when they came back to the woods.

After several heartstopping minutes, the trees suddenly cleared, and there was a large river with a rocky bed.

Rose looked up and down the bank. Off to her right, there was a small cottage. She turned and headed towards it cautiously. There were no candles in any of the windows, because no one was there or because they were asleep. Rose didn't know.

She passed under a large sycamore tree, stopping in the darker shadows of the leaves to look around.

"Rose," came a voice from the trunk of the tree. Rose looked down and saw Evans slumped against it, holding his side.

"Evans," She hurriedly slid from the saddle and went to him. "What happened? Where are the others?"

"We lost Trip and the girl in the woods," He said. "Three came after Trent and me. We killed them and made it here. When you and Garrett didn't show up, Trent sat me here and went to look for you." He tried to sit up and grimaced, clutching his side.

"You're hurt," She said. She went to his side and gently pulled up his shirt. There was a piece of cloth tied tightly around a wound, but it was already soaked with blood.

"It's just a scratch," Evans tried to joke.

"It is not," Rose took her knife and cut a long piece of her dress hem.

She wrapped it around the bandage that was already there and tied it tightly.

"Perfect," Evans said. "Now you can't see the blood."

Rose snorted, "Because that makes it better. Stay here, I'm going to get you some water."

She stood and went towards the river. She looked in the windows of the cabin, but it looked abandoned. Even if there were people inside, she didn't know if asking for help would be safe. She tried the door, but it was locked.

She looked around the cabin and found a bucket near the back steps. She took it to the river so she could fill it for Evans.

She went to the other side of the cabin and saw four canoes tied to a stake sticking out of the ground. There were several larger rafts pulled up onto the bank, also tied to stakes.

She untied the canoes and pushed them as close to the water as possible without them being taken by the current. She saw that each had two oars tied to the underside of the bench seats.

She stooped to fill the bucket and shivered as the frigid water touched her hands.

Rose went back to Evans and had to shake him to get him to answer her. She got him to take a few sips of water, but that was all he could manage.

His weakness frightened her. She had always known him as the strong commander and warrior. She checked his wound again and was slightly encouraged that it had not yet bled through the second bandage she had put on.

"Evans," Rose asked gently. "Can you stand? There are some canoes by the river, and we should get you in one so we are ready to leave when the others get here."

Evans nodded, and to her surprise, he could stand. He leaned on her heavily, but he managed to make it to the cabin.

"Here, take a rest," Rose said, sitting him on the back steps. "I don't hear anyone coming, just rest a minute."

Evans didn't protest.  He sat and took a few deep breaths, "Not exactly the trip we planned, is it?"

Rose looked at him and forced a laugh, "No, not exactly."

"Ah, well," Evans said, turning to look at her. "If I remember correctly, you always wanted to go on adventures as a girl."

"The longer I'm on this adventure, the more I think all the storybooks lied," Rose said.

Evans gave a small chuckle, "They do tend to leave out the messy bits, don't they?"

Rose sighed, "They do indeed."

"You can't blame the stories, though," Evans said. "People do it too. People have a way of remembering the good and forgetting the bad. I'm sure when we get back, Trent will take immense pleasure in telling all the nobles about this tale."

Rose couldn't help but laugh, "We'll have to keep him honest, I suppose." She looked towards the river, "Can you make it the rest of the way?"

Evans nodded and reached for her to help him up. With his arm over her shoulder, they made it the rest of the way to the canoes, and Rose helped him step into the closest one.

She had just settled Evans into the bottom of the canoe when she heard a horse approaching behind them. She looked up, her eyes widened when she saw who it was.

"Wee flower, He's been looking for you," Steven said with an evil grin on his lips. "He's going to be very happy when I give him your dead body."

***

Garrett turned to face the riders who had just entered the clearing on the south side. There were three of them, and they didn't look very organized.

One had a mail shirt and a sword, another had a metal breastplate and a mace, and the last had only a bow. They all looked like they had been yanked out of bed and thrown on a horse with whatever they could grab on their way out the door.

Good, he thought to himself. The less organized, the better.

"Evening, Gentlemen," He said loudly across the clearing. "What brings you into the woods so late?"

The man with the sword sneered, "Think you're funny, do ya? Well, we'll see how much laughing you do when we drag you back to town and string you up in the square."

The other men chuckled darkly. Garrett shook his head and clucked his tongue, "Now, I wouldn't want ya to have to go through all that trouble. I'm a big man, ya see, it would be awful for ya to have to drag me all that long way. S'there any way we can work out our differences here, do ya think?"

"Aye, there might be," said the man with the sword. He nodded to the man with the bow, "Kill him."

The bowman raised his weapon, and before he could draw back, Garrett threw a small knife. The knife hit the horse in the shoulder, causing it to rear and bolt. The man was thrown off the horse while his companions charged towards Garrett.

Garrett drew his sword and waited. At just the right moment, he ducked and kicked his horse forward, sending him harmlessly out of the way of the charge.

He quickly slid out of his saddle and pulled a dirk from his belt. He held the dirk in his left hand and the sword in his right. He turned to Valdar and gave him a command in his native tongue.

The horse reared and charged toward the rider with the mace. The other horse tried to skirt away, but his rider pulled fiercely on the bit, trying to get it to stand.

Valdar kept after it, turning so he could kick with his back legs. The man with the mace was soon thrown from the saddle, and the horse bolted.

The other rider came after Garrett. Using his dirk and sword together, he was able to block the man's blows from above. After several blows, Garrett managed to catch the man's sword on his sword hilt and use his dirk to cut the saddle girth.

He grabbed the man's foot and sent him sprawling off the other side of the horse. Garrett sent the horse off into the woods with a slap on the flanks.

Garrett had to give the man credit; he didn't give up easily. The man was already on his feet and ready to fight again.

They exchanged blow after blow, neither one gaining an advantage until they went hilt to hilt. Garrett dropped to one knee, taking the weight of the man with one hand, and stabbed upward with his dirk into the man's stomach.

The man went rigid and fell. Garrett stood panting. He turned to find the other men and had to jump back to miss the swing of the mace.

Most of the blow glanced off Garrett's shoulder, but it was enough to knock him to the ground. He tried to shake off the blow, but his vision was fuzzy and he couldn't get to his feet. He managed to block a few blows with his sword, but it wouldn't take this kind of abuse for long.

There was a shout from behind the man attacking Garrett. The man jerked around and screamed. Garrett tried to stand again but was too off balance.

"Are you alright?" a voice asked. "Where's Rose?"

A man stooped to help Garrett to his feet. Once he could focus, he saw it was Trent.

"Bless your impeccable timing, lad," Garrett said, breathing a sigh of relief.

"Don't mention it," Trent said. "Where's Rose?"

"She went to the river," Garrett said. "It's not far through the trees. That way," he pointed north.

Trent led Garrett to their horses that were waiting patiently on the edge of the clearing for them.

"Can you ride?" Trent asked.

Garrett shook his head to clear it, "I'll be fine. Let's go."

They were just about to kick their horses to the north when they heard a young girl's shrill scream to their left.

They looked at each other for only a second before they both turned and rode towards the scream.

***

"What are you talking about?" Rose said in the bravest voice she could muster. "Who's been looking for me?"

"I don't know his name," Steven said, slowly walking his horse towards her. "All I know is he's willing to pay highly for you."

"Why?" Rose asked. "I'm no one, I'm not worth anything."

Steven gave a dark chuckle, "I didn't ask questions. I just asked how much."

Rose didn't know what to do except keep him talking, "I thought you were Garrett's friend. Why are you doing this?"

To her surprise, Steven stopped, "Why should this not make me Garrett's friend? Wasn't the plan to ransom you?" He shrugged one shoulder casually, "I don't see any difference between this plan and the next. They both have the same result, money in my purse."

"How can you say that?" Rose asked incredulously. "You know he wouldn't turn me over to be killed."

Another shrug, "What Garrett doesn't know won't hurt him." He kicked his horse towards her.

She only had a fraction of a second to act. She dropped as he rode past her and stuck out her knife, slicing his horse's legs.

The horse screamed and fell forward, throwing Steven onto the rocks. Rose stood quickly, but Steven had already gotten up and was coming back towards her.

Despite his fall, he was only limping slightly. He pulled a sword from his belt, which was richly decorated with jewels on the hilt.

Anger burned in her, "It wasn't enough to kill Carlos? You had to rob him, too?"

He laughed, "What does it matter? He was dead anyway. You could almost argue I did the man a favor."

He was close enough now that Rose could see his eyes. They were pitch black. Not just the iris, his entire eye was as black as the night.

He swung, she ducked, and stepped back quickly. There was no way she was going to be able to fight him; all she had was a knife.

She dodged another blow and slipped on the loose rocks of the riverbank. He quickly grabbed for her legs. She kicked out at him, but he managed to hang onto one of her ankles.

She grabbed a smooth stone in her right hand. Sitting up, she struck his head right on the temple. He bellowed in fury but let go of her leg. She scrambled back to her feet, grabbing more rocks.

He stood as well, but Rose could tell he was off balance. She threw some of the rocks at him and ran back towards the canoes. He scrambled after her, unsteady from the blow to the head and the rocky ground.

She went to the canoe next to Evans and grabbed an oar.

"I'm going to kill you for that, you little..." He wasn't able to finish his sentence. She swung the oar with all her strength, hitting him with the sharp side of the paddle directly in the neck.

There was an awful crack, and Steven dropped instantly. Time froze around her as she looked at his limp body. His eyes stared unseeingly into the night sky. They had returned to their normal blue. A small wisp of dark smoke went up from his slightly open mouth and hovered in the air above him.

"Hmm," a voice said. It seemed to reverberate all around her, even though it was almost a whisper. "You're proving much more trouble than I thought you would. Until next time, little flower."

The smoke shot off towards the woods. Rose watched it go. She stood shaking, still holding the oar in her hands. Whatever that thing was, it was the same voice as the darkness in her dreams.

Rose didn't know how long she stood there looking towards the woods. It could have been a second, it could have been an hour, she didn't know.

Suddenly, there was shouting from the edge of the woods. The sound broke her from the daze. She strained to recognize the voices, but she couldn't. A second later, an arrow missed her by inches and bounced off the rocks at her feet.

She ran towards the canoes. She hesitated. She couldn't let them follow her, but she didn't want to leave the others stranded either.

She quickly went to each canoe and pulled out the oars from under the seats, throwing them into the river. At least the others would have the canoes to use. They would just have to fashion their own oars.

She shoved the canoe with Evans into the water. She cringed when her feet stepped into the freezing water. She went in as far as her knees, then climbed into the boat. Trying to stay low, she used the oar to steer them into the swiftest part of the current.

There was a thunk on the side of the canoe. She looked over the side, thinking she must have hit a hidden branch in the water. There was an arrow stuck in the wood.

She risked sitting up further so she could paddle faster. She looked back at the shore and saw at least six men on horses watching her go down the river.

The archer notched another arrow and let it fly. Rose ducked again, but the arrow fell well short of the canoe.

They were moving very quickly now. Thankfully, the river was deep as well as wide, so they didn't hit anything, and Rose didn't have to steer around any rapids.

"Hold on, Evans," She said, reaching down to make sure he was still sitting up.

He gave a faint grunt, "Aahva help us."

Rose still didn't know who Aahva was, but she silently echoed Evans' prayer, not caring where the help came from, just as long as they got some.

# Chapter 22

Trip and Malcolm were fighting for their lives. Trip had managed to get Ade to a small clump of trees before the men overtook them. It was so dark he was hoping they wouldn't find her, but his heart ran cold when he heard her scream.

He was not a particularly grand talent with a sword, but he knew enough not to die within the first few blows of a fight.

He chanced a glance at Malcolm, and he seemed to be taking on two men with almost no effort. Trip wished he had his bow. This would have all been over with three easily placed arrows.

Thankfully, the man he was fighting wasn't very skilled with the sword either, although he was extremely large and brutish.

At the moment, though, that was working in Trips' favor. The man was tiring quickly, and it was easy for Trip to skirt out of the man's way.

He looked around when he heard two more horses thundering towards them. If they were enemies, they would be done for.

The man he was fighting looked up also, there was a surprised look on his face for only a second before he was cut down by the rider.

Trip looked up at the rider and saw Trent, "'Bout time you showed up." He said, immensely relieved.

Trent smiled and turned his horse to help the other two, but they had already taken care of the men they were fighting.

"Where's the girl?" Garrett asked. "We heard her scream."

Trip nodded, "This way." He swung back up on his horse and led them to where he had left the girl.

They found the clump of trees and stopped. A man was lying on the ground, his legs twisted at a strange angle.

"Help me," he rasped. He held out an arm but quickly dropped it.

"Where's the girl?" Garrett demanded.

"I'm here," came Ade's voice. They all looked around but couldn't see her. "Up here."

They looked up into the trees. Ade was in the highest branches of a large oak tree.

Garrett gave a relieved laugh, "Are you part squirrel? How did you get up there?"

"Climbed," Ade said. Her voice was shaky and small.

"Are you stuck?" Garrett asked more seriously.

"No," Ade answered.

"Come on down," Garrett called. A few moments later, they heard the branches moving and saw a small figure working its way down out of the tree.

"Right then," Garrett said. He turned and looked at the man on the ground. "We have some questions for you."

The man on the ground snorted a laugh, then winced in pain, "You can ask whatever you want, lad, I don't know nothing."

"I'm sure your lack of knowledge will astound us," Trent said. "But you do know some things. Such as, why are you out here in the middle of the night?"

"They said we was to come help if the bell rung," The man said.

"Who said?" Garrett asked.

"The short man," he said. "Don't know no names. He just paid the men in town and said we was to come to the brothel if the bells rung."

"What about the jeweler?" Garrett asked.

"What jeweler," the man asked. "I don't know nothin' bout no jeweler. Told ya, didn' I? I don't know nothin 'cept we was supposed to come if the bell rung."

"And you didn't ask any questions," Trent asked. "You just did whatever this man you don't even know said?"

"Ya don't ask questions when someone pays ya," The man said, like this was the most obvious thing. He coughed and jerked, "I can't feel me legs. Why are we all standing around talking, help me or kill me, I say, and have done with it."

At that moment, Ade came down to the last branch of the tree. Garrett went to help her to the ground, "Are you alright?"

Ade nodded, "I'm fine."

"What happened?" Trip asked.

"I was hiding in the bushes where you left me," She said softly. "He must have seen you put me down because he came right after you left. I climbed into the tree and he followed."

She looked at the man on the ground, "He grabbed my ankle and tried to pull me down. I was pretty high in the tree and kicked at him. He lost his balance, then tried to grab a branch, but it wouldn't hold his weight, and he fell."

Garrett looked back at the man, disgusted, "And did your orders tell you to chase after little girls?"

"That ain't no little girl," The man spat. "She lives at the brothel. I was goina take the little whore back to Madam and get me a handsome reward."

Ade stood straighter, "I'm not a whore."

Trip was impressed. This girl had some grit to her.

Garrett knelt and whispered in the man's ear, "You know, where I'm from, it's a hanging offense to call a lady a whore. But I think tonight we'll just let you suffer the consequences you've made for yourself." He stood and went to Valdar, "Let's go." He swung up into the saddle.

Everyone else followed. Trip put Ade onto their horse and swung up behind her.

They turned to go. The man spat again and yelled, "You can't leave me here like this!"

Garrett stopped and turned in his saddle. He looked like he was debating with himself. He reached into his belt and pulled out a knife. He tossed it towards the man, "You caused your suffering, you can choose when to end it."

He turned and kicked Valdar north towards the river.

***

Trish was walking down the hallway towards the kitchen when she heard a strange noise.

"I'm sorry," came a voice from behind a closed door.

Trish slowed her walking. Of course, she had been raised to never eavesdrop, but...

She stood outside the door for a moment to see if she could hear anything else.

There was a quiet, oily voice speaking, but she couldn't make out what it was saying. She moved closer to the door.

"You've done nothing, nothing at all helpful to me," The oily voice said. "You seem to have managed to acquire your own desires, however."

"I only desire your will," The voice said. "Ask it of me and it will be done."

There was a soft chuckle. It made the hairs on the back of her neck stand on end, "I've asked you to do many things that have yet to be done."

"We are working on the girl, I've sent men after her," he was cut off.

"Your men have failed," The oily voice said. Trish could hear anger in the voice now. "The incompetence of your followers shows your incompetence. If I do not have the girl soon, I will be extremely unhappy." There was a choking sound, "And you don't want that." Said the oily voice.

There was a gasp and a thud, "No, of course not."

"Good," said the oily voice. "I have work to do elsewhere. Do not call me again until you have the girl."

Trish stepped back from the door and quickly went back up the hallway. She calmed her breathing, and once the door opened, she walked towards the kitchen again.

She looked up and saw the Duke. "Oh, hello," he said. He was pale, and a sheen of sweat was on his brow. "Headed down to dinner?"

She smiled and nodded, "Care to join me?"

It took him a second to put a smile in place, "Of course." He held out his arm to escort her.

She took it and managed a glance into the room he had just exited. There was no one there.

***

They came to the river and looked around. No one was there. They saw several hoof prints that came to the river's edge, but they went back into the woods.

"I left Evans here, under this tree," Trent said, pointing towards the sycamore tree.

"Well, he's not here now," Trip said.

"He couldn't have gone far by himself," Trent said. "He was too badly injured."

"Maybe Rose found him," Ade said.

"It's possible," Garrett said. He was looking at the ground with Trip. "It's hard to make out any tracks in these rocks."

"We need to go after them," Trent said, heading towards the large barges.

"We don't know if they went in the river," Garrett said. "If Evans was badly hurt, Rose might not have been able to move him."

"If she didn't move him, someone did," Trent said, getting angry. He ran his hands through his hair.

"Exactly," Trip said. "They might have taken them back to town. If we go down the river, we could be going farther away from them."

Malcolm said something to Garrett. Garrett nodded, "We have to at least check." He put a hand on Trent's shoulder. "We don't have a choice."

The sun was just starting to turn the sky pink. Trent looked out over the river. It was large, far bigger than any they had in the eastern kingdom. He hated to think of Rose going down the river alone. Evans wouldn't be in any condition to help. As he stood looking over the river, Raul came up and bumped him with his nose.

He turned and rubbed the horse's soft face, "We'll find her."

Raul's nostrils flared, and he whinnied. He tossed his head and sniffed at the ground.

"Come on, boy," Trent said, getting into the saddle. "Let's go."

He turned Raul back towards the woods. The horse stopped when they were about to enter the trees. He turned his head back towards the river and tried to go back.

Trent pulled gently on the reins, "Come on, boy, I know, I know." He patted Raul on the neck and managed to turn him back towards the woods. "We'll find her, I promise."

Raul whinnied again and went extremely reluctantly, but they eventually caught up to the others.

"Everything alright?" Trip asked Trent.

"He must have smelled her at the riverbank," Trent said and patted the horse again. "He's fine."

"You know, we can't just ride into town," Trip said.

"Malcolm can go," Garrett said while Malcolm nodded. "As big as he is, he is remarkably good at going unseen. He also looks the closest to the locals."

"Right," Trent said. "Let's go."

***

Rose paddled until the sun was fully risen. She checked on Evans frequently and did not like what she saw. His breathing had become shallow, and he winced in pain every time a wave hit the canoe.

"We'll stop in a little bit," Rose told him. "I can take a closer look at that wound."

"No," He croaked from the bottom of the boat. "We need to get as far away as possible."

Rose had no idea how to tell how far they had gone. She was constantly looking at the bank, trying to see if anyone was following them. So far she hadn't seen anything, but the farther they went down the river, the steeper the banks were.

"We need to check it," Rose said. "At least we can clean it and dress it better."

Evans gave a small shake of his head, which Rose ignored. She kept looking for a spot to take the canoe ashore, but the rising banks didn't give her many options.

After another half hour of paddling, Rose heard something. She sat up in her seat and turned her ear towards the noise. For a moment, she couldn't place the sound. Then it hit her, it sounded like a rushing creek after the spring rains made it swell.

She shook her head. Of course she heard rushing water; she was on a river. She sat back down and began paddling again. The sound was slowly getting louder. It was slightly higher-pitched than the other river noises around her.

They went around a bend in the river, and Rose gasped. The calm, though fast-flowing, water they had been in before suddenly changed to foaming, roaring water.

She frantically tried to paddle towards the shore, but she knew she wasn't going to make it.

"Stay in the middle," Evans said. He had managed to sit up slightly and could see the rapids. "Don't fight the water, just try to steer around the rocks the best you can."

Rose swallowed hard. She had always hated boats. A flat river was one thing, but this? There was no way they were going to make it.

"I don't know how to steer this thing." She said frantically to Evans.

"Paddle on the left side to go right and on the right side to go left," Evans said.

Rose didn't have time to lament how unhelpful that advice was just now. The canoe went over the first few rapids easily enough, but she could see it was about to get much worse.

Two large rocks made a narrow passage in the middle of the river. Rose tried to steer the boat around them, but Evans suddenly said, "No, go in between them."

Rose didn't know how much steering she was actually doing, but she put her oar to the right side of the boat and paddled hard. They went in between the two rocks quickly, and the canoe's sides scraped against them a little, but to Rose's surprise, they made it through.

"It's better to go with the rapids than around. The water on the sides will push us sideways and capsize the boat," Evans said.

Rose gave a nod that Evans didn't see and looked for the next rapid. This one was wider, but right after it was another rapid to the left.

"After you go through the first one, stick your oar in the water on the right side of the canoe and just hold it in the water," Evans said.

Rose did as he said. They went through the first rapid, and she held the oar down on the right side of the boat. The front of the boat turned, and they went down the second rapid. Water splashed into the boat, but they had made it through.

"I think it's over," Rose said, amazed they hadn't drowned.

"There's one more," Evans said softly enough that Rose almost couldn't hear him.

She looked and saw he was right. There was one more rapid, but there wasn't a place she could easily put the canoe through. In fact, the closer they got, Rose could see that it wasn't a rapid at all but a small waterfall.

"Evans," Rose breathed. "What do I do?"

"We just have to go over it," Evans said. He held onto the sides of the canoe with both hands.

Rose tried to find the easiest way over, but there wasn't one. They came to the edge, and the nose of the canoe went down. Rose screamed as she and Evans were thrown out of the canoe.

Her head went underwater, and she could feel the pounding of the waterfall pushing her down. The water was ice cold, and her body seized with the shock.

She blindly reached out for Evans, but she couldn't find him.

She kicked hard, and her head broke the surface of the water. Gasping, she looked around and yelled, "Evans!"

The current was pushing her swiftly away from the waterfall. She frantically looked around for Evans. She turned to her right and saw his head barely above the surface of the churning water.

She swam towards him and grabbed hold of him. She was being drug down by the weight of her dress, but she didn't dare take it off. It was the only clothing she had, and she would be freezing without it when they got to land.

"Evans," Rose said, shaking him.

He didn't respond, "Evans!" She shouted, no response.

She couldn't swim with the weight of him and her dress, so she focused on keeping his head above water and let the river take her in its current.

She kicked out, and her leg hit something in the water. A sharp pain in her calf told her it was either a sharp rock or a tree branch.

In the moment of pain, her and Evan's heads went underwater. Evans jerked and grabbed hold of her. She kicked out again, and they resurfaced.

"It's alright," She tried to say. She choked on the water in her throat. "I've got you."

Evans was a little easier to keep above water now that he was helping her kick, but it wasn't much. Rose's back suddenly hit sand.

They had washed up against a small sandbar in the middle of the river. She quickly dragged Evans further up so he was completely out of the water.

She examined him, and her heart sank. He was struggling to breathe. Rose was sure he had inhaled some water.

"Evans," her voice cracked as she spoke.

He opened his eyes and looked up at her, "We'll make a sailor out of you yet, girl."

She smiled down at him as a tear rolled down her cheek, "I think I'll stick to horses."

He reached up and wiped the tear from her cheek, "You look just like your mother."

Rose's eyebrows knit together in confusion, "What?"

"You look just like her," Evans said again.

"Evans," Rose said with a sigh. "Don't talk, just rest a moment."

No one knew her mother. She was an orphan. Evans couldn't possibly have known her mother. He was delirious.

Evans shook his head, "No. I was there when Queen Millesant took you from the homeland. Her sister had written her a letter begging her to come."

"What are you talking about, Evans?" Rose asked. Her teeth were chattering with the cold. "The homeland is a myth."

Evan shook his head once, "It's real."

Rose noticed that Evans wasn't shivering. He almost looked peaceful.

"Stop it, Evans," She said. "It's not real. I'm an orphan," her voice broke. "I'm an orphan, and the queen found me and took me in out of pity."

"No child," Evans said softly. "Queen Millesant was your aunt. You look a lot like her, too, you know that at least is true."

"You need to rest, Evans," Rose said. "Let me get you out of these wet clothes."

Evans grabbed her wrist as she started to tug at his shirt. His grip was so weak she could have easily broken it, but she didn't. "What?" She whispered.

"I've watched you grow into a strong woman," Evans said. He took another rattling breath, "You have to be strong now. You have to," He coughed, his whole body shook with it.

Rose pulled his head onto her lap. She propped him up, trying to help him breathe.

"No one's returned," Evans choked out. "Not since the day we took you."

He looked into her eyes, "You have to go back, you have to find out why they stopped sending messengers."

"Evans, I don't know what you're talking about," Rose said helplessly. "What messengers?"

"You have to go," Evans whispered. "Go..home."

"Evans," Rose said. "Evans." She shook him gently, but he didn't move. "Evans," She said louder and shook him harder. He didn't move. "No," She gasped. "Evans, you can't leave me."

His eyes stared, glassily reflecting the sunrise. She held him and sobbed.

The sun crept higher into the sky, but she didn't move. She just rocked Evans' body back and forth, sobbing.

When her tears finally ran out, she looked around. Her eyes were almost swollen shut, but she saw something that was out of place. A small mouse was sitting a few feet from her, looking at her.

"Go away," She said, swatting at the mouse. It didn't move.

"Go away," She yelled and kicked at the mouse, sending sand flying.

The mouse scampered back a few feet but sat back down and looked at her.

How had a mouse gotten here? There was no way it could have swam out here. She looked around. Maybe there was a way back to shore. She saw something, floating just beneath the water line.

She looked down at Evans, "I'm sorry." She said as she gently lowered his head to the sand. She stood and went to the edge of the sandbar.

It was the canoe. It was wedged between the sand and a fallen tree. She stepped into the water and tried to drag it onto the shore. It barely moved. She could only get it far enough onto the bank to raise the edges out of the water.

She started bailing water with her hands until she could drag the canoe further onto the sand. Once she was able to pull it all the way out of the water, she tipped it over, spilling the rest.

She sat down, exhausted. She looked over, and the mouse was still sitting on the sand, looking at her.

"Now what?" She asked the mouse. "I don't have an oar. The canoe isn't much good without an oar."

She stared at the mouse. It, of course, didn't answer her, being a mouse and all. However, it turned and ran along the sandbar.

Not entirely knowing why, Rose got up and followed the mouse. On the far end of the sand, there were several large branches piled up in a log jam.

Rose went over and inspected several of the logs. Most of them were far too big for her to even hold, let alone use as a makeshift oar. She dug into the pile and eventually found one that would work. It wouldn't be very efficient at paddling, but it was slightly spoon-shaped and had a long handle.

Rose turned back, looking for the mouse, but it was gone. She shook herself, "If you start talking to rodents, you're going to have bigger problems than you already have."

She went back to the canoe and put the stick in the bottom. She then turned towards Evans' body.

She got on her hands and knees and started digging in the sand. She thought as she dug. The homeland, her dreams, the strange black smoke that had come out of Steven when he died. What did it all mean? And what did it have to do with her?

The longer she thought, the angrier she became. If what he had said was true, why would Evans have waited all these years to tell her? Why hadn't Millesant told her anything? She was supposedly her niece, and Millesant never said anything?

She looked down at the hole and stopped digging. It was bigger than she had meant to make it, but that was fine. She stood and pulled Evans as gently as she could into the hole. She started crying again as she pushed the sand back over him.

Once the hole was filled, she stood staring at it. There wasn't a marker. She couldn't leave him here without a marker. She went back to the logs and found a short fat one. She couldn't lift it, but she managed to roll it over to the grave.

She pulled her knife out of her belt and roughly carved into the top of the stump.

Commander Evans

Husband

Father

Friend

It fell so horribly short of what he deserved. He deserved a statue, a monument. Some place where his children could visit him and tell others how wonderful their father was.

Rose wiped new tears from her cheek. She couldn't stay here forever, and she didn't want to spend the night here.

She went to the canoe and slowly pushed it out onto the water. She tested her oar, and it worked relatively well for what it was.

She didn't know where she was going. She didn't know how long it would take her to get there. For that matter, she didn't even know who she was anymore. The only thing she knew was she needed answers, and she wasn't going to stop until she got them.

# Epilogue

She saw the lights of a town in the distance. It was the first town she had seen since leaving Seawald.

She paddled her canoe towards some wooden docks and got out. She had been on that river for three terror filled days. Every time she thought she had control of the canoe another current or waterfall would come up. After the first day of trying to get to the banks, she realized even if she could, she had no idea how to get back to Trent and Garrett.

The entire second day, and most of the third, she was in a gorge with sheer cliffs at least fifty feet on both sides.

"Excuse me, uh," The man looked her up and down, clearly struggling to be polite. "Ma'am, you have to pay to dock your boat here."

She knew she looked horrible. She was wearing what was left of that ridiculous red dress. After being torn for bandages,  dunked in the river, snagged on brambles, and worn for three days, it was not looking its best.

"I don't have any money," She said flatly.

The man fidgeted with his papers, "I'm afraid I won't be able to let you take it back until you've paid the fee, ma'am."

"You can keep it," She said, barely looking at the man. She never wanted to see that boat again. She walked down the dock towards the town without another word. The man stammered after her but didn't follow.

She went into the first building she saw with people. It was a tavern. She looked around at the patrons and almost walked right back out. It was clearly a rough crowd.

Heads turned to see who had entered, and several catcalls ensued. She ignored the noise and went straight to the bar. "I need to speak with the owner." She said to a young serving girl.

The girl looked her up and down with wide eyes. Rose was surprised someone so innocent-looking was working at a place like this.

"I'll get him for ya," The girl said and walked back into the kitchen.

A moment later, a rather large man with an apron came out, wiping his hands. "Can I help you?" He said. He stopped talking when he saw her and gaped.

Ignoring his stare, she said, "I need a room. Do you have any available?"

"I do miss, but I'm afraid I require payment upfront," He looked doubtful that she would be able to do so.

"Are you willing to trade?" Rose asked.

The man looked at the serving girl, then back at Rose, "Some decency please, miss, I'm a married man."

It took Rose a second to realize what he was talking about, "No, no, you misunderstand me, sir. I have jewels I can trade, once I get some new clothes, that is."

She stood back from the bar so the man could see her dress better. The opals that were still attached glinted in the candlelight.

The man went slightly pink, "Ah, yes, I think something could be arranged." He turned to the girl and said, "Take this lady to your mother for some new clothes. When you come back, we can work something out."

"Thank you," Rose said to the man and turned to follow the girl upstairs.

There was more cat-calling as she left, but again she ignored it.

"Mama," The girl called once they were on a landing.

A middle-aged woman came out of one of the rooms with a load of bed linens on her hip, "Yes, dear?"

"Papa asked me to bring you this lady to get her some new clothes," The girl said.

The woman looked Rose over. Rose could see the initial shock at her appearance, then it quickly went to sympathy, "Of course, follow me, dear." She turned and went down a back set of stairs into a scullery.

"I'll just get one of my old dresses for ya to try on," The woman tossed the linens into a wash basin and went to a line where several pieces were drying.

"If it's not too much trouble, could you bring a shirt and britches?" Rose called after her.

The woman stuck her head around a large bed sheet, "If that's what you would prefer."

She came back to Rose with a pair of thick blue pants and a white long-sleeve shirt, "There you are. They might be a trifle big, but I'll find you some rope to use as a belt. You can change in that room over there, dear."

Rose nodded her thanks. She went to the room to change. She wished she could have a bath before putting on the clean clothes, but she would have to work out the room situation first.

Once she changed, she went back to the scullery. She cut the remaining opals from the dress and gave the dress to the woman, "I'm not sure what good it'll do, but there's quite a bit of material there. You can have it. Use it, throw it out, it doesn't matter."

The woman took the dress, holding it out from herself slightly, "Uhh, right then. Let me take you back to my husband, and you can work out your room payment."

Rose followed the women back through the dining room towards the bar.

"Wait here," She said and left Rose at the bar while she went into the kitchen.

The man soon came back out and looked at Rose, "Well, now let's see what you've got."

Rose laid ten opals down on the bar, "This should more than cover a room, food, and the clothes."

The man's eyes widened slightly, "It does indeed, miss, in fact, it's quite a bit more."

Rose nodded, "The rest is for information. I need to hire a ship that can take me to the eastern kingdom."

The man shook his head, "I'm sorry, miss, but no one will be going that way this time of year."

"You can't think of anyone willing to risk it," Rose asked, laying two more opals on the bar.

The man smiled and pushed the jewels back to her, "There's no need, miss. The only person who might be willing is the man sitting in the corner by the fire. Don't know his real name, everyone just calls him Kieran or Captain."

Rose looked towards the fire. She couldn't see the man, just his outline. She turned back towards the barman, "Thank you. Can I have dinner in my room in an hour? And a bath would be most welcome."

The man smiled, "Of course, dear."

Rose went over to the booth in the corner. He was sitting alone, smoking a pipe, listening to the music from the stage.

"I need to hire a ship to the Eastern kingdom. I hear you might be willing to take me," Rose said by way of introduction.

The man looked up at her. He was wearing black clothing from his shirt and jacket to his black leather boots. Even his hair was black. He looked like a giant raven.

"That's quite a request," He said, taking another pull of his pipe.

"I can pay you," Rose said. "May I sit down so we can talk it over?"

His lips twitched, and he held his hand out, gesturing for her to sit. He studied her for a moment without saying anything. He leaned back on his bench and took another puff from his pipe.

"You know, lass, you seem like a very interesting lady," He said. "You sure caused quite a stir in here just by walking in the door." He leaned forward and folded his hands on the table. "The Eastern kingdom, hmm. That's a mighty far trip for this time of year. Why do you need to get there?" he tilted his head and waited for her to answer.

"I have my reasons," Rose said. "I can pay you, just tell me how much."

"While I do appreciate your eagerness to give me endless riches, I'm a practical man," He narrowed his eyes slightly. "It'll take more than gold to get me out on these seas at the moment. So tell me, why do you want to go?"

Rose grit her teeth. She couldn't tell if he was making fun of her. "To save the world," she said sarcastically.

He barked a laugh, "Now that there's a good reason! That's an adventure I might just be willing to go on."

He looked at her a moment longer, "What's your name, Love?"

She met his gaze, "Rose."

# Acknowledgements

Thank you for making it to the end. I especially want to thank my Mom and Kayla, who had to suffer through reading this chapter by chapter as I wrote. They endured almost two years of my giving them three chapters in a week, then having to wait two to three months before the next one came their way.

Thank you to my wonderful husband, who got to listen to me hem and haw over whether anyone would even read this book and if it was worth finishing. He gave me the courage to finish this book for myself. Even if for no other reason than to prove that I could.

This book is for everyone who used to read all the time as a kid, then life hit them, and they lost their reading spark. May this book bring at least a little of that spark back. I hope you fall into this world and find yourself in at least one of the characters. Learn from their strengths and weaknesses and strive to learn from their mistakes.

# Book Two of the Homeland Series

Here's a quick preview...

# Prolog

"The world used to be a simpler place. Believe it or not, that made my goals much much harder. Those pesky little humans used to band together, they used to teach their children to fear me, they used to know who I was."

It smiled and glided to the center of the room, "Not anymore though." The smugness radiated from him.

"They are stupider than ever and, although that does make finding competent help much harder, it makes my goal that much easier to attain."

It looked down at a large table. The table top was a detailed map of the three kingdoms. It glided a hand over the table without actually touching the surface, "Where, where are you."

The three humans in the room glanced at each other nervously but didn't dare to answer.

"We lost track of you didn't we," it mused. "An all together impressive feat I must admit.

"Please Master," a shivering voice said. "Might she be dead?"

"That is possible," It said. Its hand came down on Seawald. "Last we saw her though, she was still alive. So we must continue as if she is, until we get the happy news."

"Of course Master, you are wise, of course," The shaky voice said.

"Thank you for that assessment Edmund, you know I so desire your approval," The once silky voice grew harder as it spoke. "If it weren't for you I would already have her wouldn't I."

Edmund dropped to his knees, "forgive me master, I was over eager for your works to be accomplished. Please, tell me how I can make it right."

"Make it right," It scoffed. "You can't even seduce the girl."

Edmund bristled slightly, "It is hard to accomplish when she half thinks she's been kidnapped."

"She has been kidnapped," It said, a smile creeping back into its voice. "She came willingly but all the same," It trailed off.

After long moments of silence, Edmund gathered the courage to ask, "Master, what, what if the old man talked?"

"And," It asked.

"And," Edmund had to stop and swallow his fear. "And told her about the homeland."

"Ahh," It hissed. Its hands went to the western most part of the map. There was nothing but sea to the edge of the map but he knew there was much missing. "How nostalgic of you Edmund. Tell me, do you consider that place your homeland?"

"No master," Edmund said quickly. "That's just what it's called. I've never been there of course, but it's said to,"

It raised a hand and Edmund's words were cut off as quickly as if he had been gagged.

"I do not care what the humans say about the place," It's smoky form seemed to darken with its words. "They are mostly wrong anyway. It's no matter, if she does learn where she's from, there is nothing to go back to."

There was silence. A very long, very uncomfortable moment of silence. "Nevertheless," it said. "Everyone is to keep a lookout."

"Yes master," Edmund 's voice quivered slightly. "And if we find her?"

The figure turned and looked at his pitiful servants. He hated that he was reduced to using these pathetic beings. He used to control armies of the most fearful beings in existence. But now, now he had to hunt down the one thing that had even the slightest hope of stopping him, and it was a little girl.

It glided towards Edmund and ran its shadowy hand down his cheek. It's hand went to his throat and slowly started to tighten.

"Kill her."